REVERSE PURSUIT

A Jason Mulder Thriller

Robert Goluba

Evertouch Publishing

ISBN: 978-1-7330513-8-5 (Paperback)

ISBN: 978-1-7330513-9-2 (eBook)

Edited by Ryan Steck and Lisa Davis

Cover Design by Miblart

Sign up for my email newsletter at **RobertGoluba.com/newsletter**

CONTENTS

CHAPTER 1

Phoenix, Arizona

Special Agent Jason Mulder inhaled the dry night air and welcomed the surge of adrenaline to fuel his fight for justice. He tightened his black tactical gloves and trained his gaze on the north entrance of the alley from the darkness inside his black pickup truck. The cracked, sun-bleached asphalt in the alley was strewn with trash, and gang graffiti peppered the cinder block fencing behind each home. Jason steadied his breathing to calm his nerves.

A rusty, late-model sedan rumbled under the flickering streetlight minutes later, shifting Jason's senses into high alert. Rattles and high-pitched squeaks pierced the cool desert air as the vehicle's tires sunk into canyon-sized potholes. He caught a glimpse of the driver and passenger as they passed his truck. They were scouts, simple minnows for the big fish following behind from a safe distance, but that didn't reduce the tension in Jason's neck.

"Any sign of Titan?" Alpha One asked over his headset.

"Bravo one. Negative on the seller."

"Charlie one, also negative. I have eyes on scouts circling the area, but not our guy," Jason responded.

Nine months earlier, Special Agent Andre Mercer, also known as Alpha One, had penetrated a ring of meth dealers in a gang-ridden neighborhood four miles west of downtown Phoenix, Arizona. During this time, he'd earned their trust with frequent and growing purchases of methamphetamines. Mercer pushed to meet the top dog to purchase a substantial quantity of the addictive stimulant, which led him to Titan.

Titan hailed from Cottonwood, Arizona, a city of twelve thousand residents, one hundred miles north of Phoenix. He'd been on Jason's radar since Jason started at the United States Drug Enforcement Agency duty office in Camp Verde a year earlier. Jason's team served warrants and arrested dozens of small drug peddlers in the Verde Valley, but the infamous Titan proved elusive. The DEA team out of Camp Verde could never lure the primary source of narcotics out of his secure fortress... until now.

Jason joined Special Agent Holland, who recruited him into the DEA, on the nine-man operation to nab the drug kingpin from Cottonwood. Holland saw the potential in Jason, so he made him the lead for Charlie team while he led Bravo. Jason appreciated the confidence of his mentor to lead a team on the highest stakes operation since leaving the DEA Academy in Quantico, Virginia, ten months earlier. His experience in the US Air Force Special Warfare as a pararescueman prepared him for many aspects as a DEA special agent, but the learning curve on the unique tactics and culture of the DEA was steeper than he expected. As a PJ, Jason and his team were thrust into every mission to rescue or retrieve an injured soldier, sailor, Marine, or airman with little notice. He didn't have time to overthink a mission or consider the million ways an enemy could kill him. DEA stings were the exact opposite. They planned a takedown of a target for days or weeks, and once on site, Jason laid in wait like a leopard waiting to snare its prey.

Jason made frustrating but minor mistakes during more routine busts in Verde Valley and was growing anxious about how he could screw up the mission to capture Titan. He couldn't mess this mission up if he wanted a successful career in the DEA.

Jason glanced at his watch and blew out a long breath. He couldn't wait for Titan to show up with his security team and guns to get the sting underway.

Several blocks away, a car turned onto the street toward Charlie team. Jason could tell by the ultra-bright halogen headlights that this car wasn't like any other from the neighborhood. He slumped down in the passenger seat of the rented Chevy Silverado truck and watched the sports car pass. It was impossible to mistake the sleek lines of the black-on-black Maserati Quattroporte Trofeo and the sweet purr of its V8 engine. The chances of the Italian sports car being anyone but Titan in this neighborhood were a million to one, but Jason still confirmed the license plate.

The vehicle parked half a block ahead of Jason, and they set the alarm with a distinctive chirp. Three shadowy figures emerged from the car with hoods pulled over their heads and hands in their pockets. The trio strode past a house on the corner and turned into the alley. Jason pulled his black balaclava down and spoke into his throat mic.

"Lock and load, fellas," Jason whispered. Three special agents from Charlie team followed him out of the truck. The only evidence of men under black tactical clothing was their eyes.

"Charlie One copy all."

"Go ahead, Charlie One," Special Agent Holland replied.

"I have eyes on the vehicle and confirmed the make and license plate. Titan approaching Alpha One in the alley with his muscle. Total headcount is three. No evidence of long guns, but assume all three to be armed. We've dismounted and are trailing Titan from a safe distance in the north entrance to the alley," Jason shared on the radio.

"Bravo One also dismounted. Covering the south entrance," Holland reported.

"Good copy. I see them coming. Switch to radio silence," Alpha One whispered.

Bravo and Charlie team could hear Alpha One, but would refrain from using their radio headsets until the mission ended. Or if something went wrong.

Jason took a position next to a cinder block wall that ran the entire length of the alley with limited interruptions in the sea of concrete. He found cover thirty yards from Alpha One while another of Charlie team settled in ten yards behind him. The remaining two members of Charlie chose positions on the opposite side of the alley. They took advantage of the extra column of blocks at the openings in the wall that allowed homeowners access to the roadway through their weathered wooden gates. This was Charlie team's only defense if Titan or one of his bodyguards turned around to check their six.

Titan and his men stopped close enough to touch Alpha One. The conversation between the undercover special agent and Titan streamed into Jason's ear. He heard the usual questions of distrust from Titan and felt Special Agent Mercer tap-danced nicely to allay his suspicions. The positive feeling didn't last long when the posture of the bodyguards and Titan's tone signaled Alpha One was not as convincing as Jason hoped. His vest felt heavy and tight as his heart pounded faster. Jason raised his LWRC M6A2 carbine rifle and trained the red dot visible through the holographic sight on the back of the taller man in the middle of the three sellers. He kept his eyes on Titan except to confirm the rest of Charlie team had their M6A2s raised and ready to fire. Before Jason could regain his target, he caught a flash of movement, and a pistol report stabbed his ears.

The three drug dealers turned and darted away from Charlie team as the gunshot echoed through the alley.

Alpha One collapsed, and Jason's PJ instincts took over. He rushed to the undercover agent, fell to his knees beside him, and turned on his headlamp. He observed Special Agent Mercer holding his left hand, writhing in pain.

"Are you hit?" Jason shouted.

"Yeah," Mercer groaned. "My hand."

"Let me see."

Jason dragged Mercer's left hand away from his body and saw blood dripping from the entry wound in the palm of his hand. It looked like a 9MM round. He suspected Mercer put his hand up and deflected the slug from hitting his body at center mass.

"It's a clean through and through," Jason reported. He reached for his first aid kit when Alpha One grabbed Jason's collar with his good hand.

"I'm good. Go get him."

"What?" Jason asked.

"Go get him!"

"I will. Let me bandage you up first."

Jason had replaced the standard issue gauze in his first aid kit with Celox rapid hemostatic gauze pads impregnated with a substance that would stop the bleeding in under a minute. He placed it over the entry wound in the palm of Mercer's hand and pulled his fingers over it.

"Apply pressure, and I'll be back once we get him."

Jason turned to pursue Titan and noticed a USB drive on the pavement. He snagged it from the asphalt and secured the drive in his pocket as he sprinted toward the north entrance. Jason turned the corner and saw five DEA agents wrestling two hooded men on the ground.

"Is that all of them?" Jason asked over the radio.

"Negative. We have the bodyguards, but Titan is still on the run," a member of Charlie team replied.

Jason turned in the only direction Titan could have gone and resumed the chase. A minute later, he turned a corner and observed a hooded man running forty yards ahead. He kicked hard as he did in high school track to close the gap with the shooter when a special agent from Bravo leaped from behind a parked vehicle to tackle Titan. The drug dealer dodged the agent's arm tackle and pushed him to the ground like an all-pro running back. Titan slid to a stop, drew his 9MM pistol, and raised it toward the agent. Jason stopped and raised his M6A2 to fire, but before he squeezed the trigger, Jason heard the report from another weapon.

He expected Titan to run away again, but he collapsed on the rough pavement instead. Jason bounded toward Titan with his weapon at the ready until he reached the limp drug dealer. Blood oozed from a hole the size of a quarter in his forehead just above his nose.

Special Agent Holland appeared from behind a truck with his rifle still locked on Titan. He kicked his pistol away and lowered his weapon.

Jason bent down and put two fingers on Titan's carotid artery. "He's dead."

"No shit Sherlock. He has a bullet in his tiny brain."

Jason did not know how to reply and stared back at Special Agent Holland.

"Where were you? The rest of Charlie team pursued the sellers immediately after shots were fired."

"I checked on Mercer after they shot him."

"You know our protocol is to eliminate the threat before rendering aid. You're not a combat medic anymore," Holland barked.

Jason shuffled back to his vehicle with his shoulders slumped and his eyes on the ground. Taking Titan off the streets should have been a reason to celebrate, but Jason added another mistake to his growing list. He ran scenes of the operation through his mind hundreds of times during his two-hour drive home. Jason knew that protocol dictated he should eliminate threats first, but he resorted to his role as a PJ when bullets started flying.

He slunk quietly into his bedroom and undressed. Jason removed his car keys and felt the USB drive in his pocket. He removed it and examined the navy blue plastic driver. Jason flipped it over in his hand multiple times but saw no discernable marks.

"Shit. I better add this to the evidence file now, or I'll never hear the end of it from Holland," Jason whispered.

Jason punched the PIN to access his phone and logged into a secure server. His phone screen dimmed after he opened the evidence entry app, and Jason noticed his battery was nearly dead. Two seconds later, the screen went dark, so Jason placed the phone on his nightstand next to the USB drive and plugged it in.

I'll enter the USB drive into evidence as soon as I get into the office tomorrow.

Jason crawled into bed next to his wife. He stared at the ceiling, unaware of the extensive chaos the three-inch piece of circuitry and plastic on his nightstand would bring into his life.

Chapter 2

One Year Earlier near Payson, Arizona

Jason gazed at the picture of his little brother on the fireplace mantel, and the familiar deep, dull ache of excruciation loss hit him like a gut punch.

I wish you were here, Josh, to see what we did. It looks great, and you'd love it.

Five months after Jason buried his brother, he began construction of his home in Whispering Pines, Arizona, that he'd dreamt up with Josh. Jason poured himself into the off-grid house to take his mind off his brother and build his new life. A quarter of the way into the four-month project, the peace of mind and satisfaction Jason hoped would accompany the rise of the new structure remained elusive. He didn't just lose his brother to a drug cartel but also his sense of purpose after he left his role as a full-time pararescueman in the United States Air Force.

Jason had to fill the growing void in his life, so he enlisted in the Drug Enforcement Administration. Special Agent Holland planted the seed to join the DEA after they chased down the La Palma cartel in the forests of Arizona the previous summer. The two unlikely partners worked in tandem to capture and kill members of the cartel responsible for the death of Josh Mulder. Jason testified to put the remaining members of the El Salvadoran gang behind bars, along with corrupt Navajo County Sheriff Kellerman. During the hunt for the cartel, Holland recognized Jason's unique skill set and disdain for all involved with narcotics.

The initial step to becoming a DEA special agent required Jason to pass the highly selective and demanding hiring process. First was the grueling Physical Task Assessment or PTA, which only five percent of applicants passed on the first attempt. Fortunately for Jason, his training regime as a pararescueman was well-suited for the PTA. Even while building a home every day, Jason joined the rare group of applicants that passed the PTA on the first attempt after he gained all the necessary points on the sit-ups, 300-meter run, push-ups, and 1.5-mile run.

The panel interviews, physical and psychological assessments, polygraph, and background investigation followed the PTA, which Jason passed without problems. Next, they slotted Jason for BATP, or Basic Agent Training Program, at the DEA Academy in Quantico, Virginia.

Thoughts of Josh's young life ending at age fifteen by a drug cartel always put Jason in a foul mood, so he went outside after the mid-winter sun rose above the pine trees surrounding his yard and split logs for the wood-fired stove. Once Jason built a waist-high supply of kindling, he carried an armful inside and inserted several pieces of wood into the belly of the cast-iron beast that demanded regular feeding to keep his Whispering Pines home warm. Ten miles north of Payson, Arizona, the tiny residential community contained a cluster of summer homes and full-time residents nestled among a thick stand of Ponderosa pine trees in the Tonto National Forest. Jason's property bordered the meandering East Verde River, delivering abundant wildlife and breathtaking vistas of the rugged Arizona High Country.

Jason returned to his back patio, turned a chair toward the river, and stared into the forest. He would have continued for hours if his phone hadn't buzzed in his pocket. His dad texted a confirmation of when he'd pick Jason up and drive him to the airport in Phoenix. Jason didn't have time to sulk about the lost future with his younger brother. He had to get his affairs in order before leaving for one hundred and fifty days.

The Boeing 737 landed at Dulles International Airport on a sunny but frigid February afternoon two days later. He secured his luggage and boarded a shuttle bus for the ninety-minute trip to Quantico, Virginia, thirty-five miles southwest of Washington, DC.

At twenty-six, he was several years older than most of his BATP class's fifty-four basic agent trainees. For some, this posed a problem.

At the Academy, Jason's roommate was Andrew Cohen, from Lauderdale Lakes, Florida, and they immediately hit it off. Jason suspected he'd get along with everyone, but quickly sensed one guy he'd have to put into place. Anthony Russo, from East Rutherford, New Jersey, strutted up and down the dorm hallway on the first night like he was the top peacock in the class. The only encounter with Mister Russo happened two days after moving into the Academy.

"Move your ass, Grandpa. I need to fill up and don't have all day," Russo ordered Jason. The twenty-two-year-old was six feet tall, so Jason had a two-inch height advantage, but the buff Jersey boy had thirty pounds on Jason's one-hundred-and-ninety-pound frame. Russo's quip at the water filling station drew laughs from other trainees, but Jason didn't acknowledge the jab. He'd seen this movie a hundred times in the Air Force. Men thrown together in a new environment always have some that test their position in the unspoken hierarchy. Jason chose not to challenge the young buck and continued to fill his water bottle for defensive tactics training. He'd deal with the annoying gnat more discreetly later. Russo made the mistake of taking the delayed response as a weakness.

Later that evening, Russo barged into Jason's room.

"They assigned me latrine detail tonight, but I'm not doing it. I need one of you two ladies to finish it in the next thirty minutes."

Mulder and Cohen looked at each other and then back to Russo without saying a word. Russo marched over to the former PJ sitting on his bed. He bent down until his face was ten inches from Jason's nose.

"You better get going now, old man. It may take you a little longer."

Jason stared into Russo's eyes and saw the fear behind the bravado. He stood slowly and kept his eyes locked on his challenger.

"We're not cleaning anything," Jason said. Russo attempted what Jason guessed was supposed to be an intimidating smirk, but Jason wasn't concerned, so he turned and opened his wall locker.

"Don't turn your back on me," Russo chirped.

Russo grabbed Jason in a bear hug from behind, and Jason's instincts kicked in with lightning-quick speed. He elbowed Russo in the gut, which caused him to lose his grip and bend over, so Jason followed with the same right elbow under his chin. Jason spun around as Russo fell back, catching the Jersey boy by his shirt and left arm. In the blink of an eye, Jason had his left hand at the top of Russo's back, pushing his head down toward Jason's waist. During his Krav Maga training, Jason was taught to finish attackers in this position with an elbow or hammer fist to the back of the neck, but that could cause a lethal injury, and this situation didn't warrant a deadly response. Instead, Jason swept Russo's right leg and slammed him to the ground. Russo's face connected squarely with the freshly waxed tile floor, which sent a loud slapping sound into the hallway. This drew observers to the dust-up like moths to a flame.

Jason recalled Holland's advice for the Academy as the crowd grew.

"Keep your nose clean, and don't attract attention to yourself," Holland advised.

Jason knew that ship had sailed, so he switched into crisis management mode in front of a growing audience.

"Are you alright?" Jason asked.

Russo shook his head and stared blankly at nothing particular on the gray wall.

"You have to be careful not to slip on the slick floors."

Jason helped Russo up when an instructor charged into the room.

"What the hell is going on here?"

He looked at the growing black and blue bump on Russo's forehead and then at Jason, helping his former aggressor to his feet.

"He rushed into this room too fast and did a nosedive into our floor."

The instructor stared at Jason for several seconds and then turned to Cohen. "Is this true?"

"Yes, sir," Cohen replied.

The instructor looked at Russo and seemed to recognize the stars swirling around his head.

"Don't run in socks on these floors, dumbass. That's why we issue your boots. Everyone, back to your rooms."

Russo never spoke or made eye contact with Jason over the next five months. Nobody else challenged the elder trainee in the class.

Jason's remaining time at BATP was less dramatic. The instructors filled his days and nights with hours of classroom instruction sandwiched between hands-on training from early mornings deep into the evening. He spent over 1,000 hours on the grounds in Quantico, learning the skills and replicating the conditions DEA special agents encountered in the field.

Jason graduated and earned his gold and blue DEA badge. He became one of over 5,000 special agents in the lead agency for federal narcotics investigations and enforcement. Jason returned to Payson, Arizona, in time to watch the night sky light up with red, white, and blue fireworks for Independence Day. While the pyrotechnics burst in the air, Jason lowered his gaze and watched the splashes of color dancing in the eyes of his girlfriend, Shanna. He continued to stare until Shanna turned toward him.

"Is everything okay?" Shanna asked between the booms.

"Everything is fine."

"Are the fireworks bothering you? Do you not like them?"

Jason loved how Shanna cared deeply about him and other people. She was genuinely kind to her core, and he knew she'd make a great mother and wife.

Jason took her hand and looked back to the sky to catch the barrage of bright, multicolor explosions during the grand finale. After the sky turned quiet and black, he got down on one knee and proposed to Shanna. She nodded, jumped into his arms, and buried her face in his chest. Jason held her tighter than any embrace in his life.

One year after they met, it was time to upgrade Shanna's title from girlfriend to fiancée. His time at the DEA Academy taught him how to become a special agent, and he also learned that he wanted to spend the rest of his life with Shanna.

Neither Jason nor Shanna desired a large or complicated wedding, so he rented a tux, and she borrowed a dress made by her aunt on the Fort Apache Reservation. They married at sunset at the L'Auberge de Sedona resort in Sedona, Arizona, a month after the proposal. Shanna and Jason's immediate family and a handful of friends joined them under a canopy of cottonwood trees along Oak Creek with Sedona's mystical rusty red rocks surrounding the venue.

After a honeymoon on the beaches of Nuevo Vallarta, Mexico, Jason moved his new bride into the home he built in Whispering Pines. Days after Shanna moved in, Jason started his career as a special agent at the DEA Post of Duty Office in Camp Verde, Arizona. The office required a one-hour commute each day he wasn't in the field, but it allowed Jason to remain in Whispering Pines and not relocate to another city like Phoenix or Tucson.

Jason's boss, Special Agent Holland, immediately thrust him into the overflowing number of cases at the district office. He worked tirelessly on narcotics investigations and deciphering information from informants in the busy Central Arizona corridor. The Verde Valley was outside the Arizona HIDTA or High-Intensity Drug Trafficking Area, which seemed to attract narcos like Titan that wished to elude the brightest DEA spotlight yet maintain easy access to Phoenix, Tucson, and the lucrative east-west Interstates to California and the East Coast.

After his year-end review with Special Agent Holland, Jason remained in the office after everyone left for home. He pushed himself away from his laptop and strolled to the window. He peered outside at the snow flurries swirling in the wind under the streetlights as he reflected on his evaluation. Holland gave him an average rating, which is positive for a new agent on the job for less than a year, but for Jason, it stung.

Average is not good enough. Average is the same as failing.

The former Air Force pararescueman demanded excellence from himself in everything he did, and for six years as a PJ, he operated at a high level every day. He expected a learning curve during the transition from combat search and rescue medic to a federal law enforcement agent dedicated to eradicating illegal narcotics, but it was steeper than he envisioned. Mastering the DEA special agent mindset and daily duties was challenging, but it also came with rewards and benefits important to Jason. His new position as a special agent provided the things he lost after transitioning from full-time Air Force to a part-time PJ in the Air Force Reserve. He missed the teamwork and camaraderie with his fellow PJs while helping innocent civilians and citizens. The DEA provided a similar purpose, so he wanted to make his new job work. He yearned to react as decisively as a DEA special agent as he did a PJ. Jason needed the opportunity to make a statement to Holland and change his current trajectory within the DEA. He returned to his desk, unaware that his opportunity was around the corner, but the result would turn Jason's and Shanna's lives into hell.

CHAPTER 3

3-Days after the Titan sting in Whispering Pines, Arizona

The muffled crackle and hiss of logs in the wood-burning stove were the only sounds in Jason Mulder's home minutes before sunrise. The aroma of pine sap and freshly brewed coffee filled the dimly lit dining room as Jason stuffed his laptop into his work backpack. He filled his 32 oz travel mug, leaned against the granite counter, and blew on the steaming black liquid before taking his first sip. It was Monday, and his mistakes during the Titan sting were days old. Jason took to heart the advice a Combat Rescue Officer gave him after several bloody missions in Afghanistan.

"We see too much shit out here to stay sane if we don't let go of things quickly. After a tough mission, you need to face it, process it, learn from it, and then flush those memories down the toilet like a giant turd."

The sage advice helped Jason cope overseas, but back in the States, his quiet time savoring a cup of coffee in the morning before the rest of the world woke up did the trick. It ranked in his top five things he loved just after family, friends, country, and the outdoors.

Jason added two fresh logs to the wood-burning stove before sticking his head into the bedroom to visit Shanna, who was getting dressed for work.

"It got pretty cold last night, so watch out for black ice on the road when you drive to work," Jason warned Shanna. "I put a couple more logs in the stove, so it'll be nice and toasty until you leave."

Shanna stopped brushing her hair and stood on her tiptoes to kiss her husband.

"You take such good care of me."

Jason turned to leave, but Shanna snagged his arm to stop him.

"Do you know what today is?" Shanna asked.

Jason's body tensed as he tried to figure out what important date he missed.

"Ummm. It's the first day of spring?"

"That's not wrong, but that's not what I was thinking. It's our eight-month anniversary."

Jason chuckled. "I didn't know eight months was a big milestone for anniversaries. What's the gift? Bath salts and a bottle of wine?"

Shanna bit her lower lip. "We can take a bath together with that bottle of wine."

Jason scooped his wife into his arms and kissed her.

"We better stop now, or we're both going to be late for work," Shanna whispered into Jason's ear.

"I've always thought arriving on time for work is overrated."

Shanna tilted her head to let her silky black hair cover one eye. "Maybe later."

He stared at Shanna to verify she wasn't planning to change her mind. Once she resumed brushing her hair, Jason left.

Jason arrived at the DEA duty office at Camp Verde a few minutes after eight. The newest office in the Phoenix district occupied a converted former retail print shop into a workspace with two private offices and enough desks for fourteen special agents and support staff. Jason unpacked his laptop, placing it on his open-air desk positioned face-to-face with Special Agent Carlson's desk.

"Holland is looking for you," Carlson told Jason as he sat down.

"Me? What does he want?"

"Don't know. He came by a few minutes ago and told me to tell you to stop by when you get in."

"Alright, I'll go see him in a minute."

Jason wondered why Holland wanted to see him so early in the day. He had an idea it had something to do with the Titan sting last week and that it wouldn't be a pleasant conversation. He strolled to Special Agent Holland's office and knocked on the open door.

"Come in," Holland yelled from his desk. "Did Carlson tell you I was looking for you?"

"No, he never said a thing." It was common for special agents to pull pranks and bust each other's balls. This was Jason's turn to get back at Carlson for all the times he pranked him.

"I just told him ten minutes ago to tell you. Let him know when you return. I want to see him next. Sit down."

Jason faced Holland perched behind his desk. Holland tapped several keys on his computer and then turned to Jason.

"The Use of Force Review Board already justified my shooting of Titan, so that's behind us, but we still haven't discussed what you did. In the future, will you follow protocol if an active threat exists before giving aid?"

Jason looked down at his boots and then up at Holland. "Yeah, I understand what I can and can't do in the future. My instinct is to help, but I'm more conscious of DEA protocol now, so I won't do it in the future."

"Good to hear. Would you like to get your chance to prove it sooner than later?"

Jason straightened up in his chair. "Sure. What are the details?"

Holland stood and walked to a poster-size map of Arizona. He pointed to the eastern part of the state about halfway up the map.

"The Flagstaff office has a sting in Show Low, Arizona, tomorrow night. The intel says a lot of coke is involved, and they're short on manpower, so they asked us to send an extra body or two. They asked specifically for someone familiar with the area, and I know you've spent some time in Show Low, so I recommended you. They immediately approved."

"Is this a joint sting with local law enforcement?" Jason asked.

"Yeah, Show Low PD."

Jason leaned back and exhaled a deep breath of relief. Although former Sheriff Kellerman was in prison, he was popular in the county and still had supporters working as deputies at the Navajo County Sheriff's Office. He testified against the sheriff and helped put the old lawman in prison, so Jason knew he might not be in good standing with some of the NCSO deputies. Jason didn't want to second guess whether the local officers there to support the DEA were an ally or an enemy during an active sting.

"You'll be working with Special Agent Donaldson and Special Agent Cruz. I believe you met them before during the sting in Flagstaff a few months ago."

Jason nodded. "Yeah, I remember those two. They were an odd team but seemed like decent agents."

"Odd?"

"Not in a bad way. It's just that Cruz is a gym rat in his mid-twenties who spends more time on his hair than my wife, and Donaldson reminds me of the stereotypical old guy who yells at kids to get off his lawn."

Holland chuckled. "I can't argue with either of those descriptions, but they always get the job done. Will you help them out?"

"I'm in."

"Great, I'll let them know."

Before Jason exited the office, Holland stopped him. "Hey, Mulder, one more thing."

Jason stopped in the doorway and turned toward his boss.

"This is an opportunity for you to shine in front of special agents from another office and could be good for your career. No pressure, but don't mess this up."

Jason stood tall in the doorway, flashed a grin, and responded confidently. "I won't. I promise you'll hear nothing but good things about me after this mission."

He strutted out of the office, comfortable with his prediction. It was a promise Jason would not keep.

CHAPTER 4

Show Low, Arizona

The streetlamps illuminated the nearly empty parking lot outside the largest grocery store in town when Jason arrived. A few customers loaded their bags into their vehicles after the store closed for the day, leaving plenty of room for DEA parking. Stately ponderosa pine trees surrounded the property and soared fifty feet into the air, giving the parking lot a canyon-like feel.

Jason turned down the classical music pumping softly through the truck speakers he traditionally played when he required optimal focus. During the ninety-minute drive from Payson, the DEA special agent thought about his promise to Holland and was optimistic he'd step up and deliver on the moonless night. As instructed, he pulled next to a cluster of vehicles parked at the far end of the parking lot.

Jason recognized the balding Special Agent Donaldson and beefy Special Agent Cruz talking to a handful of Show Low police officers, so he parked his new truck next to the Flagstaff team. It was a lifted black Ford F-150 Raptor pickup truck with front and rear LED light bars on the roof. This turned several heads, but Cruz was the first to arrive, with Donaldson a few steps behind.

Cruz extended his hand. Jason shook with Cruz and then Donaldson when he arrived. Donaldson introduced himself when Jason stopped him.

"I worked with you guys before. It was at a sting in Flagstaff with both of you just off the Northern Arizona University campus. I look forward to working with you again."

Donaldson's forehead creased as if he was trying to remember, and then he nodded. Cruz smacked Jason on the shoulder. "Oh yeah, I remember. That tweaker thought he could take me. I think his jaw is still wired shut today."

The younger Cruz was the talker of the dynamic duo, while Donaldson maintained a near-permanent look of indifference. The fifty-four-year-old veteran DEA Special Agent had an athletic build for his age but looked older with his patchy, short, gray hair and weather-beaten face. Jason imagined a lifetime of drug stings contributed to his thousand-yard stare.

Cruz stepped toward Jason's truck.

"Nice ride, Mulder. Does that have the 5.2-liter V8 under the hood?" Cruz asked.

Jason laughed and shook his head. "I wish. That's in the new models. Mine has five years and seventy thousand miles on her."

"Still looks like new. How does she look on the inside?"

Jason checked his watch. It was an unusual request before a sting, but Cruz seemed very interested, and Jason still loved to share his baby.

"I guess we have a few minutes. Hop in, and I'll give you the nickel tour."

Cruz climbed in, and Jason started his commercial that he'd pitched dozens of times. "This model has a twin-turbo V6 engine, standard all-wheel drive, and sits on—"

"Whoa, this has the console shifter that folds down and turns into a desk inside your truck like a transformer," Cruz interrupted. "I wish my Mustang had this. I'd do all my reports in my car instead of driving into the field office."

Jason nodded slowly. "Yeah, it's nice. I probably don't use it as much as I could."

The back passenger door swung open, and Jason looked in the rear cabin to see who was coming inside for the tour when Cruz sounded like he'd just opened his favorite Christmas present of all time.

"Mulder, that instrument panel is sick! That digital gauge cluster with all the special graphics and aluminum trim is my favorite thing in this truck."

Jason turned from the dashboard to Cruz to ensure he wasn't joking. The instrument panel was nice, but it didn't make the top twenty things Jason liked about his off-road truck.

"Wrap it up, fellas," Donaldson told the duo.

Jason turned and saw the senior special agent standing with the rear passenger door open.

"We need to focus on the upcoming task at hand."

Jason and Cruz exited the truck and caught up with Donaldson as the rest of the team reviewed the final details of the sting.

After the briefing, Jason joined Cruz, Donaldson, and another special agent from Flagstaff in one vehicle as they drove through town until they reached a neighborhood with no streetlights and vehicles parked on the front lawns. Two beat-up pickup trucks parked in front of a mobile home with a DIY front porch addition confirmed they found the right property.

All four DEA special agents exited their vehicles, and four additional Show Low police officers joined the team.

"Everybody's home," Donaldson whispered.

Jason's role in this sting was back up with Show Low PD. He took his position behind the open truck door and directed his M6A2 rifle toward the front door.

"Let's go."

The trio moved in unison up the warped steps of the patio. Donaldson placed his back against the right side of the door, and the other special agent mirrored him on the left side. Cruz held the battering ram, swung it forward on Donaldson's signal, and obliterated the flimsy metal door.

Neighborhood dogs barked and howled as Jason peered through his red dot reflex sight at the front door. He was prepared to neutralize any threats that appeared.

It took less than a minute, but it felt five times longer. First, Jason saw a bright light and then heard the flash-bang grenade, followed by shouting from DEA agents. A tall man with long blond hair burst through the former front door hanging on one hinge, crossed the short patio, and jumped to the rocky soil below. Jason tracked the fleeing drug dealer with his rifle while searching his hands for weapons. He raised his M6A2 when Special Agent Cruz emerged from the home and tackled the man like an all-pro linebacker. Jason watched Cruz give the man several elbows to the face and then yank the cuffed man to his feet with one arm. The house fell silent and the other Show Low police officers lowered their weapons, but Jason kept his eyes locked on the front door. Minutes later, a whistle and laughter proceeded shouts of "all clear" from inside the house, so Jason followed the Show Low officers inside.

He found Donaldson holding a black gym bag in one hand and a bag of white powder half covered by tin foil in the other. He had a smile that accentuated his missing incisor tooth.

"I count forty-two kilos of coke, boys. This was a big one," Donaldson said. "Let's get all this into evidence and write this one up. The Phoenix District Office will be excited to hear about this."

Donaldson handed Jason one of the gym bags while Cruz took the other one. He followed Cruz to the locked Pelican case in the back of the SUV.

"Should we count it?" Jason asked.

Cruz looked at Jason as if he'd asked the dumbest question in the history of man. "I thought you said you've done this before."

"We usually count it. That's why I asked."

Cruz shook his head. "We counted it twice and came up with forty-two, but by all means, if you feel the need to check our work, go right ahead."

Jason felt heat creep up his back into his neck. He knew he should count the bags, but the pressure not to ruin a successful bust was too great to overcome.

"Forty-two it is," Jason replied.

Jason and Cruz handed the bags to a Show Low PD sergeant kneeling in the back of the SUV and watched him place all the cocaine into the secure case. The sergeant locked the case and the vehicle. All three men returned to the trailer.

Donaldson and the other special agents completed their inventory of the remaining cash and guns while Jason watched. He did very little during the sting and questioned why he even had to be there, but in the end, Jason felt satisfied he contributed in a small way. Nobody got hurt, and they took a substantial quantity of drugs off the street. A win was a win.

Everyone returned to the grocery store parking lot and strode to their vehicles.

"Are you taking the evidence in tonight?" Donaldson asked the Show Low PD sergeant.

"Yeah, I'm heading in right after I leave here."

Donaldson turned to Cruz and Mulder. He seemed reinvigorated by the operation. "Good job, guys. Let's go home and celebrate another successful sting."

"I will," Cruz replied.

Cruz jumped in his Mustang GT first and pulled forward so a member of the Show Low Police K9 unit could run the black and tan German Shepard around his vehicle. Donaldson followed in his Chevy Truck, and it was Jason's turn to have the narcotics detection dog walk around his truck with his handler—a standard operating procedure after every sting to prevent drug thefts.

Jason pulled forward and waited for the officer to complete the revolution around his truck, followed by a wave that cleared him to leave. When the dog reached the vehicle's passenger side, it stopped and barked to alert its handler. The K9 officer pulled the excited German Shepard away, walked in circles several times, and returned to the passenger side of Jason's vehicle. It barked wildly again. Jason leaned over in his seat to get a better look at what was going on when he heard a tap on his window and rolled it down. A sergeant from the Show Low Police Department stood outside with a disappointed look.

"Special Agent Mulder, please step outside your vehicle."

Jason smiled and looked around for Donaldson and Cruz.

This must be some rookie initiation, Jason thought. When he didn't see anyone from the DEA office in Flagstaff, he leaned out the open window.

"What's the problem, sergeant?" Jason asked with a playful smile.

The sergeant stepped back and motioned for another member of the Show Low PD to join him. He widened his base and moved his hand closer to his service pistol.

"Turn your engine off and step from your vehicle. Now!"

The facial expression, stance, and tone told Jason all he needed to know. This wasn't a prank, and he was in serious trouble.

Chapter 5

Show Low, Arizona

The parking lot seemed to come alive. Members of Show Low PD buzzed around Jason and his vehicle as the German Shepard barked continuously at the Ford Raptor pickup truck. It was disorienting as Jason slid from his truck onto the asphalt pavement. A Show Low police officer put on black nitrile gloves, opened the rear passenger door, and disappeared from view.

Why is the K9 barking? Why are they searching my truck? What are they looking for?

Questions scrolled through Jason's mind like a movie on fast-forward. He'd seen enough drug busts to know they were searching for drugs, but his brain couldn't accept that it was happening to him. No drug, narcotic, or illegal substance has ever been inside his truck.

"Hey, man," the Show Low officer said. "Please turn around and put your hands behind your back."

"What's going on?" Jason asked.

"'It's the job, man. You understand."

Jason stared at the officer for several seconds, pondering his next move. He saw the flashlight beam in his rear cabin changing angles and heard plastic bending and breaking. Jason turned around and pushed his arms out, so he was easier to cuff.

"Now, will you tell me what's going on?" Jason asked.

The officer applied the cuffs, but not too tight.

"Got a hit from the K9. As you know, getting a false positive is not uncommon, so we'll check it out, and if everything is clear, you'll be on your way."

Jason had witnessed false hits by K9 units before and took a long breath at the thought of driving away soon. The officer walked Jason away from his truck and leaned him against an SUV owned by Show Low PD. A black and white police cruiser with SERGEANT written below the City of Show Low logo arrived. The man dressed in a black uniform with a gold badge exited the cruiser and joined the search inside Jason's rear passenger door. Each minute that passed eroded Jason's confidence of a simple misunderstanding.

The repeated barking of the K9 unleashed a range of emotions inside Jason. After shock and confusion, his muscles tensed as a wave of anger washed over him.

"This is bullshit. There are no drugs in that truck," Jason said aloud to nobody. He pushed away from the SUV and shuffled back to the Show Low officer who put him there.

"You need to uncuff me and let me go. The K9 hit and search is bullshit, and you know it."

The officer observed Jason approaching; his response was cool and far less cordial now. "Stay back by the vehicle, or you'll find yourself in the back seat."

Jason's new vantage point allowed him to see officers sink behind his truck and up again like ships in a storm. Their expressions were grave, and their eyes accusatory. The entire scene emitted a tension that Jason felt he could touch, and his stomach turned sour.

Why would the dog register a hit?

A minute later, he had an answer.

A Show Low police officer left the rear cab and carried something to the front of Jason's truck. Two bags of white powder and an envelope bulging with foreign currency bills landed on the black hood. Another officer took pictures of the evidence while the sergeant moved toward Jason. Four Show Low police officers converged around Jason.

"Did you forget to put all the contraband in the evidence truck?" the sergeant asked.

"No. Why?"

The sergeant nodded and pursed his lips. "Come on, help me help you. Did you intend to examine some of the evidence or take it somewhere else for analysis?"

Jason understood why he was asking and wanted to give him an answer to make everything go away, but he still couldn't wrap his mind around Show Low PD finding drugs in his truck.

"No, I took my bag straight to the truck and handed it to your evidence guy without opening it. Cruz and your evidence guy can vouch for me."

The sergeant looked around the parking lot and back at Jason. "Neither of them is here right now, so that doesn't help."

"Can you tell me what's going on?" Jason asked.

"We found two kilos of what appears to be cocaine in the underseat storage area on the passenger side of your rear cabin. It's in a package similar to the wrapping material seized earlier tonight. You're still pretty new. Are you sure you didn't mess up transporting the coke to evidence?"

Jason considered lying but knew that could get him into more trouble. He was innocent, so this crazy misunderstanding would eventually get sorted out.

"No, I did everything by the book," Jason lied. He wished he counted the cocaine in his bag before handing it over as evidence.

The sergeant shook his head and grabbed Jason by the arm. He led him back to the police cruiser and turned him until their eyes met.

"You're under arrest for possession of cocaine with the intent to distribute. Read him his rights."

Another officer put Jason in the backseat and left the grocery store parking lot. Jason watched familiar buildings pass by from his unfamiliar position in the back of the police cruiser. The reality of his predicament grew clearer with each passing block, and the impact of an arrest for possession of cocaine settled around Jason like a descending fog. It was like the turmoil of what lay ahead heightened his senses. He grew keenly aware of the metal restraints digging into his wrist and how he had to sit at an angle with his hands behind his back. Each breath grew more challenging. It was like he was trying to breathe through a straw.

Jason watched the eyes of the driver look back and forth from the rearview mirror and the road. The Show Low police station was less than a mile away, and his arrest was imminent, so Jason formed a plan for an even greater concern. He couldn't be in the same prison as former Sheriff Kellerman.

Jason leaned forward and spoke through the metal grate separating the front seats from the back.

"Where are you taking me?"

The eyes returned to the mirror.

"Show Low police station."

"Is that where I'll be until my attorney arrives?"

"I don't know. I just provide the transportation."

Jason looked out the window and turned back to the driver.

"I don't use or sell any drugs. Call Special Agent Holland with the DEA, and he'll—"

The driver cut Jason off before he could finish.

"I wouldn't talk if I were you. Talk to your lawyer first. You're in a lot of trouble."

Chapter 6

Jason leaned back in the cruiser as the driver drove through the well-lit parking lot to an oversized garage door on the side of the building. A large white sign above the door said: Central Booking. Law Enforcement Entry Only.

The driver helped Jason out of the back seat, and the metal garage door creaked as it descended and slammed shut. The next stop was Booking, and ninety minutes later, he was ready for Holding. Before entering his cell, Jason called Shanna with his one call, but it was after two in the morning, and she didn't answer. He left her a voicemail with a brief explanation and instructions to find an attorney.

After the call, they transferred Jason to his cell. He was happy to see nobody else was on the narrow, rusted, metal bunk bed in the corner. Jason laid down on the thin, worn mattress with a lumpy pillow and thought of the sleepless nights endured by those who had occupied the cell before him. Although Jason was awake for over twenty-four hours, sleep wasn't possible, so he sat up and waited for the sun to rise.

The next day, Jason remained in his cell until after lunch. A guard took him to a small room with cream-colored concrete walls and a metal table bolted to the middle of the floor. He sat by himself for several minutes until a man in his fifties with a medium build dressed in a tan suit, wavy, dark hair parted on the side, and a thick gray mustache about the same color as stainless steel resting under a broad nose entered the room. Jason did a double-take to ensure he correctly saw the dichotomy in hair color.

"Jason Mulder?" the man asked.

"Yes."

"Good."

The man took the chair in the room on the opposite side of the table. He opened a leather briefcase and placed two manila file folders on the table.

"I'm Dom Bertelli with Kalil, Pratt, and Dean PLC. I'll represent you in your initial appearance later today."

Mr. Bertelli opened the file folder to his left and selected a document.

"You're being charged with possession of a controlled substance with intent to distribute over 9 grams. That's a class-2 felony."

The attorney looked up as if he expected a rebuttal, but Jason said nothing.

"What happened?" Bertelli asked.

Jason focused on the peeling paint on the table for several seconds and shook his head. "I'm not sure. We busted a known group of dealers in Show Low and found a bunch of coke. It was a textbook operation until I went to leave in my personal vehicle. I went through the standard K-9 checkpoint like I've done dozens of times. Only this time, the dog alerted them to something in my passenger door. That's when they claimed to find coke in my truck door."

"How'd it get there?"

"I don't know."

The attorney eyed Jason for several seconds. "We can't help you if you don't tell me the truth."

"I don't know how else to say this so you'll understand. I didn't put it there."

The attorney leaned back in his chair but did not break eye contact with Jason.

"Fine. They'll get the tox results in a day or two. What are they going to find?"

"They won't find anything. Zip. Nothing. Nada."

"What about the Hong Kong currency? That looks like distribution."

"I didn't put any coke or Hong Kong money in my truck."

Mr. Bertelli dropped the stapled pages onto the table and breathed a long sigh.

"This isn't good, Jason. If this was your first offense of simple possession, you might walk with probation, treatment, and a shit-ton of community service, but you know as well as anyone that you're facing jail time. They have physical evidence of two kilos of cocaine in your truck. Do you know the sentence if you get charged with possession and distribution of that much coke?"

Jason shook his head.

"Five to ten years. Maybe twelve if they find aggravating factors like that SIG in your glove box. Although you were on duty, that's your personal weapon, and it becomes an aggravating offense if they deem you were committing a felony with a firearm. Are you sure you don't have a better answer for the drugs and foreign currency found in your truck? Did you lend your truck to someone? Could someone else have put it there? Anything?"

Jason looked down at his hands and then at Bertelli. "No. I don't know anyone else who could have put it in my truck. I went through another K9 checkpoint last week after a sting in Phoenix and passed with flying colors. It had to be put in my truck recently."

Bertelli unbuttoned his suit jacket and leaned forward. "I have to ask this to cover all my bases, so don't get offended, but are you sure you didn't accidentally take it from the sting? It was a lot of coke, so it's understandable if some got mixed up. Is it possible you picked it up in another sting? Were you transporting it to the district office as evidence? That is something a judge may understand," Bertelli said. His voice rose in intensity with each additional question.

"That would break every protocol in the book," Jason responded.

"You're not leaving me with many options for a defense. Our best option may be to negotiate a plea deal."

Jason slammed his fist on the table. "I did nothing wrong. This is a colossal mistake. I'm 100% innocent, and I'll prove it if we go to trial."

Bertelli held up his hand. "Let's not put the cart in front of the horse. Today, the judge will notify you of the charges and decide on bail. I will push your impeccable military record and lack of priors to see if she'll let you go on your own recognizance. The foreign currency may show you're a potential flight risk, so I'll do my best to push the bond down as far as possible if it goes that way. Can you scrap together up to five or six grand if needed?"

Jason ran his fingers through his short hair. Money was tight after building the off-grid house, stocking his new armory, and buying the Raptor truck. He'd also have substantial bills from his new attorney due soon.

"I forgot to ask when you came in. How did you find out about me?" Jason asked.

"Your wife contacted your brother Kevin at the Colorado Springs Fire Department. My brother Michael worked with Kevin in Phoenix before he moved to Colorado, so he knew I was a defense attorney. I work with a lot of first responders."

Jason nodded. He trusted his older brother Kevin's referral and just hoped he offered a friend and family discount. Jason's thoughts returned to finding the funds for bail. He suspected he could borrow some money from his parents if he had to. He hated to owe people anything, especially money, but they'd transfer him to the Navajo County Jail if he couldn't make bail. Jason knew that as a federal law enforcement agent, he'd have a target on his back among the inmates. He was likely also on the shit list of any Navajo County corrections officers that found out he testified against the former sheriff of Navajo County.

"Do whatever you have to do to keep me out of jail."

Jason knew going to federal or county jail would put him inside the lion's den. The length of the sentence didn't matter. Any amount of time was a death sentence. Federal police officers who become inmates don't walk out of prison.

Chapter 7

A white midsize SUV sent puffs of gray exhaust smoke over the sidewalk as it idled near the entrance of the Show Low Police Station. Shanna sat with the music turned low and twirled a tuft of her hair as she eyed everyone who exited the adobe building. She sat straight in her seat and pulled forward when her husband appeared outside the entrance.

Nineteen hours after the K9 alerted its handler, Jason was out of police custody.

"Thanks for coming up with the money so fast," Jason said as soon as his butt hit the seat. The judge set his bail at $25,000, and Shanna scraped together ten percent within an hour to post the bond to spring her husband.

Shanna leaned over and hugged him.

"What happened?"

"Let's get out of here. I'll tell you on the way home."

"Do we need to get your truck?"

"Not today. It'll be in evidence for a few more days. I want to go home."

The first five minutes of the two-hour drive to Whispering Pines were quiet. His current predicament still agitated Jason, but he knew Shanna had questions, and she deserved answers. He cleared his throat and shared the entire story from the request from Special

Agent Holland until the judge set his bond. Shanna kept her eyes on the road and listened with occasional glances at her husband, nodding to confirm she understood. Jason wondered if she was in shock like he was hours earlier. It was still hard to believe they had charged him with a crime he didn't commit.

The following day, Jason woke up grateful to be in his own bed and that it was Saturday. He wasn't sure he had a job, but he wouldn't have to worry about it for a couple of days. After feeding the wood-burning stove another log, Jason sat at the kitchen table and ran the previous forty-eight hours through his mind for the millionth time. He still couldn't pinpoint how two kilos of cocaine could spontaneously appear in his truck. His head throbbed, and his neck grew tense as he mentally racked his brain for answers. Fortunately, Shanna entered the kitchen and ended his self-torture.

"How did you sleep?"

"Pretty shitty, but better than I would have in a cell."

Shanna helped herself to a cup of coffee and sat at the kitchen table across from Jason.

"What are your plans for today?"

"It's nice out today, so I'll probably go fishing."

"Fishing?" Shanna asked. Her nose pinched, and her brow furrowed.

"Yeah. I'm going crazy thinking about everything that's happened the past two days, and fishing will help take my mind off it. I'll see if Kai can go with me."

Kai was Shanna's younger brother and the biggest fan in the Jason Mulder fan club. Jason's victim and grief counselor wife encouraged the relationship between her husband and his new brother-in-law. She shared with Jason that he was the responsible male role model Kai hadn't had since their father died when he was eight years old. Now Kai was an intern at the San Carlos Indian Community Game and Fish Department and needed strong male mentorship as he entered a pivotal crossroads. Shanna admitted to Jason that she believed the friendship with Kai also benefitted him. She was concerned about Jason's inability to grieve the loss of his younger brother, Josh, after his untimely death. Kai gave him the eager mentee and partner in crime Jason lost after Josh died. Initially, Jason was reluctant, but he spent more time with Kai after he graduated from college the previous year and now considered him like a little brother.

"Okay, but we need to figure out what's happening with you. Do you still have a job, and when do you have to go to court?" Shanna asked.

"My attorney has a status conference with the county attorney in the next few weeks. That will determine if they dismiss the case or proceed with charges, and yes, I still have a job."

"How do you know?"

"Nobody called to fire me yet."

Kai stared straight ahead through the windshield as Jason guided his truck higher into the heavily wooded Coconino National Forest. Once they climbed over 7,000 feet of elevation, they turned off the highway onto the gravel forest road that led to the serpentine Blue Ridge Reservoir. It was a favorite destination for local anglers, and Jason and Kai were admirers of the lake stocked with rainbow and brown trout. They'd fished together at the Blue Ridge Reservoir twice before, but today, Jason turned onto a different forest road instead of taking the typical path to the lake.

"Where are we going?" Kai asked. His long, midnight black hair, pulled back into a ponytail, smacked his tan and rust-colored flannel shirt every time he looked right and left.

"I'm not in the mood for crowds today, so we're going somewhere more secluded."

"How far?"

"Just a little farther."

Thirty minutes later, Jason pulled into a paved parking lot with ten of the twenty available parking spaces open.

"This is Kinder Crossing," Jason shared as he exited the truck. "We're about a mile east of the dam at Blue Ridge Reservoir as the crow flies." He took several steps and pointed to the waist-deep, meandering stream. "That's East Clear Creek. It has excellent wild brown trout a half mile from here."

Kai and Jason alternated back and forth from warm sun to cool shade as they hiked on a game trail through the dense pine trees to a broad section of the creek with calmer, deeper water. Crows notified the forest of the intruders from their lookout positions six stories above. Jason was the first to cast his line toward the brown trout darting to and from their rocky underwater shelter. He interrupted the rhythmic sounds of the gentle cascading stream when he turned to Kai standing five feet from him.

"I have something important to tell you, Kai, and I want you to hear it from me first," Jason opened.

Kai turned his full attention to Jason. "What is it?"

"The police arrested me for possession of cocaine after a sting in Show Low."

"What?" Kai shouted.

"It's a mistake because you know I'd never take or distribute drugs. Right?"

"Right," Kai replied. "Especially after what happened to Josh."

Jason nodded. "I'm telling you because I'll be spending a lot of time digging for the truth about what happened, so I may need your help."

Kai straightened up. "Sure, how can I help?"

"I may need you to help your sister if I can't be around."

Kai's shoulders slumped. "I'll help, but I was hoping for something more adventurous."

"If I need you to do something adventurous for me, something went drastically wrong. I do have something else I need you to do."

Kai turned toward Jason. "Okay."

"Remember how to get here."

"Here? Why?"

"So, you can drive here next time, you freeloader."

A blank expression remained on Kai's face for a couple of seconds until his lips curled up, and then he pushed his brother-in-law.

Jason feigned an angry look. "You better watch yourself."

Kai pushed him again, and Jason dropped his pole and snared Kai in a headlock before he could get his arms up to defend himself.

"Come on, Kai, you can do better than that."

Kai struggled to escape Jason's vice-like grip around his neck until he succumbed to deep belly laughs. The snorts of joy from Kai's mouth squished against Jason's chest reminded him of Josh. Jason needed to hear the sweet sound he had missed over the last two years. His face melted into a genuine smile for the first time in forty-eight hours.

Monday morning, Jason rose at five-thirty like every other workday. He hit the weights in his home gym next to the garage, showered, and made coffee as though the Show Low PD had never arrested him for felony drug possession. He didn't know what to expect once he arrived at the office because he'd never seen another special agent accused of a crime during his short stint with the DEA. Jason hoped the men and women in charge would know the cocaine found in his truck had to be a mistake. However, Jason wasn't betting on that ideal outcome and prepared himself to be fired on the spot.

The first hour in the office gave Jason hope. His digital key opened the secure front door, and he logged onto his computer. His hope for a resolution rose after another agent stopped by his desk to ask about the sting last Thursday night.

Did he not know what happened?

Jason stood to get another cup of coffee and saw Special Agent Holland leave his office and turn toward him. He knew in a nanosecond that he was coming for him by Holland's body language, and the shit was about to hit the fan.

"Mulder, in my office," Holland barked.

The thirty steps to his office felt like a mile. Hundreds of scenarios flashed through his mind.

"Sit down!"

Once Jason sat down, Holland got up and closed the door to the small office containing a desk, a file cabinet, and two chairs.

"What the hell happened in Show Low?" Jason observed Holland's neck transition to dark red below his square jaw.

Jason cleared his throat. "The K9 handler got a hit on my truck, and they found cocaine under the seat of my rear cabin."

"No shit, Mulder. I can read a report. Why the hell did you think you'd get away with stealing coke when you know every personal vehicle goes through a K9 inspection?"

Outrage replaced shame and embarrassment.

"That coke isn't mine! I know how it looks, but I didn't take anything from the crime scene. I'll fight all charges, and when I do, I'm positive I'll be exonerated!" Jason shouted back.

Holland stood behind his desk and crossed his arms. "So, what are you saying? Someone planted the coke in your truck?"

"The thought has crossed my mind."

"Okay then, who planted it?"

"I have no idea. If I knew, I'd beat their ass and serve them to you on a platter."

Holland raked his fingers through his buzzed blond hair that was thinner than when Jason first met him and leaned forward over his desk with his fingers supporting him.

"Everybody in the history of my time with the DEA says someone else planted the drugs on them. I know it's a long shot that it's true, so I'll open an internal investigation to see if we can find something."

"Thank you."

"Don't thank me yet," Holland chirped.

"I just heard from Virginia. You're on paid administrative leave until we complete the internal investigation, and you're either convicted or acquitted at trial. You're banned from this office and any DEA facilities until further notice. Leave your badge and your entry card to the office on my desk."

Jason reached into his pocket and placed a gold badge and a white RFID card on Holland's desk.

"What now?" Jason asked.

"Go home and pray the internal investigation finds someone else planted the coke."

"And if they don't?"

"Life as you know it will never be the same."

Chapter 8

Whispering Pines, Arizona

A gust of wind forced the sounds of rustling pine needles and the scent of rain through the open windows of the family room in Whispering Pines. Instead of its typical indigo blue, the afternoon sky featured a turbulent mix of white and gray, signaling an incoming spring storm. Jason welcomed the smell of anticipation the forest emits when rain is imminent, as he sat on the couch opposite Shanna, who was curled up on the other end, reading her book. He also had a book, which was closed while he stared at the wall with his feet propped up on an ottoman. Jason had formed a new habit of staring into nothingness since his arrest.

Jason's phone rang, and his eyes darted to Shanna.

"I have to take this."

Jason went into the bedroom and shut the door.

"Hello, Mr. Bertelli. Have you heard anything?"

"Yes, I spoke with the District Attorney in Phoenix during our status conference. I have some good news and some bad news."

Jason inhaled deeply. "Okay. Let me hear it."

"The good news is that he will not challenge the bail, so you are free until your trial. The bad news is that he will not drop charges, so the next step is a preliminary hearing."

"What happens then?"

"At a preliminary hearing, the prosecution presents evidence to prove the drug possession charge, and the judge will decide if there is sufficient evidence to go to trial. The judge can rule that the DA did not establish grounds for a criminal case and can dismiss the charges against you. I already have my team scouring over the evidence to see if we can find something to contest."

"What happens if the judge says the prosecutors have enough evidence for a case?"

Jason asked the question, but his mind raced to the worst-case scenario. He pictured a judge declaring him guilty, then sitting in a cell with a half dozen thugs cornering him with shanks. Jason figured he could handle one or two inmates, but it would be him against the entire prison population. He couldn't allow himself to go to prison.

"You'll be arraigned, and that's when you know the specific charge against you and when you'll plead guilty, not guilty, or no contest. If you—"

"I'll be pleading not guilty," Jason growled.

"Of course. If we don't get a dismissal at the preliminary hearing and you plead not guilty at the arraignment, then the judge schedules a trial."

"What do you need me to do?" Jason asked.

Bertelli exhaled loudly. "Not much you can do right now. Keep your nose clean and let me know if you come up with anyone else who may have had access to your truck before the sting in Show Low."

"I will," Jason said.

Jason ended the call and tossed his phone onto the bed. He turned to the wall, made a fist, and cocked his arm back to punch a hole through the drywall. Jason held it briefly and let his arm drop back to his side. He'd run everyone who came into contact with his truck before the sting through his mind over the last week. Jason considered crooked cops at Show Low PD, disgruntled co-workers at his office in Camp Verde, and he even ran his conversation with Donaldson and Cruz through his head again. They all had access to his vehicle, but nobody rose to the top as a prime suspect.

Jason returned to the family room and found Shanna sitting on the edge of the couch cushions. "What did he say?"

"It appears the DA is proceeding with the charge, but I get to stay home until the trial."

"When will we know for sure?"

"The deadline for the arraignment is April 6th, so we'll know next week."

Jason sat next to Shanna, put his elbows on his knees, and cupped his chin between his index fingers and thumbs. Shanna scratched his back over his shirt.

"What should we do now?" Shanna asked.

Jason pushed Shanna's hand away and jumped up from the couch.

"Sorry, Honey," Shanna whispered.

"I'm just pissed that we're going through all this because somebody is framing me."

Jason moved to the open dining room window overlooking the patio and backyard. "I need to find out who is behind this."

Shanna rose from the couch and joined her husband at the window. An expanse of freshly cut grass separated the house from the tree line and the river sixty yards from the bottom step of the deck. It was common for Shanna and Jason to see deer, elk, and javelina grazing near the river at sunrise, with coyotes and the occasional black bear using their backyard as a shortcut after sunset.

Large raindrops dotted the thirsty wood planks on the patio.

"I know you don't want to say it because of what it could mean, but you have to consider that someone planted those drugs, knowing you'd be caught. Someone you may have arrested before. Even someone you know and think you can trust."

"I know, but even when I expand my mental list of suspects, I don't know who would do it. A lot of people had access to my truck, but who had the motive to frame me?"

"Don't look for motive. I see it all the time with my patients. Some people do terrible things with no clear motive."

Jason closed his eyes, turned his hands into fists, and leaned his forehead against the screen. Outside, sporadic raindrops morphed into a downpour that obscured the trees surrounding the property. A fine mist penetrated the house through the screen and clung to Jason like morning dew on grass. The sudden fury of the storm and cool liquid awakened something inside him. It was time to slip out of his woeful funk and find the people responsible for putting him and his family into this terrible situation.

Jason opened his eyes and stepped back. "I'll find out who did this."

Chapter 9

Davis-Monthan Air Force Base, Tucson, Arizona

Jason arrived at Davis-Monthan Air Force Base with streaks of violet and gold on the horizon above the rising sun. He parked and walked past a sign containing a Pegasus image with 943rd Rescue Group written in a scroll underneath the winged horse logo. Jason entered the building for his weekend drill with the Air Force Reserve. A ritual he's repeated monthly since he left his full-time role as a pararescueman two years ago.

Donning his Air Force uniform transformed Staff Sergeant Mulder into a different person. His ABUs, or Airman Battle Uniforms, transported him to the challenging but less complicated four years after becoming a PJ before life turned for the worse. Multiple deployments to Afghanistan and the sudden loss of his little brother six weeks before his contract ended left scars that would never heal. After Josh's death, slipping into his ABUs was the only thing that made Jason feel normal. It always brought a sense of clarity and purpose, and this time was no exception. No matter what happened with his trial, he was still a PJ in the 943rd Rescue Unit. At least for now. News of an arrest travels slow from law enforcement to the military, so his commanding officer would eventually find out, but it could take weeks or months, unless Jason told the CO himself. He had no intention of prematurely informing the Air Force Reserve of the current misunderstanding with the DEA. Jason hoped to have his situation resolved before his CO received the news of his arrest.

After morning formation, a safety briefing, and an hour to get kitted up, Mulder joined his team leader and six other PJs near the helicopter pad. The rotor wash from the twin-engine HH-60 Pave Hawk helicopter and the familiar smell of grease snapped Jason into tactical mode. He clicked into his safety harness and joined the rest of the team on the short flight to the Coronado National Forest forty miles southeast of Davis-Monthan Air Base. The 1.8-million-acre national forest encompassed plateaus covered in golden grasses and mountains rising from the high desert floor. The isolated and rugged peaks and valleys were ideal for rotary-wing aircraft fast rope and vertical lift hoist exercises in hostile terrain. This was a situation PJs found themselves in regularly during combat and civilian rescues.

The first mission on a cloudless April day focused on fast rope infill onto a narrow ridge. Once every PJ clung to a sliver of flat granite along a sheer cliff with a two-hundred-foot drop to jagged boulders and small juniper trees, they hoisted back into the helicopter for the next mission. They moved from maneuvering along a cliff like the native bighorn sheep to a narrow basin, but now they had to render aid to simulated injured personnel. A mission with injuries always generated more adrenaline; training was no exception. Jason tightened his gloves and slung his M-4 over his shoulder before he fast-roped to the valley floor to a waiting patient.

The first two PJs went opposite directions to set up a perimeter while Jason scrambled with Airman Cahill to evaluate the male victim. He dropped to his knees and began a blood sweep of the victim's legs, arms, and torso while Cahill checked his vitals.

"Vitals?" Jason asked.

"Pulse is normal, but his pupils are dilated."

Jason scanned the area and saw an overturned quad ATV. He pointed with his thumb toward the all-terrain vehicle. "Looks like we have an ATV accident with a possible head and neck injury."

"Don't forget my broken ankle," the victim said.

Jason's head jerked toward the simulated victim, who broke character, and he laughed when he recognized the victim's face. It was Senior Airman Clay Landry. He wasn't a PJ, but was the unit's lone Special Recognizance specialist. While Clay didn't have the same medical training or skills as most others in the rescue unit, he provided advanced Unmanned Aerial System or UAS operator experience. Jason could attest that his specialized expertise was invaluable for a combat search and rescue squadron. Clay was instrumental in helping Jason find the cartel responsible for his brother's death two years earlier.

Clay held up his hand, and Jason secured it.

"Just relax, sir. You're going to be okay, but we'll have to set you up for a full rectal exam when we get you to the hospital," Jason deadpanned.

Clay's eyes widened, and he moved his hands from his chest to cover his behind. Cahill and Mulder laughed.

"Okay, enough fun for now. Let's get this vic in the bird and get out of here," Jason said.

Jason approached Clay in the locker room after training ended. "We haven't talked since last drill weekend. How is everything?"

Clay shook his head. "Busier than a one-legged man in an ass-kicking contest. A lot of UAV work for the county lately."

"Good to hear," Jason replied.

"How about you?"

Jason hoped Clay would ask this question. He scanned the locker room to verify that nobody else was within listening distance.

"I'm in a bit of trouble, but I can't discuss it here. Do you have time to grab a drink?"

Clay looked at his watch. "I have some work to do at my apartment, but I have a few cold brewskis there if you're okay talking while I put together the UAV kit I need on Monday."

"Perfect."

Jason followed Clay through Tucson, and fifteen minutes later, they parked in a sprawling apartment complex. Clay lived alone in a one-bedroom apartment on the third floor.

"It's not much, but it's home for now," Clay said after Jason entered.

Clay snatched two bottles of beer from the refrigerator. He popped off the top and walked a bottle to Jason. The SR specialist disappeared briefly and returned with three hard-top cases.

"Grab a seat while I mix and match these. I'm looking for the vehicle of a college student who has been missing for over a month. A rancher says he saw a new glare in a wash five miles off Interstate 10, so I need my best infrared and 4K cameras on my biggest drone."

Jason nodded and leaned against the kitchen counter.

Clay took a swig of beer and opened all three cases. "So, what kind of trouble are you in?"

Jason had rehearsed his answer across town, but he forgot his fine-tuned spiel in the heat of the moment.

"This could be my last weekend drill in the Air Force Reserve."

"That's not that big of a deal. We all have to move on from the military at some point. My time may come up soon, too."

"It's not that. I was arrested for trafficking cocaine."

Clay dropped the tool in his hand and stood straight. "I never took you for someone that touched drugs, let alone deal drugs, especially since—"

Jason held up his hand to stop Clay. "I don't use or distribute drugs. I'm confident someone framed me, but I can't prove it, so the district attorney plans to prosecute me. He wants to make an example of a DEA special agent gone rogue."

"Who do you think framed you?"

"I'm not sure. That's the problem."

Clay moved away from the table with the UAVs and leaned against the counter next to Jason.

"I imagine you've made a few enemies working for the DEA."

"Yeah, I've made a few."

Clay stepped back from the counter. His eyes opened so wide that Clay's baby blue irises looked like tiny marbles lost in a sea of white. "Do you think it was the cartel from two years ago?"

"That option crossed my mind, but I can't link it to anyone involved. Sheriff Kellerman is in prison, Victor Romero is dead, and I confirmed with our Central American DEA office that El Jaguar is still in town. It could be someone else I don't know about, but my top three suspects are accounted for."

"Anybody from a previous bust that recently got out of prison?" Clay asked.

"I couldn't find any. I've only been a special agent less than a year, so most people I've busted just landed in prison or are still working through the court system."

The room fell silent as Clay and Jason took several pulls from their bottles.

"What about an inside job? You skip anyone over for a promotion or something?" Clay asked.

"Anything is possible. I'd guess probably nine or ten DEA special agents and Show Low police officers were involved in the sting."

Clay raised his hand. "Back up. Did you say Show Low?"

Jason nodded.

"That's Kellerman country up there. Do you know if any Show Low officers are tight with the former sheriff?"

"Not that I've been able to find. It's hard to do high-quality background research from home, but so far I can't find anyone with a connection to Kellerman or a motive. So you see my dilemma?"

Clay nodded, moved back to the table, and started working again. "Does the CO know?"

Jason understood Clay was asking about the commanding officer of their Air Force Reserve unit. "Not yet. I plan to let him know once I have more answers."

He swirled the final inch of beer in the bottom of his bottle. "I guess I'm in no hurry because I don't know what happens after someone in the Air Force Reserve is charged with a crime and waiting for their trial."

"I do."

"What?"

Clay tilted his head and looked up. "A guy in my old reserve unit caused an accident while he was drunker than a skunk. He put a couple in the hospital, so he got charged with some type of vehicular aggravated assault. The Air Force involuntary discharged him within a few months of the accident, so it happened quickly."

"Where is he now?"

"Who?"

"The guy that caused the accident."

"He's serving six years in Texas State Prison."

Jason opened his mouth, but did not respond. He pulled out a chair from the kitchen table and sat.

Clay placed the drone on the table and moved next to Jason.

"I'm sorry for the bad news and the pickle that you're in right now. They have served you a real shit burger on a platter. I don't know how to help you this time, but I'm here for you if you need anything."

"I know. Thank you, Clay."

Jason departed Davis-Monthan Air Force Base on Sunday evening, reinvigorated by the weekend with his PJ brothers but deflated with the prospect of an involuntary discharge. The past two days reminded Jason why he loved being a PJ. He didn't get the same sense of purpose with the DEA he enjoyed over the past eight years as a pararescueman. It was doubtful he could continue his career in the military once Jason shared his arrest with his commanding officer.

He had many reasons to clear his name as soon as possible, but preventing an involuntary discharge from the Air Force Reserve was high on his list. Everything Jason loved was at risk of being ripped from his life, but he wouldn't let that happen without a fight.

CHAPTER 10

Flagstaff, Arizona

The brisk morning air accompanied Special Agent Donaldson as he entered the DEA field office dressed in blue jeans and a black polo shirt. He closed the wobbly metal door behind him and hurried through a flurry of associates kicking off their day in the cramped workspace. Male and female voices rose and fell over the sounds of phones ringing and side conversations over cubicle walls. He passed through the commotion with a cup of coffee from a nearby coffee shop in one hand and his laptop bag in the other. Donaldson set both on his desk, tilted his head, and bent forward to listen to a faint noise from his office. His body stiffened when he confirmed it was a cell phone buzzing in his top drawer.

"Oh no, not this asshole first thing in the morning," Donaldson said to himself.

The DEA special agent knew only one person would call that number, since it was a burner, and quickly shut his office door. After pressing the answer button and moving the phone to his ear, he stood behind his desk.

There were no greetings or pleasantries. The caller launched directly into a question the moment Donaldson answered the phone.

"What are you doing about the missing drive?"

Donaldson exhaled loudly. He knew this call was coming, but dreaded the answer he had to provide.

"I'm still working on it."

The caller paused for several beats. "How could you let this happen?"

"Everything was going as planned until Titan tried to—"

"No names!" the caller roared.

Donaldson pulled the phone away from his ear, cleared his throat, and started over. "Um, the package was out for delivery as planned, but the driver made a detour before reaching the final destination. He lost the package during a scuffle with our suspect and his friends. That's when our suspect picked up the package and took it with him."

The line fell silent, so Donaldson waited. After several seconds, which felt like minutes, the caller spoke again.

"The information on that drive is encrypted, but it could still lead someone back to our friends overseas. They are paying us to prevent that. It won't be good to disappoint them."

"I understand," Donaldson replied.

The voice of the caller grew louder and more agitated.

"I hope I don't need to remind you about who we're dealing with and the consequences of disappointing them. It's on you if anyone uses that drive to put two and two together, leading to our friends."

Donaldson was in one of the few offices in the temporary building that housed the DEA field office on the Coconino County grounds. His workspace was tiny, but came with windows with blinds and an old, flimsy door for slightly more privacy than the cubicles outside his office. Donaldson snuck a glance through the closed blinds to ensure nobody was listening to his conversation.

"I know. I just executed a plan to take our suspect's attention off the drive to buy us more time to retrieve it. They charged him with trafficking cocaine, and he is in a shitload of trouble. He's out on bail, but I don't think he'll do anything with the USB drive while trying to figure out how two kilos of coke ended up in his truck."

"Will he suspect it was you?"

"Suspect it was me? Probably, but it won't matter. All the evidence points to him, and my story is airtight."

"I still want that drive!"

Donaldson exhaled loudly. "I will, but we have to do this right. If he catches me or my guys snooping around his house now, he'll be on to me. I just need a little more time."

"Do whatever is necessary to get it back!"

"I will."

"Whatever is necessary," the caller repeated slowly.

"Yes, sir."

The caller hung up, so Donaldson opened the top drawer and returned the burner phone. He slammed his fist on the desk, causing some of his coffee to splash out of the cup and douse a stack of files.

"I don't care how much money they throw at me. Nobody talks to me that way," Donaldson muttered to himself.

He raised the stack of files and tilted them to allow the coffee to run off onto the worn carpet floor when a soft knock came from his office door. Donaldson saw a middle-aged woman in a black pantsuit standing outside his closed door. It was his assistant, Judy.

Donaldson straightened his shirt and cleared his throat. "Come on in."

"Is now a good time?" Judy asked. "I found something interesting in the files you gave me yesterday that I want to show you."

"Yeah, sure, come in. I spilled coffee all over my files, so give me a second to clean this up."

Judy rushed to his desk. "Can I help you?"

"No, I've got it. Grab a seat, and we'll get started in a minute."

Donaldson cleaned up and sat down behind his desk. Judy launched into her findings, and he nodded as if he was listening, but his mind was elsewhere.

I will get that drive from Jason Mulder, no matter how much pain I have to inflict.

Chapter 11

One week after Jason's arrest in Whispering Pines, Arizona

Jason's fingers moved over the keyboard while he listened to the ticking of the antique clock crafted by Shanna's grandfather. It was the only sound in their Whispering Pines home while Shanna was at work, and each day grew quieter since Jason's arrest. It was rarely noisy before his arrest since they didn't own a TV, and Jason agreed to listen to his 80s and 90s rock music with his earbuds. During their eight months together in the house, Jason and Shanna settled into the routine of reading next to each other on the couch after dinner. On most nights, Shanna crossed her legs on the couch while she read, and Jason would close his book, lie on his back, and rest his head on her lap. He loved the closeness he felt to his wife in that position, and sometimes, he'd remain there for an hour and listen to the rhythmic sounds of Shanna breathing. Each breath made Jason feel at peace, like a baby in the womb. Neither said a word, but the non-verbal communication of their love and trust in each other spoke volumes.

The antique clock showed it was a quarter after three in the afternoon, and Shanna wouldn't be home from work for another two or three hours. It pained Jason that she had to work extra hours to stash away additional income and could no longer stay awake late enough to read her books at night. Jason tried relieving some of Shanna's stress by making dinner several nights a week. The reheated frozen meals did not impress him, and Shanna wasn't happy with the cuisine either, but was too nice to tell him. Jason missed Shanna's cooking, especially her mom's traditional White Mountain Apache recipes, but most of all, he missed the closeness they once had. He was drifting from his new wife months before their first anniversary.

Jason laced up his shoes and went for a run. He typically used his daily run to clear his head, but now they allowed him to consider new suspects that could have framed him. Jason recalled Clay's question about whether it could be an internal job. He weighed the possibility of Special Agents Donaldson, Cruz, and everyone in the Show Low police department present before, during, and after the sting. Although Sheriff Kellerman was the former Navajo County Sheriff, he still had close ties to men and women on the Show Low police force.

Questions flooded Jason's thoughts.

Where was the K9 officer during the sting? Could the K9 officer get his dog to signal a false hit? If yes, what was his motive? Does he have a relationship with Kellerman?

Jason put every man and woman at the scene through the same line of mental questioning until he completed his run.

After he showered, Jason returned to his laptop to conduct more research.

The Show Low K9 officer and the young buck who drove the evidence van with the cocaine Jason loaded after the bust were his primary suspects. Cruz was also high on the list because of his extreme interest in Jason's truck before the sting, but he couldn't imagine a motive for a fellow DEA special agent to frame him.

Jason scrolled to an article in the White Mountain Independent, the local Show Low newspaper. He stopped at the top of page three when his eyes zeroed in on a picture with former Sheriff Kellerman and the Show Low K9 officer behind an open semi-trailer filled with pallets of narcotics. The story was two years old and proved the K9 officer and Kellerman knew each other.

"I have to let Holland know," Jason said aloud. He typed a quick message to his former boss.

```
Be sure to have your investigators check
out the K9 officer from Show Low PD. He
knows Kellerman. You should also have them
take a closer look at Cruz. He was in my
truck acting strange before the sting.
```

Jason hit send and returned his attention to his laptop when his phone buzzed with a message. He didn't expect a response from Holland, but an immediate reply was a shock.

```
Mulder, we have good people on this, so
let them do their job. I know you're eager
to get involved and investigate everyone,
but if your lawyer hasn't already advised
you to stop meddling, I will. Don't dig
yourself a deeper hole. If someone framed
you, my guys will find it. Let them do
their job!
```

Jason stared at his phone when another call came through. It was his attorney.

"Hi Jason, can you talk now?"

Jason closed his laptop and sat up straight. "Yeah. What's going on?"

Bertelli cleared his throat. "I just left your arraignment and pleaded not guilty like we discussed. The judge set a trial date, so now we have to work on presenting our case in court."

"What's the date?"

"September 16th," Bertelli replied.

Jason quickly did the math in his head. "That's less than six months from now."

"I know it's quick, and we'll get started immediately. If we find any additional evidence, I'll make pre-trial motions to dismiss or delay, but we need to prepare for the 16th of September."

The line went silent for several seconds until Bertelli spoke. "If you have questions, give my office—"

"Should I do my own research on the people that framed me? Can that help you help me?"

Bertelli sighed. "Why do you ask?"

"My instinct is to immerse myself in researching everyone at the scene that night, but my old supervisor, Special Agent Holland, said that was a bad idea. He said to let their internal investigation play out."

"I agree with your old supervisor. If you say or do the wrong thing, they can charge you with interfering with an investigation, but more importantly, you can jeopardize your case. As your attorney, I advise leaving the investigation up to the DEA and my team."

Jason stared at the phone, but did not respond.

"Are you going to follow that advice?" Bertelli asked.

"Probably not."

Doing nothing wasn't an option, so Jason hung up and paced throughout the family room and kitchen. On his third trip past the couch, he stopped abruptly.

Where did I leave that USB drive?

He found the USB drive from the Titan sting and inserted it into his laptop. A single digital folder appeared, and he clicked on it, uncovering the only file on the drive. Jason expected a prompt for a password or PIN to come up with each click, but none did.

A text file with random letters and numbers assembled in columns and rows like a word search puzzle filled the screen. He scrolled down the equivalent of several pages, and it was the same.

"Is this some kind of code or encryption?"

Jason stared at the letters and numbers until it brought on a dull headache.

I bet Holland knows someone in cybersecurity who can figure this out.

Jason typed the first four words into a new text to Holland and stopped. He recalled the last text from his boss and the fact that he'd never turned in the USB drive as evidence from the Titan sting. A minute ago, he was sure the USB drive held the answers to all his questions, but doubt crept into his thoughts.

Am I sure Titan dropped this USB drive? Could Mercer have dropped it? Would I get into deeper trouble or screw up my case if I turned it in now?

Jason weighed his options carefully, ultimately deciding to stash the USB drive back into the top dresser drawer. It would only make matters worse if he turned in evidence that didn't provide answers to who framed him. He sighed and slumped in his chair at the lack of information gleaned from the drive. Jason opened a new browser and resumed digging for answers online. He had to do something.

Chapter 12

Whispering Pines, Arizona

Saturday morning, Jason woke early to split more logs for the wood-burning stove. The early April afternoons were getting warmer, but the nights and mornings were still brisk at one mile above sea level. He found Shanna drinking tea at the kitchen table when he entered. She smiled at the sight of her husband. "Good morning."

Jason wanted to return the greeting but couldn't. He'd waited to tell her about the trial and couldn't withhold the news any longer.

"I have something to tell you."

Shanna must have detected the ominous nature of the news because her face changed from a bright smile to a concerned frown like the flip of a light switch.

"What is it?"

Jason sat down next to her.

"Bertelli asked for a dismissal at the preliminary hearing, but the judge sided with the prosecution."

"Okay. He told you that would probably happen," Shanna said.

"I know, and now we have a court date."

"When is the trial?" Shanna asked.

"September 16th."

Tears immediately welled up in Shanna's eyes and cascaded down her cheeks. Jason moved closer to hold her, but she got up and moved into the family room. "I need a minute," Shanna choked.

Each sniffle and tear wiped from Shanna's face were like daggers piercing Jason's heart, and he felt powerless to help. With a heavy sigh, he went outside and sank into a patio chair. He rested his chin in his hands and stared at the East Verde River behind his property for twenty minutes before returning.

Shanna was no longer in the kitchen or family room, so he entered the bedroom and found her. She was sitting on the bed, staring at the wall.

"Is everything okay?" Jason asked.

Shanna nodded.

"I know you well enough to know that's not true. What's wrong?"

Shanna stood and faced Jason.

"I still don't understand why they arrested you. It doesn't make any sense."

"Simple. I was framed. I can't find much information online, so I'm still trying to piece everything together."

"Do you have anyone in mind?"

Jason didn't want to share his theory about the K9 officer until he had more evidence. "No, not yet."

Shanna put her hands on her hips. "You can't go to jail, Jason. If someone planted those drugs to frame you, you must find them."

"I'm trying!" Jason snapped—his face and neck flushed red.

"You have to try harder."

Jason tossed his hands in the air. "I can't win. You're telling me to get more involved, and Holland and Bertelli are telling me to stay out of it. Bertelli says I can jeopardize my case if I poke around too much. What the hell am I supposed to do?"

"You should do what your attorney tells you," Shanna whispered.

"I don't know if I can do that. Am I supposed to sit on my hands while the DA builds a case to put me in prison?"

Shanna sat back down on the bed and turned away from Jason.

"What is it?" Jason asked. He wondered if his wife was finally cracking under the pressure of the unanswered questions and possible adverse outcomes. Jason felt it himself but could easily compartmentalize it like he always did with traumatic events.

Shanna extended her hand toward Jason. She held something like a flat pen with a display screen at one end.

Jason moved next to her and leaned over to see the plus sign on the display better. He looked at Shanna and back at the digital display. It took a few moments for the realization to sink in, but as soon as their eyes met, any lingering resentment quickly disappeared.

"For real?" Jason asked.

Shanna nodded. "I've thought for a while that I might be pregnant, and this confirms it."

Jason pulled Shanna from the bed, picked her up, and spun her around. Then, after two rotations, he quickly put her down.

"I'm sorry. I just got excited. This is awesome news."

A smile twisted up on Shanna's face. They'd discussed getting pregnant and starting a family before Jason got arrested. The timing was horrible, but it was still the best news Jason had heard in years.

He pulled Shanna into his arms, squeezed gently, and stepped back.

"We're having a kid!" Jason shouted.

Shanna laughed.

"We're having a baby," Jason whispered.

I wonder if we'll have a boy or girl. Either way, I can't wait to show him or her how to ride a bike, fly a kite, and cast a reel.

Jason's thoughts about his future child were swirling out of control like a tornado. A new human that wouldn't breathe the same oxygen as him for another eight months rocketed up in importance in Jason's life. An hour ago, raising a son or daughter wasn't even a passing thought, and now thoughts of his future child pushed out every other thought in his mind.

It was the emotional high Jason needed.

But it would be short-lived.

CHAPTER 13

Six weeks before Jason's trial in Scottsdale, Arizona

A palm tree cast a welcome shadow over Jason's truck while he stopped at a red light after exiting the freeway in Scottsdale, Arizona. Heat radiated off the street, creating mirages of distant water holes in the relentless early August sun. Jason looked at the temperature gauge in his truck and shuddered at the 108-degree reading. He wondered why Bertelli requested his physical presence at the firm's office in the Phoenix suburb and subjected him to scorching temperatures twenty degrees warmer than what he left in Whispering Pines.

Once the light turned green, Jason followed his GPS directions to the posh office complex of the Kalil, Pratt, and Dean law office. It was his first visit to Bertelli at the firm's office, and he arrived early, so Jason opened his phone to review the remaining tasks on his to-do list.

After Shanna shared she was pregnant, Jason switched from framed defendant to future father mode. He spent his days building the nursery and baby-proofing the house. Jason took advantage of his free time while on leave from the DEA and attended all doctor's visits with Shanna. He smiled at the memory of their conversation during her twenty-week ultrasound.

Jason held her hand while the technician guided the probe over the clear gel covering her belly. The technician worked silently as Jason tried to make out the black and green blobs zooming in and out on the screen.

"Everything looks good. The heart, lungs, and brain are all progressing nicely. Do you want to know the gender?" the technician asked.

Shanna turned to Jason. "Do you still want to wait to find out?"

Jason looked into her brown eyes. "I do. There are so few surprises left in this world, so I still want to wait, but I can be swayed to find out."

Shanna bit her lip. "I'm torn. I want to wait, but I kind of want to find out."

Jason squeezed her hand. "I know. I do, too. But I say we wait. It will make his or her birth that much more special."

Shanna turned back to the technician. "We'll wait."

Jason stole a final glance at the monitor to see if he could sneak a peek of the gender before the technician turned the screen away from his prying eyes. Knowing the gender months before the baby was born would be fun and practical from a planning standpoint, but he didn't care if he had a boy or girl as long as the baby was healthy.

No matter what happens with this trial, I will be the best father I can.

Jason snapped from his memory, checked his phone, and saw it was time for his 2:00 appointment. He rode the elevator to the fourth floor of the five-story building next to a golf course and outdoor shopping mall. A young female receptionist with thick blond bangs and a pointy nose ushered Jason into the corner conference room with floor-to-ceiling windows and 180-degree views of the Valley of the Sun. Bertelli stood when he entered and introduced

Jason to his staff assisting with the case. Amber, an attorney who appeared to be in her upper forties, remained seated and tossed her strawberry blond hair to the side to offer Jason a smile. Next, Bertelli pointed to Jacob, a junior attorney with a neatly trimmed goatee who looked to be barely thirty years old. He stood on the opposite side of the table, waved, and sat back down.

Bertelli started before Jason sat down. "You're probably wondering why I asked you to drive two hours to our office instead of discussing this on the phone."

"I am."

"Have a seat, and we'll share everything with you."

Jason sat down, and Amber pushed several file folders across the table. She opened each of them and explained the pre-trial motions they filed to dismiss the case or withhold evidence from the prosecution.

"This seems very thorough, but we could have reviewed all this on the phone with everything else. Is this why you asked me to drive down here?"

"Thank you, Amber," Bertelli said. "There is something else. We know you're looking forward to telling your side of the story to convince the jury of your innocence, but we don't think you should take the stand."

Jason turned to Amber, and her face dropped, so he glared at Bertelli. "Why?"

"The prosecution has a solid case against you. The physical evidence and testimony from the officers who witnessed the K9 hit, and vehicle search will be impossible to dispute, so we'll focus on your character to create reasonable doubt. I'll review your impeccable military service and lack of a criminal record to win the jury over."

Jason leaned back in his seat and exhaled. "I don't understand why I can't do that on the stand. I have to tell them how I was set up to clear my name."

Bertelli cleared his throat. "The general attitude against members of law enforcement accused of crimes is not very sympathetic right now. The public is tired of people who feel they are above the law and want someone to pay, especially if they carry a badge." He turned toward Jacob, sitting to his right.

"Jacob, what happened in a similar federal case in South Florida?"

Jacob looked down at a yellow notepad on the table. "A jury convicted a DEA agent for possession of fentanyl after four hours of deliberation. The initial lead came from an anonymous tip that was never identified, leading them to the drugs in his locker."

Bertelli stood and walked over to the expansive wall of windows. The blinds were open, but he pulled one slat down and leaned closer as if looking for something outside. After a few seconds, he let the slat snap back and turned toward Jason.

"It sure looked like a setup, and the defendant took the stand to tell his side of the story, but the DA tripped him up during cross-examination, and he lost his cool in front of the jury. He laid out exactly how a DEA agent and ex-husband of his current girlfriend could have planted the drugs in his locker. His attorney proved the ex had motive and opportunity, but the jury heard fentanyl and saw an angry, defensive cop, so they convicted."

He turned around to face Jason. "I don't want to risk that with you."

"But I won't get defensive or lose my cool on the stand," Jason argued.

The three members of his legal team exchanged glances. Bertelli flashed a smile, and then his face turned serious.

"I'm sure you would keep your cool, but the DA will try to poke holes in everything we present to the jury, including your exceptional character. They know how to push the right buttons to trip people up. We can't risk the DA putting any holes in your reputation as an honest man who's served our country with honor. It's the foundation of our case."

"But I can't clear my name if I don't take the stand and tell the jury how they framed me."

"First things first, Jason. Our number one priority is an acquittal and keeping you out of jail. It only takes one juror to do that. We'll work on restoring your reputation and career after you're cleared of the possession charges," Bertelli responded. "We racked our brains on this for several days before coming to this recommendation. In our professional opinion, it's the best option."

Jason leaned back in the black leather chair and exhaled. He knew little about the finer details of the legal process other than what he learned at the DEA Academy. "If that's what you think is the best way to keep me out of prison, I'm in."

Bertelli nodded. "Okay. We'll finalize our defense without your testimony. We still have a lot of work to do over the next six weeks, so we'll see you again at the Phoenix Federal Courthouse in mid-September."

CHAPTER 14

One day before Jason's trial in Whispering Pines, Arizona

The sun cleared the tallest trees surrounding Jason's property, bathing his bedroom in soft white light the day before his trial. It didn't wake Jason because he never fell asleep. He left the room quietly to not wake Shanna, went outside, and took deep breaths of the pine aroma he had long associated with home. It could be the last time Jason inhaled the comforting scent for many years.

Jason stepped off his back patio onto the grass and let the late summer sun warm his cool skin as he strolled to the headwaters of the East Verde River behind his house. He stopped at the bank, closed his eyes, and listened to the water lapping gently over the smooth boulders. Jason recorded the soothing sound in his memory to play back in case prison was in his future.

A slamming door pulled Jason from his thoughts. He turned and saw Shanna standing with two cups of steaming liquid next to the back door. Jason joined her on the patio and sipped his coffee in silence until Shanna asked a question. "How are you doing?"

"Good."

"You're doing good?"

Jason nodded.

"Really?"

"Yeah. I'm doing as well as someone can be the day before they stand trial and potentially serve a long sentence in prison if found guilty."

"You don't have to get nasty with me. I just wanted to know how you are feeling."

"I'm not angry or depressed if that's what you really want to know." Jason leaned over and kissed Shanna. "I don't want to spend my last potential day of freedom talking about how I may feel about losing it."

"Fair enough."

The patio was quiet again until Jason finished his coffee and stood.

"What time is everyone coming over tonight?" Jason asked.

"I told everyone to be here around five."

"Okay. I have to run a few errands. I'll be home after lunch."

"You're going to run errands today?"

"Yeah. It may be the last day I can leave and go anywhere I want. If I'm found guilty, I'll be transferred to county jail for sentencing, so I'm going to take advantage of this opportunity while I still have it."

"They're not going to find you guilty, Jason. Think positive."

"I'm not being negative. I'm just being realistic and prepared for the worst if it happens."

"Okay, I'll stay positive for the both of us."

Jason smiled at Shanna, but left without a reply.

Two hours before family arrived, Jason returned home, showered, and rechecked the nursery to ensure it was perfect. He sat in the glider his parents gave them as a gift and pushed himself back and forth.

I can't believe my trial is here and I still don't know who framed me.

Jason tried to research as much as possible himself, but his texts with investigative suggestions for Holland were no longer returned. He hated leaving the research up to other people, but as time passed Shanna grew increasingly upset whenever he attempted to leave and investigate another online lead. It wasn't good for Shanna or the baby, so Jason let the DEA internal investigation team and Bertelli and his team do their job. He hoped it was the right decision.

The future father looked down at the padded armrests and wondered if he'd ever rock his future son or daughter in the glider or if he'd be rocking on a prison cot. He swayed back and forth, taking in everything he could soon miss out on until he heard a knock at the door.

Jason's mom and dad, Celeste and Phillip, arrived first. Phillip hugged him quickly while Celeste held onto her son like it was the last time she'd ever see or touch him. Once she let go, Jason noticed the tears in her eyes.

"Don't cry. I'll be okay."

"I know they'll find you innocent, but I just hate the idea of you going away if they get it wrong."

"It's a little like my deployments with the Air Force. It was tough, but we got through all of those," Jason said.

"It's not fair that this is happening to you."

Jason agreed but ran out of energy pleading his innocence weeks ago. He didn't want to dwell on the horrible injustice bestowed on him the night before his trial. After several beats of awkward silence, Jason left his mother's embrace to open the door after a soft knock. His younger brother Noah entered next while Kai followed him in with his mom, Judy, and his younger brother, Evan.

Everyone moved into the cozy dining area and stood around the table. Jason grabbed a beer and listened to the banter among his guests. He knew the conversations he'd hear if convicted and sentenced to prison would not be about baby showers and problems with the poor quality of bananas at the grocery store.

"You're awfully quiet, Jason," Noah said. "Has your attorney found any more information about who is framing you?"

Jason turned away from Noah to the discussion between his mother and mother-in-law.

Noah didn't notice Jason's apparent discomfort with the topic, or he didn't care. He pressed on. "He's going to expose the people that planted the drugs, right?"

"I'm sure my attorneys are doing all they can," Jason whispered.

"You're innocent. You can't just accept this."

Jason tried to stop himself before the words on this tongue left his mouth, but he couldn't.

"It doesn't matter if I accept it or not. In less than twenty-four hours, I'll be sitting in front of a jury that could find me innocent or guilty. I don't know what they'll decide, but if they find me guilty, nobody can do a damn thing about it!"

All the conversations in the room stopped. Jason thought of every plausible scenario of who framed him and couldn't stand wasting another second on the topic. He'd accepted that his fate rested with a jury of his peers and resigned to accepting whatever judgment they rendered.

"Jason, he's just trying to support you. You don't have to yell at him like that," Shanna snapped.

"I know." Jason turned and cupped hands with his younger brother. "It's not your fault. I don't want to discuss the trial, lawyers, or verdicts tonight."

The room remained quiet until Jason snagged a jacket from the back of the chair and started toward the door.

"Where are you going?" Celeste asked.

"I need some fresh air," Jason replied.

"Nobody is going to talk about that stuff anymore," Shanna said.

"I know. I need a little time to clear my head. Kai, grab your jacket and come with me."

Kai did as he was told, and they disappeared into the darkness.

Shanna walked from the family room to the window overlooking the backyard every five minutes. Jason loved to sit by the river when he needed to think, but she didn't see him or Kai anywhere.

Celeste and Shanna's mom, Judy, joined Shanna at the window after Jason and Kai were gone for over an hour.

"He must be so worried about potentially going to prison," Celeste stated.

"I know he's concerned that he may not be here for the birth of his son or daughter. For Jason, I think that would be worse for him than being locked in a prison."

Celeste nodded. "The stress of a trial and facing prison time while innocent could cause depression, right?"

"It's possible."

The response lingered as the two women continued to look out the window. Moments later, two silhouettes appeared in the moonlight.

"Looks like they're back," Celeste announced.

Jason hung up his coat and moved into the family room. Nobody dared to bring up topics related to the judicial or legal system, but Jason did not engage in any conversation. Thirty minutes after returning from his walk with Kai, he shuffled to his mom and hugged her.

"I'm sorry, but I'm not in the mood to talk anymore tonight. I'm going to turn in early," Jason said while Celeste squeezed her boy tight. She turned to Shanna with a concerned expression splashed across her face.

"Honey, it's only nine o'clock. Are you sure you need to go to bed this early?" Shanna asked.

"Yeah, I'll see everyone at the courthouse in Phoenix tomorrow."

Jason went around the room and hugged everyone else. Tears flowed from every family member, but it didn't faze Jason. The thousand-yard stare remained on his face until the last person departed.

After all the guests had left, Jason locked the door and found Shanna sitting on the couch. She began to scoot next to him, but Jason stopped her. "Just stay there."

He knelt on the floor and put his head on her belly while Shanna stroked his hair.

"What are you doing?"

"Listening to your heartbeat."

"Oh. Why?"

"I just want to remember the sound of it if I have to go away."

"Baby, you're not going away. Keep thinking positive."

Jason didn't respond as he climbed onto the couch beside Shanna and laid his head on her chest. He sensed prison was in his future and wanted a memory with his wife to take with him.

Chapter 15

Phoenix, Arizona

Day one of the trial began with the morning sun beaming through the windows and creating a grid of narrow shadows on the floor at the Sandra Day O'Connor courthouse in downtown Phoenix. Jason entered the courtroom in a charcoal grey suit with a maroon tie and sat with Mr. Bertelli and the junior attorney, Amber. Jason's parents and Shanna sat in the row behind them.

Everything seemed to be happening in slow motion. Jason felt like he walked slower than normal, and the people in the room seemed to speak at half speed. He knew his senses were on high alert and took several quick breaths to calm himself.

Everyone stood as United States District Court for the District of Arizona Senior Judge Kimberley Chen entered the courtroom and sat on the bench. Bertelli felt their gamble received a boost after Judge Chen was selected. She'd been on the bench for thirty years and garnered a reputation as a fair arbiter of the law over those three decades.

The District Attorney kicked off the proceedings with his opening statement, followed by Mr. Bertelli on behalf of the defense. Jason found himself nodding in agreement with the key points of their defense. Next, the DA called their first witness, Special Agent

Holland, Jason's direct supervisor and Supervisory Special Agent of the Camp Verde DEA office.

The DA started with general questions on Holland's role and responsibilities, and then they turned to Jason Mulder's character. Jason leaned forward to hear every syllable of the DA's questions and Holland's answer.

"How did you first meet the defendant?"

"I worked on a case that involved the injury of his mother and death of his brother by a Central American drug cartel," Holland responded.

"Did the defendant cooperate with the DEA and local law enforcement?"

"Yes, he did. I learned of Jason Mulder's personal integrity and military record when I met him, and he cooperated throughout the investigation. He was the primary reason a growing drug cartel no longer operates in our Northern Arizona communities. When I saw his passion for removing drug dealers from our streets, I suggested he consider a career in the DEA."

The DA rose from his seat and walked closer to Holland on the stand. "Let me rephrase the question. Did you or any other members of law enforcement have to warn the defendant to stop pursuing the cartel on his own?"

"I don't recall having a conversation like that with him."

The DA turned to the table behind him, picked up several stapled pages, and held them high.

"That's not what we found in the Navajo County Sheriff and White Mountain Apache Tribe Police reports. They both say they warned him multiple times, and WMAT PD even detained him for trespassing. Does any of that sound familiar?"

Holland glanced at Jason and then turned back to the DA. "Yes, it sounds accurate."

"Does the defendant have a problem with authority?"

"No."

"Does the defendant believe he is above the law to do whatever he wants for his own personal gain?"

"No!" Holland shouted.

"Then why do we have this pattern of Mr. Mulder disobeying numerous orders to stay out of the forests and leave the cartel investigation up to law enforcement?"

"Objection, leading," Bertelli barked to the court.

"Sustained. Rephrase or move to another line of questioning," Judge Chen said to the DA.

The district attorney took a drink from the glass of water on his table and moved back to Holland. "Did your office conduct an internal investigation of the incident involving the defendant?"

"Yes, we did."

Jason leaned forward as his knees bounced wildly under the table. This was the wild card Jason had been waiting months to hear. If the internal investigation found the K9 officer, Special Agent Cruz, or any member of the Show Low PD tampered with his truck or the evidence, nothing else mattered. Bertelli could move to strike all testimonies and evidence presented by the DA and file for an immediate dismissal of the charges against Jason. If the investigation failed to identify another party responsible for the drugs found in Jason's vehicle, his fate was sealed.

"Please tell the court the results of your internal investigation."

Holland cleared his throat. "We did not find any wrongdoing by DEA special agents or the Show Low police department during the search, seizure, and collection of the cocaine that led to charges against the defendant."

Jason's head dropped, and he stared at the wood grain on the table until Holland left the witness stand.

That was my best chance for a dismissal. This doesn't look good.

"Keep your head up, Jason. It'll go better during cross," Bertelli whispered.

Jason watched three Show Low police officers who found the cocaine, including the K9 officer, take the stand. Each methodically described their roles and the actions of everyone present at the sting until Jason was arrested, but none of them dropped any new bombshells during their testimony. He waited for the K9 officer to lie or embellish what happened that night, but he never did. Jason exhaled when the last Show Low officer left the stand. He didn't get the dismissal he hoped for from the internal DEA investigation, but the district attorney also didn't score any further points.

The DA called their last witness of the day—Special Agent Cruz. Jason leaned back in his seat and relaxed his shoulders for the first time. Although he had his suspicions about Cruz, Jason felt good about day one of his trial with a fellow DEA special agent on the stand.... until Cruz answered the DA's questions.

Chapter 16

The courtroom seemed to close in on itself and the air grew warm and stale with Special Agent Daniel Cruz on the stand. Jason wasn't sure if it was the giant witness or the impending doom Cruz's responses meant for his defense. The witness leaned back in his expensive Italian-made suit with the collar open like he was discussing whether he should order the fish or beef dinner special from a five-star restaurant. The DA also appeared to enjoy himself with a smug look on his face while asking each question to his witness.

"What happened after the breach team found the drugs in the home? Did the defendant bring the other gym bag filled with cocaine with you to the evidence truck after the sting per seizure protocols?"

"Sort of. He didn't walk next to me like he was supposed to. He disappeared for a minute, and then he showed up at the evidence truck with his bag for evidence," the beefy special agent replied.

"Did you see where he went and if his bag had the same amount of cocaine when he returned?"

"No, I didn't see where he went. I wanted to ask him, but I was in shock after he darted away with a bag full of coke for a minute. Looking back, I wish I would have said something sooner."

Jason wanted to scream, "You're lying your ass off, Cruz! Every word coming out of your mouth is complete bullshit," but he restrained himself. Instead, he leaned over to Bertelli. "He's lying about everything. I walked next to him every step to the evidence truck after Donaldson handed me the bag of cocaine. Can you object?"

Bertelli shook his head. "Not yet. Let him perjure himself, and we'll catch him in the cross-examination."

Jason clenched his fists tighter and pounded his legs under the table with each lie. Finally, when Special Agent Cruz stepped down, Jason felt physically beaten. The court adjourned for the day, but Jason remained seated. He couldn't take his eyes off the empty witness stand.

Did Cruz plant the coke by himself? Who else is in on it?

Special Agent Donaldson took the stand the following day, and Jason's bad dream turned into a full-blown nightmare. Donaldson weaved a remarkable story of fiction that could make Stephen King jealous.

"Did you see the defendant walking with Special Agent Cruz to the evidence truck after you handed him one of the seized bags of cocaine?" the district attorney asked.

"I saw them walk off the front porch together, and Special Agent Cruz proceeded straight to the evidence truck while the defendant turned right and went out of view for about a half minute. I saw his head bobbing up and down behind another vehicle, and then he returned to the evidence truck."

"Did you notice anything else suspicious about the defendant after he disappeared for thirty seconds?"

Donaldson turned to Jason. His face pinched together as if he had eaten something disgusting. "Something seemed off with his body armor. His waist area was bulging a little, and he seemed nervous. He kept looking around and seemed jumpy whenever anyone spoke to him. It caught my attention because the dangerous part of the mission was over."

Jason waited impatiently for his attorney to conduct the cross-examination and highlight Cruz and Donaldson's fabrications to the judge, but when the time came, Bertelli failed in both attempts. The Flagstaff duo remained steadfast in supporting their tales of the sting in Show Low, and Jason sensed the jury was buying it. He peeked at the twelve men and women to his left several times and noted they seemed attentive and engaged when Cruz and Donaldson were on the stand.

Court adjourned for the evening, and Jason met with his legal team deep into the night in the lobby of his hotel, reviewing every detail of the sting in Show Low. The following morning, Bertelli tried more unique angles to expose the perjury committed by Cruz and Donaldson, but they never cracked. The indignation pumping through Jason's body dissipated like a deflating balloon when the defense rested. He couldn't compete with people who wanted to frame him and could flat-out lie about everything under oath. Jason believed honesty and integrity were paramount in every situation, and he couldn't lie like Cruz or Donaldson, even to save his own skin. It was clear the two special agents from Flagstaff were involved in the effort to frame him, but knowing that offered Jason little solace.

Why would Cruz and Donaldson need to frame me? Did someone else give them the order?

The DA opened his closing arguments with a string of damning evidence against Jason. The list was long, backed by seemingly credible law enforcement witnesses.

Bertelli stood, removed his suit jacket, folded it, and placed it carefully on the back of his chair. He rolled up his shirt sleeves as he sauntered over to the jury.

"Ladies and gentlemen, you've seen the evidence and heard testimony from a litany of law enforcement officers who all confirm they found two kilos of cocaine in my client's truck. We don't dispute that. What we haven't heard during this trial is why. Why would a man with a distinguished military record who has dedicated his adult life to protecting others steal cocaine? Why would a man who saved dozens of lives in a war zone in Afghanistan take drugs from a sting? Why would a man who risked his life tracking down a murderous drug cartel responsible for his brother's death want anything to do with drugs? Why would a man who built his own home and still has money in his savings from his Air Force career get into the drug trade? The fact is, he wouldn't. Someone else placed the cocaine in my client's vehicle. My client is not guilty of cocaine possession, and he vehemently disagrees with the testimony of multiple witnesses at the sting in Show Low that night. That alone creates enough reasonable doubt not to send an innocent man to prison, so I ask this jury to find the defendant not guilty of the charge."

Jason felt a pang of hope as Bertelli returned to the seat next to him. The prosecution did not offer a rebuttal, and Judge Chen instructed the jury to begin their deliberation.

After a deep breath, Jason turned to his parents and his pregnant wife. "Let's go outside. I need some fresh air."

He held hands with Shanna as they found shade under a Palo Verde tree on the sidewalk outside the courthouse. Jason saw her eyes glistening with salty tears and couldn't bear to meet her gaze. "How are you and the baby feeling?"

"We're okay. I'm worried about you."

Jason put his hand on Shanna's belly. "I'll be okay," Jason whispered.

Nobody else spoke for a long time as they sat and watched the people of Phoenix walk and drive past them, oblivious that a man's freedom was on the line.

"I'm sorry," Shanna said.

"For what?"

"I shouldn't have been so against you doing more research and investigating who framed you. You're good at it, but I thought a DEA investigation would surely find out who placed the drugs in your truck without you having to get involved. I was worried you—"

Shanna trailed off, so Jason pulled her next to him. "Don't blame yourself. I made the same mistake, and trust me, I'll never do that again."

Jason continued to hold Shanna until Amber appeared on the sidewalk. "The jury is returning. We have to head back now."

Jason looked at his watch. "They were out less than two hours. That's not good."

The expression on Bertelli's face when Jason returned to his side told him his lead attorney was also concerned.

Everyone stood as Judge Chen appeared in her flowing black robe and sat once she took her perch on the bench. She shuffled some papers and turned to Jason.

"Will the defendant please rise?"

Jason stood along with his counsel.

"Has the jury reached a verdict?"

"We have your honor."

"Please share your verdict with the court."

Jason's hands balled up in fists, and he looked down at the floor. *Please be not guilty.*

"On the charge of Possession of a Controlled Substance with Intent to Deliver, we, the people of the jury, find the defendant guilty."

After the jury foreman said the six letters that crumbled Jason's world, his outward expression remained composed. But his head spun with a flurry of questions and potential outcomes. The nausea in his stomach continued to swell, yet the worst news was still to come.

"I'll see everyone in a week for sentencing. Bailiff, see that the defendant is put under house arrest until the hearing."

Judge Chen smacked her gavel, and Jason Mulder was a convicted felon. The only remaining question was how long he'd sit in prison.

Hopefully, I get the minimum sentence of five years. Maybe I could get out in three with good behavior and return home to Shanna and my son or daughter sooner.

Jason chuckled out loud at his thoughts. He couldn't believe he'd reached the point of rooting for less prison time, but it was his best option with a new wife and a baby on the way.

One hour later, Jason was fitted with an ankle bracelet and instructed not to leave his house until the sentencing hearing.

Seven days after his guilty verdict, Jason returned to the courtroom in Phoenix for sentencing. Jason watched the eyes of Judge Chen closely for any foreshadowing of her pending decision. She telegraphed nothing, so Jason hoped her reputation for being fair would change to being lenient for his sentence.

"Will the defendant please rise," Judge Chen commanded.

Jason stood simultaneously with Bertelli. His legs felt like he'd just run a half marathon, and butterflies the size of eagles battled each other in his stomach. Jason cleared his throat and focused on the judge's lips. The next words from the judge could dictate the next decade of his life.

"Mr. Mulder. Last week, a jury of your peers found you guilty of possession of a controlled substance with intent to deliver over 9 grams. Do you have anything to say to the court before I hand down your sentence?"

Jason cleared his throat. "Your Honor, although we could not prove it during this trial, I'm innocent of the charge against me. Somebody else planted that cocaine. I've never consumed or possessed cocaine for any reason. I'm not a criminal. I like to think I'm one of the good guys. When I joined the Air Force, I did it to protect people. When I joined the DEA a year ago, I did it to remove drugs from the streets. I married last year and my first child is due in a month." Jason's voice cracked, and he paused.

Judge Chen never took her eyes off Jason while he composed himself. He cleared his throat and resumed.

"I despise drugs and have a track record to back that up. I hope you see the man that I really am and consider the utmost lenience at your disposal when you issue your sentence."

Jason took a step back and exhaled. He made the best case possible for the minimum sentence of sixty months.

She nodded. "Thank you, Mr. Mulder. I took your clean record and insistence of your innocence into consideration. Still, I must also consider the damage to the institution and the public when a jury convicts a special agent from the Drug Enforcement Agency of a drug-related felony. As a just society, we cannot take this breach of trust lightly. As a result, I remand you to Phoenix Federal Corrections Institution in North Phoenix for ninety months."

Jason's stomach dropped worse than parachuting from a high-altitude plane. Seven and a half years was thirty months more than the minimum sentence. She made an example of Jason.

Judge Chen made her final judgment. "We'll transfer you to Fourth Street Jail in Phoenix until US marshals can escort you to the Phoenix FCI within the next seventy-two hours."

Jason's gaze fell to the floor as he shook his head.

I'll never survive in Phoenix. I'm as good as dead.

Chapter 17

Judge Chen lifted her gavel, but Bertelli stepped forward and raised his hand to stop her.

"Your Honor, may I approach the bench?"

"What is it, counselor?"

"Can I approach?"

Judge Chen nodded, and Bertelli rushed to the bench. He stood next to the United States District Court emblem with the bald eagle holding an olive branch and arrows in its talon while Judge Chen leaned toward him to listen. Bertelli left the bench and nodded to Jason as he returned to his side.

"What did you say?" Jason asked.

"I bought us a little time to appeal before you're sent to Phoenix."

"I'll be there in two or three days. Is that enough time?"

Bertelli held up his index finger as Judge Chen straightened to speak.

"In light of the defendant's recent position with the US Drug Enforcement Agency, I'm granting the request of his counsel for Jason Mulder to be transported to the Coconino County Jail in Flagstaff until he can be transferred to the Phoenix FCI by US Marshals."

Her gavel struck the bench. "This case is closed."

Jason rolled over on the thin mattress in his dark cell to watch for activity in the lighted corridor. He barely slept the last two nights after his sentence and expected his transport to Phoenix FCI to arrive soon. He wondered if the steps echoing off the concrete and iron walls were coming for him.

Two Coconino County Corrections officers stopped in front of his cell, and the door opened.

"Get ready. Your limo will be here soon," the heavily tattooed guard said with a chuckle.

Two Coconino County corrections officers guided Jason in his navy blue pants that looked similar to hospital scrubs and matching shirt with COCONINO COUNTY JAIL printed on the back in white. They placed him in a holding room used to transfer inmates with nothing but concrete walls and metal doors painted a sandy yellow color. Two men were waiting inside when Jason arrived. They wore khaki cargo pants and black long-sleeve shirts under assault vests with US MARSHAL printed in white below a five-point star within a circular ring. One marshal was in his lower thirties and about the same height as Jason but with a lean runner's build. The other man was a year or two younger and several inches shy of six feet with a thick neck and forearms.

The taller one stepped forward. "I'm Deputy Cosgrove with the US Marshal Service, and this is Deputy Bilski. We're here to escort Jason Mulder to the Phoenix FCI."

The Coconino County corrections officer handed the transfer paperwork on a clipboard to the marshals. Once Cosgrove signed everything, the guards pushed Jason to the marshals and spun him around. Deputy Bilski placed his handcuffs around Jason's wrists and let the corrections officer remove his restraints.

Two secure doors and a row of razor wire later, Jason was back in the early morning sunlight. Bilski led Jason across the parking lot until they reached a black SUV.

Jason spoke to the marshals for the first time. "Can you cuff me in the front? I was a DEA special agent before all this. It's a long ride."

Bilski's turned to Cosgrove. The senior marshal rubbed his chin and nodded. "That's fine, but any resistance out of you and they're going behind your back."

Jason flexed his fingers after Bilski unlocked the cuff on his right wrist under the watchful eye of Cosgrove.

"Put your hands in front of your waist."

The cuffs dangled off Jason's left wrist as he moved his hands in front, and Bilski secured both wrists in the metal shackles. The clicking sound of the teeth of the single metal strand interlocking with the double strand reverberated throughout Jason's body.

Here we go.

Bilski guided Jason to the rear doors of the SUV and pushed his head down to help him inside while Cosgrove held the door open. Jason felt the shade inside the Chevy SUV replace the sun on his face. He scanned the people going about their daily lives around the Coconino County complex as Cosgrove put the vehicle in drive and drove to Interstate 17 for the two-hour commute to the FCI in North Phoenix.

Jason didn't speak until they passed within a half mile of his old duty office in Camp Verde an hour into the ride.

"That was my old office right there," Jason muttered aloud.

Deputy Bilski chuckled. "Your new office won't have the same mountain views unless you count the rolling hills on Bubba's fat-ass trolling the block for a new boyfriend."

The Phoenix FCI was a medium-security facility so that reduced the number of "Bubbas" looking for a prison wife, but it didn't eliminate them. He'd need to keep his head on a swivel and overcome any challengers, especially his first few weeks, to ensure he didn't project signs of weakness. The predators devour the weak in any prison, like an injured gazelle on the African savanna.

I'm running out of time. I have to do something soon.

Jason stared through the windshield in a trance-like state as the SUV consumed miles of interstate freeway until the sign for Sunset Point Rest Area exit two miles ahead appeared. He was thirty minutes away from his new prison home.

Do something now.

Jason leaned against the rear passenger door, panting and moaning.

Bilski turned around in the passenger seat and looked at Jason through the metal grate separating prisoners from the marshals. "What's wrong with you?"

"I'm sick," Jason replied between groans.

"You've got to do better than that. Everyone feels sick on the way to the big house."

"My stomach is cramping, and I think I'm going to puke all over your backseat."

Cosgrove didn't take his gaze off the road ahead. "Suck it up, buttercup. We'll be there in under thirty minutes."

"I probably shouldn't have eaten all those runny jail eggs they gave me," Jason said. He panted louder and faster.

Deputy Bilski's head snapped around toward Jason. "Why the hell did you do that? Sit up, and you'll feel better."

Before Jason straightened up, he bent over further to be out of view of both marshals and stuck his finger down his throat. He dry-heaved several times and threw up on the floor behind Deputy Bilski in the passenger seat.

Bilski slammed his fist on the dashboard. "Ah, man, now I've got to clean that up. Sit up now!"

"I can't. It's getting worse. I need to go to the bathroom."

"We're not stopping. So, you'll have to hold it," Cosgrove barked.

Sell it. Do whatever it takes to make them stop.

Jason continued to groan, gag, and cough. The smell of his vomit made him throw up again. "I don't think I can. It will come from both ends soon, and your entire vehicle will smell like shit."

Bilski's eyes widened. The younger marshal looked like he was told to enter a den of rabid wolves. "Come on, Cos, we've got to stop. I will lose it if that guy shits himself in our backseat."

"We're less than thirty minutes out. We can't stop."

Jason let out his loudest groan yet. "Please stop. I can't hold it much longer."

"Cos you've got to let him go. There's a rest area a mile ahead. We can take him in there. Please!"

"Fine! If it will make the two of you shut up. I'll stop."

The marshals pulled Jason from the back seat and escorted him into the Sunset Point Rest Area twenty miles north of Phoenix, along Interstate 17. It was aptly named for its perch on a plateau with one-hundred- and eighty-degree views of the Bradshaw Mountains for travelers stopping between Flagstaff and Phoenix. It provided breathtaking vistas of the sun descending behind the pine-covered mountains three miles to the west.

Jason shuffled into the stall, closed the door, and sat down. Both marshals stood outside the locked door. He moaned again as he considered his next move. Jason didn't think he'd get this far, and now he had to execute the most dangerous and critical part of his escape.

"Let's go. You've been in there long enough," Bilski said. He pounded on the stall and shook the metal door to confirm the locked door. Jason remained silent and stood quietly.

"It won't take much to break this door down. If we have to come in there to get you, you'll come out hog-tied."

Jason did not reply. He assumed a ready position, like a football linebacker preparing to tackle a running back. Jason lifted his cuffed hands to eye level next to the locked stall door. He needed the marshals to make one more move, and then he'd pounce.

Deputy Cosgrove's voice boomed from the other side of the door. "You've got three seconds to come out. One, two, three."

A right hand appeared on top of the stall door. It was the signal Jason had been waiting for. He just hoped his assumption that the marshal was right-handed was accurate. Cosgrove pulled on the locked door once, and then Jason quickly unlocked it when he attempted to yank it open with all of his might. The door swung out with the force of Jason's one-hundred and ninety pounds behind it. Cosgrove didn't fall but stumbled backward until the middle of his back collided with the stainless-steel sinks. He yelped in pain and reached for his holstered weapon with his right hand. The extra second to get his hand into place to remove his Glock .40 caliber pistol was all Jason needed. He raised his cuffed hands over Cosgrove's head and pulled his face down into his rising knee multiple times with the force of a grizzly bear and the speed of a rattlesnake. Cosgrove fell limp and dropped to the tile floor. He likely suffered broken cheekbones and a shattered nose based on the dark red blood pooling under his face pressed against the gray and white mosaic tile.

The junior deputy marshal froze. Instead of running or attacking, Deputy Bilski stood like a deer that wandered onto a freeway. He didn't go for his weapon until Jason was within striking distance. Bilski's fingers found his Glock as Jason stepped forward and caught the marshal under the chin with his right elbow while clasping Bilski's rising shooting arm before reaching his waist. Jason knew it took less force to push an arm down versus up from his Krav Maga training, so he pinned Bilski's shooting arm against his own hip with the barrel of the gun pointed toward the floor. Bilski looked up at Jason wide-eyed and struggled to release his arm from his attacker. Jason eyed Bilski's nose between his ping-pong-like eyeballs and slammed his forehead into the target three times. The headbutt caught Bilski square across his nose and mouth, but one of his teeth cut Jason's forehead above his right eye when he screamed. Bilski dropped his gun, wobbled, and bounced off the concrete wall as blood poured from his nose like a dam break. He swayed forward, glanced at Jason, and spit blood onto the floor. Jason lost his grip on the marshal as the pain from his gash reached his brain, and Bilski seized the opportunity. He ripped his arm free and staggered out of the bathroom.

Jason moved to the dull mirror above the sink to evaluate the injury on his forehead. Blood dripped into the sink basin, but once Jason splashed water on his face, he could see that it was an inch-long gash, but not too deep. He knew head wounds bled more, and he'd be fine with some pressure on the wound.

Deputy Cosgrove stirred, so Jason bent down and pulled the deputy up to a sitting position against the cool concrete wall. Jason took the Glock from his holster, removed the magazine, and tossed the pistol into his lap. He stepped over Cosgrove to gather Bilski's firearm and tossed his empty pistol beside the other handgun. He put both loaded magazines in the front pocket of his prison shirt.

A man with grey hair and brown sandals over his white socks shuffled into the bathroom. He looked down at Cosgrove and then to Jason standing over him. The older gentleman's eyes widened before he spun around and darted out the door.

I don't have much time.

Jason reached into the deputy's pocket and removed his keys. He checked the key ring for a handcuff key and recalled that Bilski cuffed him, so he secured both pistols, rushed into a stall, and dropped the guns and keys into the toilet bowl. Jason didn't want either marshal to have easy access to a weapon if they pursued him, but Jason also didn't want to take their loaded guns. He knew that "armed and dangerous" escapees drew a more robust response than unarmed fugitives. Jason noticed Deputy Cosgrove's eyes flutter and then open. His glassy eyes moved around the room and then focused on the inmate he was tasked with transferring to Phoenix FCI.

Jason returned to the stall, yanked on the toilet paper until he had a wad, split the bundle in two, and wet them under the sink. He placed one on Cosgrove's nose and pulled the deputy's hand up to keep it in place.

"Keep this on your nose. It'll help stop the bleeding."

Jason did the same with his wound while Cosgrove stared at him.

"I'm sorry this had to happen to you. Sometimes bad things happen to good people."

Cosgrove tried to talk, but Jason held his hand up to stop him.

"I was framed, and let everyone know I'm going to find the people who did it," Jason growled. He turned and tiptoed to the door to see if Bilski was waiting for him outside and saw the deputy pulling on the door handles in his attempt to get into the locked SUV.

Jason turned to leave but stopped and evaluated his oversized jail-issued tennis shoes and uniform. He regarded the similarly sized Cosgrove on the bathroom floor.

"I hope his shoes and pants fit," Jason said.

He removed the semi-conscious marshal's boots first and then his cargo pants. Jason tried them on after stripping off his jail bottoms. The boots fit perfectly, but the pants were a little snug.

I must have put on a few pounds while on leave.

Jason left the top button to his pants unfastened and darted from the restroom with toilet paper pressed on his forehead. He hurried as casually as possible to the scenic overlook. Jason reached the end of the property, looked over the cliff at the four-hundred-foot drop to the valley floor, and tossed one leg over the waist-high stone wall.

That slope has to be at least a forty-five-degree angle. Maybe worse. This will not be easy.

He looked left and right to see if the steep angle improved, but it only worsened. This was his only option.

The sound of shattered glass informed Jason that Bilski must have broken a window to access his vehicle. Jason was out of time.

He swung his other leg over the wall, looked down, and jumped.

CHAPTER 18

Sunset Point, Arizona

Jason tumbled uncontrollably down the rocky slope for what felt like several minutes. He stayed on his feet for three-quarters of the way down but couldn't stop his forward momentum once he fell. The handcuffs wouldn't allow him to extend his arms and turn his body into a giant X like they taught him in SERE school. Waves of pain shot throughout his body with each collision against the large and small boulders strewn along the steep slope. It was like he was inside a clothes dryer filled with sharp, hard stones until he landed on the valley floor with a loud pop.

At first, Jason thought it was the marshals shooting at him, but then his brain registered fiery pain shooting up and down his spine. He dislocated his left shoulder.

"Ah, son of a bitch!" Jason cried out as he attempted to move his tethered arms.

He took several deep breaths, held the last one, and rolled onto his side. Jason attempted to push his shoulder back into the socket using the ground. He exhaled loudly after it failed, pulled his knees underneath him, and stumbled to his feet. Every part of his body screamed in pain, but he forced himself to shuffle further into the valley to assess the situation.

A large gathering of travelers pressed against the stone wall forty stories above Jason. He scanned the clothes and faces but saw neither deputy marshal at the overlook. Jason knew that wouldn't last long and he had to move immediately. The desolate basin offered little concealment or cover but also lacked the infrastructure for vehicles to pursue him. It would take time for the US Marshals to scramble helicopters and dogs to track him down, and he had to be in the Bradshaw Mountains before they arrived.

Jason turned west and took several shaky steps with his left shoulder dangling lower than his right. He talked to himself to push back the pain and doubt.

Suck up the pain. If you get caught now, you'll do a lot more than seven years in prison.

Jason grew more sure-footed with each step and soon walked at a 3 MPH clip. Five minutes after hitting the earthen floor, he jogged the best he could while handcuffed with a dislocated shoulder. It was two and a half miles to the tree line in the foothills of the Bradshaw Mountains, and Jason had to get there in under thirty minutes. He'd be a sitting duck in the open basin for any aerial search launched to capture him.

Twenty-five minutes later, Jason felt the shade cool his body and collapsed a dozen feet into the woods. It was the first day of October, and even at the elevation of 6,000 feet above sea level, the temperatures in the high desert were in the high eighties. Jason was glad he pre-hydrated before the marshals arrived because he wasn't sure he could reach fresh water before dehydration set in. Water was not his number one priority yet; it was his shoulder. He'd never cover the ground needed to avoid the search teams until it was back in the socket.

Jason stood and sized up a few pine trees with sturdy trunks and no branches under seven feet. He lined up his left shoulder and used his legs to push. Jason bared his teeth as the pain ratcheted up to the point he almost yelled out, but it didn't work. The PJ knew what to do, but he was avoiding the inevitable. He had to slam his throbbing shoulder into the tree trunk to get it back into place. The pain would be excruciating, but there was no other way with his hands cuffed.

After drawing in a big breath, Jason exhaled and counted down. "Three, two, one."

Instead of resetting his shoulder, the fugitive stepped back and rolled his neck. He had to trick himself into inflicting imminent agonizing pain.

"Okay, do it this time," Jason muttered. "On one. Three, two—"

His shoulder collided with a tree trunk that felt more like a brick wall. The pain was instant and electrifying. It felt like someone hooked jumper cables onto his spine and started the engine. Even his legs wobbled from the pain, but it worked. Although his shoulder screamed in anguish, he rotated his arm the best he could in cuffs to confirm he'd regained a full range of motion.

It was time to move again. Directions were easy because he knew the Bradshaw Mountains were due west of Interstate 17, which ran north and south. Jason turned in all directions and considered his next steps.

Phoenix had the resources to hide out long term, but law enforcement would expect him to go there. Jason ruled out the big city but wanted to give his pursuers the illusion he was headed toward Phoenix.

Jason climbed another two hundred yards into the woods and turned south. He heard sirens in the distance and checked his watch. It was a quarter past twelve, giving the search teams six hours before sunset. In previous stings with the DEA, a couple of suspected drug dealers escaped, and they had to call for a search team. Jason knew the local police would arrive quickly, but it took time to assemble dogs and helicopters. If he could make their search area as large as possible during daylight, he stood a chance of making it through the night. Jason found a game trail and resumed jogging. He also knew the search teams would base their radius on how far the average person could travel on foot in mountainous conditions. Jason couldn't be average. He had to be exceptional, and fortunately for him, traversing twenty miles through hills and mountains was something he'd done on multiple occasions in the Air Force. Of course, he'd had better gear and fellow PJs to push him when his body felt like giving up, but Jason had the best motivation possible. Getting caught meant decades in prison.

The shadows in the pine forest grew longer as Jason plodded south. He arrived at a dirt road and knelt inside the tree line to assess the situation. The forest was completely silent, so he approached the road slowly, and that's when he noticed two old signs on opposite sides of the forest road. The sign for the southbound track said: Horsethief Basin Recreation Area 1 Mile. Jason turned around and saw the northbound sign proclaiming campgrounds were also 1 mile away. This meant people, and that was exactly what Jason needed. He could use the human activity in the area for cover and scavenge their camps.

Jason had never been to Horsethief Basin, but he'd heard friends talk about taking their OHVs or Off-Highway Vehicles there and riding them all day in the basin. He went north, hoping to find empty camps of people out riding their OHVs, but he had to hurry. Most of them would return before sundown.

A half-hour later, Jason crept toward a campsite. He saw two tents, a seven-passenger SUV, and a toy hauler.

"Jackpot!"

He waited in the underbrush for ten minutes to confirm nobody was in the area. Once Jason was confident the toy hauler owners were out riding their OHVs, he bolted for the SUV. He shielded the glare with his cuffed hands and peered inside the passenger side window. Jason saw a cooler and bags of groceries in the SUV, but it appeared locked. He didn't want to risk setting off a car alarm, so he moved to the rear hatch. He pulled on the single wiper blade until it snapped off and bent it until it fit into his cargo pocket. Next, he unzipped the tents, looking for anything he could take. Upon a quick examination, he found sleeping bags, pillows, and an extra-large black long-sleeve T-shirt with a white logo of a popular powersports manufacturer emblazoned on the front. Jason snagged the T-shirt and moved to the open toy hauler. It was mostly empty, but it had built-in cabinets. Jason opened the bottom doors and found tools, gloves, and a helmet. He took the gloves, opened the top doors, and pumped his bound fists. It contained a 32-ounce bottle of Smart Water and a box of Clif Bars. He left one bar in the box and put the rest in his cargo pocket.

Jason checked his watch, saw it was close to four o'clock, and figured some OHV riders might return to camp soon. He started back into the forest but stopped. Although it was a warm day, Jason was at an elevation similar to his home in Whispering Pines and knew the temperature would drop thirty to forty degrees at night. Jason galloped back to the tents and dove into the first one. He grabbed the first sleeping bag he saw and pulled it into the sunlight. It was large enough for him to fit, but the pink color with a Disney princess print caused him to pause. He returned the sleeping bag and moved to the other tent. Jason pulled a larger, brown sleeping bag out with both hands and slung it over his shoulder.

"It looks like the mister and misses are going to get real close tonight."

Jason found flat ground underneath a dense canopy of ponderosa pine trees three hundred yards from the campsite. He laid the sleeping bag down and sat on it so he could work on his windshield wiper. Once comfortable, Jason peeled the rubber off the flat metal insert. He hoped the story he heard at the DEA Academy from one of the blowhard candidates about making a shim from windshield wipers to escape from handcuffs was true. Jason bent the metal at the perfect angle, but before he could use it, Jason heard the sound he'd been waiting for since he jumped off the Sunset Point overlook—a helicopter.

Determination washed over Jason like a storm-driven wave. He brought the shim up to his left hand with his right and worked it into the cuffs. The metal shackles dug into his wrist, but Jason never lost focus. He worked the shim over the teeth until he felt a freedom that was never so sweet. His left wrist was free, and now he could remove the cuffs altogether.

The sound of the helicopter got closer as Jason trekked deeper into the mountains and away from any forest road. He didn't hear any dogs yet and hoped by the long shadows they wouldn't come for him today.

As the sun set, the temperature dropped quickly, so Jason pulled over the long-sleeved T-shirt he found in the tent and climbed into his sleeping bag. He stared up at the stars emerging in the night sky. Jason had thought about this day hundreds of times since his conviction and almost every waking moment since his sentence. It felt surreal to escape from the marshals and be on the run. Although the forest was calm, Jason knew the US Marshal's office in Phoenix was buzzing with activity. They would come aggressively for him tomorrow, so Jason ran through his plan again.

He'd skirt past the mountain community of Crown King five miles away and push to Prescott, another twenty miles further north in the Prescott National Forest. The route was virtually impenetrable by vehicle, so that would limit the reach of the K9 units and reduce his primary concern to the aerial search that was sure to grow by morning.

It was a safe and solid plan, but Jason's thirst and cold surprised him, so he reconsidered his destination in Prescott. Initially, he hoped to link up with an old friend in the Air Force who owned one of the largest outdoor gun ranges in the state. Technical Sergeant Bentley was no fan of the government and would welcome the opportunity to stick it to Uncle Sam. Jason joined Bentley on Whiskey Row in the Courthouse Square in Prescott every day they went to the range, and he hoped to catch him at his favorite watering hole to ask for help. He wasn't sure he could get there before the marshals closed the net around him.

Jason laid back and listened to the crickets. Suddenly, he jerked and sat up. He remembered the perfect place with ample resources outside of Prescott. He'd leave before sunrise if he eluded the intense manhunt through the night.

Chapter 19

Four hours after Jason Mulder escaped near Sunset Point, Arizona

Senior Deputy US Marshal Deshon Whittaker took in the land-scape of the pine-tree carpeted Bradshaw Mountains jutting above the arid sandy brown basin from the passenger seat of the SUV. The driver of the black Chevy Suburban jumped the curb of the rest area parking lot and skidded to a halt. Whittaker hopped out as dust enveloped the vehicle. The lead investigative marshal in Arizona, dressed in a graphite gray sport coat and faded blue jeans, emerged from the cloud like a superhero walking away from an explosion. He strutted into the command center, barely sixty minutes old, and let his eyes adjust to the dark.

Men and women from the US Marshal Service hurried in and out of a house-sized white tent like worker bees in a hive. The USMS team constructed the temporary command center on a bluff south of the Sunset Point Rest Area three hours after Deputy Marshal Bilski called in the escaped inmate.

"I need a sit rep!" Whittaker barked.

Everyone under the tent stopped for a beat when Arizona's head of the local fugitive task force spoke and resumed their activities, except Deputy Marshal Jennifer Miley. The twenty-eight-year-old member of Whittaker's team had grown up in San Diego with three older brothers who loved to push their baby sister to be independent and tough. Despite her rugged interior, Miley drew attention from her single male coworkers in the Phoenix USMS office with her blond hair, bright blue eyes, and toned figure. However, her boss seemed to be oblivious to her beauty. Despite his reputation as a smooth-talking ladies' man, Whittaker never flirted with Miley. Instead, Whittaker challenged her to improve, like her older brothers, while tapping into her intelligence that other supervisors overlooked because of her attractive appearance. In return, Miley turned down promotions and rewarded Whittaker with loyalty and superior analytical skills for someone in her position.

Miley stepped forward with the requested information.

"The fugitive is Jason Mulder. He escaped just before eleven during transport to Phoenix FCI. We completed the command post set up at fourteen hundred and deployed our ground resources, including K9 units."

"Do we have an airtight perimeter established around the fugitive yet?"

"That's not possible. Based on the terrain, the active search area is one-hundred and sixty square miles, and 95% of it is not accessible by our vehicles. We're working with the Yavapai County Sheriff's office to secure a few off-road vehicles, increasing our accessibility by another 20%."

"Holy shit, we're in the boondocks out here. Whose bird is that I saw coming in?"

"That's also Yavapai County. We're working with Arizona DPS to secure one or two more helicopters."

Deputy Marshall Whittaker left the tent without warning and turned toward the Bradshaw Mountains. Miley followed him.

"Does EDAS out of Spring, Texas, have any resources on the way?" Whittaker asked. EDAS was the acronym for the Early Detection Alarm System or the front name for the contracted aviation resources for the US Marshals Service. EDAS aircraft were outfitted with the most advanced surveillance technology available.

"Not yet. The Spring office won't send anything unless you request them."

"I'm requesting them now. Tell them to send all they have."

Whittaker took several steps away from the commotion in the tent and turned to Miley. "Who are we dealing with?"

"Jason Mulder roughed up two of our guys transporting him to Phoenix for a drug charge and then jumped over the cliff to escape. He's a former DEA Special Agent and claims someone framed him during a sting six months ago. He maintained his innocence throughout the trial and told Deputy Cosgrove, after he assaulted him and stole his pants, that he escaped to find the people that framed him."

"Stole his pants?"

"And his boots."

"That's cold. Did he take anything else? Did he get any of our weapons?"

Miley shook her head. "No. He removed the magazines but left their Glocks in a toilet. One of our searchers found the magazines with all the ammo near the bottom of the cliff Mulder descended to escape."

"This was no spur-of-the-moment escape. He's been planning this for a while."

Whittaker did a quarter turn and stared at the emerald swath of trees carpeting the Bradshaw Mountains across the canyon from their command center.

"Do you think he's innocent?" Miley asked.

"Don't know and don't care. Walk with me."

Strands of blond hair slipped from Miley's bun as she bounced behind Whittaker until he stopped fifty yards away on a rocky bluff. He conducted a one-hundred-and-eighty-degree scan of the Bradshaw Mountains and then turned around to do the same with the I-17 freeway behind him.

"I know we can't set up a complete 360-degree perimeter, but do you have the southern trails and roads toward Phoenix covered?" Whittaker asked.

"We do, but I don't think he's headed to Phoenix."

Whittaker tilted his head. "Why not?"

"Before he joined the DEA, he spent six years in the Air Force as a PJ, so he has extensive training to survive in the wilderness."

"A PJ? Never heard of them."

Miley, a former Senior Airman in the US Air Force Security Force, flashed a quick grin. "PJ is short for pararescueman or, specifically, pararescue jumper. Pararescuemen are combat EMTs who rescue Marines, soldiers, sailors, and airmen injured in combat zones. Initially, PJs focused on retrieving downed Air Force pilots behind enemy lines, but over time, they've added responsibilities to assist any branch of service, plus civilian rescues. They have some of the longest and most intense training of any special operations force in the DOD. He'd have no trouble traversing through these mountains and living off the land for days or weeks."

Whittaker shook his head. "So, we're going after a real John Rambo or something like him out there?"

Miley smiled again. "PJs are certainly capable of offensive assault, but most of them are combat medics that shoot back only when they have to."

"What about this guy? He roughed up our guys pretty good."

"We're not sure yet on motive, but he insists that he's innocent and doesn't appear to like the idea of prison. He grew up in a mountain town about two hours east of here. This is his backyard, and I'm sure he has the advantage in these mountains."

"You've got to be shitting me," Whittaker muttered. The Chicago native and former college defensive back was not a fan of the vast Arizona forests.

Why did you have to run and hide in the forest, Mulder? I will not be happy if I have to go in the woods to drag your butt out.

Deshon Whittaker's father was a beat officer for the Chicago PD, and his mom babysat for the other working moms in the neighborhood. Deshon grew up in a humble brick Tudor-style home in the Rogers Park neighborhood on the north side of Chicago. He struggled with grades in junior high and even got a taste of street life, but then he discovered football in high school. He loved it and was better than most boys his age, so Deshon focused more on his schoolwork to be eligible to play football. It paid off with a full-ride football scholarship at Augustana College, a Division III football program in Rock Island, Illinois. His six-foot frame, long arms, and quick burst allowed him to snag five interceptions and lead the conference his junior year. This led to the confidence and swagger that Whittaker still possessed today. Offensive coordinators and quarterbacks smartened up and avoided the rangy cornerback during his senior year. His interception rate dried up, and so did his opportunities to play football after college. Deshon had to pivot, so instead of covering wide receivers, he tackled criminals with a career in law enforcement. Deshon's father showed him the pros and cons of being on the city police force, so he applied to the US Marshal Service.

After a tough eighteen weeks at the United States Marshals Service National Basic Training Academy in Glynco, Georgia, Whittaker reported to his post in Phoenix. Four years after he joined the USMS, Deshon Whittaker rose to Senior Criminal Investigator Deputy US Marshal. His tenacity and wit helped him land attractive assignments on fugitive and HIDTA task forces. The 34-year-old was involved in the capture of several high-profile fugitives, including two on the top fifteen most wanted list, which earned Whittaker the respect of his peers within the Phoenix District Office of the US Marshals Service.

"I have to check on something back in the tent. Is there anything else you need me to do?" Miley asked.

Whittaker nodded. "Yeah. I want every K9 unit in the mountains and every aerial asset in the air ASAP. This cool cat is not going to walk into our net."

Whittaker continued to gaze over the million-acre Prescott National Forest extending as far as he could see. He sensed this fugitive was unique, not just because he was former federal law enforcement or made unwavering claims of his innocence, but because of his unique ability to thrive within Arizona's vast network of pine forests.

This guy will be a challenge, but I'm always up for a challenge. Victory is sweeter when the opponent requires your A-game.

Miley stood quietly as Whittaker was lost in thought and started toward the tent until Whittaker stopped her.

"One last thing. We have a fugitive out there in a massive hiding place, and I expect every resource available to the USMS to be utilized. If we don't catch him soon and he goes all mountain man on us, we could be in for a long and tough pursuit."

CHAPTER 20

Near Crown King, Arizona

Jason stared at the Milky Way displayed brightly with millions of stars sparkling in the moonless sky, interrupted only by occasional charcoal-colored clouds on the black canvas in the clearing above him. Crisp, cold air suspended the pungent smell of pine that Jason tasted on his lips. He watched the east horizon for the first signs of twilight while shivering inside his sleeping bag.

The day-old fugitive was eager to move toward his destination before his pursuers, so he checked his watch and noted it was twelve minutes after five. He had to begin his journey to Prescott early to bypass Crown King before most of the two hundred residents in the former gold mining haven started their day. Although it was still dark, his eyes adjusted enough to see, and if he started now, he could be on the other side of Crown King before eight.

Jason headed northwest after rolling up the sleeping bag and slinging a strap over his shoulder. He bushwhacked through a half mile of undergrowth and then passed over a sea of tailings from previous mining operations. Warmer muscles and bones, plus the benefit of fewer trees, allowed Jason to move faster through the exposed area under the cover of twilight. Jason reached the main forest road as the sun rose. The dirt trail sat atop the spine of the Bradshaw mountains and was the only way to navigate through the summit pass with treacherous slopes on each side. Jason traversed through the woods parallel to the forest road to remain concealed without risking a tumble to the mountain's base. It was slower than hustling along the improved road, but cover was critical if a search team appeared in the area.

A pickup truck and an early bird family on OHVs passing by on the forest road was the only activity Jason encountered in Crown King. He skirted past the general store and the Crown King Saloon & Cafe, which looked well over one hundred years old. Next, he passed a restaurant, and the smell of bacon wafting through the forest clutched Jason like an invisible hand. He'd forgotten his hunger until he smelled the smoky pork goodness. He recalled the numerous breakfasts his dad had made for him when he came home from the Air Force. Growls from his stomach grew louder as each virtual plate loaded with eggs, bacon, hash browns, and toast flipped through his mind.

A vehicle pulled into the central village, which snapped Jason from his dream of a hearty breakfast. A man in a US marshal uniform exited his white government-issued truck and approached a worker sweeping in front of the restaurant. Jason was one hundred yards away and could see the marshal start a conversation and then hand the worker a sheet of paper. Jason dropped to the forest floor and observed the situation. His pulse thumped in his neck as he watched the worker and marshal discussing the flyer's contents. Jason knew more law enforcement officers would soon arrive to canvass the area, and this marshal was the first of many.

The fugitive didn't move a muscle until the marshal returned to his vehicle. He caught a break when the marshal turned south toward the direction he'd left. Jason rose with caution and increased his pace through the forest. His best chance of avoiding the wide net of the search team was to be faster than they would ever expect a person to traverse the craggy Bradshaw Mountains. Jason knew it was possible if he pushed through his mental doubts and physical pain for the next twenty miles. He pulled his stolen gloves tight and embarked on the most critical hike of his life.

Jason's march to Prescott slowed, and his muscles were on fire. The salty sweat dripping from his skin stung all the cuts and scratches he sustained pushing through the woods. He last heard the bark of a K9 dog eight hours ago, and the beat of helicopter rotors had been absent for the last ninety minutes. His goal of pushing farther and faster than they expected seemed to pay off, but it came at a cost. He'd finished the bottled water and last Clif Bar hours ago and felt the looming effects of dehydration. When Jason tried to push harder, his body resisted. He'd passed mind over matter miles ago. His physical exhaustion was real, and Jason had to find food, water, and shelter soon, or he could pass out on the side of the mountain and die from exposure.

The game trail turned north, and Jason's legs suddenly felt stronger and the sleeping bag lighter. The early autumn sun dipped in the west, and a dim glow of city lights emerged between two mountains. He recognized he was only a mile away from his destination outside Prescott.

Jason trekked twenty miles up and down mountains and through dense woods until the church camp he attended as a young teenager was in sight. The cooler summer air, multiple lake reservoirs, and vast forests for endless outdoor activities attracted dozens of summer camps to the outskirts of Prescott. Although the camps were brimming with people from Memorial Day through Labor Day, students and staff visited infrequently the rest of the year. He knew they kept pantries stocked with canned goods and bottled water with little to no security to prevent an unwanted visitor. If he could push his body for one additional mile, he could get the food and water it critically needed.

The decades-old lock on the door to the main cafeteria at Emerald Pines Christian Camp was no match for Jason's good shoulder. Moments after entering, he found his way to the food shelves he had stocked a dozen summers earlier. He flipped the switch by the pantry door and a single bulb cast a yellow light on the restaurant-size packages of nonperishable foods. Jason pushed aside five-pound bags of rice and gallon-size plastic jars of ketchup to find something edible with limited preparation. The growl in his stomach transformed from bobcat to lion as he struck out on each shelf.

"Come on. There has to be something to eat in here," Jason groaned.

Behind a giant bottle of mayonnaise, Jason struck pay dirt. He snared a 32-ounce can of beef chili and then a similarly sized can of peaches. Seconds later, he was at the counter-mounted can opener in the kitchen and quickly opened both cans. Jason raised the room-temperature chili above his head and tipped the contents into his mouth like he was chugging a beer at a frat party. Next, he fished peaches out of the light syrup with a plastic fork he found still in its protective wrapper. He closed his eyes and stopped chewing for a second after each bite. Jason couldn't recall canned food ever tasting so good. After filling his stomach with chili and peaches, Jason lowered his head under the kitchen tap and drank for two minutes. The exhausted fugitive lay flat on the stainless-steel island in the center of the kitchen to let the cocktail in his stomach settle. He stared at the rafters in the ceiling.

"I'll have to give this place five stars on Yelp when I get home," Jason said aloud with a chuckle.

It was Jason's first opportunity to stop and reflect on his situation since he bolted from the marshals. He was happy with his choice to push hard to the summer camp outside Prescott. No place was 100% safe as a fugitive, but he was in a secluded area, though it wasn't unusual to see a person on the grounds fixing up the facilities for future campers. He couldn't risk staying there too long but figured he could hole up in the kitchen for a night or two while he figured out his next move.

Jason rolled out his sleeping bag between two long picnic tables in the dining room. This gave him an unobstructed line of sight to the main door while keeping him hidden from prying eyes looking through the screen windows covered in seasonal glass. Jason dozed off once his butt hit the sleeping bag, but thoughts of his pregnant wife alone at home jerked him awake. He stared up at the blackness and thought about Shanna. A million questions flooded his mind.

How is Shanna doing? Is the baby, okay? Are the authorities harassing her?

Jason clenched his jaw and secured the end of the sleeping bag into his curled fists. The desire to rush home and be with Shanna was overwhelming.

The following day, Jason woke shortly after sunrise. He rose gingerly and limped to the window. His body ached as he scanned the grounds and the adjacent paved road for signs of human activity. Seeing none, he wobbled back to the picnic table and plotted out his next move.

He finished the giant can of chili and washed up the best he could in the kitchen sink. Jason found a baseball cap on a seat in the dining room, so he put it on and left the camp. He hiked two miles to Goldwater Lake, a fifteen-acre reservoir in the Prescott National Forest that attracted hikers, fishermen, and kayakers. It should have been a thirty-minute trek, but it took Jason over an hour. His back, feet, and knees barked at him with every step, and he knew he'd never reach downtown Prescott in time to catch Bentley, so he altered his plan.

Jason waited at a picnic table near the day-use parking lot at Goldwater Lake to find the right person to ask for a ride. He watched families and young couples return to their vehicles but was afraid they'd recognize a fugitive with his face plastered all over the news. Finally, a single man with white hair shuffled up the trail and strode toward a rusty pickup truck. He placed his fishing pole and tackle box in the bed, and Jason approached him.

"Excuse me, sir. I locked my keys in the car but have a second set at my house in Prescott. Could—"

Jason noted the blank expression on his face like he didn't understand a word he was saying.

"Hablas Español?" Jason asked.

The man, who looked to be in his sixties, smiled. "Si. Si"

Jason told him about his lost keys in Spanish and asked for a ride to downtown Prescott. The old fisherman nodded and waved for Jason to jump into the cab.

Fifteen minutes later, the fisherman dropped his passenger off at the Courthouse Plaza in historic downtown Prescott. Jason walked across the grassy park dotted with mature elm trees surrounding the county courthouse like wooden sentries until he found a bench facing the famous Whiskey Row. He strategically sat on a bench across the street from The Palace Restaurant and Saloon to look for his old friend and gun range owner, Scott Bentley. Jason knew Bentley loved The Palace and darkened its doorway daily after the range closed. He loved to tell Jason that Arizona's oldest business opened in 1877 and that Doc Holliday, Wyatt Earp, and his brother Virgil were frequent visitors to The Palace Restaurant and Saloon. Bentley had a well-documented problem with authority in the Air Force, and Jason was counting on his distrust of the government to ask him for help.

Jason looked at his watch and noted it was a quarter after six. It was time for Bentley to leave The Palace and drive home for dinner. He pulled his cap down over his face and watched the front door from the corner of his eye. His knees bounced despite Jason's best efforts to appear relaxed. Each minute felt like an hour, and it seemed like every pedestrian stared longer at Jason than anyone else when they walked by. He was more exposed than he preferred, but the time to retreat had passed.

A sturdy man around six feet tall exited The Palace and stopped on the sidewalk. It looked like Bentley, so Jason stood and waved to catch his attention, but when the man looked in his direction, Jason realized his mistake. The brim of the man's cowboy hat rose and locked in on Jason as he scurried back to the bench. Jason's heart beat faster, and he removed his ball cap to run his fingers through his hair. When the man pulled a phone from his Wranglers, Jason considered bolting for the neighborhood south of the courthouse, but then another man left The Palace with the same broad shoulders and staccato gait as Bentley. He turned left toward the parking garage while the cowboy looked back and forth from his phone to Jason.

Jason's chance to catch Bentley was slipping away, but now a cowboy appeared to have recognized the most wanted fugitive in the state. He debated whether to flee or try to catch his friend when the cowboy forced Jason to decide. Cowboy returned his phone to his pocket, pushed the brim of his hat up two inches, and marched straight toward Jason.

CHAPTER 21

Prescott, Arizona

Jason bounded away from the cowboy and saw cars and trucks backed up at the stoplight near the courthouse in Prescott. He slunk closer to the wall of vehicles that offered temporary concealment while maintaining visual contact with his pursuer. Cowboy waited on the sidewalk for a break in traffic to cross the street, so Jason used the screen of Chevys, Rams, and Fords like smoke on a battlefield. He skirted to the opposite end of the park and crossed the same street as Cowboy to pursue Bentley.

Once Cowboy crossed the street and entered the park, Jason walked briskly away from the potential vigilante. Jason picked up his pace and, minutes later, was on the parking structure's ground floor. He wasn't sure if Bentley parked in the garage but knew that his GMC Sierra 3500HD with dual rear wheels wouldn't fit in any parking spots around the park.

Jason walked behind the vehicles on the first level of the garage and listened for the signature sound of the diesel engine in Bentley's truck. He shuffled toward the stairs and slowed his breathing until he heard a roar and the classic knock of a cold diesel engine. Jason took two steps at a time to the second floor, but the sound was still too faint, so he continued up to the third floor. As he passed the top step, he saw the pickup truck disappear down the ramp to the second floor. Jason raced down the steps and ran onto the second floor, only to see Bentley's taillights disappear around the corner.

"Damn it, Bentley, slow down."

He did an about-face and raced to the first floor, but instead of Bentley, he ran into the cowboy and stopped. Jason saw the GMC Sierra exit the garage over his shoulder. The chance to get in touch with Bentley vanished quicker than a ship in the night.

Jason tried to play it cool with Cowboy. He slowed and transitioned into a casual walk like he was looking for his vehicle. He felt his ruse was convincing until Cowboy turned and marched toward him.

Jason saw the face under the black fur-felt cowboy hat when Cowboy got closer. The young man with splotchy growth in his goatee was barely old enough to drink, but he looked more muscular than Jason had observed from the park. Jason surmised by his broad chest and tanned pockmarks on his cheeks that he was a legitimate cowboy who probably worked with cattle or horses on the hundreds of ranches in the Prescott area.

"Are you the guy on the news?" Cowboy asked.

He stood in a wide stance, but Jason could tell by the high-pitched crack in his voice that he was nervous.

"What guy in the news?"

"The one that escaped from the police that everyone is looking for."

Jason chuckled. "I wish my life was that exciting."

Cowboy didn't crack a smile. He took a step closer to the potential fugitive, and that's when Jason noticed the tattoo of two military-style rifles in an X pattern with infantry written underneath. Now Jason understood his boldness. He was in the Army as an infantryman in the not-too-distant past.

Jason tried another approach with the cowboy.

"Look, man, I'm a vet and ran into some tough times. I don't have a place to live right now, but I'm working on something. I don't cause trouble, and the police aren't after me. You probably just saw me hanging out in the park before."

Jason watched Cowboy's face soften. He could tell his attempt to gaslight the former Army Infantryman was under consideration. Seconds later, his nose pinched, and resolve returned to his eyes.

"I don't know if I've seen you before or not, so we'll let the police sort this out."

"Why do you care so much if the police are after someone?" Jason asked.

"I don't want a fugitive running around and threatening my town. Plus, they have a reward for anyone that turns you in."

"You'll look stupid if you take me to the police claiming I'm some fugitive."

Confusion returned to Cowboy's face. Nobody wants to look stupid.

"Maybe I should look for this fugitive character if they're offering a cash reward. How much is it?"

"I think it's five thousand dollars."

"That's it?" Jason asked, insulted by the paltry reward.

Cowboy's forehead filled with wrinkles as he tilted his head. "Enough talking. Let's go."

The cowboy reached toward Jason, wrapped his hand around Jason's arm above the elbow, and yanked for him to follow like a horse on a lead rope.

Jason didn't budge. He looked down at his hand and then up at the cowboy.

"You don't want to do that."

"Is that right? Why's that?"

"I'm not going to the police station with you."

Cowboy let go of Jason and reached for his phone.

"I guess we'll invite them to come down here."

Cowboy tapped a few keys before Jason smacked the phone out of his hands. It flew the width of the car behind them and collided with the concrete pavement before sliding under a Toyota sedan. The smartphone left a trail of glass and plastic in its wake. Cowboy stared at the destroyed phone for several seconds and spun around. His face flushed fire engine red.

"Now you've pissed me off!"

He clenched his fists and charged Jason while he wound up like a pitcher preparing to deliver a roundhouse punch. It was the easiest punch to see coming and block. Jason raised his left arm above his ear to block the punch while he stepped forward and pushed him back with his right hand.

"This is your last chance. Walk away now," Jason warned.

"I ain't walking away from shit. You owe me a new phone."

The cowboy launched a jab that caught Jason in the cheek and knocked him back several steps. The former infantryman could pack a punch, so Jason had to be careful of taking too many hits.

Jason moved into a defensive stance and prepared for Cowboy to attack. He didn't have to wait long. Cowboy attempted a right hook that Jason blocked and countered with four quick strikes to his midsection. Cowboy gasped and backed up. He adjusted his hat and spat on the floor. Jason twisted his right foot onto the dusty concrete pavement to maximize his leverage for what was about to come. Cowboy geared up like an angry bull, ready to charge.

He lunged toward Jason and delivered a barrage of right and left hooks, one after the other. Jason tucked his chin to his chest, stepped back to keep his distance, and covered his face so his fore-arms took the brunt of everything Cowboy delivered. The rate of his punches slowed, and Jason knew Cowboy was tiring, so he waited patiently for his opportunity.

Cowboy pulled his hands back to his waist, squinted, and reared back to deliver a roundhouse right with all he had left in the tank. Jason saw his chin sticking out like Florida into the ocean. Everything was in slow motion for Jason as he unleashed a straight punch into the bullseye. Jason's first two knuckles connected squarely with Cowboy's chin, and the reaction was instant. Cow-boy's eyes rolled back as he fell backward into a Chevy sedan and slid unconscious to the pavement.

Jason moved next to the limp lump on the parking garage floor to check on him when the distinct sound of high heels filled the first level of the parking garage. Jason couldn't risk being discov-ered standing over a man out cold with blood dripping from his bottom lip, so he grabbed Cowboy by the collar and dragged him several car lengths into the stairwell. He leaned the unconscious man against the railing on the stairs leading up to the garage's second level. Jason wanted to ensure he could breathe and not choke on his vomit. He couldn't help being a PJ, even if someone just tried to kick his ass and drag him to the police.

The footsteps grew louder, so Jason dashed out of the parking garage. He knew someone would find Cowboy, or he'd wake up soon, and the Prescott Police would swarm to the city center to apprehend the assailant.

The next few minutes would determine if Jason could escape or if he'd spend his next night in prison.

CHAPTER 22

Rust-red colored bricks and green foliage passed Jason in a blur as he sprinted across the street and cut through the courtyard of a closed coffee shop until he reached Granite Creek. He jumped over a chest-high stone wall and slid down the muddy bank until he splashed down in the shallow stream. The depth ranged from knee deep to waist high, allowing Jason to distance himself from the parking garage. He passed underneath roads with cars speeding by, the drivers unaware anyone was using the creek as an escape route below. Fifteen minutes later, Jason left the heart of town and jogged in the shallow stretch of water until the landscape transitioned to a riparian wetland. Towering cottonwood trees with green leaves speckled with splashes of yellow, foreshadowing the coming winter season, formed a leafy canopy above the creek.

Jason stopped to catch his breath and to listen for any pursuers. A stiff breeze made the dense stand of trees sound like a coastline, with waves breaking every time a gust of wind ruffled the leaves.

Sirens!

Somebody must have found Cowboy because the sleepy sirens of the Prescott Police Department woke up. Fortunately, the sirens grew faint, and Jason could relax, knowing they were moving away from him.

Jogging became tricky as the water rose above his knees and his waist. It was too deep to wade through the creek at any speed and too shallow to swim, so Jason climbed up the bank and pushed through the overgrown shrubs between the thirsty cottonwood trees. Jason strode quickly through the dirt path, then froze when he heard a noise behind him. He couldn't believe someone got on top of him so fast, without warning. Jason turned around and saw two men on mountain bikes peddling hard toward him. He looked around to find a place to hide, but jumping into the creek to his right would have aroused more suspicion. They may have even stopped to help. His only chance to avoid detection was to act like the average citizen out for a walk in nature. Jason slowed his pace and breathed through his nose. His heart didn't understand the rapid change and continued to beat in Jason's chest as the mountain bikers closed within twenty yards.

"On your left!" the first biker shouted. He coasted by and then began peddling fast again before warning Jason. "One more coming."

The bikers passed Jason and continued down the path. Jason watched them continue ahead and noticed a large body of water.

Watson Lake.

Jason was familiar with the man-made lake formed after the city dammed Granite Creek. He'd fished and kayaked there a few times and knew that the dam on the other side of the seventy-acre lake led to a narrow canyon a couple of miles long. Jason's route through the creek with a swim across the lake would prevent search dogs from catching his scent. It was practically a freeway for a fugitive to escape town undetected.

At the mouth of the creek, Jason waded into the cool but tolerable water. He dove in and swam swiftly with no sound or splashing to attract attention. Jason pulled himself ashore one hundred yards before the diversion dam and wrung out his shirt. He shivered in the cold but kept moving until he reached the canyon previously carved by Granite Creek. Jason plodded through the mostly dry creek bed hundreds of feet below the top of the granite cliffs. As the cliff walls descended, Jason heard traffic from a nearby street. He knew he was about to lose his cover when he noticed a building cut into the former volcanic lava flows.

After further recognizance, Jason spotted a shuttle bus parked on the east side of the two-story structure. He wanted a better look, so he darted from tree to tree around the parking lot until he was parallel with the folding bus door. He raised his head and scanned the parking lot. A white sedan pulled under the covered porte cochère, and a passenger exited the vehicle. They were one hundred and fifty yards away from the shuttle bus and did not know they were being watched from the tree line. Jason leaped from his position and pushed the folding bus door inward. It opened without resistance, and Jason climbed inside. He noticed keys in the ignition and pumped his fist.

Jason hopped into the driver's seat and slammed his knees on the steering wheel. He mouthed "ouch" without sound and found the lever to lower the seat. Whoever drove it last time couldn't have been taller than five and a half feet. He adjusted the side mirror and noticed the hunter-green letters on the white bus. It was backward, but Jason soon deciphered that the bus belonged to Granite Dells Assisted Living.

An unwelcome wave of guilt washed over him. This was the only shuttle bus he saw on the property and the only mode of transportation for many residents inside the building. Jason was cold and wet from the swim and had to dry off and warm up before nightfall, or he could face hypothermia. He justified boosting the shuttle with the assumption that the facility must have insurance and could replace the shuttle within a day or two. Satisfied that he wouldn't hurt any senior citizens, Jason rubbed his hands together and reached for the keys, still in the ignition with his right hand.

He couldn't do it.

Jason slammed his fist on the steering wheel and tossed his head into the headrest. He turned to the north side of the property and shot up from his seat. A front loader with a backhoe and a dump truck sat motionless beside the parking lot. It looked like they were digging a trench earlier and stopped for the day. This was an even better option because it was more likely they wouldn't return until morning. Five minutes later, Jason was outside the construction equipment. He tried to get inside the dump truck that had probably been responsible for moving tons of gravel and dirt, but the driver's side door was locked. Jason tried the passenger door, which was also locked, but the small triangular-shaped vent window was open. Jason pushed the window open, sticking his arm far enough to unlock the door. He moved into the driver's seat but saw no keys. Jason was grateful his former squad leader with the 22nd Special Tactics unit at Joint Base Lewis McCord insisted they all learn to pick locks and hot wire vehicles. Just like his algebra class in high school, Jason had wondered if he'd ever need to use his new skills in the future. Now he could hug his old Technical Seargent.

He connected the wires beneath the steering wheel, and the dump truck roared to life. Jason shifted the manual transmission for the Peterbilt dump truck into first gear, cranked up the heater to high, and rumbled off.

Jason drove the speed limit as the sun set behind him. He had narrowly escaped the cowboy and the cops, but didn't have a plan about what to do next. It was the first time in hours that he wasn't running from somebody trying to take away his freedom, so he used it to plot his next move.

It was dark when Jason arrived at the entrance ramp to Interstate 17 thirty minutes later. Jason figured his best opportunity was to keep the search area as large as possible so the US marshals couldn't focus all their resources in one spot. Dumping the vehicle in a dirt lot near the primary north-south transportation artery running through the state's center would force the searchers to account for all directions. Instead of taking the faster but higher-risk interstate north to Flagstaff or south to Phoenix, Jason planned to continue east on foot through the unforgiving mountains toward the Verde River.

First, Jason examined the interior for resources but found little more in the cab outside the seats, an instrument panel, and a steering wheel. He noticed a balled-up hoodie on the passenger seat and picked it up. A thermos sat under the sweatshirt. Jason opened it and found it was half full of cold coffee. The chilled beverage meant to be served hot was not Jason's first choice, but it would quench his thirst. He pulled the oversized 2XL hoodie over his head and wedged the thermos into the front pocket.

Jason hesitated to turn off the engine because his bones were finally warm after several days of fighting a constant chill. The most wanted fugitive in Arizona was only a hundred yards off the freeway exit and a sitting duck if anyone from law enforcement pulled into the adjacent dirt lot.

Jason stepped out of the vehicle and pressed the door until it clicked shut. He scanned the freeway exit and parking lot a final time.

Time to do this.

Jason crept into the dark forest, determined to reach Shanna and their unborn baby.

Chapter 23

Whispering Pines, Arizona

Shanna shifted her weight in the chair to get comfortable as the morning sun beamed through the dining room window, casting three additional shadows across the hardwood floor. Her brother, Kai, sat beside her, while Senior Deputy Marshal Whitaker and Deputy Marshal Miley occupied two chairs on the opposite side of the table. The baby had been more active lately, and sleep was elusive for the first-time mom. She was not in the mood to be grilled by the men and women hunting her husband and needed an energy boost to get through their line of questioning. Shanna put a kettle on the stove for herbal tea.

"Kai, it's getting chilly in here. Please add a couple of logs to the stove," Shanna said.

"Sure." Kai bounced up from his chair and inserted two white oak logs into the stove. While he was up, the tea kettle whistled, and Shanna attempted to get up. She placed both hands on the table and leaned as far forward as her thirty-seven week pregnant body allowed to pull herself up, but Kai dashed into the kitchen.

"I'll get it."

Kai returned to the table and poured hot water into the empty cup in front of Miley.

"Thank you," Miley said. She added the tea bag and stirred in some sugar while Whittaker fidgeted with his pen and bounced his knee so rapidly it shook the table.

"Mrs. Mulder, I have several questions for you, so I'd like to get started."

Shanna turned toward the senior marshal and took a sip of decaffeinated tea.

"I'm here to ensure your husband returns safely, so withholding information will not help him. Do you understand?"

Shanna nodded.

"Has Jason tried to contact you since his escape?"

"No, he hasn't."

"Are you sure he hasn't tried to reach you in some way? Text? Instant message? Email? Message through a friend?"

Shanna adjusted herself again after the baby moved positions. "No, and I'm as surprised about this as you. Jason seemed stressed before the trial, and his mom thought he might be depressed. I don't think he is, but I never suspected he would try to escape."

Whittaker stared at her for several seconds as if considering her response and continued.

"Did he have a favorite place he liked to go to be alone and get away from it all?"

Shanna nodded. "Yes, he did."

Whittaker smiled and exchanged a glance with Miley. "Where'd he like to go?"

"The forest," Shanna replied.

"The forest? That's only about ten million acres we'd need to search in Northern Arizona. Could you narrow that down a little further, Mrs. Mulder?"

"I can't. He loves exploring all over. Jason has been to each corner of the state and everywhere between, so he could be almost anywhere."

Whittaker stood and paced between the family room and dining room table while Shanna, Kai, and Miley remained seated. Miley sipped her tea while Whittaker seemed to consider his next question.

"He must have a favorite spot. What about you? Has he shared any favorite places with you?" Whittaker asked Kai.

Kai looked at Whittaker until his forehead wrinkled. "I can't think of a favorite place. I know he prefers places that don't have a lot of people."

Whittaker tossed both hands in the air. "Thank you for that useful nugget. That will help narrow down our search to a manageable 9.9 million acres. I was hoping to get more cooperation from both of you."

Shanna sensed Whittaker's growing frustration and decided it was time for a bathroom break. She excused herself at the same time Whittaker received a call. He was in the family room when Shanna returned. Miley, Kai, and Shanna waited patiently for Whittaker to get off the phone.

Whittaker ended his call but remained standing. "Does your husband have any weapons in the house?"

"I'm sure every Arizonan in this area has weapons in their house," Shanna replied.

"Can I see them?"

"Why would you need to see the weapons in our house when my husband is hiding in the forest?"

Whittaker's expression turned cold. He snagged a chair, spun it around, and sat down so close to Shanna that she could smell his coffee breath when he spoke. "Look, I'm going to get straight to the point. I know you're stonewalling us, which will not end well for either of you. I want to know why Jason Mulder escaped and where he's going, and I'm betting you know more than you're telling us."

Shanna leaned closer to Whittaker. "You're right. I know why he escaped."

It was in Jason's DNA to protect people, especially his family and Shanna knew it was killing him not to be home for her and their future child. Shanna surprised herself that she was so calm even though her husband was a fugitive hiding in the Arizona mountains in early fall. Of course, she was concerned for the safety and well-being of her husband, but Shanna couldn't help feeling confident that he was okay. She trusted Jason more than any other man she'd met and had complete confidence that he had a plan and was executing it right now. She sensed he was coming back for her and their baby but wouldn't put his wife and future child in danger until he had everything figured out and it was safe to return. None of this information would be shared with the marshals, though.

Whittaker leaned back and raised both palms like a conductor leading an orchestra. "Okay then. Enlighten us."

Shanna looked at Kai and then at Whittaker. "They framed him, and he's out looking for the people responsible."

The chair fell over as Whittaker sprung up again like he sat on a tack. "What is it with this conspiracy that someone framed your husband? He told my deputy the same thing. Your man had his day in court, and a jury of his peers found him guilty. What evidence do you have to back up your ridiculous claim? Do you have any?"

"We don't have any evidence yet. My husband is innocent, so we know somebody else planted the drugs to look like they belonged to Jason. He escaped so he could find the people that framed him. You may not like it, but that's the truth."

Whittaker formed a wide, toothy smile. "That girl's number on my phone isn't mine. That text message wasn't for me. The drugs in my car aren't mine. You really believe that?"

"If it's Jason Mulder. I believe it one hundred percent," Shanna replied. Her tone oozed with confidence.

Whittaker shook his head and resumed pacing for a few beats before returning. "We got interrupted a few minutes ago. Let's get back to your husband's weapons and hunting gear. You were about to show me where your husband stores everything."

"I'm not showing you anything else unless you have a warrant."

Whittaker turned to Deputy Miley, "Tell her how easy it is for us to get a warrant."

Miley tensed and appeared shocked to be put on the spot but regained her composure and responded.

"It's pretty easy to get a warrant for the personal contents of a fugitive. It only takes a phone call to a judge and a few pages of paperwork, and we'd have a warrant in under an hour."

Shanna's lips formed a forced, fake smile. "If it's that easy, I don't know why you are still here. I'd make that call so you can get that warrant because we're through until you have one."

The marshals from the Phoenix District left, and Shanna moved to the couch and put her feet up. She felt light-headed after a string of sleepless nights. Shanna knew she had to relax for the next three weeks until the baby was born. It was hard to relax without Jason.

Kai went outside to chop wood for the stove until he returned thirty minutes later. "Someone just pulled up."

Shanna pushed herself up from the couch and shuffled to the patio door. "I don't believe they got the warrant that fast." She looked out the window and noticed it was an unfamiliar vehicle, so she walked out to the back patio to investigate.

"Good morning, ma'am. We want to ask you a few questions about your husband." It was special agent Donaldson and special agent Cruz from the DEA.

Shanna clenched her fists, and her skin prickled with rage the moment she recognized the men. She was in the courtroom and had listened to them lie on the stand about her husband. The baby kicked violently in the womb as Shanna's pulse quickened and her heart pounded inside her chest. Shanna felt faint again and knew she couldn't let herself get too angry, but she couldn't help it.

"Why are you here?"

"We want to come inside and ask you a few questions about your husband," Donaldson replied.

"Haven't you done enough? Get off my property."

Donaldson and Cruz looked at each other and took several steps toward the deck stairs.

"I said, get the hell off my property!" Shanna yelled.

The outburst caused both men to stop, but it cost Shanna her consciousness. Blackness closed in, and Shanna put her hand over her stomach to protect her child. She slowed her fall by clutching the railing with her opposite hand until she fell limp on the patio planks.

The DEA special agents stood in stunned silence, their eyes wide in disbelief, until Cruz spoke. "You want me to hurry inside and look around while she's down?"

Before Donaldson could reply, Kai appeared on the patio and noticed his sister lying on the deck.

"Shanna?"

He dropped to his knees and brushed away her hair until he could see her face.

"What happened?" Kai yelled. "What did you do?"

Cruz stepped back, and Donaldson raised his hands to his chest with his palms facing Kai. "We didn't do anything. We worked with Jason and came here to make sure everything was okay. She passed out while we were walking up here. Are you going to call 911?"

Kai put his index and middle fingers on Shanna's neck, held it for several seconds, and nodded. "Yeah, I'm going to call right now."

He went inside while the two special agents scurried to their SUV. Kai returned with a pillow from the couch and put it under Shanna's head. He watched the two men from the DEA speed off and shook his head in disgust.

The ambulance arrived twenty minutes later, and paramedics stabilized Shanna. They placed her on a gurney, and Kai remained beside her while she lay semi-conscious, arms crossed over her chest. He kissed Shanna on the forehead before they loaded her into the back.

Kai watched the flashing lights disappear past the trees as they sped to the nearest emergency room.

"I wish Jason was here," Kai muttered. He jogged to his car and followed the ambulance with his sister and future niece or nephew in grave condition.

CHAPTER 24

Coconino National Forest, Arizona

Jason made his way down from the hilltop as the morning sky brightened to a sapphire blue. He spotted a game trail and followed it through the forest to pick up speed or conserve energy. Jason wasn't sure which was more important with fatigue dulling his mind after trudging through the forest all night. His breath was visible as he passed through the cool shade of the pine trees and welcomed the warmth on his body once he reached an open area. The trail continued from the woody ridge into a golden alpine meadow splashed with morning sunlight. Jason closed his eyes, turned to the sun, and stood as still as a statue.

Jason was exhausted but grateful he wasn't already in a cell or custody of the US marshals. After several minutes, the warmth of his skin and clothes provided a burst of energy, and Jason resumed his journey to subtract another mile from the marathon distance ahead of him.

The forest thinned out, and loose rocks became more of a problem as Jason dropped in elevation. His legs refused to take another step when the midday sun was directly overhead, and he collapsed underneath a juniper tree. He drained the rest of the liquid in the thermos and fell asleep. Jason slept deeply and uninterrupted until the sun dipped below the horizon in the west. The downtime did wonders for Jason. His legs were fresh, so he resumed his journey until a familiar sound caught Jason's attention. A helicopter thumped in the distance. The sounds of its rotors alternated from barely loud enough to hear to so loud Jason expected to see it over the treetops. It was clear to Jason that the helicopter was flying in a grid pattern, which meant they were likely looking for him. Jason increased his pace while simultaneously searching for any natural structure that could conceal him from the eyes of the crew in the helicopter. As the sun set, Jason stopped to listen closely. If the helicopter stopped searching, he knew they were conducting a visual-only search. If they continued to search, they would be using their infrared cameras.

He remained motionless and let his breathing slow as the shadows engulfed the surrounding forest.

Is the helicopter getting louder or moving away?

Jason tilted his left ear toward the sound.

Is that getting louder?

He repeated the process with his right ear.

"Shit!"

Jason bolted like a sprinter leaving starter blocks and darted through the monochrome forest. The emergence of the blue hour colored everything in light and dark shades of gray under a blue-black sky. It was difficult for Jason to see, but if the helicopter flew over him, he'd light up the infrared cameras like a Christmas Tree in the town square.

Tall pine trees gave way to low-slung juniper trees as Jason continued to descend from the summit. Jason hoped to reach the Verde River after he ditched the dump truck, and based on the changing terrain, he knew he was getting close. He moved swiftly but cautiously through the maze of coniferous trees as the helicopter seemed to track him. Jason felt like the actors in the dinosaur movies trying to outrun the larger and faster T-Rex. He couldn't go any faster in the low light without risking serious injury, but he had to keep moving. If he could reach the bend in the Verde River he'd visited once before, he might avoid the infrared eye in the sky.

The horizon ahead of Jason seemed to lighten until he saw a clearing. He pushed his burning legs to move faster, and a minute later, he was at a ledge overlooking the Verde River. Jason looked up and saw the blinking lights of the helicopter a quarter mile away bearing straight toward him. He looked down at the inky black ribbon two stories below, surrounded by an unrecognizable landscape in hues of gray. The helicopter was less than a hundred yards away, and Jason was out of options. He pushed off the ledge and felt the wind on his face.

Jason closed his eyes and let his feet inform him whether he jumped far enough to avoid the rocky bank. He felt his boots penetrate the water, and a split second later, they smacked the bottom in seven feet of water. Jason immediately noticed the water temperature. He'd jumped into the main bath at Verde Hot Springs with water at a constant ninety-nine degrees.

Jason spun in the water to get familiar with his surroundings. The remaining twilight revealed the man-made concrete foundation of the former hotel built around the hot springs. Now, only the former concrete floor and several graffiti-laden walls remain. He was in a hot spring the size of a residential swimming pool, which might help distort his heat signature.

Minutes later, the helicopter returned, tracking to fly right over Jason. He dove to the bottom of the spring and curled up in a fetal position. Jason didn't know how it would look on the infrared camera, but he knew the less human it appeared, the better the odds of them missing him. One minute after drifting to the bottom, he heard the beat of the rotors overhead. His lungs screamed for oxygen, so Jason rose slowly until his head was out of the water. He breathed copious amounts of cool air as he watched the helicopter lights disappear behind the trees. Jason considered climbing out of the hot spring when the helicopter grew louder again.

"Damn it. They're coming back."

Jason dove back to the bottom and tried his best to resume the same position in the same place as the last time. Seconds after he found his spot, the helicopter flew over. This time, Jason ignored his lungs and stayed for nearly ninety seconds. He resurfaced but remained in the water for twenty minutes until he was sure the helicopter would not return.

The following day, Jason undressed into his boxer briefs and slid into the hot spring after sunrise to warm up after sleeping beside the former hotel pool. The warm water soothed his aching muscles, and he used the relaxing time to create a plan to retrieve his go bag. An hour later, Jason heard voices. He turned around and saw a man and a woman enter the Verde River from the opposite bank. Jason hurried out of the water and pulled a shirt on when the couple reached the hot spring near him.

"Don't worry, honey, we don't bite," the lady said.

The couple looked like they had arrived in a time machine from the sixties. They both had long, curly gray hair, and the man had a matching beard. The lady had dozens of metal bracelets on each arm that rattled with every step. She arrived first, removed her robe, and lowered her naked skeletal body into the hot spring.

"Ah, this hits the spot."

The man also disrobed and followed his mate into the pool. He doggy paddled to the other side while the lady remained near the steps.

"Come back in. We didn't mean to scare you off."

Jason considered his options. He doubted they recognized him, but running away could draw their suspicion. He got back in with his boxers on.

"Feels good, doesn't it?" the lady asked.

Jason moved to his corner of the pool. "Yeah."

The woman kept her eyes on Jason while the man leaned back and closed his eyes. He had no interest in Jason, but the lady seemed determined to start a conversation.

"You out here camping or something?"

"Sort of. I was hiking and decided to stay here last night after it got dark."

She took his response as an invitation and swam over to him so close that Jason could smell the cigarette smoke on her breath.

"You out here all by yourself?"

Jason watched the wrinkly woman move closer in horror. He froze in disbelief as she reached down and tugged at Jason's boxer shorts.

"We don't judge out here. Why don't you take those off and relax?" Her yellow teeth appeared in a smile under her witch-like nose.

Jason's heart was beating like he'd sprinted a mile, and relaxing was the last thing he could do. He jerked away and swam to the steps.

"I—I have to go."

Twenty minutes later, Jason was a mile away from the hot springs and one of the more uncomfortable moments in his life. He'd heard stories of the nudists descending on the hot springs in the area, but his first-hand experience was shocking. He turned a bend and noticed an older model, Subaru Outback.

I'd bet a hundred bucks that's their car.

He approached the vehicle and observed that the rear hatch area was full of tie-dyed clothes and hand-woven blankets. A guitar and a tambourine rested on another pile of clothes in the back seat. Jason opened the door and sat in the driver's seat. The aroma of marijuana and cigarettes was so overpowering he kept the door open. He searched for car keys and found them in the cup holder.

Would it really be this easy?

He turned the key, and the car started. His shoulders relaxed as he exhaled pent-up tension from his body. It was a much-needed break for the fugitive. Jason rolled down all the windows and put the car in drive. This would save him a two to three-day trek across thirty-five of the most rugged miles in Arizona to retrieve his go bag.

Two hours later, the car sputtered and died after it ran out of gas. Jason couldn't risk traveling on the main paved roads, so he'd only covered half the distance to his destination on the unpaved forest roads.

Jason rummaged through the car for resources. He pulled the musty clothes from the backseat until he found a can of iced tea and a box of Ritz Crackers. Ravenous, he tore into the crackers. They were stale, but Jason didn't care. He had consumed no calories in over twenty-four hours and was growing weak from the lack of food and water. The food in his stomach provided a boost of energy, so he continued to search the car. His jaw dropped when he opened the glove box.

It contained an old flip phone. Jason snatched it from the glove box and examined the device. It didn't look like they had used it in the last decade, and Jason figured it had to be broken or contained a dead battery. He took a deep breath and pressed the power button. His eyes widened when he saw the number keys and screen light up. Jason pumped his fist when he checked the signal and saw three of the five bars light up. He was close enough to Strawberry, Arizona, to get a signal.

Jason stared at the phone for a minute. It was time for plan B, so he dialed a number.

A male voice answered.

"Kai, I need your help, so stop whatever you are doing and don't mention any names," Jason commanded.

"Where are you? Shanna is worried sick about you. She just—"

"I said no names. They may be listening," Jason barked.

"Sorry. What do you need?

"I put together a go-bag and hid it the day before my trial. It's a camouflage rucksack, and I need you to retrieve it for me."

"Where is it?"

"I need you to memorize this. Don't write it down. Go back to the place where we both caught a couple of brown trout earlier this year. Walk one hundred and twenty paces southwest from where we parked the truck that day. You'll find it in a cluster of juniper trees about your height. You got all that?"

Jason was nearly out of breath from talking so fast. He stopped and waited for Kai to respond. After several seconds of silence, Jason spoke again.

"I don't have a lot of time. Do you know where to go?"

"I—I can think of a couple of places we caught brown trout this year, or at least I think it was this year. I guess I'm not sure where to go," Kai stammered.

"Remember where I said you need to pay attention because you'll have to drive there next time?"

"Yes," Kai replied enthusiastically. "Holy shit, did you have this planned all those months ago?"

"That doesn't matter. I need you to get the pack as soon as possible and contact my Cajun friend. I left a note inside for him in case I couldn't get to my go bag, so he'll know what to do with it. Your sister has his number."

"Got it," Kai replied.

Jason exhaled and slowed down. "How's my wife and the baby?"

Kai started to speak but stopped.

"Is something wrong?"

"They just got home from the hospital. She and the baby are fine, but she went into premature labor. The doctors said the stress was terrible for her and the baby. If it gets any worse, they'll have to put her on bed rest to reach full term. I'm going over there every day to check on her."

Now, it was Jason's turn to be silent. His worst fears were becoming a reality. He heard a snapping sound and put the phone down to scan the forest. Once he confirmed nobody was in the area, he returned the phone to his mouth.

"Have you watched the news lately?" Jason asked.

"Yeah."

"What are they saying about me?"

"They're saying that you assaulted the marshals and are armed and dangerous. They put a number on the screen to call if anyone sees you or has information that can lead to your capture."

"The news said armed and dangerous?"

"Yeah."

"Hmm. What picture are they using of me?"

"They're using an old picture of you in the Air Force. You had really short hair and were probably twenty years old."

Jason smiled. Now that he knew the public was looking for a much younger and thinner fugitive, he could use that to his advantage.

"I've got to go but tell your sister I love her and will see her soon."

"Will you really see her soon?"

Jason didn't respond to Kai's question.

"Take care of her and let my parents know about your sister. They're closer and can help her out. Do you still remember how to find the backpack?"

"Yeah."

"One last thing and this is extremely important. After you hang up, wait forty-five minutes and call the US Marshal's District Office in Phoenix. Tell them I called you. They'll—"

"Why would I do that?"

"Let me finish. Eventually, they'll find out about this call, and I can't let you get in trouble. The marshals will ask what we talked about. Be honest and tell them I asked about my wife and the baby. Then tell them I asked if you know of any hunter cabins deep inside the Fort Apache Reservation. Say that you didn't know of any but promised to check for me and then search for some on your computer. Tell them I said I'd contact you again in two days and hung up before you could say anything else. They'll be less suspicious and believe you more if you call them before they come to your work or home to question you."

"Makes sense."

"Get that backpack as soon as possible."

"I will."

Jason hung up and let his fingers hover over the phone. He wanted to call Shanna with every fiber in his body. Hearing her voice would help boost his morale, but he couldn't risk a call. Not yet, anyway.

If his plan worked, Jason would see Shanna soon.

Chapter 25

Flagstaff, Arizona

Gunshots blared from the television, startling Special Agent Ken Donaldson as he jerked awake in his recliner. A solitary floor lamp that struggled to illuminate the tiny family room cast the room in a dull, golden glow. He had dozed off after eating dinner while waiting for Special Agent Cruz to arrive. Yawning, he adjusted his chair to an upright position and grabbed a glass from the side table. His gaze fell upon the blank wall above the TV as he slowly swirled the amber liquid inside it. By now, all the ice had melted, leaving only lukewarm whiskey.

But that didn't stop him from gulping it down with a quick jerk of his head.

The twenty-five-year US Drug Enforcement Agency veteran returned his attention to the blank wall. It was like a movie screen, and Donaldson watched a lifetime of regrets unfold before him. He appeared older than his fifty-two birthdays due to years of drinking and hard living. Eight years of service in the Army resulted in two tours in Iraq and dozens of near misses with IED blasts. He returned to the States with PTSD but refused treatment beyond self-medicating with Wild Turkey 101 Kentucky straight bourbon whiskey.

After his second wife filed for divorce, Donaldson grew bitter and cynical toward everyone and even contemplated suicide. He resigned to become another statistic. One of the twenty-two veterans who loses their battle to post-traumatic stress every day. Donaldson prepared to take his own life and would have if it weren't for his granddaughter.

Natalie was the lone bright spot in Donaldson's life, and he'd do anything for the spunky little girl with blond curly hair. Unfortunately, his son, Natalie's father, didn't feel the same paternal sense of commitment. He chose pain pills instead of alcohol like his father and failed to hold down any job. Natalie's father was unemployed and broke, while her mother was nowhere to be found. She'd lived that way for almost her entire half decade on earth, but now she needed responsible adults more than ever. Doctors diagnosed Natalie with leukemia.

Her doctor said her prognosis for a full recovery was good with proper treatment, but adequate care would be a challenge for Natalie without health insurance. This led Donaldson to fight daily with his son, and the DEA special agent doubled his consumption of Wild Turkey. One morning, after a cup of coffee to dull his throbbing hangover, he raised his eyes to the ceiling and cried out to the Almighty. He vowed to do anything to help his granddaughter get the treatment she needed, and a darker spirit answered Donaldson's plea. Natalie started her treatment days after Donaldson negotiated a deal with the Devil, and now it was his turn to honor his half of the commitment. It was why he was in his current predicament with Special Agent Cruz.

A robust knock on his front door stirred Donaldson from his thoughts.

"Door's open," Donaldson shouted.

The twenty-nine-year-old Puerto Rican strutted in like a bull. The six-foot-tall gym rat was easy for Donaldson to recruit. They had become partners two years earlier, and he saw how Cruz loved nice things that were out of his price range on a government salary. Donaldson also saw that Cruz lived comfortably in the gray area of the law. While in college, he attempted to date a seventeen-year-old girl from his former high school, although he was four years older than she was. Her father intervened to prevent his daughter from dating Cruz, and he didn't like to be told he couldn't have something he wanted. Cruz made his feelings known to the father by beating the shit out of him in a parking lot, leaving the protective father in the hospital with broken cheekbones, a mangled jaw, and a severe concussion. Daniel Cruz of the Castle Hill neighborhood in the Bronx continually found himself in trouble for his temper. He had one assault charge that nearly prevented him from joining the DEA, and he'd collected a handful of complaints for unnecessary use of force over his six years as a special agent.

Cruz had no philanthropic reasons for his involvement in the operation with Donaldson. He had over $23,000 in credit card debt and was two payments behind on his beloved Ford Mustang GT. Cruz needed the money to get out of debt and fuel his expensive tastes, so when Donaldson offered him forty grand to help clean up the Titan mess, he jumped on it. Cruz was on board solely for the money. A paid mercenary and proud of it.

Cruz stopped and stared at an empty pizza box on the couch perpendicular to Donaldson's recliner.

"This place is a shit hole, man. How can you live like this?"

Donaldson didn't respond, so Cruz pushed the cardboard box off the couch and sat down. He gazed at Donaldson until his brow furrowed in concern.

"I see we've already started drinking."

"Is that why you wanted to come over here? To bust my balls?"

"No. I want to know what we will do about Jason Mulder?"

Donaldson peeled himself from his recliner and took his empty glass to the kitchen table. Once full of ice and whiskey, he took a long sip. "I got a call from our guy yesterday."

"The boss in Kingman?" Cruz asked. He referred to the man pulling the strings from his cell in the Arizona State Prison Complex in Kingman, Arizona.

Donaldson nodded and returned to his recliner. Cruz moved to the edge of the couch.

"What did he say?"

"He wasn't happy. He reminded me that the operation is at risk every day that Mulder is free. He expects us to recover the USB drive soon."

"Do you think it's still at Mulder's house?" Cruz asked.

Donaldson shrugged. "Don't know. We know he picked it up after the sting that took out Titan and never turned it into evidence, so we'll start with his house."

A smile spread across Cruz's face. "Should we take out his wife and brother-in-law?"

Donaldson tilted his head as if he was contemplating the question.

"We'll do what we have to do if they get in the way, but right now, everyone still thinks Mulder is guilty, and slaughtering his family may move the spotlight off of him and onto someone else like us."

Cruz stood and moved to the front window. He pulled down one slat in the sun-warped blinds and peered through the glass. Seconds later, he turned back to Donaldson.

"Have you heard anything about the hunt to find Mulder? How's that son of a bitch avoiding all those state police and US marshals?"

The crime show ended on TV, and a news anchor appeared on the screen. She stood outside Flagstaff Medical Center talking about an officer-involved shooting. Donaldson snagged the remote, and the screen went black a second later.

"I talked to a guy I know at the US marshal's office in Phoenix that used to be DEA, and he said they are on his trail, but he's gone every time they get there. He says they are close, but Mulder's hiding in the forest, and he knows the area better than any of the marshals. They'll catch him soon," Donaldson reassured Cruz.

"Should we go out and see if we can find him? We could solve all our problems if we find him first, if you know what I'm saying," Cruz replied with a sinister smirk. "I could really use my cut before they repossess my Mustang. I'm willing to hunt him in the woods and beat some answers out of him. He can't be that hard to find."

Donaldson stood from his chair, stretched, and walked over to the fridge. He grabbed a bottle of water, opened it, and chugged it half down in one go. Donaldson leaned on the open refrigerator door and exhaled loudly.

"Let's focus on recovering the USB drive. We'll start at his house, and if it's not there, we'll talk about hunting for Mulder ourselves."

"And if someone interferes while we're looking for the drive?"

"I'll let you handle it any way you want."

Cruz nodded and rubbed his hands together. "Now that's a plan I can get behind."

CHAPTER 26

Coconino National Forest, Arizona

Jason ascended a ridge overlooking granite boulders and pinyon pine trees growing in the shadow of the canyon walls. The haggard fugitive leaned against a tree and scanned the area after pushing through the forest eight hours after ditching the car and calling Kai. He searched for a space to hide from airborne searchers and sleep before night descended on the remote area above the Mogollon Rim.

A depression underneath a sandstone overhang appeared darker than the rest of the area, offering hope it was deep enough to evade infrared cameras. Jason slid into the canyon, climbed up to the depression, and found the cave two body lengths deep. He'd be invisible to the air search, and it provided easy access to Potato Lake to look for the rucksack Clay would deliver soon. Jason found his home for the night.

During Jason's trial and sentencing, he considered every contingency for Clay, Kai, and himself to retrieve and deliver his go bag. Once he heard Cruz lie on the stand, Jason knew he was right to prepare for the worst-case scenario, and it was time to see if his preparation paid off. Plan A called for Jason to retrieve the rucksack himself, but he suspected it might be fraught with risk and problems. Plan B involved other people, and Jason wanted to limit the involvement of others but needed Clay and Kai to help. Jason knew they'd both assist without hesitation but would be taking enormous risks with the US Marshals and law enforcement if his plan was intercepted. To protect them, Jason built plausible deniability and escape routes into the plan. The trickiest part was the note he left for Clay in his rucksack. The note said:

```
Thanks, brother. If you get this note,
I've moved to Plan B. You can launch
a long-range drone from 34.27.10 N and
111.22.42 W. It's an observation tower
and shouldn't create suspicion for using
a drone there. I'll be enjoying a potato
and washing it down with some chocolate
milk near the maximum range of your drone.
The farthest point from the access road is
best.
```

Jason hoped his message wasn't too cryptic for Clay or too easy to decipher by authorities if they captured Clay before he could deliver the rucksack.

The sun vanished behind the horizon and darkness arrived like a light switch was flipped off. Jason wrapped himself in a wool blanket he'd taken from the Subaru, pulled the hoodie over his head, and curled up in the rear of the depression. He shivered on the cool rocky floor and thought about the rucksack's contents to take his mind off his numb fingers and toes. He'd filled his go bag a month earlier but the cold weather gear and Meals Ready to Eat or MREs were top of mind. Jason salivated at the thought of eating the vacuum-sealed kit of military rations, something he never thought was possible when it was his primary food option on several missions during his deployments in Afghanistan. His vacuum-sealed gourmet dinner would have to wait until Kai and

Clay retrieved the rucksack and delivered it to Potato Lake. Jason dozed off despite his splitting headache and hunger pangs that felt like he was getting stabbed from the inside.

Jason rose from the icy floor after light entered the depression entrance and emerged to witness the sun climbing above the tree-tops in the canyon. He only slept a few hours because he had to continually do pushups to stay warm. Jason feared he might suffer from hypothermia as temperatures dipped into the low forties. It was early October, and at his elevation of 7000 feet, Jason knew nighttime lows would fall below freezing soon.

The rucksack consumed all his waking thoughts, so Jason traversed to Potato Lake to wait for his delivery. Jason sat thirty yards inside the tree line and listened for a drone and vehicles. He dropped into a prone position several times to avoid detection from trucks and SUVs that stopped to look at the shallow, muddy pond, but the buzz of a quadcopter UAV never tickled his ears.

Jason ambled back toward his shelter as fatigue, thirst, and hunger dulled his situational awareness. He couldn't recall if he covered his disturbed soil or swept away his tracks near Potato Lake. Finding food and water was paramount, so he dropped farther down the canyon near the depression. Ten minutes later, he stopped to rest. He felt dizzy, while brain fog dulled his thoughts and senses. His head felt too heavy to hold up, so Jason let it drop until he saw the pebbles by the heel of his boots. He closed his eyes and took in short breaths.

Jason heard something and jumped to his feet. He hopped from boulder to boulder until he found the source of the sound. It was a trickle of water percolating from under a boulder the size of a hatchback car. The liquid flowed down a flat rock, descending a couple of inches until the drops kissed another flat piece of granite.

It was similar to a leaky kitchen faucet, but to Jason, it sounded like Niagara Falls.

It was too shallow to collect water, so Jason unscrewed the top from the thermos he swiped from the dump truck and followed the canyon down until he found a shallow pool of water a foot deep. Jason plunged the thermos into the cool liquid and closed the lid. Like a little devil on his shoulder, Jason's thirst tempted him to drink the water straight from the source, but he didn't want to risk contracting a water-born illness.

He descended farther along the narrow stream bed until he found an old beer can. Two minutes later, he spotted an Emory oak tree a few feet up the canyon.

"Jackpot!"

Hundreds of fresh acorns were on the ground, which wasn't unusual with the number of oak trees in the area, but all the other acorns contained undesirable amounts of bitter tannins. Emory oak acorns were sweet and a favorite of the local deer and javelina. He'd wash and soak them to be safe.

Motivated by the acorns, he felt a surge of energy and picked up his pace to search for more resources and was rewarded with a batch of green purslane succulents growing between rocks. Shanna had used purslane in salads before, and Jason knew it would provide essential nutrients to further boost his energy. He searched for another ten minutes as shadows consumed the canyon, and Jason knew it was time to return to his shelter. As he climbed out of the canyon, he grabbed a rock that came loose and tumbled past him.

"Oh shit," Jason yelled.

A striped scorpion with its tail at the ready darted within an inch of the hand Jason put down to steady himself. It ran in circles, looking for a new shelter, so Jason picked up another rock and smashed it. Although it was only two inches long, scorpions were around eighty percent protein and quite tasty if desperate for food. Jason pulled up more rocks in the area and was treated to another striped scorpion.

Jason reached his temporary home for the night after the orange disk disappeared behind the trees. The high for his successful hunt and forage for food was short-lived when the evening chill foreshadowed another dangerously frigid night ahead.

Jason exited the depression and gazed at the tall pine silhouettes shimmering in front of the dark blue twilight sky. He'd traveled over one hundred miles over the past four days, with half of them on foot. Jason was beyond grateful for the dump truck and Subaru that helped him put miles of distance between himself and his pursuers, but he was running out of time, energy, and strength. He knew staying put the past twenty-four hours to wait for the rucksack would dramatically shrink the gap he'd built between him and the marshals. Jason also understood that he needed a decent meal and a night of sleep to continue his pace to stay ahead of them. The beat of a helicopter rotor or howl of search dogs had been absent the last few hours, so Jason knelt at the depression entrance and dug two holes two feet apart and one foot deep. He pushed a sturdy stick through one hole until it came through in the other. Next, he collected small twigs and dry grass and placed them in the hole nearest the entrance. Jason removed his watch and pulled out the flint fire starter in the band. After several strikes, a flicker appeared on the grass, and a small flame sprung to life seconds later. Jason started a Dakota fire hole to boil his water and keep warm with as little smoke and visible light as possible. It was a tremendous risk for Jason to start a fire that would show up for miles on a helicopter mounted infrared camera, but so was dehydration and hypothermia.

Jason finished soaking, drying, and crushing his acorns two hours later. He turned the acorns into flour tortillas and toasted them on a flat stone over the fire. After his acorn tortillas were done, Jason wrapped himself in the blanket and devoured his dinner of scorpion tacos with a side of purslane.

The rucksack has to arrive tomorrow.

The freezing fugitive didn't know how much more of the cold, hunger, and thirst he could take with his lack of gear and resources. For the first time, he considered the possibility of surrendering himself and reattempting to prove his innocence in court to make the pain go away.

Chapter 27

Coconino National Forest, Arizona

Jason scrambled up the slope of the bluff overlooking Potato Lake. He woke with refreshed legs and stronger resolve after feeding his hunger and quenching his thirst. Eagerness to see if the life-giving package arrived quickened his pace. It was like descending the final steps on Christmas morning to find a big present wrapped in colorful paper and a bow.

At the edge of the tree line, he dropped into the prone position and peered cautiously over the foliage. Jason rose to scan the area and was slapped with the pungent smell of fish and rotten eggs. He understood the hydrogen sulfide assaulting his nostrils meant the wind had shifted directions and threatened Clay's drop. Jason hoped the sudden gusts wouldn't impede the drone's ability to make the crucial rucksack delivery.

The shadows in the mid-morning sun receded while Jason edged closer to the tree line of the two-acre lake. His eyes darted from left to right, looking for movement and signs of recent human activity. Jason focused his search on the east side of the coffee colored body of water and then moved his gaze slowly to the west until he spotted a dark bundle ten yards from the water's edge. His pulse quickened, and he considered darting from his cover toward the unidentified object but caught himself. Instead, Jason maintained his cover as he crept through the trees until he was parallel with the bundle. He knelt in the underbrush for five minutes, and once Jason was sure it wasn't under surveillance, he scampered to the lumpy object. Jason smiled at the sight of his rucksack but pinched his nose when he picked it up. It seemed fuller and heavier than before, but he didn't have time to worry about it now. He dropped to a knee, pulled the straps over his shoulders, and centered the rucksack on his back. Once he tightened the straps, Jason tossed operational security out the window and rushed back to his shelter. Jason couldn't wait to dig into his fresh supplies.

Under the late morning sun, Jason opened his rucksack with cold weather gear on top. A moment later, a stocking hat, gloves, wool socks, thermal blanket, and a box of hand warmers he used while hunting were lying on the rocky soil beside his rucksack. That's when he noticed the next item that he didn't pack.

Jason stood up and tapped his index finger on his lips while eyeing the foreign item. He pulled the soft plastic object from the rucksack, and a piece of paper fell out. Jason opened the folded paper and found a handwritten note. He moved closer to the entrance, and once the sunlight hit the note, Jason let out an audible laugh. He continued to laugh under his breath as he read the message.

Stay strong and safe, brother. I added a friend to keep you company in case you get lonely out there all by yourself. Ashley isn't much of a talker, but she knows how to keep you warm at night. On a serious note, I joined the security detail for Senator Conrad for his next election run. I'll be out of pocket for a while, but come find me once you clear your name.

Jason unfurled the inflatable lifesize blow-up doll and reread the note three times. He wished he could have been there to congratulate Clay in person.

Next, Jason removed a knife with a four-inch blade, two hundred feet of rappelling rope, a LifeStraw personal water filter, and four MREs. It took all his willpower not to tear into a MRE and consume all its contents, but he resisted the primal urge. His current shelter was no longer safe, so he'd eat once he found a new location.

Under the survival gear, Jason reached the evasion section of the kit. He unveiled five hundred dollars in cash, hair dye, scissors, razors, shaving cream, a mirror, and two temporary tattoos. A burner phone in a Faraday bag was under the hair dye.

He looked at the pile of goods on the cave floor and nodded. He was satisfied with his tools to change his appearance. It was imperative that his new look be convincing enough to avoid capture by anyone searching for him.

After repacking his rucksack, including Ashley, Jason left the cave to find water when he heard a stick snap further up the canyon. The hair on Jason's arm stood up at the potential threat. He dropped to the ground and crawled to the edge of the canyon. Two men in black tactical uniforms bounded down the side of the canyon toward Jason. The US marshals had arrived.

Jason's heart pounded in his chest as he ducked behind a cluster of boulders, adrenaline surging through his veins. His eyes narrowed, scanning the canyon for any sign of additional pursuers. Seeing none, Jason tuned his ears to the marshals' conversation as they bounded closer to him.

"Should we head back now? I don't think anyone is out here," one marshal asked.

"In a few minutes. The drone hovered for a while somewhere around here before it vanished. Let's confirm it's nothing, and then we'll grab lunch," the other replied.

The marshals jumped from boulder to boulder without concern for operational security. Their weapons were holstered, and they jabbered on as if they were standing at the office coffee maker. Jason's mind raced, calculating his options. His hands clenched into fists and his body tensed to prepare for what lay ahead.

Jason lay flat on the ground next to a van-sized boulder and let the first marshal pass by him undetected. The second marshal followed his footsteps and slid across the boulder thirty seconds later. Jason lunged like a silent predator and launched his strike the instant the marshal's boots touched the ground.

The second deputy marshal, a burly man with salt-and-pepper hair, was caught off guard as Jason's fist connected with his jaw in a lightning-fast strike. Jason immediately grabbed the marshal by the back collar as he slumped forward unconscious and dragged him behind the boulder before his limp body hit the ground with a thud. Jason crept behind another boulder down the canyon and waited.

The first deputy marshal, a lean and agile figure, stopped and turned around a minute later.

"Hoff? Hoff, where are you?"

He removed his Glock 9mm pistol and raised it to the ready as he carefully retraced his steps. Near the enormous boulder, he turned toward the unconscious deputy marshal. He stared at his comrade, lying awkwardly for a few beats, and spun around to encounter Jason Mulder's left hand, wrapped around the barrel and slide while his right hand arrived on top to secure full control of the weapon. Jason turned the barrel up and then toward the marshal's body and drove it into his chest armor several times. Seeing it did not have the intended effect, Jason aimed higher and struck the marshal's shoulder with the barrel three times before ripping it from his grip. Jason removed the magazine and tossed it into the canyon.

The marshal grabbed his shoulder and looked up and down the canyon for a second. Jason thought he might turn and run, but he locked his eyes on Jason and widened his stance. He put up his hands like an eighteenth-century bare-knuckle boxer. Jason moved into his defensive stance and waited for the marshal to launch an attack, but it never came.

Jason inched forward, and when the marshal delivered a right jab, he blocked it with his left and lunged forward. He kneed the marshal in the thigh while simultaneously moving behind him. Jason secured the marshal's neck in a chokehold between his forearms and slid backward to remove the marshal's feet from under him. The marshal pulled and slapped at Jason's forearm to release the python-like grip, but nothing worked. Jason held onto the marshal a few additional seconds after he stopped resisting and laid him on the ground. He turned to the first marshal and noted both men were out cold, so he pulled the radios off their chests and stomped them into pieces with his boot. Next, he removed the magazine from the first marshal's Glock and tossed it in a different direction than the first one. He searched both men and found each had a second loaded magazine in their vests, so he removed them. Jason ditched both magazines on his way back to the cave. Now, neither man could immediately shoot if they regained consciousness before Jason escaped the canyon.

Jason snagged his rucksack, and sprinted up the canyon's sheer walls. Jason didn't look back before he disappeared over the ridge, leaving the incapacitated marshals in the rugged canyon behind him. He knew an army of marshals and aircraft would mobilize soon and fan out across the area to capture their fugitive. They'd be more determined than ever to catch him and make Jason pay for injuring two of their own.

Chapter 28

Coconino National Forest, Arizona

A gust of wind caught the dry soil and swirled until it deposited a layer of red-brown dust in Deputy Marshal Hoffman's open mouth. He coughed, spit, and winced at the pain in his face. Hoffman laid awkwardly on his back and slid his hand over his aching jaw. His fingers confirmed the growing lump above his neck, and his nerves confirmed it hurt like hell. The first man taken out by Jason Mulder opened his eyes and blinked repeatedly at the bright blue sky. He attempted to roll from his back to his stomach, but his arm was numb from lying on it for several minutes. Hoffman shook his arm for thirty seconds and turned onto his stomach to prop himself up on his hands and knees on the rocky ground. He stayed on all fours for several beats and then scanned the area to get his bearings. The pounding in his head slowed, so he rocked back until he was on his knees. Hoffman opened and closed his mouth multiple times to ensure his jaw still worked. That's when he heard moaning further down the path. He wobbled to his feet and found Deputy Marshal O'Neal curled up in a fetal position.

"Hey, Shawn. You okay?" Hoffman asked.

O'Neal turned his head toward his partner. "My—my shoulder is killing me."

Hoffman nodded in response but said nothing more. He was too dizzy to bend over and help.

O'Neal moved to a seated position. "What happened to you?"

Hoffman reached for his jaw again. "I'm not sure. I feel like I was hit by a bus."

"Not a bus. Jason Mulder," O'Neal replied.

Hoffman tilted his head, and his eyes widened. "Are you sure? He knocked me out before I saw anything."

"Yeah, I'm sure. After he dropped you, I went back to help, and then he jumped me. I didn't know he could fight like that. I met a couple of PJs when I was in the Marines, but they were more like combat medics. He learned that John Wick shit on his own," O'Neal noted.

Hoffman let go of the boulder he leaned against for support and offered O'Neal his hand to help him, but his beaten comrade waved him off.

"It would have been nice to have seen his martial arts background in his profile," Hoffman said. He continued to examine the cuts and scrapes on his hands from falling to the ground after the powerful strike to his jaw by Jason Mulder.

O'Neal finally stood and joined his partner on the boulder. "How long do you think we were out?"

"I'm not sure. I am thinking ten to fifteen minutes. Maybe more," Hoffman replied.

"What should we do now? Should we go after him?"

Hoffman's head snapped toward O'Neal. "And get our asses kicked again?"

O'Neal raised his hands in mock surrender. "I was just asking."

"Let's police the area for signs of where he may have gone. He can't be too far yet, so once we have a direction, we'll call it in to send an airborne team after Mulder."

O'Neal stood and then winced in pain. He rubbed his chest and muttered, "Damn, that hurts," under his breath.

Hoffman saw the broken radios on the ground and spun around toward O'Neal. "He smashed our radios."

Both marshals reached for their holsters and removed their Glocks. "He took my magazine," Hoffman said.

"Mine too," O'Neal reported. He patted his vest. "And he took my back up magazine. We're sitting ducks right now, so let's find out which direction he ran and get out of here."

"I'm pretty sure he came from the other side of the canyon, so I'll go over there and look," Hoffman replied.

Ten minutes later, Hoffman yelled for O'Neal. "Over here. I think I found his trail."

O'Neal traversed the boulders across the trickle of water in the canyon until he reached Hoffman. He was standing near the entrance of a cave.

"He was hiding in here for the last few days. I found evidence of a Dakota fire and some food prep." Hoffman pointed to a flat rock with flour on it.

"Follow me," Hoffman said with a wave. He led O'Neal out of the cave and bent down twenty yards away. "See the boot prints on this path?"

O'Neal nodded.

"They lead northeast over that summit, and he was clearly running through here. I think we found the direction he's headed. Let's get the hell out of here and call it in."

Two hours after leaving their US Marshal Service SUV to investigate a drone reported in the area, Hoffman and O'Neal returned to their vehicle. They climbed inside and called into the dispatcher.

As they waited for a response, Hoffman turned to O'Neal with a look of concern. "Are you going to tell them what happened?" he asked. The senior marshal knew the crap they'd get from their fellow deputy marshals if they found out a fugitive took out two men.

"You mean how Mulder jumped us from behind?" O'Neal asked with a wink.

"That's true for me," Hoffman replied.

"Same for me. At least, that's how I remember it."

Hoffman nodded. They both needed to save face.

The radio crackled to life. "This is dispatch. Go ahead."

Hoffman grabbed the radio. "This is Deputy Marshal Hoffman and O'Neal. We found the trail of our fugitive, but he jumped us and escaped."

"Please confirm the fugitive. Was it Jason Mulder?"

"Affirmative."

"Hold one," the dispatcher replied.

Hoffman and O'Neal sat without talking until the dispatcher returned.

"Senior Deputy Marshal Whittaker wants to see you."

EMTs treated Hoffman and O'Neal for deep bruises and lacerations and guided them to another room in the newly constructed command center. They erected the white, circus-like tent near the tower where Clay launched the drone.

"Deputy Marshals O'Neal and Hoffman?" Deputy Marshal Miley asked.

"Yes, ma'am," Hoffman replied.

She moved across the dark room in the center of the command center with her hand extended, but pulled it back.

"Are you two okay? Have you seen the medics?"

Hoffman rubbed his jaw. "Yeah, we just left. We're both banged up, but we'll live."

"I'm glad it wasn't worse."

Hoffman and O'Neal nodded in unison.

"Whittaker will see you now."

Miley pushed a canvas curtain aside that revealed Whittaker sitting at a round table with three open chairs. He looked up at the battered men and waved them in.

"Ladies and gentlemen, take a seat."

The three deputy marshals found seats around the table. Whittaker's eyes darted back and forth from Hoffman and O'Neal until he spoke.

"So, what happened, guys?"

Hoffman shot a glance at O'Neal and cleared his throat. "We got a tip of a drone dropping something near Potato Lake shortly after sunrise. After we got there, we found fresh boot tracks on the far side of the lake, so we followed them through the woods and into a canyon. Next thing we know, Mulder jumps out from behind a tree and clocks me before I can draw my weapon. He hit me square in the jaw, and everything went black. I'll let O'Neal tell you what happened to —"

Whittaker held up his hand. "It's clear that you both got your asses whipped by Jason Mulder, so I want to move on to finding him. How far away from the lake did this happen?"

Hoffman looked at O'Neal, and he shrugged. "We walked for a while, but it was pretty rugged. I'd guess we were a half mile away."

"Did you see where he was hiding out or which direction he went?"

"Yes, sir," Hoffman replied.

"After we came to, we investigated the area and found the cave he was hiding in. It had a Dakota fire, and we found some type of crushed grain or flour on a rock inside the cave."

"And you saw which direction he was last headed?"

Hoffman shook his head. "We didn't see him but found the same bootprints running over the ridge. He's heading east."

Whittaker stood and moved to a 4x3 foot map on an easel against the tent wall. He crossed his arms and stared at it. A minute later, he slapped the map with his open hand, causing Hoffman and O'Neal to jump in their chairs.

"He's headed home. I felt he might try this, but now it's clear as day."

Whittaker turned to Miley. "Get at least two birds in the air to search the corridor between Potato Lake and Whispering Pines as soon as possible. I want infrared cameras used on all visible caves in that corridor and beefed up patrols near Mulder's house."

Whittaker fell back into his chair and locked his fingers behind his head. He stared at the top of the tent for several seconds and smiled. "Now we know where he is going and that he likes to hide in caves. We'll have him in custody within twenty-four hours."

Chapter 29

Jason slid down a rocky hill and continued his hurried pace on another game trail. Two hours after knocking out both marshals, he marched ahead on autopilot while his mind raced through scenarios on how they discovered him. It would be understandable if the marshals had dogs, surveillance listening devices, or handheld infrared cameras, but it was just two men on foot. Jason thought he'd covered all bases to avoid detection and wondered if he was slipping physically and mentally due to fatigue or if the marshals were closer to capturing him than he imagined. His pace increased upon the realization that it could be both. His eyes bounced up from the path and spotted a cave on a ledge overlooking the canyon. Two juniper shrubs concealed the opening in the side of the ridge.

Jason climbed into the cave and investigated its suitability as his next hideout. It wasn't as deep as he had hoped, but he sat down for a break. He figured the US marshals he roughed up were awake and sharing their stories by now, so Jason wanted to put as much rugged wilderness between himself and his pursuers as possible. Jason left the cave and pushed himself for another hour until he stumbled and fell. The heavy rucksack and physical exhaustion drove Jason's face into the rocky path. He spit out dusty pebbles as he moved to his hands and knees.

Jason took a deep breath and raised one knee to resume his journey when a small opening on a south-facing slope caught his eye. The juniper trees outside the entrance resembled the last cave he investigated.

He grunted as he pushed himself upright and dusted himself off. The faint trickle of a stream in his right ear confirmed a source of life-saving water was also nearby. Jason turned one-hundred and eighty degrees to track his progress. The enormity of the ridge he conquered since beating up the US marshals surprised even him.

Jason had traveled over two miles since he explored the first cave, so this one was considerably farther from the marshals' primary search area. He used his last reserves of energy and climbed up to the cave. He peered inside and noticed it went further back than the sunlight allowed him to see. It reminded him of the cave he traversed with Clay and Tarek while they were pursued by the La Palma cartel. He'd give anything to have those night vision goggles now. Jason knew the determination of the US marshals to find him would shoot up to a new level after the beaten comrades returned. If their resolve rated a seven or eight before the beatings, it would be no lower than an eleven out of ten now.

Jason let the rucksack slide over his arms and fall to the ground onto the rocky soil inside the cave. It was like removing the saddle and harness from an old workhorse. He rolled his neck and shook out his hands. Jason opened his rucksack and snagged the materials needed to change his appearance from the top. With the mirror in his hand, he moved near the cave entrance to see himself better. First, Jason shaved his head to begin his transformation. He ran his hands over the stubble on the top of his dome and moved the mirror high and low to see himself from different angles. Although he'd worn his hair short for the last decade, Jason was encouraged by how different he looked with a bald head. Next, he attacked his seven-day-old beard with a razor and formed it into a goatee. After washing his face with water from his thermos and letting his facial hair dry, he applied hair dye to his goatee and eyebrows. The marshals and law enforcement were looking for a clean-shaven fugitive with short brown hair based on the picture of Jason circulating the local TV news stations. Now, he was a bald man with a blond goatee, but the biggest change to his appearance was yet to come.

The next item in his pile was a black scorpion with its tail raised high and ready to strike. He held the first of two temporary tattoos on the right side of his neck. He didn't want to order anything that signaled military service, so he chose the most outlandish designs he could find. Jason approved the placement and applied the tattoo. It looked menacing, and Jason cringed as he placed it just above a t-shirt line on his neck. The scorpion tattoo looked tame compared to the second patch of temporary ink. It was a skull and crossbones with a serpent coming out of one eye. Blood cascaded off the snake's fangs, poised to strike its next victim. Jason spent an hour meticulously applying his temporary tattoos. It was the most critical component of his disguise. Even more than his bald head and beard dye. He knew the tattoos would draw the eyes and attention of anyone looking at him, including law enforcement. It was impossible not to stare at the ink art on his neck.

He raised his mirror to admire his handiwork and stared at the strange man in the reflection. He turned to the left and then to the right. His lips curled skyward at the successful transformation. Jason lowered the mirror and a frown clouded his face. He paced from the bright entrance of the cave to the rear, where he fell out of view into the darkness of the cave.

Am I really going to live in the woods until the marshals call off the chase?

Jason returned to the entrance and stared out of the cave south toward Whispering Pines. He knew he was less than ten miles away from his wife and unborn child. A half a day for him if he pushed himself. Jason turned away, kicked some rocks, and then turned back south again. He wished he was going home instead of perfecting his appearance to go on the run for as long as possible. Shanna was two weeks from her due date, and Jason should be there for her. The thought of not being home for the birth of his first child crashed over him like a rogue wave.

Jason was ecstatic to become a father the moment Shanna told him she was pregnant. It elated him to learn the good news, but he didn't understand until now just how important having a child was to him. He did everything necessary to prepare for a new baby, but the trial and fight for his freedom distracted him from fully appreciating the preparation for his child. If he was honest with himself, Jason had assumed the court would find him not guilty, and then he'd focus on fatherhood. Now, the prospect of missing the birth of his first child churned up emotions buried deep in his core. The need to be a good father swelled inside him like a mushroom cloud. Jason's parents were outstanding role models, but it was more than that. His relationship with his younger brother Josh had aspects of a father-and-son relationship before he died. Because of the ten-year age difference, a sibling rivalry never existed between the brothers. Josh looked up to his older brother for wisdom and mentorship, and Jason wanted to give his little brother the best life possible. He understood nothing would bring back Josh or fill the gaping hole in his heart, but rising to the occasion to be a good father was as important as protecting his family for Jason.

A good father doesn't miss the birth of their child unless he is overseas fighting for his country.

Mentally exhausted as he was physically tired, Jason slid down the side of the cave and leaned against his rucksack. He used the last of his energy to open and heat an MRE. Jason devoured the ready-to-eat meal while plotting how to avoid law enforcement to see Shanna.

The following day, Jason woke up committed to returning to Whispering Pines. He had to know if Shanna was okay and be present for the birth of his first child. Jason was aware the marshals would stake out his house, and his chances of getting caught were high, but his will to see Shanna trumped all other concerns. He mentally confirmed his plan to return home. He just had to execute it.

Jason pulled the rucksack over his shoulders and checked his mirror to ensure his disguise remained. He shuffled to the entrance of the cave and stopped. The familiar sound of beating rotors filled the air and was getting closer. Soon, Jason could tell it was two helicopters. The marshals were sending the cavalry to catch their fugitive.

Jason swallowed hard. The odds of getting through the gauntlet of state police, sheriff's deputies, and US marshals on his tail to see Shanna before she went into labor just plummeted.

Chapter 30

Coconino National Forest, Arizona

The walls of the command center moved in and out with the morning breeze as if the structure were alive and breathing. Senior Deputy Marshal Whittaker leaned back in his chair with a file folder in his hand under the white light of a floor lamp. He opened it and scanned the report on Jason Mulder for the twentieth time since he got the call to apprehend the elusive fugitive.

"What makes you so special, Jason Mulder?" Whittaker asked himself.

He saw the six years of exemplary service as a pararescueman in the Air Force, including his deployments to Afghanistan. Jason's brief history with the DEA was also in the report, but he still couldn't understand how Jason Mulder could avoid capture by the best fugitive hunters in the world. His eyebrows raised at a single sentence, and he put the file down.

"Miley, please come in here."

Miley pushed through the white canvas wall separating her workspace from Whittaker. "Yes?"

"Have you read this report on Jason Mulder?"

"Yes. Probably a hundred times."

Whittaker cocked his head. "Okay, that's a few more times than me. I'm asking because I noticed this sentence on the last page about citizen recognition by the DEA for his efforts with the La Palma cartel. Do you know what that's about?"

"I saw that too, so I contacted the DEA District Office in Phoenix for additional details. They told me a cartel caused an accident that killed Jason's youngest brother, and when local law enforcement couldn't find the cartel hiding in the White Mountains, he went after them himself and found them."

"Jason Mulder captured a cartel by himself? I find that hard to believe."

"He had help from the White Mountain Apache Tribe Police Department and Special Agent Holland with the DEA in the physical apprehension of the cartel, but apparently, he tracked them down with a couple of other civilians when nobody else could find them."

Whittaker nodded and leaned forward in his chair. He stared at the wood-grain table for several beats until he looked up at Miley standing beside him.

"So, what you told me earlier is true. We have a real mountain man on our hands."

"It appears so."

"Good work, Miley. I think there's still more to Mulder, so keep digging. Talk to Special Agent Holland at the DEA and see if he can shed more light on our fugitive."

"Do you think he's innocent?" Miley asked.

Before Whittaker could respond, a young marshal burst into the room, and the flap slapped shut behind him. "Sorry to barge in like this, but we just got a call from one of the pilots. They got a hit on the infrared camera, and it's in a cave."

Whittaker jumped to his feet. "Where's the cave?"

"Due east of here, about two miles. It's in the new corridor we've been searching."

"Get one of those birds back here and load up the strike team."

Twenty minutes later, Whittaker's boots hit a patch of pale, yellow grass in a clearing. He bent at the waist and rushed into a stand of nearby shrubs to join men in tactical gear who arrived in the lead helicopter. Whittaker donned a tactical helmet and a ballistics vest under his black windbreaker with US Marshal emblazoned in gold on the back. Silence fell upon the shallow canyon once the last helicopter lifted, and the grass stopped swaying. The morning sun cast shadows across the west-facing wall of the ridge. The air was crisp and cool, and the pungent aroma of juniper tickled his nostrils.

Another man in tactical gear arrived next to Whittaker and took a knee. He leaned in and pointed twenty yards up the slope to a shadowy entrance.

"It's up there."

"Is Mulder inside?" Whittaker whispered.

"We think so. The bird got a hit on the infrared camera about twenty feet inside that cave."

"Has he come out or moved at all?"

"No movement yet."

Whittaker pursed his lips. "Hmm. What's the plan?"

"I'll lead a team of six. We'll approach with three on each side and assault the cave with overwhelming force. If he's in there, we'll get him."

Whittaker nodded.

The lead marshal signaled for the team to move out. They stalked through the underbrush, their weapons at the ready, and crept up the ridge toward the mouth of the cave. The minutes ticked by slowly, each one feeling like a day. Whittaker's hands were curled into fists as he swayed back and forth with his eyes locked on the cave. He couldn't be still. He loved the adrenaline rush he got just before they apprehended a fugitive. It was the best sixty seconds of his job. Nothing else made him feel like he was back in the ring as a competitor. His stomach fluttered again like it did when he stepped on the football field in college.

As the marshals neared the ledge flanked by junipers, the leader used hand signals for the assault team to fan out on both sides of the entrance. Whittaker watched from below as three men gathered on each side of the cave entrance.

Whittaker could hear the blood rushing through his ears as he waited for the six deputy marshals to enter the cave. Relief rushed over him when he saw the hand signal displaying five fingers, and everyone raised their weapons. Six men disappeared in a coordinated move like the cave sucked them down a drain. Whittaker braced for yelling or gunshots, but it was eerily silent.

"What's going on up there?" Whittaker asked himself.

He drifted toward the base of the granite wall that hosted the cave. Whittaker considered climbing to the entrance when he saw the lead marshal exit the cave. His shoulders slumped, and his head hung low.

"Is he in there?" Whittaker yelled up.

"You better come up here and see this."

Whittaker's eyes widened, and he bolted up the slope until he reached the cave entrance. He peered inside and saw five men gathered in a circle.

"Is he dead?" Whittaker inquired.

"No, not dead. Worse."

Whittaker stared at the deputy marshal for several seconds and then let the cave's darkness wash over him like a wave. He scanned the faces of the men surrounding an object, looking for a clue to what he was about to witness. They all maintained blank stares until Whittaker squeezed through a wall of men and saw what lay in the center.

It was a brunette blow-up doll dressed in a naughty nurse outfit. She had hand warmers placed up and down her inflated limbs and core to project an image of a human to the infrared cameras.

"What the hell is this?" Whittaker yelled.

"It's a blow-up doll, sir," an anonymous voice responded. A few chuckles wafted from the group.

"I know what the hell it is and what it is not. It's not our fugitive."

Whittaker kicked dirt inside the cave and stormed to the entrance. As soon as the sunlight hit him, he returned to the rear.

"Are you telling me our infrared cameras can't tell the difference between a human and a freaking plastic blow-up doll?"

The lead deputy marshal cleared his throat and stepped forward. "Out in the open, it would be obvious, but we were looking through a small entrance inside a cave. He did a good job with the hand warmers to make it look like a human."

Whittaker shook his head. "I don't believe this. Jason Mulder should be in cuffs right now, but instead he's having a good laugh somewhere in the forest."

"Our fugitive is toying with us."

Whittaker spun toward the deputy marshal. "No shit, but two can play this game."

Chapter 31

Jason stood on the ledge outside the cave entrance, listening to the echo of helicopters in the surrounding valley. Although they were over two miles away, he could tell they were circling a specific area. They must have fallen for the countermeasures he completed before leaving the beaten marshals in the canyon. Minutes before he left for Potato Lake, Jason ran out of the cave in an eastern direction until he reached the ridge's summit. He veered off the rocky path and stepped into the impressionable soil to leave boot prints. His tracks left the signature of someone running away in a panic. Then came the tricky part. Jason walked backward to the cave. He only stepped on a gravel surface or reused the same boot print he left on his initial dash up the side of the hill. After neutralizing both marshals, Jason returned to the cave and walked backward again for fifty yards, but this time, he went south. If his efforts worked as planned, his pursuers would focus on his tracks rushing eastward from the cave toward his Whispering Pines home. It was the most direct route and the path Jason preferred to take, but the marshals were getting too close. He had to put some distance between himself and his pursuers.

A sinister grin replaced the intensity on Jason's face at the thought of US marshals with dogs and rifles charging into the cave to find Ashley waiting for them. He returned to his rucksack in the cave and removed a burner phone from the tablet-sized Faraday bag. After powering up the phone, Jason returned to the cave entrance to get the best signal.

First, Jason confirmed all the location tracking settings were off, and then he opened the Virtual Private Network or VPN app before connecting to a search engine that did not track personal information. He found the US Marshal's office's phone number and opened his VOIP app for his call. This would hide his identity and location from anyone trying to trace the call.

Jason pressed zero after a short, automated message confirming he called the US Marshal's office in Phoenix and waited. After two minutes of instrumental jazz music, a human answered.

"How may I direct your call?" a female voice asked.

"I'd like to speak to the person in charge of the search for Jason Mulder."

"I'm sorry. Who are you looking to speak with?" the woman asked. She sounded less robotic with her question this time.

"The US Marshals are searching for a fugitive named Jason Mulder. I want to speak to the person in charge of the search."

"Are you calling to share information or provide a tip to the search team?"

Jason smiled. "Yes, I have an excellent tip for the searchers. Can I speak with the person in charge?"

"He's not available at the moment, but I can take any information you have to share and ensure it gets to the proper individuals."

"Sure. This is Jason Mulder, the fugitive they're looking for, and I'll hold until the person in charge is available to talk."

The line went silent for several seconds.

She must be in shock. I wish I could see her face right now.

Jason heard her breathing faster over the phone.

"Go ahead and reach out to him. I'll hold."

The Jazz music returned, so Jason sat on a boulder and waited.

Eight minutes later, the music ended, and a male spoke in a booming voice.

"Who is this?"

"It's Jason Mulder. Who am I speaking with?"

"How do I know this is really Jason Mulder?"

Jason cleared his throat. "Have you come across two marshals on the wrong end of a scuffle near Potato Lake?"

"Anyone with a scanner could know that information. That proves nothing."

"How's Ashley doing?"

"Who the hell is Ashley?"

"I'm sure you've met the resident nurse in my old cave. Don't tell me she's deflated that I left her behind."

The man did not respond, confirming he had found the companion Clay left for Jason.

"Okay, now that we've confirmed I'm Jason Mulder, who am I speaking to?"

"This is Senior Deputy Marshal Whittaker."

"Nice to meet you, Deputy Marshal Whittaker. I need you to call off the search because I didn't do what they accused me of doing. I'm innocent."

Whittaker laughed. "Oh, another innocent man on the run. That's the first time I've heard that one."

"It's true."

Jason waited for Whittaker to counter his statement but never did, so he continued.

"Don't bother trying to trace the number or find me. I believe the VPN I'm using will say I'm in Virginia right now, which we both know isn't true, but I am already miles away. So, call off the search while I clear my name, and I'll fill you in on the details later."

"Not going to happen, Mr. Mulder. Don't let my perceived sunny disposition on this call fool you. I'm a lion, and this isn't my first hunt. I'm very good at what I do, and I have a team that's as good as me, so we'll find you. When we do, it'll feel like an entire pride of lions pounced on you," Whitaker hissed.

"Sounds like I have a challenge ahead of me," Jason replied.

"Once I start hunting, I don't stop until I'm fed. I'm hungry now, Mulder, and I'm locked in on you," Whittaker growled.

Jason stood and took several steps forward until he was at the end of the ledge overlooking the canyon. "So, you don't care that I'm innocent? Don't you even want to hear my side of the story?"

"Nope, I don't care. You had a trial, and a judge and jury declared you guilty. My only job is returning you to prison to serve your sentence. Oh, plus a few more years now," Whittaker chuckled.

"Federal agents lied on the stand about me. I'm not guilty."

"You'll have a new day in court again soon, so tell it to the judge, Mulder. Tell me where you are, and we'll come get you."

"See, that's what you don't understand. I'm not going to prison for a crime I didn't commit. Save yourself the trouble and stop looking for me."

"No trouble at all, sir. It's inevitable. A lion is on your scent, and it's only a matter of time before this apex predator tastes your blood."

"Have you ever seen a jaguar in the wild?" Jason asked.

"Can't say that I have."

"They're the largest cat in the Western Hemisphere. Jaguars hunt and live alone. They're expert climbers and swimmers, but humans rarely see them. Some wildlife photographers spend months trying to get a single glimpse of the elusive jaguar and never see so much as a whisker of the stealthy feline."

"What's the point of this PBS wildlife special?" Whitaker asked. "Good luck finding me, Simba."

Jason hung up and returned the phone to the Faraday pouch. Trolling the man trying to lock him up in prison brought Jason some pleasure, but the actual reason for the call was to confirm Whittaker's exact location. Now Jason was sure that Whittaker and his team of marshals were miles north and east of him. The diversion worked and gave Jason a solid head start south on his indirect and more difficult journey toward Whispering Pines. The Mogollon Rim would be steeper and more challenging on his new route, but the extra distance between himself and the marshals was worth it.

Shanna was due to have their first child in a little over a week, and Jason had to return home to be with her. She needed Jason, and he'd been so focused on eluding the marshals that he got sidetracked from what was truly important. Being there for his family when they need him most.

Jason was done running. In less than 24 hours, he'd either feel the warmth of Shanna's body against his or lament the cold steel bars of his prison cell separating him from his wife and baby. Jason couldn't imagine any other outcome.

Chapter 32

A triangle of sweat darkened the front of Jason's shirt as he pushed himself to move faster through the stand of ponderosa pine trees. Shade was scarce as high noon approached, and the sun cast a pale gray tinge of color across the forest. He'd covered two miles from the last cave in under an hour, and his back and legs protested the pace. It wouldn't usually be an issue because Jason continued to run and workout every day, but he was malnourished, dehydrated, and exhausted. The fifty pounds he lugged in the rucksack contributed to the rubbery feeling in his legs. Jason was used to carrying sixty to seventy pounds of gear as an active-duty PJ, but that was two years ago. The DEA didn't have as much equipment to tote around on foot, and his weekend drills with the Air Force Reserve weren't enough to rebuild his prior stamina.

The rhythmic crunch of the pine needles below each footfall allowed Jason's mind to drift. First, he recalled his training and deployment to Afghanistan with the 22nd Special Tactics Squadron based at Joint Base Lewis–McChord outside Tacoma, Washington. Despite the intense training and live combat, life was simpler in those years. Jason was surrounded by combat medical professionals willing to die for others, especially their fellow PJs. The bond with his team was strong, and Jason considered them family. For Jason, nothing was more sacred than family.

After sliding down a smooth granite slab and navigating through a dry canyon, Jason's thoughts turned to his current team with the 943rd Rescue Group at Davis-Monthan AFB in Tucson, Arizona. His bonds at the Air Force Reserve unit were strong, especially with Clay Landry, but one weekend a month and two weeks during the summer wasn't enough time to forge the ties he enjoyed while on active duty with the Air Force. His status in the Air Force Reserve was also marred with complications and uncertainty. Jason stopped attending weekend drills after he told his commanding officer, Captain Goodwin, of his arrest. It was difficult enough to share the news, but the eyes of his CO still haunted him. Jason had hoped Captain Goodwin would be more understanding if he told him in person, so Jason had driven to Tucson to tell him face-to-face. He didn't expect his CO to be happy with the news, but the look of betrayal and utter disappointment wasn't something Jason expected to see from Captain Goodwin. It wasn't a look Jason had ever experienced before.

Captain Goodwin informed Jason that he had no choice but to start the paperwork for the involuntary discharge. Jason understood and asked for only one concession.

"Could you take your time with the paperwork? I'd like some time to clear my name."

"I'll put you on the bottom of my stack. That will give you another month or two."

Jason failed to clear his name before his trial and was sure the involuntary discharge papers were signed, sealed, and delivered. Because of his time of service and rank as a staff sergeant, a board of officers and senior noncommissioned officers would hear his case. His fate in the Air Force was with that board, and Jason hoped he could clear his name and return home before the board made a final decision. This thought caused Jason to pick up his pace. If he wanted to stay a PJ, he had to find the people that framed him soon.

A change in the horizon snapped Jason from his thoughts. Patches of light blue replaced the browns, greens, and grays that dominated the northern Arizona forest. He'd reached an opening carved by an unpaved road. The aptly named Rim Road ran along the edge of Mogollon Rim for forty miles. It was not a heavily traveled route, but it was the perfect spot for a patient marshal or sheriff's deputy to stake out and wait for a fugitive to cross.

Jason approached with caution. He took a knee ten yards inside the tree line cover and waited. After seeing or hearing nothing for five minutes, Jason darted across the gravel road and found cover in the trees on the other side. He remained still and listened. Once he was sure he wasn't spotted, he continued toward his destination.

He felt it before he saw it. The breeze swirled around him, and Jason sensed the enormity of the vast landscape ahead. He stopped at the edge of a granite slab, aware that one more step would be his last. The refreshing air chilled his skin as he gazed across the sweeping vista. Jason looked out over the pine trees from his perch two thousand feet high, blanketing the mountains and valleys. It looked like an emerald ocean.

Jason had stood on the edge of the rim hundreds of times, and his admiration of the natural beauty below never waned. This was the first time he approached the edge with the plan to reach the bottom on foot. The escarpment was the last obstacle between Jason and his chance to see Shanna again.

The first section of the rim he encountered was a sheer drop twice as tall as two Eiffel Towers stacked one on top of the other. Jason only had two hundred feet of rope and walked west to find a more suitable path to the bottom. A quarter mile later, he leaned over the rim. It was better than the earlier spot because it contained several ledges to break up the distance, but the drops were still farther apart than Jason's two hundred feet of rope in his rucksack. He continued until he found a ravine carved into the rim. It had boulders scattered throughout the ravine that made great anchor points for his rope and a more manageable slope for Jason to descend. He couldn't see the bottom and considered walking farther west for a better spot until he heard a vehicle approaching.

Jason crouched behind a cluster of shrubs and listened. The engine shut down, and then Jason heard a vehicle door shut. Then another. At least two people were out of their vehicles, but Jason still couldn't see them. He wasn't sure if they were hikers, sightseers, or law enforcement. A half minute later, he heard a third door slam and then the unmistakable bark of a dog. A K9 unit was less than two hundred yards away, and the dog would be on top of Jason in seconds. The only exit was down, but Jason couldn't tell if his route was passable to the bottom.

The yips from the excited canine grew louder, and Jason saw movement seventy-five yards away. He was out of time, so he bolted into the ravine and hopped from boulder to boulder as fast as he could without breaking his ankles or neck. Jason heard the dog and two male voices five minutes later when he was already a hundred feet below them. The K9 barked ferociously, indicating a hit to its handler, but Jason heard the two men debating if it was a false alarm. One felt they should check it out, while the other claimed no sane person would go over the cliff to avoid apprehension. Perhaps that officer was right, Jason thought.

Jason continued down the ravine slowly for another twenty minutes until the slope turned vertical. He stopped and assessed his location and situation. He guessed he was halfway down the cliff, meaning he had hundreds of feet left until he reached the valley floor. Jason opened his ruck and removed two hundred feet of climbing rope and leather gloves. He didn't have a harness, belay, or carabiners, so he chose the Dülfersitz rappelling method, where the rope was wound around his body, and the speed of descent was controlled using friction against his body. It was far more difficult and risky than rappelling with modern tools and rarely used today, so Jason was grateful his rappelling and fast-roping instructor at Andersen Air Force Base in Guam was paranoid enough to teach his team the last-ditch rappelling technique when equipment was not available. The Dülfersitz method was effective if the braking hand never released the rope.

If it did, Jason would join his brother Josh in the afterlife.

Jason placed the rappel rope between his legs, over the left shoulder, around the back, and across the belly in the right belay hand. It was best to go slowly in this method, but Jason didn't have that option. He had to get to the bottom before the K9 officers on the top realized their fugitive was descending the near-vertical cliff. Jason created a natural anchor over a ten-ton boulder and tossed both ends of the rope over the side. It reached a ledge below with twenty feet to spare.

"I hope that works," Jason said with a tug.

Minutes later, Jason reached the ledge below and pulled the rope down from the anchor. He repeated the process six times until the tops of the majestic pine trees were at eye level. Jason was near the bottom, but now the cliff was a sheer vertical wall. He steadied himself on a granite ledge eighteen inches wide, with no anchors available. Safety was seventy feet down or nearly two thousand feet up. Jason wanted to pace as he considered his horrible options but couldn't move more than a few inches in either direction. The treetops ten feet away, grabbed his attention.

Where do I go from here?

The answer was right before him, but Jason didn't want that to be his only option. He could catapult himself toward the tree, catch a branch, and climb down to stay ahead of the searchers. If he missed a branch, he'd bounce off trees like he was inside a pinball machine until the earth broke his fall. In that scenario, a quick death was the preferred outcome.

Jason looked down and leaned forward to confirm his distance from the deadly rocks below when he felt his body tip past the point of no return. He raised both arms to form a human cross and swung them rapidly in circles to reverse his forward momentum. He felt like a basketball resting on the rim, with the hushed crowd watching to see if the game-winning shot fell victoriously into the basket or outside for a crushing defeat. Jason felt his weight shift backward, and his back slammed into the granite wall. His chest heaved as oxygen returned to his lungs after holding his breath on the ledge.

He exhaled deeply and turned to the nearest tree. The longer he debated his next move on the ledge, the better his chances of falling off. Jason dropped his arms and bent his knees slightly like a downhill skier preparing to release at the top of a mountain. He counted down as his final breath left his lungs.

"Three, two, one. . ."

CHAPTER 33

Gila County, Arizona

Pine needles whacked Jason's face, and he felt a thousand jabbing pricks on his forehead, cheeks, and neck as he hurtled through the outer branches. His forward momentum slowed, and gravity gained the upper hand. In a frantic attempt for survival, Jason extended his arms outward into the human cross position again. Flexible twigs smacked his forearms, but he couldn't secure anything until his boots collided with a sturdy branch, slowing him down a little. Jason tried to grab onto anything to stop his forward momentum, but he only hooked his arm on another branch sticking out like a woody lifeline.

The sting under his arm was uncomfortable, but it barely registered because of the eruption of pain when his left side rammed into the tree's trunk. A broken branch shaped like a medieval spear nearly impaled Jason between the ninth and tenth ribs.

Jason yelped in pain.

Instinctively, he hunched over and applied pressure to his side with his free hand as if trying to prevent his ribs from leaving his body. Tears welled in his eyes from the pain radiating through his left side. It hurt like hell, but after several painful deep breaths, Jason concluded his ribs were likely severely bruised but not broken. He tossed his leg over a branch to straddle it and pulled his sweatshirt and t-shirt up to see the injury. Blood trickled from a quarter-sized hole and moistened his pants in a pool of crimson. Jason was fortunate that his clothing prevented the jagged, six-inch branch from penetrating his lungs or organs. He slid the rucksack off his back and placed it on the branch between his legs as he leaned back against the tree. Jason planned to apply a field dressing to his wound inside the boughs of a pine tree sixty feet above the forest floor.

The reserve PJ removed his first aid kit, applied iodine to the wound and then pressed a wad of gauze against his side to stop the bleeding. He checked the bleeding every few minutes since punctures can be stubborn to clot. The kit did not have the Celox rapid hemostatic gauze pads impregnated with a clotting substance he regularly used in Afghanistan. Instead, he had to rely on pressure and time to stop the bleeding. Five minutes later, Jason removed the gauze and evaluated the hole in his side. Stitches were what a doctor in the ER would order, but Jason had not packed needles or thread, so he snared the super glue from the kit. He opened the cap with his teeth and pinched his side until the red hole disappeared under two flaps of skin. Jason bit down hard and groaned. He almost twisted off the branch as he writhed in pain, but he glued the wound shut. It would need professional medical attention once he cleared his name.

Jason exhaled once his boots hit the dead pine needles on the ground. Less than three miles from home, his thoughts turned to Shanna. Jason closed his eyes to see her face. Under his eyelids, Shanna's face glowed, and Jason felt like she was standing next to him in the forest. He swore he could smell the sweet aroma of wildflowers, coconut, and lavender on her hair and skin. Jason flinched when Shanna leaned forward in his vision to embrace him. It felt so real.

He opened his eyes, and his smile vanished. Jason didn't want visions of his wife. He wanted to hold and help her during the last week of pregnancy. Seconds later, Jason resumed his march toward Whispering Pines and Shanna.

Chapter 34

Near Whispering Pines, Arizona

Jason reached a campground a mile from his home as the sun ducked behind the hills in the west. Verde Glen Campground didn't offer any facilities or site host, so it attracted dispersed campers and day users. Jason knew it was risky to enter the campground, even with only a spattering of people. Still, it provided access to the East Verde River, and he desperately needed water and a place to rest before his final push home in the wee hours of the morning. He sat in the thick underbrush outskirts of the campground, observing the people coming and going from their tents and campers. Once Jason felt confident they weren't marshals staking out in disguise, he strolled through the campground and stopped at the river bank. He removed the LifeStraw personal water filter from his pack, laid on his stomach, and drank straight from the river. It wasn't exactly spring water from the Alps, but after a week of suboptimal hydration, Jason felt it was close. He immediately felt a burst of energy, and his headache subsided.

Shade from the stately pine trees enveloped the campground, foreshadowing the coming darkness. Jason walked around the campground, looking for a secluded site. Only a few diehard campers braved the nighttime lows that dropped into the forties, so it wasn't difficult to find a spot away from prying eyes. Jason removed his thermal tarp and used his knife to fashion tent poles and stakes. For a moment, he enjoyed the setup of his primitive camp. The forests around Payson, Arizona, always felt like home, and he'd set up dozens of campsites with his little brother Josh. Thoughts of the time Jason helped find a missing six-year-old in the forest with Josh and his high school sweetheart, Gaby, flashed in his mind. He still couldn't believe they were both gone.

Jason stood frozen next to his tent-like tarp, thinking about past camping trips when the slam of a truck door snapped him back to the present. He moved to get a better view of the vehicle parked thirty yards away, and his heart sank. It was a gray pickup truck with a star-shaped logo on the passenger door.

How'd they find me?

He turned to locate his rucksack and bolt into the forest. When Jason gauged the time to gather his items, he made eye contact with a female officer who exited the truck. She said something to a male officer who joined her in the dirt parking lot and walked toward Jason.

"Shit. Shit. Shit!"

It was too late to run, so Jason had to play the part of a camper and hope for the best. It was the first test of his new disguise as a bald, blond man.

"Good evening," the female said as she entered Jason's campsite.

"Hello."

Jason noticed the Arizona Game and Fish logos on both shirts, and his heart slowed. They may be looking for him, and both were armed, but Jason liked his chances much better with game wardens than with US marshals.

"Are you camping here tonight?" she asked.

"Yes, ma'am. Keeping it simple," Jason replied.

The female officer seemed relaxed and disinterested in Jason as she scanned his campsite.

The male officer took another step toward Jason. "You know there are no toilets or trash facilities, so you have to pack everything out with you, right?"

Jason knew this, but the tone of the male officer caused a warm, sick feeling to churn in his stomach. He seemed intense and stared directly into Jason's eyes while he waited for an answer. Jason assumed he was very serious about the leave-no-trace mandate or suspicious of him.

"Yes, sir. I'll take everything with me when I leave," Jason said with the most disarming smile he could muster.

"How?" the male officer asked.

Jason tilted his head and mirrored the question. He knew exactly what the officer was asking but wanted a few seconds to think of his answer. "How?"

"Yeah. I don't see a vehicle here, so how will you pack everything out on foot?"

A suitable response came to Jason, and he smiled.

"Oh, my girlfriend took my truck into Payson. She's not as crazy about primitive camping as me, so she's buying a bottle of wine to help her through the night."

The female officer nodded, seemingly in agreement, but the male officer's brows furrowed deeper. Jason saw his eyes dart back and forth on the tattoos on his neck.

"Do you live around here? You look familiar."

A tsunami of acid slammed into Jason's gut. The surge of adrenaline caused his heart to race, and he was afraid sweat would appear on his forehead in front of the officers, so Jason focused on his breathing. His side screamed in pain, but he couldn't show any sign of discomfort. Although a tornado of emotions swirled inside him, Jason's outward appearance remained calm.

"I get that a lot," Jason chuckled. "I was born and raised in Show Low, so I only live a few hours from here."

The male agent eyed Jason longer than he liked. Jason could almost see the wheels turning in his head as he tried to connect something that looked familiar about the man in front of him, but the connection was too murky for him to associate Jason with the fugitive he may have seen in an APB or the nightly news over the past week.

Jason kept his eyes on the male officer's hands, anticipating his next move.

A dog began barking aggressively on the other side of the campground. Seconds later, two male voices shouting at each other cut through the woods.

"We need to go check that out. Thank you for your time, and be sure to pack everything when you leave," the female officer said to Jason.

The female officer turned and strolled toward the commotion while the male officer looked Jason over one last time before joining her.

Jason exhaled loudly after they were gone. It excited a part of him that his disguise seemed to work, but mostly, he was angry with himself. He acknowledged that his proximity to home and white-hot desire to see Shanna clouded his judgment, and because of that, he nearly lost his freedom.

He crawled into his makeshift tent, pulled up his hoodie, and stared at the black tarp above him. Jason reviewed his plan in the darkness and concluded a detour was prudent. His commitment to reunite with Shanna never wavered, but Jason understood he had to find the people who framed him and clear his name if he ever expected to see his wife and future son or daughter in the future. He couldn't help Shanna or lead a family if he was behind bars.

His eyes were heavy, and Jason let sleep come. In the morning, he'd set off to find the people responsible for his fugitive status, confront them, and do whatever was necessary to prove his innocence.

The time to reverse pursuit had arrived.

Chapter 35

Camp Verde, Arizona

The hum of the fluorescent lights and Special Agent Holland's pen rapping on the desk were the only sounds in the Camp Verde DEA field office. Holland closed the file on his desk and leaned back in his chair to enjoy relative quiet before his co-workers arrived for work. His intertwined fingers supported the back of his head and neck as he gazed at the false ceiling in his office. He came in early to tackle his growing backlog of cases, but one particular case still lingered heavily in his mind.

After his promising special agent shocked him by stealing cocaine seized during a sting, Holland still couldn't understand it. He tried to find the truth, but after the internal investigation came up empty with potential involvement from another party, Holland had to accept Mulder's arrest and conviction. Some people surprise you positively and others negatively, and Mulder was the latter, he thought.

The robotic ring of his desk phone jerked Holland out of his thoughts. He looked at his watch, and he answered it after three rings. He sat up straight and swallowed hard when he recognized the voice. Naomi Dunn, the Special Agent in Charge or SAC of the Phoenix Division, was the early morning caller. Dunn was one of the 23 domestic division heads in the DEA who report directly to the top brass in Arlington, Virginia. Dunn was Holland's bosses' boss.

She got right to the point after Holland answered.

"Special Agent Holland, I'm calling you directly because we have a sensitive matter on our hands, and I want our best people on the case. Can I count on your cooperation and personal involvement?"

Holland responded a second after she asked the question. "Yes, ma'am. How can I help?"

"Arlington is investigating a rash of fentanyl overdoses across the country. They happen suddenly in every district nationwide, stop for several weeks, and then start up again. They occur nationally, and our investigators have found no connection to the usual ports of entry for fentanyl, so they're stumped. Reporters and loved ones are asking for answers, and we don't have any, so that's why each district needs to kick up our investigations of fentanyl overdoses. Are you following along so far?"

"Yes," Holland replied.

"Now, this is where I need you. The Yavapai Sheriff's Office reported two deceased high school-age females and a third in serious condition from an outdoor party in Black Canyon City last night. Deputies saved the third girl with Narcon, but it was too late for the other two girls. The girl they saved is in no condition to talk yet, so I need you to go to the site and see if you can find anything unusual about these overdoses. Unfortunately, I don't have any direction to provide on what to look for, so look for clues that may help us better understand what is behind all these overdoses. Put everything in a report when you're done and send it directly to me."

Holland cleared his schedule and arrived in Black Canyon City mid-morning. The Aqua Fria River snaked through the center of the unincorporated rural town of 3,000, nestled among steep buttes at the northern edge of the Sonoran Desert. The mostly dry washes that feed the river during the rainy season were a favorite spot for outdoor parties outside the prying eyes of parents.

Holland found a Yavapai County deputy still on the scene a half mile off the highway. He dressed in plain clothes, so he flashed the deputy his badge.

"What do you know?"

"A few of the kids came forward after we announced the deaths of the two girls, and they said about sixty high school kids were out here drinking. An hour or two after the party started, one kid passed out Molly. Almost all of them took it, but several kids reported that three girls immediately started acting sick. All three collapsed, and the other kids bolted, except for one who called 911. Two girls were gone when we arrived, but one is still alive in the hospital."

Holland nodded and scanned the dry wash littered with disposable red cups and cigarette butts.

"Do we know which kid or kids passed out the Molly?"

"Nope. A sudden wave of amnesia hit every kid at the party because nobody can remember who brought a bottle of Molly laced with fentanyl," the deputy reported.

"Where did the first responders find the girls?"

The deputy pointed to the royal blue tarp unfurled on the sandy soil of the wash. Holland thanked him and crept through the dry wash toward the tarp. Partygoers and the first responders had trampled a natural sandbar in the wash twenty yards wide and seventy yards long, so Holland knew that was the party's epicenter. As he got closer to the tarp, he saw gauze, plastic wrappers, and needle covers on the ground, evidence of the fight for the girls' lives by EMTs when they arrived.

Holland continued deeper into the wash, where the jagged granite walls grew taller and steeper, and the iconic saguaro cactus grew as dense as pine trees in Northern Arizona forests. He made a complete revolution in the middle of the wash as he looked up and down for anything unusual. That's when he spotted a white container underneath a bush. Holland put on gloves and reached into the waist-high catclaw acacia. He pulled a plastic bottle from the clutches of the thorny shrub.

Initially, the bottle looked like the standard vitamin and supplement containers on drug store shelves, but Holland immediately noticed a difference. It was heavier and felt more rigid than other plastic bottles. He examined it for any marks or printing, but it didn't contain any that Holland could find. He placed the bottle in an evidence bag and continued to search the area for additional clues.

Holland scoured the area for another thirty minutes but found nothing else. He returned to his office and typed his report with the bottle beside his keyboard in the evidence bag. He wondered if this was the evidence Naomi Dunn hoped he'd find or simply more trash in the desert.

His gut told him it was worth investigating further. He had to learn more about the people behind the unusual bottle that may have carried the substance that claimed two lives that he knew of and likely thousands more that failed to make headlines.

CHAPTER 36

Payson, Arizona

Jason reached the brow of the hill overlooking the outskirts of Payson and scanned the area. He had traversed three miles since sunrise and reached a key highway bisecting the state. As Jason assessed the situation, cars, trucks, and eighteen-wheelers buzzed past in both directions on the concrete artery. A gas station caught his eye, so Jason resumed walking as he planned his next move.

The last stop along Highway 260 between Payson and the smaller mountain communities to the west was an excellent location to steal a vehicle. He could quickly get outside the current search area of the marshals, but that would also get the local sheriff involved once someone reported the vehicle stolen. Jason had to go somewhere to get answers. He had to get out of the forest and into a city.

As Jason approached the gas station on foot, a Ram 2500 truck pulled to a pump at the gas station, and it set his plan. The white truck towed a similar colored trailer, which provided a suitable place to hide, but as a stowaway, the destination was always a wildcard. He decided the speed of leaving the area was worth the risk, so Jason meandered through the pumps while the truck owners went inside the gas station. Jason noticed sheep inside the trailer and a logo for Copper Sky Ranch on the driver's door of the truck for

Chino Valley, Arizona. The small town north of Prescott wasn't Jason's ideal destination to begin his search for the people that framed him if that's where they were going, but it was better than the middle of the forest. Jason let himself inside the trailer and slid his arm through the bars in the window to reengage the rear gate.

A half dozen black and white lambs eyed Jason suspiciously as he got on all fours and crawled to the front of the trailer. He scared away a ewe resting on a mound of hay and dove into the cut golden grass. Once he was in position, Jason's body and rucksack were hidden from anyone peering through the open side windows, ready to depart to who knew where when voices grew louder. It was the truck's occupants, and as soon as the lambs heard their voices, they started bleating.

"What's going on back there?" a girl asked. She looked through the bars in the side windows at the lambs crowded near the rear of the trailer.

"What is it?" a gruff male voice asked.

"It's just Paisley acting up again. She better have this out of her system before the show," the young lady replied.

"Settle down, girls. We've got a two-hour drive ahead," the girl commanded.

Jason was relieved when he heard the truck doors shut and felt the trailer move. For the first hour, the lambs remained near the rear gate, but after getting bounced all over the trailer, they moved to the front and lay down on the mound of hay. One got comfortable on top of Jason, and he prayed it didn't shit or piss all over him.

After ninety minutes, the trailer started and stopped frequently. Jason watched the streetlights and lamps pass through the window, but no tall buildings, confirming he was in a medium-sized town.

He wouldn't know where until the trailer stopped, and the owners exited their truck.

The vehicle came to a final halt. Jason planned to hide in the hay until all the lambs were off the trailer and sneak away later, but the people in the truck shut their doors and the crunch of gravel outside confirmed they walked away. Jason rose high enough to see outside. The area looked familiar, and then Jason realized he was at the Yavapai County Fairgrounds parking lot in Prescott for a youth livestock show. He snagged his rucksack, patted a couple of lambs on the head, and wished them luck before exiting the trailer.

The parking lot was a chaotic hive of teenage owners of sheep, goats, steers, and their parents. Nobody paid any attention to Jason as he hustled to get out of the area full of eyes that may have seen his picture on the news. He didn't have a specific destination, but it would be somewhere with fewer people. Several blocks later, he arrived at the Yavapai County Regional Medical Center entrance. The five-story brick structure was the region's primary hospital and was bustling with vehicle and pedestrian traffic. Jason continued past the hospital until something caught his eye. A taxi.

Jason could have walked somewhere secluded, but his legs and feet were beaten up after a week on the run. He removed the cash from his pack and approached the yellow taxi waiting near the visitor's entrance.

Jason approached the driver with shoulder-length white hair and a walrus-like mustache that covered his lips.

"Are you waiting for someone, or can you take me somewhere?"

"Where you headed?"

Good question, Jason thought to himself. He considered the best places to research the people that framed him.

"The Prescott Library."

"Hop in."

The scent of new carpet and fresh paint was the first thing Jason noticed when he entered the newly renovated multi-story house of books. It was a welcome aroma after spending a week in the woods. Jason ducked into a restroom to wash up and straighten out his wrinkled clothes. After freshening up, he strolled through rows of books on the first floor and found a bank of public computers on the second level, but they required a local library card with a PIN to use them. Jason considered leaving but was too close to getting answers to his long list of questions, so he approached the librarian's desk.

A petite, bespectacled, middle-aged woman behind the counter looked up. Jason approached with caution, concerned she might recognize him, but saw empathy, or maybe sympathy, in her eyes.

"Hi, I'm only in town for the day and need to use a computer for a minute."

"Sure. This is good for two hours." The librarian said as she slid a business card-sized piece of paper across the counter to Jason with a PIN.

"Come back if you need more time."

Jason fired up Google on the computer and searched in incognito mode. He wasn't sure if it mattered anymore, but it made him feel more secure with his searches.

First, Jason looked up his name. Thousands of articles popped up, and he scrolled until his cursor hovered over a link from a Phoenix-based TV station that was updated that day. Jason clicked on it, and his picture filled the screen. He quickly clicked on the X in the upper right-hand corner and looked around to see if anyone saw his face. Few people were around, and nobody was paying any attention to Jason, so he opened the article again and read a couple of paragraphs about his escape. He saw an image with a triangle in the middle, showing it was a video. Jason recognized the woman in the video as a long-time field reporter for the local Fox affiliate standing next to an African American man in his thirties outside the Sandra Day O'Connor US Courthouse in Phoenix. Jason lowered the volume and clicked play.

"This is Ally Rutledge, live with Senior Deputy Marshall Deshon Whittaker outside the US Marshals office in downtown Phoenix. It's been over a week since your prisoner Jason Mulder escaped the custody of US marshals. Do you have any new information on his whereabouts?"

Whittaker flashed a million-dollar smile for the camera and cleared his throat. "We have several leads on the fugitive that we're investigating and expect to have him behind bars where he belongs soon. I want to thank the public for—"

Ms. Rutledge interrupted Whittaker. "Should the public be concerned that Jason Mulder has been on the run for over a week and that US marshals have been unable to locate or apprehend him? Is he considered a threat to public safety?"

Whittaker's smile faded. Jason had never met the man but could tell he didn't like to be questioned. "We've located the fugitive on more than one occasion, but we could not detain him for reasons I can't divulge."

"For reasons you can't divulge? Your guys got their asses kicked, that's why," Jason whispered.

"Is he dangerous?" Ms. Rutledge asked.

Whittaker looked into the camera. "Anyone that assaults federal marshals and refuses to turn themselves in peacefully is dangerous. We're getting closer to him every day, so keep those tips coming. Thank you."

Whittaker was out of the picture before the reporter could ask another question.

Jason hit the rewind arrows and froze the video on Whittaker. He stared for nearly a minute at the man trying to put him behind bars. Jason refreshed the screen and changed his search to DEA special agents Daniel Cruz and Ken Donaldson.

Cruz was an open book on social media. He had multiple social media profiles, filled with the same four topics - working out at the gym, scantily clad women, guns, and fast cars. Despite the quantity of information about Cruz, there was little substance to glean from the social media sites, just like the man. Donaldson was a different story. Jason found an old article about multiple awards from the DEA earlier in his career but nothing in the past decade. He also found public records of his two divorces several pages deep in Google, but that was it about Donaldson.

Donaldson had a public Facebook page that had been dormant for years. Jason scrolled through his pictures and was about to give up when he leaned forward with wide-eyed astonishment. He squinted and focused on a familiar face next to Donaldson.

Suddenly, it all made sense.

A group photo from a decade earlier provided Jason with his primary suspect of who was behind the effort to frame him.

Chapter 37

Prescott, Arizona

Jason looked away from the computer monitor and rubbed his eyes. He hadn't stared at a screen for so long in years. Jason looked at the clock on the lower right side of the screen and couldn't believe he'd been in the library for over four hours. It was almost five o'clock.

He looked around to locate his backpack and noticed the librarian, who gave him the PIN numbers, walk behind him for the third time in the last ten minutes. She looked at him like she wanted to say something but talked herself out of it. Jason's jaw clenched, and he dragged his pack closer with his foot. It was clear to Jason that she wanted to approach him, and he could only assume she recognized him. He ran scenarios through his mind of the closest emergency exit to escape from the library before the police arrived. Jason hoped she hadn't already called the Prescott Police.

The librarian took a few more steps toward Jason. He tightened his grip around his pack and prepared to bolt.

"I'm sorry, but the library is closing soon. You'll have to wrap up in the next few minutes."

An involuntary nervous laugh slipped through Jason's lips. So much tension built up during his time in the library, and it had to be released.

"Ah, okay," Jason said. He looked at the clock on the computer again and feigned shock.

"I can't believe it's already five. I was just leaving."

Jason grabbed his rucksack and left the library. Whiskey Row was two blocks away, so Jason had another attempt to reach his old buddy, Sergeant Bentley. He spotted the perfect bench along the outer perimeter of the park near a stop sign. Jason knew this was the quickest way home for Bentley, so he'd try a novel approach this time. He couldn't risk getting spotted again by the guy he had roughed up a week ago in the parking garage.

For the next hour, Jason leaned on his pack to kill time until Bentley exited The Palace Saloon. Careful not to be too obvious, he monitored every vehicle approaching the intersection. As the six o'clock hour approached, a young family strolled past him, stopped, and turned back to Jason. He straightened up on the bench and tried to hear what they were saying. He couldn't make out their conversation, but they were discussing him. The parents stopped ten feet away from Jason while a little girl who looked to be four or five years old continued in her white dress to the stranger on the bench. She stopped beside him and extended her hand containing a one-dollar bill.

"This is for you," she said with a slight lisp.

At first, Jason was confused, but then it hit him. They thought he was homeless, and the little girl wanted to help him.

"Thank you, but I don't need that."

"I want you to have it so you can get something to eat."

Jason looked at the parents and smiled before he reached into his front pocket and removed the change from his taxi fare. "See, I have money, so I'll eat just fine." He handed a five-dollar bill to the little girl. She looked down at the image of Abraham Lincoln and back up to Jason with confusion in her eyes.

"I'll tell you what. Since you were so generous with your money with me, even though I don't need it, I want to get you a treat."

Jason pointed to the ice cream shop across the street. "Tell your mom and dad that you earned five dollars and that you want to buy ice cream."

Her straight lips curved skyward, and she rocked on her heels before Jason.

"I earned this?"

"Yep."

"How?" she asked.

"For being awesome."

The girl's smile expanded, and she darted back to the side of her parents. Her blond ponytail swung back and forth while high-pitched giggles accompanied each step. Seeing the little girl transported Jason's thoughts from Bentley to Shanna and his unborn child. He grinned at the memory of all the conversations with Shanna about their predictions about the gender of their first child. Jason consistently predicted a boy, while Shanna predicted a girl, but he didn't care. He just hoped they'd have a healthy baby and be good parents, like the little girl's mother and father.

The girl shared her windfall with her parents. They looked at the five-dollar bill and simultaneously turned back to Jason. He gave them a quick wave and watched them disappear into the ice cream shop. Jason chuckled at the idea they thought he was homeless, but he couldn't blame them. He hadn't showered in a week, and his clothes were in tatters.

Jason checked his watch and noted that it was five minutes until six, and Bentley should pass by soon. He wasn't sure how he'd flag Bentley down without attracting too much attention to himself. An idea popped into his head, so Jason moved closer to the stop sign and waited for his friend.

The sound of the diesel engine echoing off the facades of the buildings on Whiskey Row alerted Jason that Sergeant Bentley neared the intersection. He confirmed his friend still drove a red pickup truck with dual rear tires as he approached the stop sign. Jason had to beat Bentley to the intersection for his new plan to work.

Jason stood near the intersection and let two cars pass through. As Bentley approached, he stumbled into the crosswalk, forcing the red truck to stop. Jason wobbled across the street with his head down but maintained a visual of Bentley out of the corner of his eye. When Bentley's head tipped forward to peek at his phone, Jason darted to the passenger side door and jumped into the truck. A beat later, Bentley raised his Glock 19 in his right hand toward the intruder, but Jason was faster. He secured the barrel with his left hand and the slide with his right to control the weapon. Bentley struggled to pull the gun away or point it at the homeless man in his truck, but was unsuccessful.

"Is that any way to treat an old friend?"

Bentley loosened his grip on the Glock.

"Who are you?"

"Does the name Jason Mulder ring a bell?"

"Mulder?"

"Yeah."

"I didn't recognize you."

"That's the point."

Bentley's eyes widened in shock, and he released the weapon. His lower jaw slackened, gaping at the unexpected sight.

"What are you doing here?"

Jason placed the Glock on the seat, and the car behind him honked.

"We have to keep moving. Start driving, and I'll fill you in," Jason said.

Bentley drove through the intersection and turned to Jason.

"I was on my way home. Is it okay if we go there?"

"I know."

Bentley tilted his head. "You know?"

"Yeah, your OPSEC sucks. I know you come down here every day after the range."

The retired Air Force sergeant stared at Jason for several seconds and shook his head. "You son of a bitch. Am I really that easy to find?"

Jason laughed. "Yep."

Over the next twenty minutes, Jason filled Bentley in on the past six months while he drove to his ranch on the outskirts of Prescott. They remained in the truck after Bentley parked in his driveway.

"I want to say that I can't believe the feds framed you, but honestly, I can. I really can't believe how you've stayed one step ahead of the marshals for the past week. Those guys are good at what they do," Bentley said. "I'm not gonna lie. I'm impressed."

"The key is to keep moving. Most people get caught when they tire of running and try to hide in one spot, hoping the marshals won't find them, but they always do."

"What are you going to do now?"

"I'm going to find the people that framed me and make them pay."

Bentley raised his hand to fist-bump Jason.

"I have to let Emily know you're going to stay here."

"Are you sure she'll be okay with a fugitive on your property?"

"I think so."

"You think so?"

"Yeah, you've met Emily before. You know she can be a real wild card."

Chapter 38

Jason exited Bentley's truck and stretched his back as he took in the working ranch and residence. He noted the rustic single-story house perched like an island amid a sea of emerald grass and mature trees to his right and an eggshell white horse stable keeping watch over multiple pens to his left. Worn saddles hung on the porch rails, and the scent of leather and hay lingered in the air, highlighting the equestrian spirit of the property.

Bentley was twenty yards ahead of Jason when he stopped and turned around.

"You coming?"

Jason ambled toward Bentley but wasn't in a hurry to see Emily. During previous visits, she was always welcoming and kind to Jason, but he also knew she was very principled, ideological, and outspoken. He didn't know where she stood on harboring a fugitive and wasn't in a hurry to find out.

Bentley leaned against the metal fencing around the horse pen when Jason caught up and took the same position. Emily stood inside the pen trying to coax their nine-year-old daughter, Chloe, onto a horse.

"Mom, I don't want to ride Trigger anymore. Can't we get a different horse?" Chloe whined.

"No, Trigger is a good horse. He just got spooked."

Chloe crossed her arms and stood her ground when Bentley announced Jason.

"Emily, my old Air Force buddy Jason Mulder is here for a visit."

Emily extended her hand. "Sorry, I didn't recognize you at first. Pleased to see you again."

"It's been a long week."

Emily didn't appear to be paying attention to Jason. Her eyes and focus were on Chloe.

"Jason, maybe you can settle a debate for Chloe and me," Emily said.

He raised his hands in surrender. "I just got here. I don't think I could help you settle anything."

"We need a neutral third party, so hear me out. Chloe has been riding Trigger for a year with no problems, but earlier this week, he got spooked and took off on her. Understandably, Chloe got scared but performed the emergency dismount we taught her. Now, Chloe says she doesn't want to ride Trigger ever again. What do you think? Should she give up riding horses for the rest of her life or give Trigger a second chance?"

Jason turned toward Bentley, and he returned a nod of approval, so Jason moved his index finger to his lips while he pondered his judgment. He ran tidbits of sage wisdom through his head until he settled on his verdict.

"Chloe, what's the scariest thing that can happen when you ride Trigger?"

She shrugged and stared at Jason. He waited silently for an answer, so she responded. "I guess it would be if he bucked me off or something."

"Right. The thought of that is terrifying. Has Trigger ever bucked you off before?"

"No, but he tried earlier this week," Chloe replied with resolve in her young eyes.

"And what happened?"

"I did the emergency dismount."

Jason straightened and walked around Chloe several times, looking up and down at her with exaggerated wide eyes.

Chloe giggled. "What are you doing?"

"I'm looking for broken bones or at least some crutches. Maybe a sling for your arm."

"I didn't get hurt," Chloe stated. Her chin held high with pride.

"Exactly! So even when the scariest thing Trigger can do happens, you know how to escape it without getting hurt. You're in control of Trigger, not the other way around."

Chloe looked at Trigger trotting around the pen. "Maybe you're right. I'll give him one more chance."

Jason held up his hand, and Chloe responded with a high-five. She left for the barn to retrieve her saddle.

Emily clapped when Jason turned back to Bentley and his wife, leaning against the fence.

"Jason's going to stay in our camper in back for a night or two," Bentley shared.

"Fine by me. Anyone that can change Chloe's mind is always welcome here."

Bentley raised his hand before Emily walked away. "He's a fugitive wanted by the US Marshals, Arizona DPS, and every county sheriff in the state. He'll say he broke into the camper if they catch him here, and we'll deny that we helped him."

Emily turned and locked eyes with Jason. "So, you're running from the law?"

Jason felt a rush of heat to his face and neck. He swallowed hard and gave an affirmative nod.

"What did you do?" Emily asked. Her tone was sharp and accusatory.

"Um, I was framed for a crime I didn't commit."

"Then why run? Why not stay and fight it?"

"The people that framed me lied in court, and I refuse to go to prison for something I didn't do."

Emily's eyes narrowed. "Are the feds behind this?"

Jason nodded. "A couple DEA agents that I know of. Maybe more."

Emily stared into Jason's eyes for several seconds. Jason felt she was searching him for the truth and wanted to look away but couldn't. Finally, she broke eye contact, turned, and walked toward the barn. "You're welcome to stay here as long as you need."

Bentley laughed. "Now you know why I married her?"

"No kidding. They cut you two from the same cloth."

Jason let his heart rate slow, and his breathing returned to normal. He looked up and tracked the purple clouds in the golden sky past the stable and pens to the horses in the pasture where they roamed and grazed freely.

What I wouldn't give for that kind of freedom right now.

Bentley pushed away from the fence and shook Jason from his thoughts.

"You and Emily are helping me so much by letting me crash here, and I greatly appreciate it, but can I ask you for one more favor?"

"Sure, shoot."

"Can you drive me to Flagstaff tomorrow afternoon?"

Bentley looked to the ground as if considering the question and then back up to Jason. "Yeah, I can cut out early tomorrow. What's going on in Flagstaff?"

"Let's just say I have to meet some old co-workers to settle a debt."

"Sounds like it could get ugly. You need my help?"

"Oh, it's going to get ugly, but I need to do this alone," Jason said. His words trailed off as he considered his plan in Flagstaff.

"It's going to get real ugly."

CHAPTER 39

Flagstaff, Arizona

Black smoke billowed from the exhaust of Bentley's truck as he slammed the accelerator to pass a tractor-trailer climbing the steep incline on Interstate 17 to Flagstaff. Jason was quiet while Bentley maneuvered in and out of the two lanes, guiding his vehicle up to 7,000 feet of elevation on the Colorado Plateau. Earlier that day, Jason took advantage of a hot shower, old clothes from Bentley's closet, and Emily's homemade carne asada with refried beans for lunch. He rested until Bentley finished work early and felt physically better than any other time since he jumped the wall at Sunset Point a week and a half earlier.

Jason broke the silence once Bentley leveled off on a flat section of the highway.

"I appreciate you and Emily letting me stay over last night under less-than-ideal circumstances. Let me know what I owe you for the lunch, clothes, and backpack I borrowed to make it up to you after I clear my name."

"You PJs saved my ass while we were down range, so let's call it even. You're welcome to come back any time to pick up the rest of your gear but don't bring any feds. If Emily sees them, she could get sideways with them."

Jason laughed and then turned his attention to the snowcapped San Francisco Peaks soaring over twelve thousand feet into the indigo sky.

"How are you doing? Up here?" Jason asked, pointing to his head.

Bentley let out a long sigh. "As screwed up as the government is, I have to give them props for the VA. I found a good therapist in Prescott that I've been going to for years, and I'm in a good place now."

Jason nodded.

"You remember Upton? The Combat Controller from Bagram that was attached to my squad?" Bentley asked.

"Yeah, I remember him. How's he doing?"

Bentley turned to Jason with a look that said more than words could ever convey.

"PTSD?" Jason asked.

Bentley turned back to the road and nodded.

"Did he ever get any help?" Jason whispered.

Bentley didn't respond. He didn't have to say anything for Jason to know that Upton had the same story he'd heard too many times about men and women who served with him in Afghanistan.

"I'm glad you got the help you needed."

"Me too," Bentley replied.

Neither man spoke again until Bentley exited the freeway and drove Jason through downtown Flagstaff.

"Where should I drop you off?"

"You can drop me off at all the restaurants and bars near the county courthouse. I can walk to where I need to go from there."

"Do you need a ride back?"

Jason stared out the window for several seconds before turning to his old friend. "I'm not sure how long I'll be, so I'll figure it out."

Bentley maneuvered his truck to the curb of a bustling restaurant. Several patrons dined outside as the growing shadows enveloped the outdoor patio. Jason grabbed the door handle and then let go. He reached over and extended his hand to his veteran friend. "Thanks again for doing what most people wouldn't do for me right now."

"Don't try to make me all misty-eyed before you go. Get out there and come see me after you clear your name," Bentley replied with a gentle push.

Jason's boots hit the sidewalk, and he pulled the hood from his gray borrowed sweatshirt over his bald head. Jason fit in with all the area's college students, snowboarders, and outdoor enthusiasts. Still, he didn't want to risk detection by eating at a popular restaurant, so he opted for a coffee shop. He was happy it was open and had only one customer during the dinner hour. He ordered a black coffee and found an empty table in the back. After transferring the essential items from his rucksack that he left in Bentley's camper, Jason put his borrowed backpack on the seat next to him. His new mission required speed and agility, so a smaller pack was necessary.

Jason left the coffee shop after the sun set and the streetlights illuminated the sidewalks. He kept his head down as he passed several restaurants and bars with revelers yelling to hear each other over the music. Ten minutes later, he was at the Coconino County Complex that housed the Flagstaff duty office for the DEA. Jason had only been there once but remembered they were in a temporary trailer between the Flagstaff Police Station and the county jail. The trailer was supposed to be a temporary office until the team moved into their permanent home in the court complex. A decade later, the DEA duty office still operated in a trailer.

Jason stayed in the shadows formed by the pine trees lined up in the complex like sentinels guarding the grounds. Fortunately for him, that was the only security they had for the trailer that had previously served as an office for a construction site. He found a spot near the sidewalk that allowed him to see inside the DEA duty office without raising too much suspicion among pedestrians in the area. After ten minutes of casual observation, Jason saw lights on inside but did not see any movement. It was almost eight o'clock, and he knew that his co-workers deserted the DEA office in Camp Verde after six unless there was a sting.

Jason moved to the front door and twisted the knob, but it would not turn. It was locked, so he removed his knife and worked it into the slot between the frame and metal door. He shimmied the blade until the lock gave way, and the door opened. He turned to scan the area before entering. Seeing no one, he slid into the building, shut the door, and locked it behind him. He dropped to all fours so nobody could see him through the windows, and bear crawled to the bank of cubicles in the rear of the portable structure. Jason stood in the windowless section of the office and looked for nameplates for Cruz or Donaldson.

A framed picture of a tanned, muscular man wearing dark sunglasses in front of a red sports car caught Jason's eye. He suspected it belonged to Special Agent Cruz, so he picked up the picture and inspected it in the dim light. It was Cruz. Jason put his backpack on the floor, pulled out desk drawers, and rifled through the contents. After striking out in the drawers, Jason sifted through file folders on his desk. He wasn't sure what he expected to find. He knew Cruz wouldn't have a file that said, *Frame Jason Mulder*, but the DEA special agent was arrogant and sloppy, so Jason hoped he'd find something to link Cruz to the conspiracy to frame him. Ten minutes after Jason entered the DEA office, he found zero clues or evidence. He knew he was pressing his luck with each additional minute he stayed in the trailer, but he didn't want to leave empty-handed. Jason pulled the top drawer open, causing a dozen pens and an old flip phone to rattle around with other office supplies. It was the last area to search on Cruz's desk, so Jason scanned the room. He noticed a small office with the door closed that he thought could be Donaldson's office when something inside the top drawer caught his attention. It was a blue USB drive, like the one he found on the ground after the Titan sting in Phoenix.

He removed the drive from the top drawer and studied it. "So they are connected," Jason said to the empty building.

Jason stood still considering the possibilities for the contents to clear his name, until he realized he had to leave soon to avoid getting caught in the DEA field office. Quickly, he slipped the drive into his pocket. The fugitive moved to the office door, but before he could pry it open, Jason heard the metallic rattle of keys approaching the front door. Someone was outside, and they were coming in.

Jason spun on the worn carpet, looking for a way to escape, but there was only one entrance to the building. He heard the door handle jiggle and expected it to swing open, but it didn't. Jason's eyes flashed back and forth across the room when a toilet caught his eye, so he bolted into the tiny bathroom. Jason pushed the door shut until it was only open a couple of inches when the sound of a key inserting into a lock filled the room. His heart raced, but he slowed his breathing to listen.

The pressure change from the door opening so fast rattled the fiber tiles in the false ceiling in the bathroom, and Jason knew someone was inside. Then he heard the door shut.

"What the hell is wrong with that door?"

Jason recognized the voice. It was Cruz.

The portable structure shook when Cruz marched back to his desk. Jason was less than ten feet from the bank of desks and heard the pens rattling again when Cruz yanked the drawer open.

"There you are," Cruz said aloud. Jason heard Cruz fall back into his leather work chair and was quiet. He didn't know if Cruz had his weapon on him. The brawny agent would be a handful in a fight, but Jason didn't stand a chance if Cruz had his service weapon. Jason looked around the dark bathroom and spotted a small window above the toilet. He guessed the square opening was eighteen to twenty inches wide and high, tight but doable for him to crawl out.

The floor shook when Cruz jumped up from his chair, and Jason heard the distinct sound of a flip phone slamming shut. Cruz moved rapidly around the trailer, and Jason guessed he was pacing. Something on the phone upset him, so Jason stood on the toilet and quietly slid the window open. He tossed his backpack out, but he heard a phone ring before he could climb out.

"Yeah," Cruz answered.

"Keep your panties on. I forgot something in the office, so I had to go back and pick it up. Order me another beer so it's ready when I get there. I've got to take a piss first, and then I'll head back so order that beer now."

"Shit," Jason whispered. He raised his hands above his head and dove into the tight window like an Olympic diver. His head and arms made it through, so Jason brought his arms around the exterior to push the rest of his body out of the trailer. Once his waist was past the sill, gravity did the rest, and Jason toppled eight feet onto the grass behind the portable building. He secured his backpack and looked up at the window. Special Agent Cruz's head was sticking through the opening, and his bulging eyes locked on Jason.

"Son of a bitch," Cruz said, and his head vanished from the window.

Jason bolted. His freedom, and maybe even his life, depended on him escaping into the adjacent woods before Cruz caught him. Thirty seconds into the foot race, Jason's left side felt like it was getting stabbed by a hundred fiery needles, limiting him to only three-quarter speed. Jason turned around and saw Cruz gaining on him.

He was out of options. He couldn't outrun the hulking Jersey boy, that was for sure. This left him with one last option, and reality didn't take long to set in.

A fight with Cruz was inevitable.

CHAPTER 40

Earlier that evening in Flagstaff, Arizona

Cruz bobbed his head with the bass of the music, with each thud reverberating through the half-empty nightclub like a heartbeat. The Latin-themed club sparkled in vibrant reds, greens, and oranges, with ornate ironwork and wood carvings showcasing the Spanish influence. Large chandeliers hung from the ceiling, casting a warm glow over the entire space.

The DEA special agent sat near the entrance to scan each young woman dressed in their best club attire entering the establishment. He turned back to his table, licked the salt off the rim of the shot glass, and slammed a shot of Jose Cuervo Tradicional Añejo 100% Agave Tequila.

"Ahh," Cruz bellowed. He slammed the glass on the table and exchanged high-fives with three friends. They met him at the popular club near his office for dinner and drinks before they moved to the dance floor later that evening.

His phone buzzed in his pocket, so he removed it and read the text.

`Did you see the message from our guy?`

The text was from Donaldson, so Cruz checked his other pocket. "Damn it. I left my burner in the office," he said to himself.

He leaned over to one friend and yelled into his ear to communicate over the bumping music.

"Save my seat. I'll be right back."

Cruz strode to the county complex behind the bars and restaurants with little evidence in his gait of the three drinks he downed in the last hour. At two hundred and thirty pounds, Cruz could hold his liquor. The only sign of a slight buzz was when he tried to put his key in the front door lock of the DEA duty office. The knob seemed looser than normal, so he missed his first two attempts but finally got his key into the lock and let himself in. Cruz bounced to his desk and found his phone in the top drawer. He powered up the old flip phone and fell back into his chair until the screen lit up. The text was short and direct.

`Why is Mulder still free? We need that drive ASAP!!!`

Cruz stood and paced near his desk. The pressure to retrieve the USB drive was ferocious, and he'd have to return to Jason Mulder's house near Payson. Cruz batted the details of a plan around in his head when his phone rang. It was a friend at the club that Cruz forgot to tell he was leaving, asking when he'd be back. Cruz hung up and walked over to the bathroom. He heard a loud thud outside when he opened the door. He jumped onto the toilet, stuck his head out the open window, and couldn't believe his eyes. It was Jason Mulder!

The most wanted man by US Marshals in Arizona was on the ground outside the window, and the two men locked eyes. Mulder picked up his backpack and ran, while Cruz considered jumping through the small opening, but knew he was too big. He bolted through the front door and darted around the DEA office trailer. Cruz looked left and right until he saw movement. Mulder ran toward the wooded area on the other side of the empty parking lot.

Cruz sprinted toward Mulder and surprised himself at how quickly he caught up. When they reached the middle of the parking lot, he was ten yards behind him, and Mulder stopped and turned to face Cruz. He tossed his backpack aside and moved into a fighting position. His chest heaved, but his eyes were alert and ready.

"You're a hard man to find, Mulder," Cruz said as he raised his hands like a boxer.

Mulder did not respond. He kept his palms facing Cruz and seemed to relax as he caught his breath.

"We can do this the easy way or the hard way, Mulder. The result will still be your ass in prison tonight, but one way will be far less painful for you."

Mulder looked down at Cruz's waist, and the DEA special agent understood what he was doing. "No, I left my weapon in my car. The club doesn't allow them inside, so this will be a brute force detention."

Mulder remained in his stance without saying a word.

"What were you doing in the office? What were you looking for?" Cruz asked. Those questions generated a response from Mulder.

"Gathering evidence that you and Donaldson framed me."

Cruz felt like someone had slapped him but tried his best to maintain a look of surprise. "Is that right?"

"Yeah, that's right," Mulder replied.

Cruz moved to his right, and Mulder countered by moving left. They sized each other up like two heavyweight boxers in the ring after the bell in round one.

"We could have avoided this if you had just turned in the storage drive you took from Titan, but you got cute, and now you're in it deep. Really deep. I don't think you can outsmart Donaldson, and I know you can't go toe-to-toe with me, so I'll take my chances when you return before a judge. How'd that work out for you last time?" Cruz asked with a wink.

"I don't know how or when, but you and Donaldson will go down for this, and I'll be there to make sure scum like you stay in prison for a long time."

Cruz lunged forward with a jab that Mulder blocked. "That's some imagination you've got there, Mulder. Is that a promise?"

"No, it's a guarantee."

Tired of Mulder's mouth, Cruz launched a right haymaker punch. It was his most effective punch to end a fight. Mulder raised his left arm to deflect the blow but winced as he danced away. Cruz noticed the grimace but dismissed it as they each took turns moving in and out with jabs. The nasty New Jersey native was used to winning fights with quick knockouts, so he launched another roundhouse, but this time, Mulder responded with three palm strikes to his chin. The barrage stunned Cruz, and he backed up and shook his head.

A sliver of doubt crept into Cruz's thoughts. He wasn't used to getting hit, let alone knocked off balance, so he knew Mulder was better than most. The doubt didn't last long. Although Mulder was good, Cruz knew he was better. He just had to use his size and strength advantage and take the smaller Mulder to the ground. Just as he prepared to charge like a bull and tackle Mulder, he noticed a red stain on the fugitive's side about the size of a baseball.

That's why he winced, Cruz thought. He's injured.

Cruz threw a straight punch, forcing Mulder to block with his left arm, and that exposed his injured side, so Cruz responded with a quick right hook to his side. The blood stain on Mulder's shirt was the target, and Cruz's fist connected with the bullseye.

Mulder bent forward, took several steps back, staggered, and collapsed to the asphalt. Cruz rushed toward the fallen fugitive, ready to rain more blows, when he noticed Mulder was out cold. He stood and looked around the empty parking lot.

Why was Mulder in the DEA duty office? Did he take anything? Cruz asked himself. He calmly considered his next move when panic shot up his spine. "The drive!"

He looked down at Mulder's limp body. "That USB drive better be there."

Cruz rushed back to the DEA building and yanked the top drawer open. He pushed pens and notepads back and forth, but the USB drive was gone.

"You're not getting away with a drive this time," Cruz shouted. He stomped out of the trailer and stopped.

Should I go to my truck to get my Glock?

He could finish Mulder for good but concluded returning to his truck may take too long.

I don't need a weapon for Mulder. How hard is it to kill an unconscious man?

Cruz removed his belt as he jogged back to the parking lot. He'd strangle Mulder, drag him into the woods, and let someone else find him. He quickened his steps, invigorated by the idea of ridding himself of the pesky thorn in his side until he reached the parking lot.

Jason Mulder was no longer there.

Chapter 41

Coconino County Complex parking lot in Flagstaff, Arizona

As the cool night air descended from the mountains into the vacant parking lot, Jason's senses gradually returned, coaxing him out of total blackness. His eyes fluttered open, revealing a close-up view of the asphalt in one eye and a streetlamp in the other. He lifted his face off the pavement, igniting a throbbing pain to explode in his side, a testament to the powerful blow that rendered him unconscious.

Jason propped himself up on his right arm like a kickstand, his ribs protesting the sudden movement. With a grimace, he assessed his surroundings, his vision returning to normal to scan the area for Cruz or other potential threats.

Ignoring the pounding in his head, Jason took several deep breaths and wobbled to his feet like a newborn fawn. He wanted to run to cover, but his legs weren't ready. Jason moved a hand to his side and gingerly touched the wound reopened by Cruz's nasty right hook. It was tender and wet in a pool of blood, but the bleeding had slowed. The bandages in his backpack could completely stop the bleeding, but he had to find a safe place to reapply them. Jason found the strength to move his feet and completed two full turns in the parking lot. Still no sign of Cruz, US Marshals, or local law enforcement. He knew that wouldn't last long, so Jason hobbled across the parking lot into the wooded area surrounding the eastern flank of the county complex.

Jason moved cautiously through the pine trees rising three stories above him until he reached a busy street. He took a knee inside the tree line to consider his next move.

Did Cruz call the US marshals, or is he picking up Donaldson to help finish me off?

He didn't know where Cruz went but knew he had to flee the area fast and get as far away as possible. Jason didn't have time to properly clean his wound so he applied his first bandage over the open puncture to help clot the blood seeping down his side. After applying a second bandage, a deep rumble and a metal-on-metal screech pierced the woods around him. It was a freight train. One of the nearly one hundred trains that pass through Flagstaff between Southern California and parts East daily. If Jason could reach the train before it passed, he could hop on and stow a ride for miles until he was safely away from Cruz.

Jason waited until he had an opening in traffic speeding by on the six-lane street and bolted across the road. His side hurt less now, but he still couldn't move as fast as needed. He passed through a parking lot of two commercial buildings and saw a wall of box cars heading East. It was going faster than Jason had hoped. He guessed it was going twenty-five miles per hour, which would be challenging to board even without an injury. Jason stared at the passing train for several seconds. He knew the risk was high, but the drive to be several miles away in minutes was greater than the potential of being cut into pieces if he fell under the train. Jason started in a jog and then built up enough speed to sprint alongside the train. The vibrating ground rattled Jason's bones with each step as the train picked up more speed. The engine of the miles-long train must already be near the edge of town.

Jason turned and spotted an access point approaching two cars behind him. He veered closer to the tracks, and when the boxcar was five yards behind him, Jason raised his left arm to snag a ladder but missed. His momentum carried him toward the steel wheels turning on the iron track. It was like facing a great white shark darting toward him with its mouth open, baring dagger-like teeth capable of ripping a person to shreds. Jason lowered his left arm fast enough to push off the bottom few inches of the boxcar, and he tumbled down onto the railroad tie and gravel in a cloud of dust. He quickly scooted away on his butt and stared at each one-hundred-and-fifty-ton car lumbering past him. Once his heart slowed until Jason no longer felt it pounding in his chest, he stood and shook his head at the feeble attempt to board the speeding train. His task of getting out of the area just got harder.

Jason scampered back to the commercial buildings for cover while thinking of plan B. He noticed one hosted a dealership for motorcycles and side-by-side off-road Utility Terrain Vehicles or UTVs. Most vehicles were inside a secure building or fence, but some of their best models remained in front of the building to attract potential customers in passing cars. Jason moved closer to investigate and froze. A Can-Am Maverick X3 Turbo, side-by-side in black and silver, sat outside the front door to the showroom. A white and navy twin was next to it, with three dirt bikes completing the display. They were visible from the road, so Jason waited for a pause in traffic and darted to the shadowy side of the UTV. He tugged the passenger door handle, and his eyes widened when it opened. Jason leaned in and checked every area to hide the keys, but they were all empty.

He turned to the building and looked through a giant show-room window. Jason scanned the room until his eyes stopped on a wall behind a desk about ten feet from the window. He spotted a key safe, and it looked secure. Or was it?

Jason moved to the far left of the window, put his open hands next to his face to block the glare of the streetlights, and gazed at the safe.

I think that's open.

He moved his eyes from the key safe to the cameras and the blinking light inside the door. The dealership appeared to have a standard security system to capture video of anyone who might break in to steal a vehicle. It was a good deterrent but couldn't prevent them from being stolen, especially if the perpetrator was running for his life and had nothing to lose. Stealing went against everything Jason's parents and grandparents taught him, but the decision was simple after touching the blood pooling on his side.

The heist had to be lightning fast. Jason planned to enter the building, grab the keys to the Can-Am from the safe, and be miles from the area before the police arrived. He scanned the area and found two cinder blocks holding down an A-frame sign promoting dirt bike, RZR, and Can-Am rentals by the hour near the front window. The Air Force Reserve sergeant ran the mission through his head a final time and counted down.

"Three, two, one."

Jason slung the first cinder block through the showroom window. The breaking glass sounded like an exploding bomb. Once the final shards crashed to the pavement, an ear-piercing alarm sounded, but Jason didn't hesitate and tossed the second block through a portion of the remaining plate glass. He needed a clear path to get in and out of the dealership quickly.

Three seconds later, Jason was at the key safe. The door rested in the closed position, but it wasn't locked. When Jason pulled the door open, he found over thirty keys. He turned and saw more motorcycles and UTVs in the indoor showroom, and the safe held the keys for all of them.

"Dammit!" Jason yelled. He couldn't hear his own voice over the deafening alarm.

His chest tightened like it used to after they scrambled his team to help another soldier or civilian in Afghanistan. His body wanted to run with every fiber of his being, but Jason still had to remain calm and concentrate.

"Find a Can-Am keychain."

Jason found logos for Honda, Polaris, Kawasaki, and Can-Am in the key safe. He snagged a half dozen Can-Am keys and bolted for the side-by-side in front of the dealership. When he inserted the first key, it felt like the alarm had been going off for ten minutes. The first key went in the ignition but did not turn. The second key delivered the same result.

His fingers felt stiff, and swapping out each key got more challenging. Jason stopped after the third key and listened.

Are those sirens?

He couldn't be sure if his mind was playing tricks on him or if the police were already en route.

Stay loose and focus.

After the fourth key failed to start the engine, Jason saw he only had two more. He dropped them all to his feet while swapping out the fourth key for the fifth. The adrenaline rush he always welcomed on a rescue mission slowed him down. The constant buzz from the alarm and the potential arrival of the police caused his reflexes to slow. He reached down and found three of the six keys. He chose one, inserted it into the ignition, and paused before he turned his wrist. This might be his last chance before the police arrived.

Jason turned the key and experienced the engine's rumble throughout his body.

"Yes!"

He disengaged the parking brake, rotated the wheel, and slammed on the gas. Jason shot across the parking lot and had to turn sharply to avoid hitting the fence separating the dealership from the neighboring business. He'd driven side-by-sides before, but it had been nearly five years since he'd had a two-hundred horsepower, turbo-charged UTV under his command. Jason's lips curved upwards in a grin. Nobody would catch him in this vehicle.

Jason pulled onto the street at a legal speed and took the next right turn. He looked continually in the mirrors for flashing lights. He'd never hear sirens over the roar of his Can-Am until they were right on top of him.

A mile from the dealership, Jason stopped at a red light. He was on Lake Mary Road with only one more stoplight at the freeway ahead, separating him from the vast pine forest with hundreds of miles of cover. It was after 10:00 p.m. on the southern edge of Flagstaff, and traffic was light, so Jason exhaled and allowed himself to relax. Suddenly, the light turned green, but before Jason could move his foot from his brake to the gas pedal, flashes of red and white bounced off the rearview mirror onto his face.

A Flagstaff police officer was a quarter mile behind him and gaining fast.

Chapter 42

Jason considered slamming the accelerator to the floor to get a head start on the pursuing police vehicle. Although the Can-Am turbo side-by-side could go from zero to sixty miles per hour in five seconds, its top speed was a little over 90 MPH. That wasn't fast enough to elude a police cruiser in a long-distance chase, so Jason moved forward slowly while furiously scanning for an off-road escape in the heavily forested mountain town. He reached the last red light for the Interstate 40 exit ramp as the flashing police lights were ten to twelve car lengths behind the side-by-side. A bright red circle fifteen feet above the street separated Jason from reaching the open road in the massive Coconino National Forest. The police car sped up behind Jason and turned on the siren. Jason lifted his foot off the brake to blow through the red light and take his chances in the woods when the cruiser drove on the shoulder and passed him on the right. The black and white vehicle sped onto the freeway toward more flashing lights in the distance.

Jason exhaled, eased back into his seat, and froze. When the driver behind him honked, Jason noticed the green light, and punched the Can-Am to put Flagstaff in his rearview mirror as fast as possible. Twenty minutes later, he spotted a forest road with weeds growing on the unpaved path in his headlights. Jason knew that his unique choice of vehicle, with its loud engine and distinct shape, would be easy for the police to find on the lightly traveled roads at night, so he exited the main road. A half mile off Lake Mary Road, he found a secluded area at the top of a sandstone mound that only a UTV could climb and turned the vehicle off until morning.

Slits of sunlight cast across the Can-Am and the stone mound in the morning. Jason blew into his hands like he'd done hundreds of times during the night. It provided little warmth, so it was time to move again. He assumed that the local police and US marshals knew Jason Mulder had broken into the off-road vehicle dealership and stolen the Can-Am eight hours earlier. Jason hoped he could beat the net they'd cast to catch him with an early departure before they could get set up.

The engine roared to life and then purred like a big cat while Jason checked the gas gauge. It had just under half a tank, which Jason assumed could get him an hour or two of drive time. Jason removed the USB Drive from his pocket and stared at it. He wished he could access a laptop or computer to see what was on the drive.

Would it provide clues to all the people framing him? Was it related to him at all?

The first place he considered was the familiar bank of computers in Prescott. He wasn't sure if the same librarian would be there or if she would help him again if he returned. After further consideration, he concluded returning to the same library was too risky, so Jason considered all the other small communities in the area with public libraries. He felt someone would notice him in those small towns, but another option existed. Now was the time to leave the forests of Northern Arizona and blend in with the millions that called the Valley of the Sun home.

Jason returned to the paved highway and guided his UTV south toward Phoenix. Thirty minutes later, he approached the community of Happy Jack. The rural outpost comprised of vacation cabins, a fire department, a bar, and the Blue Ridge Reservoir, where he fished with Kai. This was practically in his backyard again, and he created a mental list of the information he wanted to find in Phoenix until he saw an SUV with a Coconino County Sheriff's emblem parked at a diagonal angle across the road ahead. He knew that meant a roadblock, so Jason eased his foot off the gas. A hundred yards from the barricade, he rolled to a stop and examined the situation. Two uniformed deputies exited the SUV, and Jason saw one raise binoculars to his face multiple times. He handed the binoculars to the second deputy, and a discussion started between them. The shorter deputy pointed toward Jason.

The short deputy jogged back to the SUV while the other stayed behind on the only road through Happy Jack to Phoenix. Jason assumed he had stop sticks, so he did a quick U-turn and gunned it. Chunks of asphalt spewed into the air like a rooster's tail as Jason sped toward Flagstaff. The fugitive let a grin slip from his lips when he looked into his mirror, and the Coconino County Sheriff's SUV was a tiny dot and getting smaller.

That wasn't so hard.

He forced the accelerator to the floor and removed his foot quickly when he came around a curve. A half dozen police cruisers with their lights on were speeding toward him from the opposite direction.

"Oh shit!"

He continued to coast toward the six-pack of police vehicles when a section of the forest caught his eye. Jason yanked on the wheel and skidded off the paved highway onto a primitive fire road. A plume of dust grew behind him as he rocketed through a recently logged part of the forest, and he couldn't tell if the deputies were still pursuing him. Jason pushed his right foot to the floor and fishtailed around a sharp curve. He looked back and saw what looked like an army of headlights barreling toward him through the opaque wall of dust.

The forest grew denser, and the road narrowed. Under normal circumstances, he would have slowed down, but he couldn't. His pursuers were coming for him aggressively, and he had to match that intensity to elude them.

Jason whizzed past craggy sandstone outcroppings dotted with juniper trees as the fire road undulated up and down like waves on a lake. The path narrowed further until jagged tips of gunmetal gray sandstone passed within a foot or two of Jason's vehicle on each side. Jason noticed in his mirror that his pursuers slowed as the canyon walls closed in around their vehicles. The fugitive skidded around a curve and leaned over the steering wheel to ensure his eyes weren't lying to him. Jason noted a small parking lot surrounded by two-story tall sandstone walls on three sides. He removed his foot from the accelerator, and the UTV slowed. The Can-Am coasted into the canyon with twenty-foot-high sandstone surrounding him like he was a gladiator in the Roman Colosseum. The cloud of dust following Jason caught up, causing him to close his eyes tight and spit out copper-colored dirt. He turned in his seat and saw the line of sheriff's vehicles appear around the curve a hundred yards from him.

"Talk about a rock and a hard place," Jason muttered.

He gave the Can-Am a little gas until he was at the far end of the parking lot. Jason noticed tracks from UTVs that had previously climbed the sandstone wall. He guessed the angle was forty-five degrees, maybe more, but Jason also knew the Can-Am could climb the wall if the front tires stayed intact on the surface. At that angle, the UTV could flip backward, and Jason would land on a Coconino County Deputy's lap.

Jason swallowed hard as he sized up the sandstone wall. When the first police vehicle entered the parking lot, Jason slammed his boot on the gas. All two hundred horses under the hood fired and roared while Jason's back pressed into the driver's seat. He was halfway up the wall when he felt his front tire lose traction. Jason instinctively braked and slowed to where he might come to a complete stop. Even the powerful Can-Am might not overcome the force of gravity at this angle, so he recovered with more throttle. Jason continued up the wall with a delicate balance of gas and brake.

He couldn't see anything but the Can-Am hood and the partly cloudy indigo sky. Jason's entire body tensed as he willed the machine to get him over the steepest part of the wall.

Come on. There's no turning back now. This has to work.

It felt like he'd been climbing the sandstone wall for several minutes, and Jason hoped a suitable landing spot awaited him at the top. Jason felt his front wheels lower as pine trees and rocky buttes came back into view. Once the Can-Am was on a level plateau, he stopped and turned around. The twenty-second climb was harrowing but worth it. Jason turned the UTV to see his pursuers as the first deputy jumped out of his SUV with his service weapon drawn. They stared at each other for a beat. The deputy reholstered his pistol and returned to his SUV, but instead of leaving, he backed his vehicle up several feet. Six other sheriff's cruisers did the same to leave an opening the width of a vehicle between Jason and the exit.

Jason's eyebrows furrowed at the scene that looked like the parting of the Red Sea.

What are they doing? Are they daring me to come back down and blow past them in the other direction?

When he saw two sets of three headlights in the shape of a triangle bouncing through the dust toward the opening of vehicles in the parking lot, he had his answer. Two deputies emerged, each on a Polaris black and white four-wheeler ATV that could go anywhere Jason could go in his Can-Am UTV.

Jason searched for an exit and looked back toward the ocean of police vehicles again after finding his way out. The ATVs screamed across the parking lot toward the same sandstone wall Jason climbed, and they'd be on him in seconds.

CHAPTER 43

Jason surged ahead of the ATVs, shaking his head. He thought he was in the clear once he climbed the sandstone wall, but now he had two deputies buzzing toward him like bees protecting their hive. Jason's resolve to end this pursuit intensified with each look in the mirror at his pursuers.

His sizeable gap ahead of the deputies dwindled when the trail turned more primitive as he neared the next stand of pine trees. Jason slowed to 40 Miles per Hour and didn't have to look in the mirror to know that the two deputies caught up with him. He could hear the higher pitched ATV engines revving behind him whenever he braked for a boulder, or a hairpin turn.

With the dense forest rapidly approaching, the landscape leveled out for the length of a football field. Jason and the deputy must have noticed simultaneously because an ATV sped up and pulled equal to Jason on his passenger side. The law enforcement officer wore a helmet with a tinted visor, so Jason couldn't see his face, but he observed his hand gesture – the back-and-forth motion across his neck like he was slitting his throat. Jason understood the deputy was telling him to cut his engine.

There's no way I'm stopping. You'll have to stop me.

Jason wagged his head at the person behind the visor and pushed harder on the gas pedal. As they approached the end of the clearing, the deputy removed his service weapon and held it high, that Jason took as a warning.

As the clearing narrowed, the deputy gunned his ATV and moved ahead of Jason by a couple of feet. He raised his pistol again, but this time, he aimed toward the front of Jason's UTV.

Pop! Pop!

Jason jumped and nearly hit his head on the fiberglass roof at the unexpected report from the deputy's pistol. He held the steering wheel tight but didn't feel any change in his speed or steering. The bumps must have caused the deputy to miss the front tires he aimed at on Jason's UTV.

The deputy raised his pistol again and aimed for another shot at the front tires just as the clearing ended, and the trio entered the pine forest packed with pine trees reaching over six stories into the sky.

My turn.

Jason yanked his steering wheel hard to the right and pushed the ATV into a tree trunk twice as thick as a telephone pole. The loud smash from the collision between the fast-moving machine and the unmovable object could be heard over the roar of two powersports vehicles. Jason glanced in his mirror and saw the ATV and deputy flip, roll, and come to rest in the trail. The former PJ cringed at the thought of the deputy's injuries but was relieved that he would no longer be pursuing him.

The terrain changed, and Jason felt himself descending on the narrow trail. He guessed he was nearing the Mogollon Rim, and this confirmed it. This was good news because the rim was the last obstacle between him and his destination in Phoenix, but it meant switchbacks were coming, and speed was no longer a tool to evade the final deputy.

Jason searched his mirrors but did not see the second person on the ATV.

Did he stop to help the other deputy?

He turned his head around as he slowed to a crawl at the first of a dozen switchbacks along the rim.

"Oh shit," Jason yelled. The deputy had jumped onto the back of his UTV and climbed toward the cabin.

Jason slammed on the gas and jerked the steering wheel right and left to dislodge the deputy clinging to his UTV. The ATV driver lost his footing, and his legs hung out from the Can-Am like a pair of pants on a clothesline blowing in the breeze, but the deputy never let go.

At the next switchback, Jason slowed and was met with a punch to his cheek by a gloved left hook. Jason shook his head more in shock than pain and turned his body to get his hands up to block another blow from the deputy outside his open window. The deputy seemed focused on hanging onto the UTV, bucking like a bronco, so Jason delivered a jab into the visor of the helmeted deputy. It didn't faze the deputy, but now Jason's fingers pulsed with pain.

The deputy scooted forward until he hovered directly over Jason, nestled lower in the driver's seat. He hung on with his right hand, and Jason felt punches hitting him in the neck, head, and face. Blood dribbled into Jason's left eye, and he blinked it away, but he couldn't navigate the UTV at thirty miles per hour and raised his arms to protect himself from the blows raining on him.

Jason entered another switchback and slowed as the stream of blood passed over his cheek and seeped into his lips. His teeth transformed from white to red, and he tasted the salty substance with a coppery tang as he exited the sharp curve.

I have to end this before he lands a knockout blow. Should I stop and square up for a fight? Or should I —

Jason released the steering wheel and turned his body toward the attacking deputy. He blocked two incoming punches and followed with an uppercut with his left hand that raised the deputy's helmet several inches to expose his neck. Jason's lighting quick straight punch hit the bullseye dead center in the deputy's throat. The deputy fell backward like a bag of sand off the back of a truck.

The UTV careened off the path, and Jason grabbed the steering wheel and turned the out-of-control machine a nanosecond before it slammed into a quartet of pine trees. Jason braked hard and slid to a stop. He stared ahead, panting from the recent near miss as the UTV purred below him. Once his breathing slowed, Jason extracted himself from the Can-Am. He saw the deputy lying on his back, holding his throat with both hands fifty yards back. He was also out of the chase, but Jason wasn't sure if another ATV or helicopter would soon appear.

Jason returned to his idling vehicle and tackled the remaining switchbacks until he reached the forest floor. He felt a twinge of hope now that he was below the rim and less than ten miles from home, but the joy was short-lived. The Can-Am sputtered and jerked. Jason checked the gas gauge, and it was below empty. It sputtered again, coughed, and died.

Jason sat in the side-by-side vehicle for a minute before leaving the machine that had kept him out of police custody in the middle of the road. His hands vibrated for several minutes after holding the wheel over rough terrain for so long.

He secured his backpack from the passenger seat and tore off a piece of his shirt. Jason pressed the shirt against the gash over his eye, stood on the gravel road, and looked in both directions.

Should I risk heading home to see Shanna when she needs me most or find out if the USB drive from Cruz can finally clear my name?

CHAPTER 44

Flagstaff, Arizona

Special Agent Donaldson lowered himself in his SUV to be less visible as the employees of Coconino County Complex pulled up and strolled into their offices. By 8:00 a.m., the lot was almost full, as most people had already gone inside to start their day. That meant Special Agent Cruz would arrive soon.

A red Ford Mustang GT raced into the lot at a quarter past eight. The tires squealed as the driver turned sharply in a spot close to where Jason Mulder had escaped into the woods. Cruz jumped from his car and darted through the parked vehicles toward the DEA office until a black Chevy Tahoe cut him off.

"What the f—" Cruz started. He stopped his protest mid-sentence once he recognized the driver. "What's up?"

"Get in," Donaldson barked.

Cruz looked around the parking lot and joined Donaldson in his SUV. Neither said a word while the senior DEA agent navigated through the heart of Flagstaff.

"Where are we going?"

Donaldson turned toward Cruz but did not respond. He saw his partner's eyes look down at the Beretta 9mm pistol in the console and shift his weight uncomfortably in his seat.

"Relax. I'm not here to shoot you," Donaldson said. "We're going to Buffalo Park to discuss what happened last night."

Five minutes later, Donaldson pulled into a nearly empty parking lot and found a spot far from any vehicles, joggers, or people walking dogs along the vast array of paths. He put the SUV in park and turned toward Cruz.

"What happened?"

Cruz shook his head and tossed his hands into the air. "I don't know, man. Somehow, Mulder broke into our office and found my desk. I caught him in the act and kicked his ass in the parking lot. After I knocked him out, I wondered why he was snooping around our office, so I left him unconscious and went back to check my desk. That's when I realized he had stolen the USB drive. When I went back to finish him, he was gone."

Cruz stared at his partner like a little boy waiting to get smacked by an older sibling. Donaldson recognized the look and tried to control his temper but couldn't. He slammed his fist on the dashboard. "Dammit. Now he has two drives. That's not good."

"I didn't know he had the drive until I went back to the office. If I'd known, I would have taken it from him while he was out cold in the parking lot."

Donaldson exhaled loudly. "Look, none of that matters right now, but we have to get those drives back, or we're both going to take permanent dirt naps."

Cruz nodded, and they both turned their gaze toward the soaring mountains with a dusting of snow on their peaks. The desolate and peaceful park starkly contrasted with the fury brewing inside Donaldson.

"I have a plan," Donaldson said.

Cruz turned toward him with a sinister grin. "Let's hear it."

"We need to use his pregnant wife as bait. We'll send a signal to Mulder that his wife is in trouble, and we'll be waiting for him when he comes home."

Lines of confusion appeared on Cruz's forehead. "How are we going to send him a signal when we don't even know where he is?"

"I'm sure he's checking on the manhunt in the news. I don't know if he has access to a radio, the Internet, newspapers, or whatever, so I'll leak an anonymous report to the press that his wife is suspected of aiding her fugitive husband. It's a believable story, so some stations will run with it, even if it's from an anonymous source."

Cruz whistled. "That will piss him off. He'll come running home to save his wife like the good Boy Scout that he is."

"I don't know how long the news will take to reach him, so I'll do it today. That means we'll have to stake out his house for a while."

"We can pull shifts," Cruz replied.

"Yeah, but we'll still need some help. When Mulder shows up, we'll grab him and his wife and do whatever is necessary to get those drives back. A couple more guys willing to rough up Mulder for a few hundred dollars is all we need."

"I know some guys at my gym that would do it for free. I'd have a line out the door for a few Benjamins."

"No, let me take care of the additional manpower," Donaldson replied. "I have a couple of guys in mind that owe me some favors, and they aren't afraid of breaking the law."

"You sure?"

"Yeah, I'm sure," Donaldson replied.

"How soon can you leak the story to the press?"

"It'll take a couple of hours to put everything together, so I'll leak the report after lunch, and we'll stake out tonight."

Shanna arched her back and pushed her belly into the air to stand up from her family room couch. She considered taking another swig from the pickle jar in the refrigerator but determined the extra steps weren't worth the effort and sat back down. She was thirty-nine weeks pregnant, and simple tasks like moving and breathing were getting more difficult. Her official due date wasn't for another seven days, but she was ready to give birth to the boy or girl, kicking inside her like an angry mule.

She leaned back on some pillows and wiggled to get more comfortable. Shanna looked at her wedding picture on the mantle above the fireplace.

Is Jason still out in the forest? Is he safe or is he hurt? Is he trying to come home? Will I ever see him again?

The doorbell pulled Shanna from her thoughts. She shuffled to the back door and invited Celeste and Phillip, Jason's mom and dad, to enter.

"How are you feeling?" Celeste asked.

"I'm okay. This baby is right on my lungs, so sleeping or getting full breaths is hard."

"I bet. You're getting close now."

"I'm so ready for this baby to be born."

Shanna turned and shuffled into the family room. "Come in and have a seat. I'd offer to get you something, but I'm short of breath right now."

"You don't need to wait on us. I can get anything you or Celeste want," Phillip said.

Everyone moved into the family room and sat in silence until Celeste spoke.

"Have you heard anything new about Jason?"

Shanna shook her head. "No, just what I heard on the news, and I don't know how much of that is true. Knowing Jason, he's probably two steps ahead of law enforcement, and I'm sure he's looking for the people who framed him. I hope he finds them soon so he can come home."

Tears formed and dropped to Shanna's cheeks. Celeste moved from her chair next to Shanna and touched her knee. She handed her daughter-in-law a tissue.

"I know this is hard. We have to pray Jason is okay and is doing what's right for you and the new baby. We'll be here as much as you need until he gets home."

Shanna wiped away the tears with the tissue. "Thank you. I appreciate it."

The back door opened again, and Kai charged in. "I split a bunch of logs for your stove. It should last you a few days. Is there anything else you need me to do?"

"No, that's a big help, and I appreciate it," Shanna said.

She tried to stand but fell back onto the couch with a groan.

"Are you okay?" Kai asked.

"Yeah, I was going to bring some split logs into the house."

Phillip stood. "Kai and I will bring in the logs. Let us do all that stuff. Please sit down."

The two men went outside to get the logs when Celeste turned to Shanna.

"How are you really feeling?"

Shanna took a quick breath. "I'm nervous that Jason won't be home when I go into labor and have to go to the hospital. I feel like I'm getting close."

"You know Jason is doing all he can to get home for you and the birth of his first child."

"I know, but I'm still nervous he won't get here in time."

Can I do this alone? It wasn't supposed to be this way for our first child. I need Jason more than ever now.

"You're a week away, so you have to take it easy until the baby is born. Phillip and I will come over every day to help you, but you also have to take care of yourself and your baby this final week. If you don't take it easy, the baby could come early."

Shanna nodded. An early delivery was the last thing she wanted. She wanted to hang on as long as possible so Jason had time to get home, but she wasn't sure anymore if that was possible.

Chapter 45

Phoenix, Arizona

Jason leaned against the Valley Metro light rail car window and watched the high-rise apartments and office buildings hosting attorneys, banks, and public accounting firms pass by like a movie reel in the mid-afternoon sun. The buildings grew taller and traffic more congested as Jason drew closer to the heart of Phoenix. He'd been to the capital city of Arizona hundreds of times, but this time, it seemed bigger and louder after spending so much time in the forest.

The hum of the electric rail car stopped at the Central Avenue and McDowell Road station, and Jason exited onto the concrete platform. With five million inhabitants, the metro area's energy assaulted Jason's senses. Cigarette smoke wafted around a group of teenagers waiting on the platform, and Jason's nose alerted him to aromatic lantana plants that outlined the city streets in gold and purple. Once the light rail car squeaked away, Jason moved cautiously across the street, scanning for threats without moving his head.

Jason felt confident that none of his pursuers were waiting to ambush him, so he pulled his hood over his ball cap and turned south toward Burton Barr Central Library in Downtown Phoenix. He timed his pace to let a group of young adults catch up with him. They appeared to be graduate-age university students, and Jason moved closer to the five women and three men to seem like he was part of the group. The fugitive kept his head down and couldn't help overhearing their conversations on the best movies to stream on a first date, fantasy football roster moves, and restaurants with the best Taco Tuesday specials. A part of Jason envied them and wished his life could be so carefree, but he was also growing impatient at the snaillike pace of the group going nowhere fast.

Come on, let's move with a little purpose.

Jason swallowed his frustration, and rode the wave of students until he reached the modern, five-story building housing a million plus books. He entered the first floor and found himself inside a canyon-like vertical atrium with elevators running up and down the open structure like nerves in a spine. Jason stepped off the elevator on the fourth floor and found rows of computers. He slid the USB drive he took from Cruz's office into the proper slot and waited for it to open, but he got an error message. All the public computers required users to punch in a valid City of Phoenix library card number to gain access, so Jason snagged his bag and walked. Two rows over, Jason saw another college-age male with unkempt hair stand up from his computer, so he rushed over.

"Are you done using this computer?" Jason asked.

The young man looked around at all the empty computers and then back at Jason. "Yeah, I guess."

"Great. Thanks."

Jason's butt was in the chair before the kid took another step.

"Can you at least log me out?"

"Yeah, in a minute," Jason responded.

The kid remained behind Jason as he inserted the USB drive and waited for it to load. A white screen appeared with a digital file folder, and the kid continued to hover over him, so Jason turned around. "I'm busy here, so can you give me some space?"

"Asshole," the kid chirped and stomped away.

The same puzzle-like text appeared. It looked different from last time, but he couldn't be sure.

"Damn it! That drive did belong to Titan."

Jason said it louder than he intended, but the confirmation that the two USB drives were related was impossible to contain. After a quick scan to verify his outburst did not bring him any unwanted attention, he turned back to the puzzle.

The results were the same as last time. A throbbing head with no clue about the contents of the USB drive.

This is crazy. I'll never figure this out.

Jason considered himself competent in technology basics, but this was beyond his knowledge. He had to get it to someone with the resources to read the encryption or break the code. The DEA still wasn't an option, so Jason had to find his answers from somewhere else. He removed his hat, ran his hand over the stubble on his head, and put the cap back on. Jason had to find answers now, so he opened the Internet browser and searched for his name. Hundreds of articles that didn't exist a week ago appeared about Jason Mulder, the fugitive. He scanned the stories for several minutes but didn't find any new information until his curser landed on a local TV station website with a live video feed of Senior Deputy Marshal Whittaker standing in front of the Sandra Day O'Connor Courthouse with several microphones pointed in his direction. Jason increased the volume and listened to the press conference.

"I have nothing new to report today on Jason Mulder. Deputies are working around the clock responding to new leads and will continue to do so until we bring the fugitive to justice."

Jason looked around at the smattering of people milling around the library's fourth floor, but nobody seemed to notice him.

"We are—"

"Why haven't US marshals been able to apprehend this fugitive? Are you short on resources or manpower?" a reporter interrupted.

Whittaker stared at the brunette field reporter from the local CBS station for a beat and responded.

"I'm in constant communication with Virginia on our resources, and they're prepared to mobilize more people and equipment, like planes and drones, to help with the search if needed. The reason we haven't caught the fugitive yet is simple. We're looking for one man hiding in a forested area larger than New England. It's a tall task, but we'll find him."

The reporter from the Arizona Republic newspaper asked the next question. "A recent news report says Shanna Mulder, the fugitive's wife, may be under investigation for helping her husband evade capture. Do you have anything to add to that report?"

"That report didn't come from my office."

"No, sir. It came from a source with knowledge of the hunt for Jason Mulder," the reporter replied.

"I can't comment on a report I've never seen."

Jason crumbled a sheet of paper into his fist and stood so fast that his chair toppled over. "You son of a bitch. Leave Shanna out of this!"

Whittaker continued to talk, but Jason no longer heard him. He stared at the keyboard for a full minute. Violent thoughts he wasn't proud of flooded his mind. Two minutes later, Jason was on the sidewalk outside the library, marching toward the federal courthouse and the location of Deputy Marshal Whittaker's press conference.

A mesquite tree provided cover for Jason as he watched every vehicle pay to exit the parking garage and then pull onto the busy downtown Phoenix boulevard. He knew everyone visiting the federal courthouse parked in this garage, and Jason hoped he wasn't too late. A white Dodge Charger pulled to the kiosk to pay, and Jason recognized the driver. It was Whittaker. Jason removed the knife from his backpack and held it inside his palm, making it invisible to anyone watching him. The gate opened, and Whittaker pulled forward. Jason put his head down and pretended he was a pedestrian, forcing the deputy US marshal to stop short of the street. Once Jason was within five feet of Whittaker's vehicle, he lunged for the passenger door. Whittaker had no time to react before the fugitive was inside with the tip of his knife in his ribs.

"Drive!" Jason barked.

Whittaker turned and tilted his head, causing Jason to push harder on the blade.

"Okay, okay, I'll drive. Where, too?"

"Just drive, or this will be the shortest trip of your life."

The Charger pulled into traffic, and Jason leaned over and removed the radio and Glock from inside Whittaker's sports coat.

"Turn right at the light."

Whittaker complied. The only sound in the cabin for the next six blocks was the V8 engine speeding up after each red light.

"Where are you taking me?"

"Leave my wife out of this! I haven't spoken to her since I escaped, and she doesn't even know if I'm alive now!"

"Is that what this is about?" Whittaker asked.

"You don't get it, do you?"

"I get you assaulted four US marshals and are facing a long list of charges that will keep you behind bars until your new baby is out of high school."

Jason's eyes moved from the road to Whittaker.

"Yeah, I know your wife is pregnant. Let me take you in so you don't get killed before seeing your first child."

"Not going to happen. They framed me."

"I don't care," Whittaker replied. His cool response was more fitting in a coffee shop after the barista asked if they wanted room for creamer in their coffee versus an armed carjacking. The stoplight turned red, and Whittaker stopped. Jason reached into his pocket with his free hand and removed the USB drive from the DEA office in Flagstaff. He tossed it on Whittaker's lap, and it fell between his legs. Whittaker looked down for a second and then back to the road.

"What's this?"

"This is a clue to who framed me and why. I don't have all the answers, which is why I'm coming to you, but I'm sure a couple of crooked DEA special agents are involved."

The light turned green, and Whittaker drove through the intersection.

"You have access to resources that can figure this out. Get the FBI involved or something, but take this seriously. That drive holds the key to who framed me."

Whittaker turned to face Jason. "I can't do anything for you with a knife in my side. Let's go to the district office to have someone look at this."

"Turn right here," Jason growled.

Whitaker turned left and stomped on the gas. Seconds later, the Charger passed every vehicle on the two-lane westbound city street.

"I said turn right!"

"If you're going to kill me, then kill me. If not, you can explain your tale from your cell."

"I'm warning you. Turn here now!"

Jason saw the federal courthouse building growing more prominent in the windshield. The US Marshal's Office in Phoenix shared the same complex.

Jason applied more pressure to the knife. It cut through Whittaker's sports coat until crimson dotted his white shirt. "Don't make me do it. I'll gut you right here, right now."

Whitaker winced but kept his eyes on the road ahead. He braked hard to stop behind a line of cars waiting at a red light. They were only seven blocks away from an army of marshals that would shoot Jason the moment they saw him with a knife to Whittaker.

"I warned you!"

Jason headbutted Whitaker and immediately followed with a jab that caught the deputy marshal under the chin. The marshal's head slammed into the driver's side window as Jason exited on the passenger side.

Jason was on the run blocks from a building that housed dozens of US marshals who weren't encumbered with the same restrictions as other local, state, and federal law enforcement officers. US marshals can shoot a fugitive on sight.

Chapter 46

Whitaker straightened in the driver's seat and shook his head. The speed of Mulder's strike and departure shocked him, and it took several seconds before he regained his bearings. He pulled his vehicle to the right, opened his door, and sprinted after Mulder.

The former college athlete had the speed to catch the fleeing fugitive, but after two blocks, he slowed to a fast walk. Whittaker continued to the next street, stopped, and did two full rotations searching for his fugitive. Mulder had his radio and weapon, so Whitaker jogged six blocks to the USMS office as fast as his aching head allowed.

The security team at the front desk froze when Whittaker stumbled in with streaks of blood on his head, cheek, and neck.

"What happened to you?"

Whittaker bent over with both hands on his knees. Five seconds later, he found enough oxygen in his lungs to speak.

"Jason Mulder just carjacked me."

"Where? Does he still have your vehicle?"

"No, I fought him off," Whittaker replied shaking his head. "He's on foot and we can't let him get away in downtown. Grab everyone you can and catch that son of a bitch."

Whittaker watched as a squad of US marshals stormed past him out the door and onto the street, amped up to apprehend Jason

Mulder. The senior deputy marshal stood upright and dabbed his forehead with a handkerchief. He staggered past the empty security desk and took the elevator to the second floor of the USMS office in the Federal Courthouse complex. Whittaker exited with his phone held high above him like a teenager snapping a selfie, but he wasn't documenting his boyish good looks. On the phone screen, he examined the cut under his chin and the growing bump on his right temple. His index and middle finger grazed across the new lump, causing Whittaker to flinch.

He could have killed me.

He stepped onto a floor humming with activity from over forty members of the US Marshal Service hard at work. The workspace was spacious and well-lit, sterile in only a way the US Government could pull off. Management tried to compensate for the blandness with motivational posters and pictures of men and women in US Marshal attire that exuded a business-like atmosphere for the professional man-hunting agency.

As he crossed the office, Whittaker strode past a row of cubicles stretched along the wall with each partitioned workspace occupied by USMS staff focused on their tasks. He kept his gaze above the inquisitive eyes on him and instead focused on the glass-walled room with a large conference table facing a messy whiteboard with an assortment of daily briefs and fugitive status updates scribbled in blue erasable marker.

Next to the conference room, Whittaker entered his private office. The modest space displayed no decorations or family pictures that showed anyone claimed the workspace. It looked like Whittaker was ready to move out at a moment's notice. After sitting in his leather desk chair, Deputy Marshal Miley entered.

"Oh my gosh, I just heard. What happened?"

Whittaker raised his eyes from the file folder on his desk.

"Mulder."

"Jason Mulder? He attacked you?"

Whittaker did not answer. Instead, he pointed to the growing knot on the side of his head.

"How did this happen? Where did this happen? Is he in custody now?"

"Slow down, and I'll explain."

Miley nodded, sucked in a breath, and exhaled. "Sorry, this is just such a shock for me."

"Imagine my shock when Mulder carjacked me and stuck a blade into my ribs."

"He what?" Miley shouted. Her eyes widened and her face formed a look of disbelief.

Whittaker scanned the workers outside his office, stood, and shut his door. He returned to his seat while Miley remained standing. He ran his fingers across his temple and chin, then recounted his encounter with Jason.

"I was leaving the parking garage after the press conference, and the next thing I know, some dude jumps in and puts a knife to my side. At first, I thought it was a random carjacking and then recognized he was our fugitive. His appearance changed, so we'll have to update our sketch for the public. It also looked like he'd lost some weight and is now bald with a blondish goatee. He also had a giant scorpion tattoo and a skull with a snake on his neck. I don't think I've seen that in any of the images of him before, so that may also be new."

"Clever," Miley chimed in.

Whittaker tilted his head. "How so?"

"People will notice those tattoos on his neck and won't pay as much attention to his face."

"Yeah, I guess. Anyway, he removed my Glock and radio before I had a chance to react, and then he pushed the knife harder into my side and told me to drive."

"Did he say anything?"

Whittaker leaned forward in his chair and put his palms on the desk. "Oh yeah. He blabbered on about how he's innocent and has proof, so we should keep his wife out of this and leave him alone."

"Do you think he could be innocent?"

Whittaker leaned back in his chair. "It doesn't matter what I think. My job is to capture Jason Mulder and let the judicial branch do their thing, and that's exactly what I tried to do."

"Is that when he assaulted you?"

"Yep. We were driving on Roosevelt, and he told me to turn right on Fifth Avenue, but I turned left to drive back here. I planned to get this over with and bring him into custody right here and now. I stopped for a red light, and that's when Mulder head-butted and punched me. Now I understand how he overtook Cosgrove and Bilski in the restroom because that boy can pack a punch. I saw stars for a few seconds, and that's when he took off. I tried to give chase, but he was gone in the wind."

Miley crossed her arms across her chest. "I'm glad it wasn't worse. I can't believe he'd risk capture by carjacking you just to claim he's innocent."

Whittaker stood, removed a USB drive from his front pocket, and tossed it on his desk. "He also gave me this. He said this has the evidence that he was framed."

Miley picked up the drive and examined it.

"Did he say what was on it?"

"No. He said he didn't have all the answers and that we may have to involve the FBI. I assume it's encrypted, and he wants someone in cybersecurity to look at it."

Whittaker moved beside his window, which overlooked the street traffic below his office. He stared at nothing in particular for a half minute and then turned toward Deputy Marshal Miley.

"He also said that some crooked DEA special agents are involved."

Wrinkles appeared above Miley's perfectly manicured eyebrows. "That's a bold accusation, even for someone running for their life. What's your take?"

Whittaker nodded. "I'm not sure, but I haven't been able to get that part of our conversation out of my mind since he said it."

"I have to ask you a question, and I know you will not like it," Miley said with her best beauty pageant smile. Whittaker knew that smile got Miley what she wanted with most men, but it had the opposite effect on him. It raised his defenses, and an involuntary scowl took over his face.

"What?" Whittaker snapped. He crossed his arms to mirror his direct report.

"I know you don't care, but are we hunting the victim of a crime and not the perpetrator?"

Whittaker's arms dropped back to his side, and he took several steps toward Miley.

"You're damn right. I don't care if our fugitive thinks he's innocent. Mulder had a talented attorney and a fair trial, and they convicted him on all charges. He could have served his sentence and appealed the ruling like everyone else, but instead, he chose to escape our custody during transport. He's assaulted four of our men, a civilian in Prescott, and probably more than we know about. Our sole focus is to capture, detain, and deliver him to the Phoenix FCI. Is that clear?"

Miley stepped back and opened her mouth as if she planned to respond but closed it. She held up the USB drive. "Yes, that's clear. What should I do with this?"

"See what you can find on it, and if it's encrypted, ask someone in cybercrimes at the FBI to do us a favor and look at it, but that's all."

"Yes, sir."

Miley exited Whittaker's office as Deputy Marshal Owens rushed into his office.

"We got a tip on Mulder. The porter at the Hyatt Hotel on Third Street just saw someone that fits Mulder's description jogging north."

Whittaker's eyes met Miley's. "Let's go!"

Chapter 47

Phoenix, Arizona

Jason transitioned from a full sprint to a walk seven blocks after escaping Whittaker's vehicle. He passed a luxury hotel busy with guests entering and exiting vehicles under the covered entrance. Jason looked down to conceal his identity and continued several more blocks until he stopped to ditch Whittaker's weapon and radio in a nearby city trash receptacle. Three minutes had passed since Jason's forehead collided with Whittaker's temple, and he knew a rage-fueled US Marshal's response team would swarm the area looking for him. He had minutes to get as far away as possible. Jason walked casually toward the largest hotel in downtown Phoenix while he considered his next move. The central part of the city was a hornets' nest of monitored public cameras and members of local, state, and federal law enforcement, so hunkering down to hide in the area was not an option. Public transportation, freeways, and city parks were slightly better but still too risky for the massive manhunt that would begin soon.

His solution came in the form of a portly man half asleep in a car. Jason noticed the long line of taxicabs parked along the street, waiting for someone in one of the 1,000 rooms in the thirty-one-story hotel to request a ride. He couldn't go too far in a cab but could exit the area quickly, which was Jason's number one objective. Although he didn't look like the prototypical business-man late for a flight, he straightened the wrinkles in his sweatshirt and raised his ball cap higher on his forehead as he approached the driver.

"Can you take me to the airport?"

The driver straightened up. "Yes, but I'm supposed to wait for the bellman to call for me."

"I don't have time for that. I'll miss my flight."

The driver looked toward the bellman unloading a family from a large SUV and then back at Jason without saying anything. The wail of a police siren erupted several blocks away, and Jason knew he was down to seconds.

Jason pulled a twenty-dollar bill from his pocket and handed it to the driver. "This is on top of a nice tip if you can get me to the airport in ten minutes. Can you do it?"

"Get in," the driver responded. Intensity washed over his face, and a minute later, Jason hurtled across Phoenix as red and blue lights flickered off the glass of tall buildings and sirens ignited across the city's center. Four minutes after leaving Whittaker, Jason slumped in the taxi's backseat as the driver raced down the entrance ramp to Interstate 10 toward Phoenix Sky Harbor International Airport.

Despite light traffic on the freeway, the driver earned his twenty dollars when he drove the five miles to the airport in nine minutes. This was another tricky spot for Jason because airports are some of the most secure areas outside military bases and federal government buildings in the United States. He had the driver drop him off at the arrivals for Terminal 3 instead of the departures because he didn't want to go inside. Once he found the location for the offsite parking shuttle, he walked to the designated area and waited. The offsite airport parking lots were owned by private companies and operated up to a mile from the airport. They'd have less security and cameras.

Jason was on the shuttle minutes later, moving further from downtown Phoenix as the sun set behind the skyline. As Jason bounced around the airport in the shuttle, he considered his next steps. Besides avoiding the US marshals eager to apprehend him, Jason had to stay warm when Phoenix temps dipped into the fifties at night. He determined he could pull down his ball cap and hop on and off the airport shuttles, constantly running 24/7 to stay warm and avoid drawing the suspicion of travelers. Another haggard-looking man among a sea of tired travelers on the last leg of their trip to retrieve their vehicles late at night was warmer and safer than wandering parking lots until dawn. Arizonans didn't take kindly to men with hats pulled low creeping around parking lots at night, and someone would surely notify the parking lot security or engage him with a weapon.

His plan worked for several round trips around the airport, and it even led to a discussion with a young man, Sebastian, who was completing his last trip with the parking lot company to start his first run with his second job at an airport shuttle service. The airport shuttle picked up and dropped off travelers in small communities around Arizona who wished to fly out of Phoenix Sky Harbor Airport but didn't want to drive or pay for parking at the sprawling international airport. Sebastian's first customer was a drop-off in Strawberry, Arizona, one hundred miles north of Phoenix but fifteen miles west of his home in Whispering Pines. Jason bought a ticket for the shuttle and waited with Sebastian outside the terminal for the middle-aged couple to arrive. Once Sebastian placed their luggage in the back, the couple fell asleep in the back row of the van while Jason listened to the driver describe all twenty-three steps in his plan to start a house-flipping business for the next two hours. He nodded often but couldn't repeat any of Sebastian's steps because Jason's mind was elsewhere.

Sebastian dropped Jason off three miles southeast of Strawberry at an empty cabin in Pine, Arizona. It belonged to the parents of Noah's girlfriend, Morgan, and Jason had visited the property with his brother and Morgan the previous spring. The ranch-style log cabin was a vacation rental, primarily for Phoenicians looking to escape the scorching summer heat in the Valley of the Sun, so Jason hoped it would be empty mid-week in October. No vehicles were parked in the driveway, and Jason didn't see any glow of indoor lights just before midnight, yet he approached with caution.

Before stepping onto the front porch, he noticed a doorbell camera and a keypad deadbolt lock. Jason knew Morgan's father owned a construction business in Payson that had frequent break-ins to steal tools, so he probably had a decent security system in the cabin. He couldn't risk breaking in and setting off the alarm for a monitored service, so Jason reached into his backpack and removed his phone from the Faraday pouch. Contacting Noah was slightly less risky than breaking in, so Jason had to be smart with his message to ensure he didn't tip off any of the three-letter federal agencies that might be monitoring his brother's phone.

The cell phone lit up, and Jason slid between the detached garage and the cabin. Jason sent Noah a message once the phone found a tower with a signal.

```
It's your favorite PJ. Don't respond with
anything but a + or - sign in case Big
Brother is watching. I need Mo's code for
the rental. It's for a friend. Can you get
it in 10 minutes?
```

Jason stared at the screen, waiting for a response. He hoped Noah was still a night owl as the text he sent floated at the top of the screen. A minute later a plus sign appeared below it. He pumped his fist and moved closer to the front porch. Jason hoped Noah would respond quickly. Every minute his phone was out of the Faraday pouch, the risk of an electronic surveillance team flagging his location grew exponentially.

Come on, Noah. Don't leave me hanging out here like this.

After ten minutes, he considered returning the phone to the pouch that made his cell phone invisible to his pursuers, but then Jason heard a ping. It contained two four-digit codes, and Jason's lips curled into a smile for the first time in days. Noah came through without typing out names or locations, which was a welcome surprise for Jason.

The codes unlocked the door and disengaged the alarm, so Jason entered the cabin without incident. After a shower and a pot of cilantro lime flavored rice Jason found in the pantry, he moved to the couch. He didn't want to mess up any of the bedding that was ready for their next guests. A soft sofa in a warm house was much better than another night outside. Jason would have slept on the bathroom floor if that was all that was available. His eyes felt heavy, but Jason's mind drifted back to what Cruz said in the Flagstaff parking lot before he allowed sleep to overtake him.

He said Jason could have avoided all his problems if he'd just turned in the USB drive from the Titan sting. The crooked special agent also said that he'd never outsmart Donaldson. Jason was sure of Cruz and Donaldson's involvement the moment they lied under oath in court, but their motives were murky. Jason wondered if his arrest and conviction were because of the contents on the USB drives.

What were the puzzles on the USB drives hiding? Did they hold the key to their motive?

Jason thought more about Donaldson. If he was honest, Jason didn't think the senior special agent was all that sharp.

Could Donaldson really be the brains behind everything? What was his relationship to the man in the picture next to him on his outdated Facebook feed?

Perhaps underestimating the wily old DEA agent might be why he was on the run today.

Jason turned onto his side, rearranged the couch pillows under his head, and faced out the window. The silhouettes of the pine trees behind the pale moon in the night sky reminded him of Whispering Pines. He thought of how great it would feel to walk into his house and hold his wife.

Jason shot to his feet.

Did Donaldson and Cruz know the drive from the Titan sting was still in Whispering Pines?

They would surely return to retrieve it if they suspected it was in his house, and Shanna would be there. Jason's hands balled into fists, and his jaw clenched until it hurt. His wife was in danger, and Jason had to return home to protect her from two corrupt and desperate men.

CHAPTER 48

Whispering Pines, Arizona

A tear ran down Shanna's cheek as she held up two newborn sleepers in the family room, littered with boxes and gift bags from the late afternoon baby shower. Red, green, and blue fish imprints adorned the full-body pajamas.

Shanna knew they were bound to have a child, boy or girl, destined to be an outdoor enthusiast like their father. The sight of the pajamas reminded her of the long conversations with Jason in bed about how they wanted to raise their children. It was important for Jason to be involved with his kids, and Shanna loved him deeply for his commitment to family. Her husband, like all parents, had many dreams for their kids. One non-negotiable skill he would pass down was self-sufficiency. It was paramount for Jason to be self-sufficient, which was one reason he built his off-grid home and honed the skills to live off the land. He wanted the same for his children but didn't just want independence from the electrical grid or to save money on meat at the grocery store. Jason wanted his family to thrive physically, mentally, and financially if all the creature comforts we enjoy in the twenty-first century suddenly vanished. Shanna understood this sentiment and supported Jason in passing those skills to their future kids. She just needed her husband back to complete her family.

Shanna's mom, Nancy, noticed her tears and moved next to her on the couch to wipe them away.

"Are you okay?"

Shanna sniffed and nodded. "It's just hard to do this without Jason."

Jason's mom, Celeste, and Nancy thought a baby shower might bring a sense of normalcy to Shanna while Jason was out. It wasn't working, so her mother and mother-in-law took turns reassuring Shanna.

"Sorry, Honey. I thought a baby shower might help you take your mind off Jason and all the stress of him being gone, but I can see this only made it worse," Nancy said.

"Mama, I appreciate it. I really do, but it's just too hard right now. Can we open the rest of the stuff later?"

"Absolutely. Let's take a break and get something to eat."

Shanna, Nancy, and Celeste moved into the kitchen where Jason's brother Noah and father Phillip were grazing on a charcuterie spread. Shanna sat gingerly at the kitchen table and dipped dill pickles into hummus when the side door opened, and Kai arrived with a guest.

"Clay!" Noah shouted to the guest.

Clay Landry strutted through the door and waved to everyone. Shanna pushed her chair back and put both hands on the table to get up, but Clay stopped her. "Hold on, Mama. I'm coming to you."

Clay placed his hand on her shoulder and kissed Shanna on the cheek.

"How are you and the baby holding up?"

Shanna patted Clay's hand. "Fine, all things considered. The baby is sleeping less lately, but I'm better now with all of you here."

Noah sauntered to Clay, extended his hand, and the big Cajun pulled him in for a hug. "Sorry, buddy, you're in the hug zone now."

Everyone laughed for a temporary break in the tension.

"Are you hungry, Clay?"

"I'm hungrier than a tick on a teddy bear. Whatcha got?"

Everyone filled their plates with appetizers and ate around the family room. The mood became somber again, and everyone knew why, but nobody wanted to broach the delicate subject until Clay spoke.

"Anyone hear from Jason lately?"

All the heads in the room snapped toward Clay.

"Is that supposed to be some kind of joke? Of course, we haven't heard from him," Shanna snapped.

She noticed Kai, Noah, and Clay lowered their faces and wouldn't look at her. She turned to Kai. "What are you not telling me? Has Jason contacted you?"

Kai's eyes widened, and his mouth opened slightly as he spun in his seat to face Clay.

"I'm sorry," Clay started as he leaned closer to Shanna. "I suspected he may have contacted others, but it makes sense that he'd only contact Kai and me. He doesn't want to put any of you in a situation that may get you in trouble. He knows I don't give a shit."

"Is that why you asked for Clay's number a couple of weeks ago," Shanna asked Kai. He looked down again and did not answer.

Shanna's face and neck flushed red. "I can't believe you never told me he called or at least let me know he was okay."

She turned to her right to face Phillip, Celeste, and her mom. "Has Jason contacted any of you?"

"No," they replied in unison.

"Promise? I'll be angrier if I find out you are lying to me."

Nancy turned to Celeste and Phillip, and they nodded.

"Honey, we're sure. Jason hasn't contacted any of us."

"What about you, Noah? Has Jason contacted you?"

Noah licked his lips, "Um—"

Shanna slid off the sofa and shuffled to Noah sitting on a dining room chair he pulled into the family room. "When did he call? Is he okay?"

"I'm sorry, Shanna. I can't say. He's only trying to protect you and the rest of his family."

Shanna let out a gut-wrenching sob as her face crumpled and salty tears streamed down her cheeks. "You can't even tell me if he's okay?"

Noah leaned forward, put his elbows on his knees, and steepled his fingers. He looked at the floor for several seconds, exhaled, and looked up at Shanna. "Jason is fine, and he's in a safe place."

"How do you know he's still safe? Kai talked to him over a week ago."

"Jason texted me yesterday. He—"

Audible gasps filled the room. "What did he say?" Shanna asked. Her tears dried up faster than rain in the desert as concern replaced sadness.

"He's concerned that our phones are being monitored, so he didn't say much. I promise Jason is okay, but that's all I can tell you."

"Can you get in trouble for talking to him?" Celeste asked her son.

"I don't know, and I don't care. Jason is innocent, and I will help my brother out, no matter what." Noah said. His voice grew louder and more intense with each word.

Clay moved next to Shanna. "I know this is hard on everyone, especially a mama-to-be, but nobody on the planet cares more about his family than Jason, and few can avoid capture by a statewide manhunt like he has for the past two weeks. I know Jason, and I bet he's planning to fix this problem right now and arrive home in time to be by your side when you deliver your baby. He wouldn't want us fussing over him and getting at each other's throats right now, so we need to give him more time to make this right. Jason will come through. He always does."

Every head in the room bobbed up and down in agreement with Clay. Shanna leaned over and hugged him. Mid-embrace, Shanna groaned and pushed Clay away gently.

"Are you okay?" Nancy asked.

Shanna winced and cupped her abdomen with both hands as she leaned back on the sofa.

"I'm fine," Shanna lied.

I hope Jason gets here soon if he tries to come home. This baby is coming any day, and I can't do this without him.

Chapter 49

Phoenix, Arizona

The morning sun hadn't yet filled the office with light, so Deputy Marshal Miley worked under the soft hum of the fluorescent lights on the growing stack of files on her desk. She arrived early at the Phoenix District Office of the US Marshals to dig out of her growing mound of case files and wanted at least an hour without interruption to make progress. She didn't open her email, check her voicemail, or look at her phone until after she cleared three files from her stack.

At eight o'clock, Miley poured her second cup of coffee and strolled back to her cubicle with a fleeting sense of accomplishment. She tapped the keys on her phone to check her voicemail and listened. The first two messages were for individuals in other departments that Miley quickly deleted, but the last message caused her to sit up straight.

"Deputy Marshal Miley, this is Rick Blankenship with the FBI National Cyber Investigative Joint Task Force. I worked late into the night on that USB drive you overnighted me, and it took me a while, but I've finally figured it out."

There was such a long pause before Blankenship spoke again that Miley thought the message had ended, but his booming voice returned barely above a whisper.

"I think you stumbled onto something big. It's too complicated to share in a voicemail, so call me back as soon as possible."

The message ended, and Miley promptly called Blankenship back. Her call went straight to his voicemail. He was three hours ahead of Miley at FBI Headquarters in Washington, DC, and probably in staff meetings, so she topped off her coffee as other USMS employees arrived to start their day.

Stumbled onto something big? What did he find?

Whittaker passed her cubicle and wished Miley a good morning.

"Good morning," Miley replied. She pondered telling him about the voicemail but knew he'd have a hundred follow-up questions she couldn't answer. It would be best to gather all the facts from Blankenship and then share everything with Whittaker.

Five minutes after her last attempt, Miley redialed Blankenship and this time, left a message. "Call me back as soon as you get this. If you don't reach me on my office line, call me on my cell phone. I need to know what you found on that drive."

Miley hung up and waited. She wondered why Jason Mulder would go to such great lengths to prove his innocence. It did not seem like something a guilty person would do, but Miley knew little about the fugitive beyond what was in her file. Learning more about Jason Mulder could help better understand his motivations and actions.

Miley recalled the look on Whittaker's face when he told her to only verify if the USB drive was encrypted and if it was, turn it over to the FBI. Overall, Senior Deputy Marshal Whittaker was a good supervisor, but he did not like his authority to be questioned. The urge to learn more was too great, and Miley justified it could provide clues to his next moves, which accomplished their number one objective. Capture Jason Mulder.

Miley made several calls to her contacts within the DEA, and they directed her to Mulder's former boss, Supervisory Special Agent Holland. She punched in the first five digits of his office number when her phone rang, and Miley saw it was coming from Huntsville, Alabama, on her caller ID. The deputy marshal considered letting it go to her voicemail but answered the call.

"This is Deputy Marshal Miley."

"It's Blankenship. Do you have a few minutes?"

"I thought you were based at FBI Headquarters in DC."

"I am."

"Why does caller ID say Huntsville, Alabama?"

"I'm on the FBI joint task force for cyber investigations. It's kind of what we do."

Miley nodded but did not respond.

"Are you standing or sitting right now?" Blankenship asked.

"Standing. Why?"

"You may want to sit down for this."

Chapter 50

Twelve Miles West of Whispering Pines, Arizona

A golden glow pierced the darkness in the vacation home, stirring Jason awake. He rose from the sofa and repositioned one of the family room chairs toward the driveway to monitor anyone approaching the property while he packed for his journey. First, he cleaned his wound and applied a fresh bandage to his side. A brown scab resembling tree bark formed over the puncture, allowing Jason greater pain-free movement. He opened his backpack and pondered the essentials for his trip when a beam of light cut across the room like a sword.

Jason leaped from the chair and pressed himself against the wall beside the window. Headlights from the slow-moving vehicle lit up the gravel driveway, but Jason couldn't see the vehicle type from his angle. He scanned the room for a weapon and settled on a fireplace poker. Jason ducked below the window and moved to the other side, closer to the front door. With the fireplace poker in one hand, he opened the front door with the other and saw an old, rusty pickup truck stopped at the end of the driveway. Jason heard a soft thud a second later and watched the truck back out and drive away.

Jason couldn't believe how close he'd come to having a heart attack when the truck pulled into the drive. His nerves frayed after twelve days of living in fight-or-flight mode.

"Damn, paper boy."

He moved back to his chair to put on his socks. Jason stopped with the second sock halfway over his ankle, yanked it up, and rushed back to the front door. He opened it slowly and scanned the driveway that cut through the tall pines for signs of movement. Seeing none, he ran to the edge of the property and scooped up five newspapers rolled up in plastic sleeves. He remembered seeing a daily newspaper on the list of amenities that Morgan's parents had left on the counter for their short-term renters. Jason also recalled seeing coffee on the list and vowed to make a cup when he returned.

In the kitchen, Jason removed the Payson Roundup newspaper for October 12th and unfurled it on the table next to his cup of coffee. He hoped to find the latest information on the search for him and didn't even have to open past the first page. Below the fold, a full-color image of Deputy Marshall Whittaker behind a podium pointing at a gaggle of reporters sat above the headline: **Marshals Call in Reinforcements to Capture Former DEA Fugitive.**

Jason shook his head and let the paper fall back onto the table. He sipped his coffee and picked the newspaper back up. Despite the ominous news, Jason couldn't resist reading the article. The reporters' use of "*disgraced DEA agent* and *fearsome fugitive*" to describe Jason in the article made him cringe, but that wasn't his primary concern. Nearly two weeks after Jason slid over the Sunset Point Rest Area wall and vanished into the Arizona wilderness, the US Marshals were pulling out all the stops to capture him. A dozen additional marshals and aerial assets like helicopters and drones were on their way to Arizona to help apprehend their number one fugitive.

The chances of Jason slipping through the tightening noose were next to impossible. He'd already eluded the marshals longer than most fugitives, but Jason could sense they were closing in. The fight with Cruz, the stolen side-by-side, and especially the carjacking and assault of Whittaker put Jason dangerously close to losing his freedom. Jason already knew what Cruz and Donaldson would do if the US marshals captured him and put him on trial for his escape. They weren't above spinning a web of lies under oath, and Jason figured they were probably manufacturing more evidence against him right now. He imagined what Donaldson and Cruz might say.

"We found evidence of his involvement with a kingpin drug dealer on the USB drive in his home and caught him trying to plant a copy in our Flagstaff office."

Would the court believe them? Of course, they would. It was plausible for anyone to believe a man convicted of trafficking cocaine would try to frame the men who caught him because most judges, juries, and district attorneys don't expect federal agents to lie through their teeth.

Jason stood and paced from the kitchen to the family room. He leaned against the stone fireplace with one hand and ran his other hand through the stubble on his head. Despite the high probability he'd get caught sneaking home, all roads led to Whispering Pines. Protecting Shanna and their unborn baby was his highest priority, and his blood boiled at the thought of his pregnant wife fighting off two dirtbags like Cruz and Donaldson. Jason's best chance of clearing his name now was to retrieve the USB drive from the Titan sting and hope someone could decode the puzzle and find the evidence to prove someone else was behind the drugs in his truck.

Shaking his head, Jason recalled tossing the USB drive to Whittaker. He thought the deputy marshal might look at the drive and help him, but that assumption was born of desperation. Whittaker only wanted one thing.

To keep me behind bars.

Jason crept to the front window facing east toward Whispering Pines. The finish line was in sight, but Jason didn't know if crossing it would result in decades behind bars or a semi-normal life with his wife and new child after clearing his name. It didn't matter. He'd leave at dusk and let the chips fall where they may.

Chapter 51

As the sun dipped below the treetops west of the cabin and the rest of the world prepared for bed, Jason, like a nocturnal predator, stirred in preparation for his mission. He rested all morning, and after lunch, he prepared his gear for the nighttime trek through the forest to Whispering Pines.

He sat at a kitchen table, bathed in the light of a solitary bulb suspended over the sink, and slid the edge of his 4-inch knife against a sharpening stone. The rhythmic sound of metal meeting stone filled the air. His movements were deliberate, his hands steady as he expertly smoothed imperfections to optimize every inch of the blade for the job ahead. Old training missions and scrambling on Pave Hawk helicopters to save his military brothers in Afghanistan flashed through his mind. A welcome tinge of adrenaline percolated through his veins in anticipation of the night ahead.

The odds of success were low, so Jason had to counter with flawless planning and execution. Everything had to be spot on, from the timing, gear, and entry point to his property.

First, he focused on his attire. Jason donned a set of old camouflage ABUs he borrowed from Sergeant Bentley. The pants and sleeves were a bit short, but the dark greens and browns blended seamlessly with the surroundings, rendering him virtually invisible in the forest at night.

Satisfied with his appearance, Jason strapped on his ankle sheath, inserted his knife, and laced up the boots he'd worn since he jumped the wall at Sunset Point. He turned his attention to the contents of his backpack. Inside were an array of essential tools and equipment—a lock pick set, a compact flashlight, and a small roll of duct tape. Each item had its purpose, chosen to aid him in his carefully planned mission.

Now that his gear was ready, Jason returned to the kitchen and moved everything off the table. He placed the toaster in the middle, the coffee maker with its cord stretched across the entire east end of the table, and Jason spread out a stack of napkins along the west end. He used the kitchen appliances to create a military-style sand table for his Whispering Pines property. The toaster was his house, the coffee maker cord represented the East Verde River, and the napkins were the road in front of his property.

Jason stepped back and added a deck of cards in the front of the toaster, symbolizing the Gila County Sheriff's vehicle he assumed would watch the house from the driveway. He entered the walk-in pantry, returned with salt and pepper shakers, and placed them on the table. Jason stared at the table with his index finger on his lips and his thumb on his chin. After a minute of consideration, he moved the pepper to the northwest corner and the salt to the southwest corner to symbolize Cruz and Donaldson.

That's where I'd set up if I planned to ambush me.

He scanned the arrangement of appliances and seasonings until he bent over and removed his knife from his ankle sheath. Jason moved closer, jamming the knife into the wooden table near the pepper shaker.

"This is where I'll enter."

The stars shone bright in the sky, so it was time to depart. Jason went into the bathroom and looked in the mirror to verify he was ready. Something was missing, so he went to the wood-burning fireplace in the family room and grabbed a handful of charcoal. He crushed the charred wood into powder in his fist and transferred the charcoal to his face until only the whites of his eyes were visible.

He washed the charcoal from his hands, pulled on his gloves, and slid a camo beanie over his bald head. Jason passed a framed picture of Morgan's family on the wall near the front door. He turned and examined the parents leaning over two teenage girls with their arms around a preteen boy. Everyone was smiling in the photo, and it took Jason back a decade when his entire family still lived under one roof. It was the best of times, and Gaby and Josh were still alive. Jason wouldn't trade those memories for anything, and now he had to chisel his mark on the world. It was a last-minute reminder of what was at stake when he arrived in Whispering Pines.

The urge to call Shanna was so great that Jason removed the Faraday pouch and the burner phone. He wanted to tell her he was coming home to ease her mind, but if he was honest, he just wanted to hear her voice. Jason stared at the phone, convincing himself that a few seconds wouldn't hurt, and it would give him a spark for his long journey.

The screen blinked and lit up after Jason turned on the phone. His fingers hovered over the numbers as Jason considered if calling Shanna was worth the risk.

Ding.

A new text message appeared, and Jason felt bile explode in his gut. Nobody had this number, but—

Jason recognized the number as Noah's, and irritation replaced concern. His younger brother always wanted to be involved, but now was not the time. Jason considered returning the phone to the Faraday pouch but read the text first, and he nearly dropped the phone.

`Hurry. She's having contractions every 20 minutes. Baby M is coming.`

His mission to reach Whispering Pines by daybreak just grew more urgent. Drawing a deep breath, Jason steeled himself for the challenges ahead. He knew the dangers that awaited him, but he had to get home for Shanna.

Jason exited the front door, locked it, and stood on the front patio amid a cacophony of crickets singing to attract mates. The stars and waxing crescent moon in the clear sky cast enough light to see through the forest once his eyes fully adjusted.

Jason pulled his backpack straps tight and took the first step toward a fierce battle he knew was waiting for him in Whispering Pines. Soon, he'd be with his wife, Shanna, or his brother, Josh. Jason understood this would be his final mission.

Chapter 52

Interstate 10 on the Arizona Border with California

Sitting behind the wheel of an unmarked black SUV parked in a rest area five miles east of the state border, DEA Special Agent Holland watched cars and trucks rumble across the Interstate 10 bridge over the Colorado River on the Arizona border with California. He peered through binoculars at a yellow moving truck climbing from the irrigated fields along the river into the graphite-gray mountains of western Arizona. He glanced at his watch and radioed a second SUV waiting three spaces away.

"This should be them."

Holland's office had received a tip from the Los Angeles district DEA office that a suspicious vehicle passed through Palm Springs, California, toward Arizona. They didn't have the resources to stop the rented yellow box truck with two drivers, so they informed the Phoenix district office, and the Phoenix team notified the DEA office in Camp Verde. Holland rounded up three special agents and a K9 from the Camp Verde office, and they sped to the western border with California to intercept the truck and occupants.

"What intel do we have on the vehicle, cargo, and drivers?" Special Agent Watson asked.

"Not much. We know they rented the moving truck in Fullerton and picked up the cargo at the Port of Long Beach. They suspect both drivers are Chinese nationals, but that's all we know," Holland replied.

"Why didn't they stop them at the port?"

"That's something that makes this cargo suspicious. LA has an asset that's adamant this shipment is full of contraband, but the dogs didn't register a hit. They want us to take a second pass with a different dog."

"Got it," Watson replied from the back seat. He prepared Torpedo, the best K9 in the Phoenix district, behind the metal mesh divider for the mission ahead.

As they waited, Holland's mind reviewed the details of the simple operation. Force the target vehicle to a stop, detain the drivers, and get Torpedo inside to inspect the cargo.

The yellow moving truck with California license plates passed the rest area and continued east toward Phoenix.

"Let's go," Holland radioed the second SUV.

Holland merged onto the Interstate and stayed ten car lengths behind the truck until it exited the mountain pass into the open desert. This location reduced the risk of drug dealers running into the hills, where they'd be harder to apprehend. He sped up, pulled behind the truck, and engaged the flashing grille lights on the unmarked SUV.

The truck continued straight ahead for a minute, then suddenly swerved into the other lane twice as if the driver was unsure which of the two lanes was best, but the truck did not slow down.

"Is he going to run?" Watson asked.

"Have Torpedo ready when they stop. These guys seem nervous."

Holland flipped on the siren for several seconds, and the right turn signal on the truck flashed. The truck pulled over, drove slowly along the shoulder, and stopped. All four DEA special agents sprung from both SUVs with guns drawn. Holland, Watson, and Torpedo approached from the passenger side in the dead ditch grass while the two DEA special agents from the second SUV approached the driver's side along the busy freeway traffic.

The driver turned off the vehicle, and the engine ticked as it cooled on the balmy October afternoon. The cab was eerily still, and that concerned Holland.

Holland issued a warning before the truck separated the two teams on each side.

"Approach slowly and be on high alert."

As soon as the words left Holland's lips, the passenger jumped out of the cab and fired at them as he ran toward the open desert. Bullets whizzed past both special agents as they hit the pavement. After the gunman turned back toward the sea of creosote bushes and cacti, Watson stood and let Torpedo off the leash. He didn't have to give the seasoned K9 a command to charge full speed toward the fleeing man. When the passenger turned around and raised his gun toward the DEA agents, a snarling ninety-pound German Shepard greeted him less than ten inches from his face. Torpedo knocked the man backward and locked his jaw on the passenger's upper arm near his shoulder. The passenger dropped his gun and wailed in agony as Torpedo thrashed around, ripping his shirt and flesh open.

Holland arrived a half minute later and cuffed the passenger after Watson dragged Torpedo from the whimpering man. Watson picked up the passenger and helped him limp to the second SUV, where he joined the driver in the secure back seat. Both men were of Asian descent, and neither claimed to speak English, so Holland grabbed the bolt cutters from his vehicle and cut the padlock from the rear door. After a quick yank, the door slid up and revealed eight pallets with boxes stacked six feet high. Holland slipped on nitrile gloves, climbed up and inspected the brown boxes wrapped in clear cellophane. He tore off the plastic shrink wrap and opened a box. It was full of the same bottles he found while investigating the overdoses of the two high school girls in Black Canyon City.

Watson arrived while Holland examined the bottle.

"Get Torpedo up here and check out every inch of this truck."

Holland jumped down to the shoulder of the freeway with the bottle still in his hand. It had a white label with St. John's Wort written in black ink. The label looked generic, with no effort to make the bottle or label attractive for store shelves.

Five minutes later, Watson and Torpedo jumped off the back of the truck and joined Holland near their SUV.

"Anything?" Holland asked.

"No, nothing. I don't understand why they'd shoot at us if the vehicle is clean."

Holland rubbed his chin and nodded. "Something doesn't add up."

"What's in the bottle?" Watson asked.

"A supplement. It says St. John's Wort on the label."

"What the hell is St. John's Wort? I've never heard of it."

"I'm not sure either. The label doesn't say much. It looks like a first grader made the label."

"Open it up. I want to see what St. John's Wort looks like," Watson said.

Holland screwed off the cap and used his knife to break through the thickest safety seal he'd ever seen. Once the bottle was open, he shook the royal blue pills inside and pointed the opening to Watson so he could see the St. John's Wort.

Watson leaned over the bottle, and Torpedo started barking furiously, indicating a hit.

"What the hell?" Watson said.

Holland lowered the bottle to Torpedo, and he bumped it with his nose and sat, confirming narcotics were in the bottle. He looked up at the pallets and shuffled toward the back bumper of the truck, deep in thought.

"Holy shit. These guys may have sneaked narcotics past our dogs and port detection systems."

Holland repeated the process three more times with bottles from different pallets, and Torpedo responded the same way each time. He removed the fentanyl test kit from his SUV and dropped a blue pill into the liquid in the container. A minute later, it turned pink, confirming the pills contained the synthetic chemical responsible for over 100,000 deaths in the United States in the most recent twelve months.

The two DEA special agents in the second SUV drove the rental truck driver and passenger to the district office in Phoenix, where an agent who spoke Mandarin would question them. After questioning, they'd transfer the suspected drug traffickers to the county jail until their date with a judge.

Holland thought about the unique nature of the bottles during the three-hour drive back to Camp Verde. He'd never encountered a container filled with potent narcotics that a veteran drug detection canine wholly missed. It wasn't due to a lack of effort by the Narcos and their mules. Over his career, Holland witnessed every imaginable method to conceal drugs carried on themselves or in their vehicles. He's seen narcotics embedded in religious candles, inside tuna cans, layered inside a cast for a supposed broken leg, and inside body orifices more times than he'd care to remember. Others tried to confuse or distract the dogs by packing their goods with dog treats, wild animal urine, soiled diapers, vacuum-sealed bags of coffee, and one desperate mule even attempted to coat thousands of MDMA pills in curry.

False positives occurred occasionally for drug detection dogs, but the dogs rarely missed the scent of a target material they'd trained for years to identify. A drug dog's sense of smell was about 10,000 times more acute than a human. They had up to three hundred million olfactory receptors in their noses compared to a mere six million in humans. This allowed canines to smell things a million times better than people. Plus, dogs had different methods of breathing. A canine nostril contained separate openings for breathing in and out and operated independently to detect distinct smells from each nostril, as if dogs sniffed in stereo. This unique ability allowed dogs to smell individual components instead of just combining multiple items. When people walked into a kitchen with someone preparing fajitas, they would smell the goodness of the entire dish, while a dog's brain would break the scent up by meat, peppers, onions, and tortillas. This unique attribute allowed a drug-sniffing dog to detect a single MDMA pill in the back of a truck.

It was after six, and the Camp Verde office was empty when Holland entered to wrap up his day. He completed his report and responded to several emails before shutting down his computer. As he stood, he noticed his voicemail light blinking on his phone. He was interested to see if it was Naomi Dunn, the Phoenix Division SAC, so he listened to the message.

"Hi, this is Deputy Marshal Miley in the Phoenix District Office. I have some questions for you about Jason Mulder. I also have some questions about a USB drive that I'm hoping you can help shed some light on for us. Please call me back as soon as possible?"

Holland sat back down in his chair.

Are Jason Mulder's arrest . . . the USB drive . . . and the impermeable supplement bottles somehow all related?

CHAPTER 53

Flagstaff, Arizona

Special Agent Donaldson's eyes tracked the blond blur racing past, emitting high-pitched giggles. A barely perceptible grin flashed across his lips at the sound of his granddaughter enjoying the playground equipment in the park for the first time since she started treatment. The stress of the mastermind behind the fentanyl operation constantly barking at him from his prison cell to retrieve the USB drive, combined with Natalie's illness, wreaked havoc on his nerves. It was the first time his lips curled upward in weeks, but Donaldson's reprieve was short-lived.

Natalie's treatment for acute myeloid leukemia (AML) resumed in two days after a brief break. Her doctors would be raising the chemotherapy dose, and they warned Donaldson that the next treatment would steal his granddaughter's laughter and sunny demeanor. He knew chemotherapy was necessary for Natalie to get well, but the thought of Natalie not giving him the smiles that warmed his heart was soul-crushing. Donaldson also had to meet Cruz that evening to begin their stakeout of Jason Mulder's house in Whispering Pines.

He'd been thinking about this day since Mulder took the USB drive six months earlier. He wasn't eager to kill innocent people like Daniel Cruz was, but wouldn't hesitate to take a life when the time came. His life and Natalie's treatment depended on him returning the USB drives. The funding he'd received so far for her treatment would dry up and disappear if he failed to deliver. They might even kill him, leaving Natalie with only her deadbeat dad, and the thought of that was unbearable for Donaldson to consider. The stakes to find and retrieve the USB drive were astronomically high. No person or thing could get in his way of succeeding.

Thirty minutes at the park was all the spunky six-year-old could handle, so Donaldson picked up her favorite fast food and drove her home. His son stood on the crumbled concrete patio with his arms crossed over his skeletal chest when Natalie pulled up with her grandpa, but Donaldson didn't even acknowledge the man.

"Natalie, today is Thursday, so make sure your dipshit dad takes you to treatment again next Tuesday. That's in four days."

"Grandpa, that's not nice to say about my daddy," Natalie said.

"I know, but it's important that you go back to treatment. I know it's hard, and you always feel sick, but that's how you'll get better. Call me if he forgets or is sleeping when it's time to go, and I'll take you."

Natalie nodded.

"Do you remember how to find my number on the phone I gave you to call me?" Donaldson already knew the answer. He'd seen his granddaughter do things with his smartphone that he still couldn't figure out.

"Yep. I'll just tell Siri to call Grandpa."

"I guess that will work."

Donaldson helped Natalie out of his SUV and handed her the brown food bag. He kissed her forehead and watched her bounce up the sidewalk and disappear into the dilapidated house. He stared at the closed door for several seconds until he realized he was late for his meeting and sped away.

Cruz sat at Donaldson's kitchen table wiping down the slide of his disassembled Glock when his partner pushed through his front door. The junior DEA agent wore black tactical pants with a tactical vest over a black, tight T-shirt, accentuating his bulging biceps. Donaldson stopped and tapped Cruz on the back of his vest.

"Are you expecting more than one person tonight?" Donaldson asked.

"What?"

"Armor for Jason Mulder?"

Cruz returned the slide to his pistol and pulled it back and forth several times before returning it to his holster. "I'm not taking any chances, and neither should you. Are you going like that? We need to leave soon."

"No. I still need to change. It will only take a few minutes."

Donaldson mirrored Cruz's attire when he returned to his kitchen. He leaned against the counter and crossed his arms.

"Are we clear on the plan for tonight?"

"Um, I think so. We take Mulder out and find the USB drive in the house," Cruz replied.

Donaldson sighed. "No, that's not the plan. We need to retrieve the USB drive, and Mulder will help us find it. We can't kill him until we have the drive, so put all those hours in the gym to good use and make sure he cooperates."

"What if he doesn't cooperate?"

"Make sure he does."

Cruz nodded. "What about the wife? Should we kill her to make sure Mulder knows we're serious?"

Donaldson moved away from the counter and turned toward Cruz. His pale skin flushed red, and he pointed his finger into Cruz's hulking chest.

"Why do you get such a hard-on hurting women? Unless she gets in the way, we don't have to do anything to her. She's pregnant, so focus on recovering the drive. That's why we're doing all this."

Cruz pushed the finger in his chest away and leaned toward Donaldson. "I don't give a shit if she's Mother Teresa. Don't get soft on me, old man. I'm prepared to do whatever it takes to return with the USB drive. Are you?"

Donaldson leaned forward until his nose was six inches from Cruz's face. "I'm not letting anything happen to Natalie. I need this drive more than you'd ever understand, so you bet your ass that I'm willing to do whatever it takes to get that drive."

Their eyes remained locked until Donaldson broke his gaze and stepped away. Cruz was essential to accomplish their mission, but sometimes, Donaldson wanted to put a bullet between the eyes of the young punk pumped full of steroids. He'd tolerate him one last time to get the drive, but this was the final straw. He'd cut Cruz loose after this.

Donaldson snagged his keys from the counter. "Grab the infrared camera and let's go."

Two hours later, Donaldson and Cruz parked behind a rusty Chevy sedan a quarter mile from the Mulder residence.

"Who's that? Cruz asked.

"Those are the extra guys I told you I would bring in for this mission."

"Are they DEA? Local law enforcement?"

"No, they're two guys from the Show Low sting. The coke we planted on Mulder kept them out of jail, so now they owe me."

"The junkies? How are they supposed to help us?" Cruz asked. His hands waved wildly in the air with each syllable.

"We can't cover three-hundred and sixty degrees by ourselves. I'll have them take the east side of the property by the river since Mulder will probably come from the west."

Cruz chuckled. "Can they shoot? Do they even know the plan?"

Donaldson turned to face Cruz. "I told them the same thing I told you. If you see Mulder, make some noise so we all know he's arrived, and then we'll have numbers. Don't just start shooting like it's the OK Corral. We need him to find the USB drive."

"You think they can do it? I mean, engage Mulder without getting killed? Or worse, get us killed?" Cruz asked. He looked as if he put a lot of thought into the question.

"Unless something has changed, Mulder has no firearms, and they have their weapons and street smarts. I'm sure Wolverine and Joker can handle an unarmed Mulder."

"Wolverine and Joker? You've got to be shitting me. My life depends on two crackheads named after comic book superheroes?" Cruz groaned.

Donaldson tilted his head toward Cruz but did not respond.

"I'll take the FLIR camera to the southwest corner, and you take the northwest corner of the property. I'll send Wolverine and Joker to the other two corners. Get your head into the game and let's go."

Donaldson slithered past Jason's only neighbor under the veil of darkness, and a hundred yards later, he stopped at a gravel driveway. The one-story home Donaldson had visited almost two weeks earlier was hard to see at night from the lightly traveled Whispering Pines Road. A light illuminating a rectangular front window was all Donaldson saw through the dense trees. It was the right house, so the DEA special agent took a dozen steps into the woods and moved to his perch in the southwest corner. He sat down on the cool earth covered in a carpet of pine needles and turned toward the Mulder residence. His eyes adjusted to the darkness, and the outline of the house and back patio came into focus. Slits of moonlight penetrated the dense canopy and fluttered like dancing ghosts on the black metal roof.

A snapping branch echoed in the stillness of the night. Then, a faint cough confirmed one of the comic book idiots was moving into the position on the eastern edge of the property.

Donaldson panned the forward-looking infrared camera, or FLIR, into the woods to the west. Knowing when Mulder would show up was impossible to predict, but Donaldson was confident the Boy Scout would return for his pregnant wife. The fugitive could return in one day or twenty. It didn't matter to Donaldson. He needed Mulder and the USB drive to receive his remaining payments, so he was prepared to wait in the woods every night until it happened. Natalie's life depended on it, and he wouldn't let anyone get in the way of the treatments she desperately needed.

Donaldson rested his head against a tree and watched the woods for Jason Mulder like a spider waiting for prey to wander into its web.

Chapter 54

Near Whispering Pines, Arizona

Jason stepped over a rocky trench and climbed through the dimly lit forest when he heard something dart through the undergrowth and pause near him. He whipped around to identify what had made the noise but found nothing. It was still too dark to spot whatever caused the disturbance. Slowing his breathing, Jason listened for more movement when the forest erupted with a piercing sound that sent chills up his arms. He'd heard the sound before and knew it was a rabbit in distress. It bolted away from Jason, and a second sound with louder, heavier steps followed close behind. He couldn't see through the foliage, but it made too much noise to be a bobcat, so Jason assumed it was a coyote. The desperation of the prey trying to escape certain death and the determination of the predator to kill and eat or succumb to starvation was palpable in the air. It reminded him of his current situation.

Silence briefly followed the struggling sounds that ended fifty yards away, and seconds later, the unmistakable yip and howl from a successful coyote hunt filled the forest. The hair on the back of Jason's neck stood up, but not because he was concerned about a coyote attack. It was an ominous sign for his mission.

I'm getting close. Time for a quick break.

Jason realized how tense he'd been trekking throughout the night, and the constant tension in his shoulders and back was draining. He slid off the backpack, removed his sweatshirt, and let the crisp mountain air cool his skin. Jason sat on a granite slab several yards from a seasonal wash and opened his backpack. His energy spiked when the cool water from his canteen hit his lips, but he remained seated. Jason was minutes from his home, with the sunrise still hours away. He had to be smart and cautious about approaching his property and home. There was little doubt someone was staking out the area, waiting for Jason to come for his pregnant wife.

Jason returned everything to his pack and marched up the last hill. He could see the clearing for the dead-end road he used to access his property, so Jason turned north. For a moment, he considered skirting around his property and approaching from the east. Jason doubted anyone watching the house would suspect he'd come from the river in his backyard, so that was a safer alternative, but he looked past the treetops at the streaks of light blue on the eastern horizon. Jason had to approach the house under the cover of darkness, and the east side approach would take too long. Instead, he maneuvered quietly past his property to enter from the northwest.

Once in the best position to cross the road onto his land, Jason knelt and faced his house. He looked, listened, and smelled for signs of a person or people waiting for his arrival. After twenty minutes of careful observation, Jason detected no signs that the house was under direct surveillance. Instead of feeling a sense of relief, concern slammed his gut. He might have had a stroke of luck and arrived between shifts among the Gila County Sherriff's deputies or US marshals, but Jason didn't believe in luck. It was too quiet and easy to enter his property, which didn't bode well for Jason. He knew the calm before a mission was the deep inhale, and the exhale brought the chaos and calamity of battle.

Despite the sense that he was being lured into a trap, Jason knew he still had to advance. He had to get inside his home to protect Shanna and retrieve the USB drive. Jason wouldn't leave until he accomplished both.

Jason sprinted across the road and onto his property. He slid under a cluster of juniper trees and pushed through the soft pine needles until his house appeared. The light bulb over the sink shone a light onto the bushes, gently swaying in the breeze outside the window. Jason lifted his nose and detected the faint smell of smoke. The fire in the wood-burning stove was out, and Jason imagined the cool air inside. This was the time of the night when Shanna scooted next to Jason and used his body heat to warm her. Jason thought about holding his wife again. She was only forty yards away, and the desire to see her drew him like a moth to a lamp. Jason sprang from his cover and scampered across a clear expanse toward his house. Halfway to his destination at the rear of his house, Jason knew he'd rushed his approach.

"I knew you'd come back."

Instinctively, Jason dropped to the ground and pressed his body against the rocky earth. The voice sounded familiar, but Jason couldn't immediately place it, with hundreds of options assaulting his brain at once. Jason looked up, and an enormous figure stepped into the moonlight from the shadow alongside the house. It was Special Agent Cruz with his Glock pointed at his face.

"I don't want to shoot you, but I won't hesitate if you try any funny business. Stand up, slowly slide off the backpack, and keep your hands where I can see them," Cruz said coolly.

Jason searched for a place to roll out of the way before Cruz could pull the trigger, but he was out in the open with no options for cover.

"Do it!" Cruz barked. The agitation was evident in his voice.

Jason moved to his feet, and a soft thud followed as Jason had no choice but to comply and drop his gear. He took a step toward Cruz with his hands held at his chest. The barrel of the 9MM pistol was only five or six feet from Jason. He was proficient with Krav Maga countermeasures to disarm a person with a handgun, but he had to get close enough to the Glock to grab it in one lightning-quick motion.

Cruz took a step back. "I know what you're doing, and if you take one more step, your wife will be a widow."

Jason stared at Cruz. He couldn't see his eyes in the darkness, but the body language of the crooked agent signaled he would pull the trigger, so Jason remained in place.

"What's going to happen now? Are you going to call the marshals?"

Cruz chuckled. "Nope. We're going inside, and you'll give me all the USB drives in your house. If not, your family can save money on a joint funeral for you and your wife."

"Leave her out of this. I'll get you what you want."

The grin vanished from Cruz's face. "I know you will. Let's go."

Cruz motioned for Jason to move with his gun, so Jason started toward the back door on the patio. Jason ambled through Shanna's vegetable garden and the uncut patch of grass behind the house. He turned his head as he walked and saw Cruz looking over his right and left shoulder as if he was expecting someone else to be there.

Donaldson must be around here somewhere.

"I better not catch you turning around again, Mulder. I know you think I won't shoot you because we both received a paycheck from the DEA this year, but if you knew how much willpower it takes not to kill you right now, you wouldn't test me."

Once Jason reached the top step of the deck, he was out of time. He couldn't allow Cruz to enter the house with Shanna inside.

"It's a good thing that you brought a weapon with you this time after I kicked your ass in Flagstaff. Smart move."

"What?" Cruz shouted. "You must be high."

"I had you beat until you got that lucky punch in."

Cruz stopped on the bottom step. "Lucky punch? I literally knocked you out. Lucky for you that you ran away before I returned, or we wouldn't be having this conversation right now."

Jason's plan to challenge Cruz's mammoth ego to distract him seemed to work. He also realized the endgame if he presented Cruz with the USB drive—he would end up dead. Taking two more steps forward, Jason grabbed a patio chair and hurled it toward Cruz when he reached the top step. The DEA special agent blocked it with his left arm, but it knocked the gun to the wood planks on the patio. The pistol came to rest on the edge of the deck. Jason could see Cruz better now in the twilight, and they locked eyes for a beat and froze. Although it was only a split second, it felt like a minute. Cruz broke eye contact and took the first step toward the weapon, so Jason went for the crooked special agent. He tried to tackle the lumbering giant, but Cruz shed Jason like an NFL running back. As Jason plummeted toward the wood deck, he reached out and snagged Cruz's foot as he bent down to secure the Glock. Cruz fell face first and knocked the gun off the porch. They froze at the sound of metal hitting the gravel below the deck.

Cruz leaped to his feet first. "It looks like we get round two from Flagstaff."

Jason rose and moved into his defensive stance.

The crown of the sun rose above the distant hills, and slits of light littered the back patio as the men sized each other up. Jason sensed Cruz was calmer this time and needed to knock the big man off his game. Instead of jabs, Jason hoped to loosen him up with taunts that would impress any teenager.

"I'm surprised you came here by yourself. I didn't think Donaldson let his lapdog do anything without him."

Cruz feigned a laugh, but Mulder could tell the verbal jab had landed.

"Laugh it up, Mulder. When the rest of them show up, you'll regret all this shit-talking."

He turned and looked toward the tree line again, and his brow furrowed over his pinched nose. Jason recognized the opportunity and lunged to tackle Cruz. He knew Cruz could box and hoped he'd be less skilled at grappling. Once Jason's arms were around his waist, he drove the muscular man backward, but he did not fall to the ground as Jason intended. Instead, Cruz grabbed Jason as they crossed the deck, crashed through the railing, and dropped three feet to the ground in an intertwined heap.

Jason hit the ground hard on his injured side, and unbearable pain radiated throughout his body. Once he caught his breath, Jason tried to get up but failed. Cruz popped to his feet and kicked Jason in his injured side repeatedly until Jason curled up in a ball to prevent further kicks.

Cruz spit and leaned over Jason. "You ain't talking much shit about me now, are you?"

Jason tried to uncurl himself, but the shooting pain up his legs and through his back made it impossible. He turned his head to find Cruz circling him like a shark until he grabbed a splintered piece of the broken railing about the length of a baseball bat. He hoisted it high and cocked it back like an oversized spring, ready to release with maximum impact.

The fugitive was just one swing away from death by blunt force trauma. Jason's mind was flooded with questions as the wood railing in Cruz's grip edged forward in slow motion.

Would the world ever know the truth? Will Shanna raise our child alone? Is this how my life will end?

Chapter 55

Jason watched the menacing shadow of Cruz drift over him, lying among the timbers of the busted patio railing. Cruz looked like an executioner ready to bring his sword down onto the neck of the condemned. He rotated his body back and forth, looking for the optimal strike zone. Jason took advantage of the brief delay and raised his left hand to block the imminent blow while his right hand retrieved the knife from his ankle holster. The crooked DEA agent paused and brought the broken railing down with all his might. Jason found the strength to roll to his right side, so the wooden weapon missed him by six inches. Cruz must have felt his armor was responsible for the near miss, so he removed it and rolled his neck. He retrieved the wooden weapon and immediately launched the second blow. Jason ignored the pain and turned his body onto his injured side as the makeshift bludgeon smashed the earth millimeters behind his back.

The impact shook the ground beneath Jason. He couldn't give Cruz a third chance. Jason sprang to his feet as Cruz returned the wooden weapon above his head. In one fluid motion, Jason lunged forward with his knife and slashed across Cruz's throat before he could bring down another blow. Jason felt no resistance from bone or muscle as the razor-sharp blade cut deep into the flesh of his neck. Cruz hesitated for a moment, staring blankly at Jason before dropping the lumber and moving his hands to his throat. His eyes widened as blood poured from his neck, and he pressed harder to dam up the crimson flood cascading down his neck and chest.

Jason backed away from the bleeding behemoth, but Cruz matched him step for step and moved toward him like a person choking on a chicken bone. One hand let go of his neck, and Cruz snagged Jason by the collar and pulled him closer. Jason heard the gurgling in his throat and felt his hot breath against his cheek.

"I'm. I'm going to kill you," Cruz stammered with each breathy word. "And then I'm going to go inside and fu—"

Cruz wouldn't complete his last threat before Jason drove his knife deep into his heart. He pushed with both hands until Cruz went limp and dropped dead with the knife handle protruding from his chest.

Jason backed away from the corpse and watched life exit Cruz's body. Confident his attacker was deceased, Jason wiped the sweat off his forehead with his arm and tugged the black tactical glove off his left hand, which quivered uncontrollably in the morning sun. Vapor trailed upwards from his warm skin in the brisk morning air.

The surrounding forest remained silent as Jason scanned for new threats. He inhaled deeply and let it out slowly to catch his breath, but it didn't help. The blast of adrenaline coursed through his veins like thick motor oil. He couldn't switch off fight mode. Two weeks on the run drained all the flight out of him, and now Jason was prepared to do one thing - find everyone that framed him and destroy them.

He knew Donaldson and potentially others were waiting nearby to pounce on him when the time was right. Jason turned slowly and examined the woods surrounding his property. The black matte Glock 17 caught Jason's attention on the pale gray granite near Cruz's body. Jason pulled his knife from the deceased DEA agent's chest and retrieved the pistol. He popped the magazine and confirmed it had one round in the chamber and sixteen ready to go in the magazine. Enough to hunt down Donaldson and any of his cronies.

Jason saw Cruz look toward the East Verde River several times as they moved toward the back deck. He scanned the tree line, forming a horseshoe shape around his backyard. Donaldson was out there somewhere, but Jason was yards away from Shanna and couldn't wait any longer to see her. He hopped onto the patio and crept to the backdoor. Jason caught a glimpse of his own faint smile reflected in the door glass just before he turned the handle. It was locked. He pressed his face against the glass but saw no movement. Jason raised his hand to knock when he heard a high-pitched yelp.

"Shanna?"

Jason shuffled to the window on his right to get a better look into the family room, but two rounds struck his house before he reached it. He dove to the deck and heard the report of a pistol coming from the eastern edge of his property.

He couldn't risk going inside the house and leading the people shooting at him to his pregnant wife, so Jason low crawled into the tree line near his home. Jason inched his way back through the dark woods under the twilight until he reached the riverbank on the east end of his property.

The river was low, but the sound of water lapping over round boulders made listening for movement difficult. Jason waited near the bank for several minutes and jumped across the narrow river to get a new vantage point. Two more shots whizzed past his head when his boot hit the soft bank on the other side. Jason dove for cover and turned simultaneously to see a lanky man with long, dirty blond hair dressed in camouflage pants and a brown shirt lower his pistol and dart into the woods. The man ran south on the west side of the narrow river, so Jason took off along the east side. Jason located the man fifty yards ahead as he pushed through the dense underbrush. Once Jason was thirty yards away, he considered firing but waited until he had a higher probability shot.

The fleeing man looked over his shoulder, his eyes wide with fear as he noticed Jason gaining ground behind him. He veered away from the river, and Jason lost sight of him until he saw two muzzle flashes behind the foliage, and the west bank erupted in gunfire. Jason found cover behind a cottonwood tree wide enough to protect three people. The gunshots arrived with no coordination or discipline. Law enforcement would fire and move while covering each other. These shooters fired indiscriminately at anything that moved. Two minutes and forty rounds later, the firing stopped.

"Why did you shoot at him by the house? You can't hit someone that far away with a pistol," a man shouted.

"They said not to let him go inside until they gave us the signal. He looked like he was going inside."

"Well, now you brought him to us. You better not miss this time."

Jason knew he wasn't dealing with professionals, so he backtracked twenty yards and crossed over to the western bank. The densest vegetation grew near the water, and the sun hadn't risen high enough to illuminate the river, so Jason slipped across the body of water undetected in his black attire. More shots rang out toward his previous location, allowing Jason to pinpoint both shooters' locations. The tall blond guy was closest to the bank, while a short but stout Black man was twenty yards behind him. The shooting stopped, and Jason heard the lapping sounds from the river again.

"Hey, Joker. I think we got him," the blond man said with apprehension.

"I don't know, man. Don't take your eye off that tree."

"I'm pretty sure we got him. Nothing could survive that."

"Let's just keep watch over by the tree."

A minute later, Blondie was ready to leave. "I think we should go back to the house and find the DEA guys. Let them check over by the tree to make sure he's dead."

"I haven't heard a call to head back to the house yet. Have you?" Blondie asked.

"I don't think so."

Jason inched closer while the two debated their next move. He crawled through the moist soil littered with thorny thickets until he was thirty feet from the blond shooter. Jason did a stealthy push-up and saw a fallen tree obstructing his shot of Blondie lying in the prone position. He couldn't risk crawling any closer, or the blond guy might hear him, so Jason had to draw the man out.

He felt around the soil until he found a smooth rock that fit into the palm of his hand. Jason waited until the two men spoke again and tossed the stone to the other side of the river, near where he had previously hunkered down behind a tree. As expected, both men fired dozens of rounds toward the landing spot of the stone. The blond shooter rose to his knees to adjust his aim. Jason grinned in satisfaction and sprang to his feet. Blondie's eyes widened in horror as he spun to face Jason, giving the reserve PJ a perfect target. Jason aimed at Blondie's forehead and winked at the drug dealer as three bullets exploded from the barrel, ripping through the air with a thunderous crack.

All three slugs connected with Blondie's face like Jason rolled a three in dice, covering the greenery behind him in bloody brain matter. The other shooter saw his partner's fate, and instead of turning his weapon on Jason, he bolted from his fallen comrade. Jason charged through the narrow stand of trees and found the other shooter sprinting toward his house. He was already thirty yards ahead and faster than Jason, so catching him wasn't an option.

Jason tightened his gloves with his teeth and raised the Glock 17 toward the running man. During PJ training, he'd hit targets fifty yards away with his SIG Sauer P226 pistol, but they were stationary. Jason wished he had his HK rifle from the safe inside his house, but he had less than two seconds to shoot the man before he was out of range and potentially escaped into the house with Shanna inside.

He aimed the metal sights of the Glock high at the fleeing man fifty yards away, putting distance between himself and Jason with each stride. Jason squeezed the trigger over and over until the slide locked. The man fell forward and slid headfirst, like a baseball player, into the rough ground feet from the back patio.

Jason jogged toward the man and saw him lying on his back with four-quarter-sized blood stains growing larger on his chest and stomach. The slugs dropped several inches from where he aimed, so Jason was grateful he fired everything he had in the magazine. The man's eyes were open, and he was taking slow, jerky breaths. Jason stood over him and watched his lips move, but no sound came out.

"Where's Donaldson?"

"Ambulance," the man sputtered.

"I'll call an ambulance as soon as you tell me where I can find Donaldson."

The man licked his lips. "He said to meet inside the house. Please call—"

Jason never heard another word from the dying man. He moved toward the house with one goal.

Find Donaldson and kill him.

Chapter 56

Darkness enveloped Jason as he dropped through the basement window and steadied himself on the concrete floor. He let his eyes adjust to the unfinished basement to locate the northeast corner below his bedroom. Jason had the foresight to build a clothes chute in his bedroom closet, and now he'd use it to climb up to the main floor undetected. Once the outline of the northeast corner came into view, he moved toward the chute. Jason climbed on top of the washing machine and heard voices coming through the floorboards when his head neared the ceiling. He stopped and listened. Jason detected movement through the floor near his patio entrance, followed by Donaldson's growl and Shanna's pleading voice. An image of Donaldson holding his pregnant wife hostage flooded his mind, heating his blood to a boil. Jason sprung from the washing machine, grabbed onto the edge of the chute, and pulled himself inside. His legs dangled as he wiggled his way into the tight opening. Once inside, he used his elbows and boots to shimmy up the chute until he emerged in the walk-in closet in his bedroom.

Donaldson's voice stirred more resolve in Jason's gut as his boots hit the carpet inside his closet. The bedroom wall was the only thing separating him from killing the corrupt DEA special agent.

"Shut up, and you won't get hurt. If your husband cooperates, you'll both walk out of here alive."

Jason couldn't tell if he was holding a gun or knife to Shanna but heard familiar sniffing sounds. He wanted to charge into the family room and shoot Donaldson dead on the spot, but he had used all the ammo in the Glock. Shanna had Jason lock up all his weapons in a gun safe in the family room, including his SIG Sauer P226, which he used to keep on his nightstand. He'd get something secure for his bedside after the baby was born, but for now, he'd have to confront Donaldson with his knife. Jason tiptoed out of the closet, pressed himself against the wall, and peered out his bedroom door.

He saw Donaldson standing beside Shanna, focused on the patio door. Shanna's shoulders slumped, and Jason could tell she was breathing faster than normal. She might be in full labor now. He knew Donaldson was waiting for him to show up, so Jason focused on the older DEA agent's hands to see the weapon he held on Shanna.

It took two minutes, but Donaldson finally raised his right hand toward the patio door. A pistol was on full display to Jason.

"I don't think your husband is coming. That was a lot of gunshots out there, so you'll have to help us find the drive if he doesn't show up."

Jason saw Shanna turn toward Donaldson and sniff. She wiped a tear from her cheek and replied, barely above a whisper. "He'll show up, and you'll pay for what you're doing to me."

"Good girl," Jason whispered.

Donaldson laughed. "You still don't get it. The only thing Jason will do is help me get paid, or he will eat a bullet." He raised his finger to push the hair out of Shanna's eye, and she smacked his hand away.

"Keep your hands off me!"

Jason couldn't listen anymore. He was glad he didn't have a weapon because he wanted to kill Donaldson with his bare hands. Jason wanted to feel Donaldson's Adam's apple attempt to bob up and down with his hands wrapped around his throat like a python. He wanted to see the fear in Donaldson's eyes as life left his body.

I have to help Shanna now.

Jason burst out of the bedroom, and six paces later, he reached a striking distance from Shanna's kidnapper, but Donaldson reacted before Jason could pounce on him. He pulled Shanna to his side with his left arm and pressed the pistol toward her head with his right hand.

"Take one more step, Mulder, and your wife's brains will be the latest artwork on your wall."

Jason stopped and raised his hands. "Don't hurt her. It's me you want, so let her go. After she's safe, I'll do whatever you want."

"You're in no position to negotiate. It's simple. You'll help me with everything I ask, and if you do, I may let you both live. If you get cute, then you'll die."

Donaldson squinted at Jason and frowned. "Where's the USB drive you stole from the sting in Phoenix?"

"I don't have it," Jason lied. "I gave it to the US Marshals."

"You what?" Donaldson hissed. The end of the barrel swung from Shanna to Jason, so he raised his hands higher but didn't move.

"You idiot! That drive was your only ticket to get out of here alive!"

While Donaldson ranted and threatened Jason, he locked eyes with Shanna. They communicated without saying a word, as they'd done many times before. She lowered her eyes toward Donaldson's feet, and Jason shook his head. Jason inched imperceptibly closer to Donaldson as spittle splattered on Shanna, Jason, and the floor during his rage-fueled rant. Jason heard sirens and knew the police were close, so he offered Donaldson something to buy him time.

"I have the USB drive I stole from Cruz's desk."

The new revelation caused Donaldson to pause. "Where is it?"

Jason saw Shanna wince and clench her jaw at the labor pains out of the corner of his eye. "It's still in my pocket."

Donaldson looked warily at Jason and shook his gun at him. "Give it to me now, and don't try anything you'll regret. I'm losing my patience with you."

"Release her first."

"Give it to me now!" Donaldson roared.

The barrel shook even more than Donaldson, and Jason knew he couldn't wait for the police to arrive. He expected to see a muzzle flash and feel the punch of the 9MM slug any moment. Jason shifted his attention to Shanna and hoped she wasn't in the middle of another contraction. He didn't want to involve his wife and baby in extremely dangerous situations, but they were out of time and options. Their eyes met for a beat, and Jason gave her a slight nod. The corner of her lips twitched, confirming she understood. It was like two clicks on the radio in the field.

"You have three seconds, Mulder. One, two—"

Shanna clenched her fist and thrust it back into Donaldson's groin with the force of an angry mule kick. He lost his hold on Shanna as she held her stomach and crumpled to the ground. Donaldson bent at the waist in pain and defensively raised his left arm to protect against a possible second assault. Jason lunged forward as Shanna crawled away, gripping Donaldson's gun-wielding arm with his left hand. He pushed Donaldson backward and pounded his stomach and head with rapid-fire knee strikes and head butts until the weapon dropped to the floor. Jason continued to deliver blows until Donaldson was nothing more than a bleeding heap sprawled across the floor.

Jason stepped over Donaldson and picked up his Glock 17 pistol. He took a step back and pointed it at Donaldson's chest.

"Give me one good reason I shouldn't kill you like I killed Cruz and those other thugs?"

The whites of Donaldson's eyes appeared through the blood streaming across his face. He made a feeble attempt to raise his hands while lying on his back.

"Don't shoot. I didn't want to do this. My granddaughter is sick, so I had to do it for her. The money is for her chemo treatments. It wasn't anything personal against you. I swear."

Jason's brow furrowed, and he tilted his head. "Are you saying you framed me for money?"

Bubbles of blood came out of his mouth when he tried to respond, so Donaldson simply nodded. Jason snagged a dish towel from the counter a step away and tossed it to him. He let Donaldson wipe off the blood from his face.

"Who paid you? Who's behind all this?" Jason roared. The pain of the last six months and the disruption of his life came crashing back to Jason like waves from a tropical storm. He moved the pistol within inches of Donaldson's face.

Shanna stepped forward. "Don't do it, Jason. Don't stoop to their level."

Jason ignored her and pressed the barrel of Donaldson's pistol into his forehead. "Who paid you?"

Donaldson smacked his lips. "You know him."

"Who? I will not ask you a—"

The door burst open before Jason could finish. Four Gila County deputies had their guns drawn and pointed at Jason.

"Drop the weapon and put your hands up!" the closest deputy shouted.

Jason didn't even look in their direction. His neck pulsed and twitched, with his eyes locked on Donaldson's sleepy gaze.

"Jason, please do what they say," Shanna pleaded.

Jason moved his index finger inside the trigger guard. He swallowed hard and never took his gaze off Donaldson.

"You put my family through hell!"

"Drop the weapon!" a deputy shouted again.

"Jason, please! I don't want to lose you!"

Jason turned to Shanna, stood up straight, tossed the pistol to the side, and moved to his wife. He cupped her face with his hands and gave her a gentle hug. "Are you okay?"

Shanna buried her face in his chest.

A deputy pulled Jason's hands behind his back and cuffed him when Whittaker arrived with two deputy marshals.

"We'll take it from here, boys. Thank you!"

The US marshals each secured one of Jason's arms while Shanna sat down in a chair and started panting.

"What's wrong?" Jason asked.

She tried to speak but responded by holding up her index finger. A few seconds later, she answered. "The contractions are getting closer. The baby's coming."

The marshals pushed Jason toward the door, but he resisted. "You've got to get her to the hospital. She's thirty-nine weeks, and all this stress put her in labor."

Whittaker turned to the Gila County deputies. "Can you get her to the nearest hospital?"

The deputies looked at each other, and then one of them spoke. "Yeah, we can get her to Payson Medical Center. It's twenty minutes away if we hurry."

"I'm going with her," Jason chirped.

Whittaker moved in front of Jason. "You're a fugitive of the law, in case you forgot. I'm not a midwife; I'm a US marshal, and I'm taking you in."

Jason used his head to point toward Donaldson on the floor, leaning against the wall with his hands cuffed behind him. "They framed me, and he'll admit it. Ask him."

Shanna moaned, and a Gila County deputy sounded concerned. "We have to get her to the hospital right now."

"Fine, get going."

The deputies helped Shanna into the backseat of a cruiser, turned on the emergency lights, and shot out of the driveway.

One of the US marshals holding Jason turned to Whittaker. "What should we do with him?"

Chapter 57

Payson Medical Center

Cries from a newborn infant only minutes old filled the delivery room. Shanna swaddled her new baby and scanned the delivery room again for her husband, who had missed their child's birth. Nurses fussed over Shanna and the baby when Jason entered the room with two US marshals close behind. A toothy smile filled Jason's face as he bent over to kiss his son on the forehead and his wife on the lips.

"Sorry, I wasn't here when you needed me. This wasn't exactly how I envisioned welcoming our first child to our family," Jason said.

"I'm just glad you're here now."

Jason turned to the marshals standing next to the open door. "Can you remove these cuffs so I can hold my son?"

The young men in their early twenties looked puzzled at the question.

"I don't think so, but I'll ask Whittaker," a marshal volunteered.

A minute later, Whittaker arrived with the other marshal.

"Say goodbye to your son, Mulder. We're going to Phoenix."

"Can I hold him first?" Jason asked.

"I've already been far more accommodating with you than any other fugitive in my career. You said you wanted to be sure your baby was okay, and we've done that. It's time to say goodbye."

Whittaker led the exodus from the room, and the marshals guided Mulder out after he kissed his wife and son one more time. They took him past Shanna's mom and brother and Jason's parents, waiting to see Jason Joshua Mulder for the first time.

Celeste rushed to her son's side. The two marshals tried to stop her, but she persisted until his arm was in her grasp. "Where are they taking you?"

Whittaker heard the commotion and returned.

"We're going to the Phoenix District Office for processing, and then he'll spend some time in a cell until he goes before a judge," Whittaker replied.

Celeste yanked her son as if she would lead a second escape. "You can't do that. They set Jason up with those drugs, and you know that."

"Ma'am, he's been a fugitive at large for two weeks, so he needs to be processed. Call your lawyer and tell him your son will be downtown Phoenix in a few hours."

"It's okay, Mom. Just help Shanna," Jason said.

Whittaker motioned for the US marshals to move their fugitive from the area. They made it to the end of the corridor when deputy marshal Miley appeared with a thick manilla file folder in her hand. She held it up for Whittaker to see.

"I have something to show you. It's important, and it can't wait."

"You should have called me before driving up here. We're just heading back to Phoenix now to process Mulder. Nothing is more important than that right now," Whittaker chirped.

"This is."

Miley let the rebuttal hang for several beats and then followed up. "Give me ten minutes, and you'll see. Can we find an empty room so I can explain?"

Whittaker crossed his arms and turned to one marshal. "I guess if it was important enough for her to drive two hours to show me instead of waiting until I got back in the office, it must be important. Go find a conference room we can borrow."

Miley straightened her blouse and pushed strands of blond hair over her ear as she meticulously arranged an array of files across the conference room table. Whittaker stood beside her while Jason stood in the corner, flanked by two US marshals.

"Okay, so what am I looking at here?" Whittaker asked.

Miley pulled a stack of papers closer to her. "Alright, I'll start from the beginning. This report is from Agent Blankenship at the FBI. He's part of the National Cyber Investigative Joint Task Force, and I sent the USB drive to him after I tried to decipher it myself but couldn't. He looked it over and then called me with an urgent message. What he told me blew my mind."

Whittaker moved his index finger around in quick circles. "Okay, let's get to the meat of this."

Miley turned to her boss. "I am, but it's a lot of information, so give me a few minutes while I lay it all out for you."

Whittaker lowered his gaze to the papers on the table so Miley continued.

"It took Agent Blankenship some time, but he finally deciphered the hidden code on the USB drive. It contained tens of thousands of random letters and numbers, but only twelve of those numbers mattered because they were for an IP address. Do you know what an IP address is?"

"Yeah, it's all the numbers with periods between them that tell the Internet servers which website to find," Whittaker said with a hint of pride in his voice.

"Yes, exactly. Agent Blankenship entered the IP address on his computer, leading him to an e-commerce website for a company based in Reno, Nevada. The site sells supplements and looks legit on the surface, but Blankenship kept digging and found they were getting abnormally high traffic after launching only sixty days earlier. The owners are shell companies, owned by a shell company, so finding the people responsible for the website was a challenge. Blankenship ultimately traced the owners to a company based in the Guangdong Province in China."

"That explains the Hong Kong currency," Jason whispered from the corner of the room.

"What's that?" Miley asked.

"The Guangdong Province is next to Hong Kong, which explains the currency they planted in my truck."

"This is all fascinating information," Whittaker interrupted. "But what does any of this have to do with Mr. Mulder? I need to get him processed."

A wide grin twisted up on Miley's face. "Hang on. This is where it gets interesting."

She pushed the largest stack of papers into the middle of the conference table and picked up a single page. "Agent Blankenship also found that nearly all the e-commerce company's sales came from two seemingly benign products - Chicory Root and St. John's Wort. He ordered several bottles and almost died when he opened them. Literally. One bottle contained meth, and the other was full of MDMA. Both were laced with fentanyl."

"In a regular supplement bottle?" Whittaker asked. He seemed more interested in the information.

"Well, not a regular bottle. Agent Blankenship sent the plastic containers to his counterparts at the DEA in Virginia. They were already working on a truckload of bottles seized in Arizona. They found that a Chinese manufacturer perfected a method to mass produce plastic bottles that make the contents inside undetectable by customs and DEA dogs. The containers have an activated carbon lining that traps and retains all scents, including narcotics. Then, they coated the inside with a petroleum-based liner that keeps the bottle 100% airtight. They pull a vacuum, seal each bottle, and put the fake supplements on a cargo ship for North America. Once the mislabeled supplement bottles evaded detection by US Customs or the DEA in the United States, they sold narcotics directly to eager customers, like a tube of toothpaste or a bottle of aspirin. They were selling narcotics to people across the country like something in a grocery store."

Whittaker leaned forward in his chair, eyes wide with intrigue. He reached out for the stack of papers before Miley and began flipping through them. "Wow, this is some sci-fi level shit, but I still don't get how this affects our fugitive."

"Here's the connection. Special Agent Holland is Jason Mulder's former boss at the DEA, and he led the bust of the truck filled with the pseudo supplements. I called him, and he shared the DEA was investigating a rash of sudden fentanyl overdoses all over the United States. The overdoses had them stumped because they did not tie to any local increase in fentanyl supply, and the overdoses started and stopped suddenly. I shared Agent Blankenship's information on the e-commerce company, so Holland provided me with a list of all the suspicious overdose victims with their addresses. Blankenship hacked into the e-commerce company's shipping records and found a strong correlation between the two, but not enough to confirm all the fentanyl came from the same company. Next, he referenced the addresses of the overdose victims with a spike in internet traffic and found the smoking gun. Blankenship identified two more e-commerce companies from the same Chinese company that sprung up, sold a lot of supplements, and then suddenly shut down. I believe that was the purpose of the USB drive. That's how Chinese syndicate distributed the IP addresses of each new site to their customers."

Whittaker stared at the open file folder, resting his chin on his thumb and index finger. "Wow, that's a lot to take in."

The room was quiet as Whittaker scanned the documents until Jason spoke. "She's right."

Everyone turned their attention to the man in handcuffs standing in the corner. He wiggled his fingers into his back pocket and removed a USB drive the same color as the one Whittaker gave her.

"I found this USB drive on a drug dealer named Titan, known for his distribution network across the Southwest. Six months later, I found another drive in Special Agent Cruz's desk. That's the one I gave to Deputy Marshal Whittaker. I've checked both out and they have the same encryption but different puzzles. I believe the Chinese were working with a couple of crooked DEA agents to help distribute the USB drives and tip off the owners of the e-commerce sites if the agency was getting suspicious. Donaldson admitted he framed me before you arrived earlier today."

Whittaker walked over to Mulder and snatched the drive out of his hand. He held it at eye level and examined it.

"You think Donaldson and Cruz framed you? Why risk their careers?"

"Money. Donaldson told me he needed to pay for his granddaughter's chemotherapy treatment, so whoever recruited him knew he was desperate for cash. Cruz was probably just an asshole that liked nice things."

"Why frame you?"

"I don't think it was their original intent, but after I found the first USB drive, I'm sure they were concerned I would figure it out and blow the whistle on the entire operation. They had access to me through the DEA and the people willing to plant the drugs and lie in court, so I was an easy target."

"Do you think Donaldson or Cruz are the masterminds of this operation?" Whittaker asked.

Mulder laughed. "No, but I know who is behind all this."

"Who?"

"I'll tell you as soon as you guarantee to drop all charges against me, including any crimes I may have committed while on the run. I'll even get the brains behind the operation to confess."

"That's never going to happen," Whittaker snorted.

Jason let himself fall back against the wood grain wall behind him. Nobody said a word for a full minute as Whittaker and Jason stared each other down, waiting for the other to capitulate.

"Put him in my vehicle," Whittaker said. "I'm leaving."

Chapter 58

Kingman, Arizona

Thin shadows of razor wire flickered across Jason's face until the thick concrete wall, soaring twenty feet high, blotted out the sun completely. Gusts of wind stirred up dust between scant patches of green grass and amplified the smell of sweat and fear radiating from the building. Jason shuffled into the Arizona State Prison Complex in Kingman, Arizona, with guards on each side.

Jason shook his head in disbelief after the first door closed behind him. "I can't believe I'm in here."

As he approached another security checkpoint, the watchful gaze of the guards seemed to scrutinize his every move. The clang of metal doors caused Jason's heart to race and legs to weaken. The weight of confinement surrounded him, threatening suffocation with each step deeper into the prison.

Jason stepped into a small, dimly lit room with a window suspended in a concrete wall that gave him a view of an identical room. Both rooms contained stainless steel tables in the center, surrounded by three chairs. Deputy Marshall Whittaker stood inches from the glass and peered into the adjacent room. Jason followed his eyes to Special Agent Holland sitting alone at the table in the other room.

"What's going on?" Jason asked.

"Holland is waiting for Kellerman."

Jason knew this because it was part of his agreement with Whittaker. He shared everything he learned about Donaldson while on the run, and the deputy US marshal gave him one chance to confirm his findings with the former sheriff of Navajo County. Jason wanted to question Kellerman himself, but Whittaker immediately shut that down and stipulated that Holland conduct the interview.

"Can we hear what they are saying in this room?"

"These are private rooms for attorneys to meet with their clients, so they have windows for guards to monitor the rooms, but no microphones for sound. I'm on a call with Holland now so we can hear everything," Whittaker replied. "He's on speaker, but we're on mute so he can't hear us."

Jason looked through the glass and noted Holland's phone on the table. The door opened and a grand figure in a blue prison uniform moved into the room with two corrections officers by his side.

Former Navajo County Sheriff Kellerman looked even more imposing in his prison garb than his former law enforcement uniform. His barrel chest and deep scowl looked more menacing than Jason remembered.

Jason opened his mouth involuntarily at the sight of the man he helped put behind the Plexiglass separating them.

The corrections officers left the room and closed the door behind them. Kellerman noticed Holland sitting at the table and hovered over him.

"Who the hell are you?"

Holland stood. "I'm Special Agent Holland with the DEA. Have a seat."

"My lawyer must be present if I'm being charged with anything."

"We have no charges to file against you at this time. I'm simply here to ask you questions about some of my agents. It will only take a few minutes. Take a seat."

Kellerman stared at Holland for a few beats as if considering his options and then dropped his considerable frame into the steel chair. The inmate locked his gaze on Holland for ten uncomfortable seconds, and Jason saw the discomfort in his old supervisor's body language.

"I haven't been in the DEA for over a decade, so I don't know how I can help," Kellerman stated. His voice was gravelly like he'd smoked a pack of cigarettes daily for the past four decades.

"Maybe not. If you can't help, this will be a short meeting."

Kellerman crossed his arms and leaned back.

"How long have you known Special Agents Daniel Cruz and Ken Donaldson?"

Kellerman didn't flinch or even blink. "Neither of those names sounds familiar. I don't know who they are."

"That's not what Donaldson and Cruz shared with my investigators."

"Never happened." Kellerman rotated his right hand as if he was reeling in a fish.

"Is that right?"

The former sheriff leaned forward. "You're fishing for information because if you had anything, my lawyer would be seated in this chair next to me, and you'd be reading me my rights. Did you fail to see the twenty-six years of law enforcement in my file? You're wasting my time."

Jason didn't like the direction of the conversation. He shared his theory with Whittaker that Kellerman was the man behind the

DEA agents that framed him. The deputy US marshal listened but was skeptical of Jason's claim and granted him one attempt to get Kellerman to confess. If he failed to get the former sheriff to admit that he ordered Donaldson and Cruz to frame him, Whittaker would have to transfer Jason to the Department of Corrections. Once inside the Phoenix FCI, Jason would have the nearly impossible task of convincing a judge he was framed while behind bars. Jason did not intend to spend a minute in prison, and his time to get Kellerman to confess was running out.

Holland looked flustered as he shuffled through a stack of files on the table.

Kellerman stood. "It looks like we're done here."

"Does RedSpruceSupplements.com ring a bell?" Holland shot back. The irony of the Chinese drug syndicate setting up a company with red in the name caused a brief smirk to crack Jason's straight face.

Kellerman's brows raised, and his jaw clenched upon hearing the web address, but his face went blank again as he seemed committed to conceal any hints of surprise. "Never heard of it."

"It's the latest pop-up website that sells meth and fentanyl-laced MDMA directly to consumers. An organization in southeast China manufactured an impenetrable plastic container that makes the narcotics inside undetectable to drug-sniffing dogs and detection devices. The Chinese syndicate had the goods but needed someone to help skirt law enforcement stateside, especially the DEA. They needed someone with a badge or previously had a badge willing to aid their illegal operation. Can you think of anyone that fits that description?"

Jason noticed the pale, blotchy skin on Kellerman's cheeks just above his greying beard transformed into a dark pink.

"That's an interesting story, and even if it were true, it has nothing to do with me."

Kellerman turned toward the exit, and Jason felt a wave of adrenaline slam into his gut. Jason's freedom and future with Shanna and his new son were in peril if the former sheriff left the room.

"I'm going in there!"

Whittaker held up his hand. "Hold on. If you go in there and try to beat it out of him, you'll jeopardize the entire case."

Jason looked through the glass and saw Kellerman moving toward the door.

"That's easy for you to say," Jason responded through gritted teeth. "Your freedom for the next decade isn't on the line."

Jason rushed out and encountered the two corrections officers waiting outside the door to return Kellerman to his cell. He split the officers and reached for the doorknob, causing one of them to protest. "You can't go in there."

Jason ignored him and pushed ahead as both men tried to restrain him as the door swung open. They were too slow, and Jason found himself nose to chin with former Sheriff Kellerman.

"What are you doing here?" Kellerman growled. The blockade in the doorway allowed the corrections officers to secure both of Jason's arms.

Jason didn't reply. He stared at a man who wanted him dead as the officers attempted to yank him out of the room.

"He can stay. This will be fun," Kellerman said. A sinister grin appeared below his blotchy cheeks.

"Are you sure?" A guard asked.

"Yeah, I'm sure. I want to hear what he has to say," Kellerman said slowly.

The guards left and the trio continued to stand between the table and the door. Jason and the former sheriff glared at each other like two heavyweight boxers at the weigh-in the day before a fight. The room fell silent, and for the first time, Jason heard the sounds of 3,500 incarcerated men living just outside the door.

Holland broke the silence. "Let's all take a seat and get back to my ques—"

"I'm not answering any more questions until I know why the Air Force medic turned narc is in here," Kellerman interrupted.

Jason bit his lip, nodded, and let a smile spread across his face. "I came in here to see if this room actually stinks."

"You what?"

"I wanted to know if this room smells like all the bullshit you've been feeding Special Agent Holland about your boys Donaldson and Cruz. We know you paid them to frame me, and now you're going to spend another decade or two in here."

Jason was tired of dancing around Kellerman's involvement. His only way out of this nightmare was to get him to confess. He knew Kellerman was a proud and boastful man, so challenging him was likely the best method to get him to talk.

Kellerman took a step closer to Jason. "If you truly suspected I was involved, I'd be in cuffs. You're fishing like your friend here."

Jason reached into his top shirt pocket and retrieved a printout of a picture with Donaldson holding a large brown trout with Kellerman's long, beefy arm around him. Jason turned it around and held it high for Kellerman to see.

"Speaking of fishing, check out this whopper. That sure looks like you and Donaldson together ten or fifteen years ago when you worked together at the DEA office in Denver. This proves you know the man that framed me and that you're lying to Special Agent Holland."

Kellerman let his eyes fall from Jason's icy glare to the bare concrete floor. Jason felt he had the former sheriff on the ropes, so he continued to push. His hand returned to the top pocket again, and he retrieved a USB drive.

"I got this from Special Agent Cruz's desk and shared it with the FBI. They cracked the code while the DEA seized a truck of supplement bottles filled with illicit narcotics. The FBI knows about the IP addresses and the rotating e-commerce sites."

"Right now, they're checking phone records, including intercepted cell phone calls made from burner phones."

This brought Kellerman's eyes back up to meet his. "Is there a chance an old sheriff from Navajo County occasionally called or texted hidden burner phones held by DEA agents out of the Flagstaff office?" Jason asked smugly.

"I had enough of this bullshit. I'm done here."

Kellerman turned to leave so Jason knew he had one final shot to coax a confession.

"I can't believe you hired Cruz and Donaldson to come after me because you're too big of a coward to do it yourself."

He couldn't touch Kellerman physically, but Jason could deliver a blow verbally. Kellerman's neck twitched as he spun around to face Jason.

"What did you say?" Kellerman growled.

"You're a coward, and you're afraid of me." Jason pointed at Kellerman's chest with his index finger as he pronounced each word slowly, which seemed to trigger the old lawman.

"You think I'm a coward? You think I'm afraid of you?" Kellerman shouted. He stomped toward Jason like a bull preparing to charge as his face flushed fire engine red. Jason took several steps back from the angry inmate until the table prevented further retreat. Kellerman looked down toward Jason and spittle dotted his face as the inmate exploded.

"The only reason I hired Donaldson is because I'm locked up in here. If I was on the outside, I would have beat you to death, retrieved the USB, and stuffed your body into a steel drum. You and your wife are lucky that I hired Donaldson. If I did it myself, you'd both be taking a dirt nap in the muck at the bottom of Willow Springs Lake now."

Jason's eyes snapped toward the window to see if Whittaker had caught the confession, but he couldn't see through the mirrored glass, so he turned to Holland. He saw his former supervisor's eyes widen and assumed it was because of the abrupt confession, but a split second later he understood Holland's reaction. Kellerman tackled Jason and took him to the floor.

It happened so fast that Jason didn't see it coming or have time to defend himself. Jason was on his back, and Kellerman was on top of him. The six-foot-five, two-hundred-and-thirty-pound mountain of rage had both hands around Jason's neck and squeezed with all his might. Jason tried pulling his arms away as black spots appeared in his vision. He saw Holland and two guards behind Kellerman trying to pull him off, but the former sheriff seemed possessed and determined to strangle Jason to death. He knew Kellerman would be successful if he didn't act in seconds.

Go for a pressure point.

Jason trained for this specific scenario during a day of Krav Maga training many years ago. The attacker was too large and leveraged for Jason to use the most common countermeasures. He had one last chance to perform a move he hadn't practiced in half a decade.

As blackness closed in on Jason and unconsciousness grew imminent, he managed to find enough strength to strike the Shousanli pressure point multiple times with a knife hand strike. The pressure point is on the inner forearm, a couple of finger widths from the elbow joint. Self-defense instructors have taught Shousanli strikes for years because the radial nerve runs below it, and hitting it just right can cause temporary paralysis of the arm. That's precisely what happened after the third strike.

Kellerman's right arm went limp, and he lost his python-like grip on Jason's neck. Jason twisted out from under the large man as he slumped forward and delivered an elbow to the temple that knocked out the former sheriff.

Jason wobbled to his feet and gasped for air. The sheriff quickly regained consciousness as the corrections officers applied shackles to Kellerman's hands and legs. Once he was back on his feet, they frog marched the disgraced former sheriff out of the room.

Whittaker entered soon after Jason started breathing normally again. "I didn't beat him up. I used the minimum force to defend myself," Jason said.

"I know. You did nothing wrong."

Jason looked at Whittaker and Holland. "I hoped you two heard everything?"

Whittaker nodded, and Holland held up his phone. "I also recorded my call."

Jason turned to Whittaker. "I got your confession. Can I please go home now?"

CHAPTER 59

Phoenix, Arizona

Whittaker stared at his computer screen, baffled by what to include in his report. Two days after the Kellerman confession, his fingers hovered above the keyboard, still unsure of the words to describe everything that happened. A moment later, Miley entered the office with a file folder, but her boss didn't look away from the monitor or take his finger from the mouse.

Miley cleared her throat. "Did you hear the news? Blankenship confirmed the second USB drive Mulder found pointed to a different IP address with another fake supplement website."

Whittaker continued to tap on his keyboard one finger at a time.

"Is now a bad time?" Miley asked.

Whittaker pushed away from his desk and turned to Miley. "No. No. I'm just struggling with parts of this report."

"Like what?"

"Well, everything is clear about the old sheriff hiring Donaldson and Cruz to frame Mulder, along with the production of narcotics in China and the distribution of those drugs on general websites in the US. The DEA investigation is still ongoing, and now I'm murky about the USB drive and how the sellers let consumers know about the new websites that changed every couple of months without getting caught. They sold tens of thousands of bottles in broad daylight. It seems as if that would have caught the NSA's or DEA's attention a long time ago. My report is due by the end of today, and I still have several gaps to fill."

Miley handed the file folder to Whittaker. "I think this will help. It's from Special Agent Holland and the DEA support team in Virginia. It covers everything, including the role of the USB drives and the communication methods of each new website."

Whittaker took the file folder and opened it. He flipped through a stack of paper thirty pages thick. "Have you already read it?"

"Yes, I have."

"Well, what's in here?"

"It's all in there. I don't want to leave anything out," Miley responded.

Whittaker closed the folder and interlocked his fingers on top of it. "Deputy Marshal Miley don't play coy with me. We both know you cracked this case; ninety percent of what's already in my report came from you. Let's make it a clean sweep, and I'll credit you with everything. Especially if something is wrong."

"Ha, ha, very funny," Miley said with a wide smile.

"Alright. If you recall, the DEA busted a major dealer named Titan six months ago. He died in a shootout, and that's when Mulder found the first USB drive. After some digging, the DEA found that Titan and a dozen others like him received USB drives to hand deliver to social media influencers around the country. Titan was on his way to pass his USB drive to a young lady in Phoenix named *InTheKnowUKnow,* who has six hundred thousand followers on social media who devour her videos of health and beauty products. The analyst at the DEA went back to all her videos this year, and the only time she recommended a supplement or botanical product was when a new website for the Chinese narcotics syndicate popped up. Multiply her video times twelve, and word got out fast."

Whittaker shook his head. "I'll be damned."

"The DEA analysts are still trying to determine how long ago this started and how they trained their buyers to follow those influencers and order from new, unproven websites."

"Didn't a normal Jane or Joe order from the website and complain when they got meth instead of Saint John's Wort?" Whittaker asked.

"Have you ever heard of anyone taking Saint John's Wort?"

"Touché."

Whittaker stood. "Good work, Miley. If you'll excuse me, I have to complete this report."

Miley rose and stopped at the door. "Can I ask you a question?"

Whittaker tilted his head, and wrinkles spread across his forehead. "I guess it depends on what you want to know."

"How long ago did you believe Jason Mulder was innocent?"

"I told you I don't care if our fugitive is guilty or innocent. My job is to catch and return them to the judicial system."

"I know. I heard you, but you've never given someone so much leeway after you captured them. You let Mulder go to the hospital to see his new baby and then gave him another day to get a confession from Kellerman. When did you know he was innocent?"

Whittaker opened his mouth to speak but stopped. He moved to the front of his desk and leaned against it.

"You first. I know you probably thought Mulder was innocent from day one. When did you know?"

"I never suspected he was innocent."

Whittaker tilted his head and raised both eyebrows. "Never?"

A shy smile tugged at the corners of Miley's mouth. "A smart man once told me it's not our job to determine if a fugitive is guilty or innocent. We catch them and let the Justice Department sort it out."

"Such discipline. I like it."

"Okay, honestly, I questioned why someone with his history and military record would take drugs from a sting. It never made sense to me. The charges and testimony from the other DEA agents seemed off to me from the beginning."

"Fair assessment, Deputy Miley."

"Okay, I spilled my guts. What about you?"

Whittaker exhaled and crossed his arms. "I suspected Mulder was innocent when he called me on the phone after he roughed up Hoffman and O'Neal."

"Why?" Miley asked.

"I've never seen someone so committed to evade capture. Most fugitives are desperate to avoid capture because they don't want to go to prison. After a few days on the run, the pressure gets to them, and they resign themselves to the fact that capture is imminent. That's when most start making critical mistakes that lead us to them. Some even flat give up and turn themselves in. None of them call to proclaim their innocence. They keep running until they can't run anymore."

Whittaker uncrossed his arms and secured the edge of his desk with both hands.

"Jason Mulder was different. He was always a couple of steps ahead of us and never gave up. It was like—"

Whittaker stopped speaking and shifted his eyes to the floor before lifting his gaze back to Miley.

"It was like he was fighting for his family's life."

"Yes, he was," Miley agreed as her voice trailed off. "Yes, he was."

Chapter 60

Tucson, Arizona

Jason sat in his idling Ford Raptor truck as the sun broke over the foothills of the Catalina Mountains, spreading its golden light across Tucson, Arizona. A week after regaining his freedom, Jason Mulder waited in the parking lot of the 943rd Rescue Unit on Davis Monthan Air Base for security to unlock the squadron door. Captain Goodwin, the Commanding Officer of Jason's unit, requested a face-to-face meeting to discuss his status with the Air Force Reserve.

A young man in ABUs, barely old enough to drink, pushed the squadron door open, so Jason locked his truck and went inside. The corridors and team rooms that usually housed a flurry of training activity were still on this weekday. Jason preferred the background noise of people preparing for training missions during drill weekends versus the sterile silence of the empty building. He found Captain Goodwin in his office, deep within the administrative wing.

Goodwin rose from his desk when Jason entered his office.

"Take a seat, Sergeant Mulder."

Jason sat across from the desk while Goodwin retook his seat.

"Glad to see you in the flesh after everything that's happened over the past six months. I heard about the judge dropping all charges against you."

Jason nodded, but did not say anything.

"You look to be in fairly good shape after two weeks on the lam," Goodwin said.

"I lost twelve pounds over those two weeks, but my wife and mother-in-law are doing their best to help me regain it as soon as possible," Jason replied, patting his stomach. "I'd love to get back here and be with the guys again during next drill weekend."

Captain Goodwin pursed his lips. "That's why I called you down here, Mulder. The hearing with the review board took place while you were out, and it did not go well. The arrest, felony conviction, and fugitive status were more than we could overcome. I'm sorry, but you've been involuntarily discharged from the Air Force."

The revelation of his discharge was not unexpected, but it still hit Jason like a sledgehammer to the gut. His face dropped to the ground momentarily, and Jason looked up with streaks of red in his eyes.

"I understand. What now?"

"Clean out your cage and take your personal items home. We will return everything still there next week to Supply. Take as much time as you need. You won't have access to this building or Davis Monthan after today."

Jason exhaled and shuffled to his cage. Once inside, he sat on a container filled with medical supplies and closed his eyes. Years of laughter, tears, disagreements, and support for fellow PJs took place in those cages. He spent hours preparing for this day in the forests of Northern Arizona, but it was still hard to believe it was his last day as a PJ in the United States Air Force.

Forty minutes later, Jason placed his last box of personal gear in the truck bed and returned to Captain Goodwin's office.

"I know you did all you could for me, and it was a pleasure serving with you," Jason said, extending his hand. Goodwin took it, and the two men shook.

"Just so you know, sir, I may never wear the maroon beret again, but I'll always be a PJ." Jason pointed to his chest. "The creed is embedded deep in my bones and will always be with me."

CHAPTER 61

Whispering Pines, Arizona

The sound of a newborn's tender grunt and a high-pitched yawn broke the peaceful hush of the Whispering Pines family room. Jason held his waking son, savoring his new title of father while Shanna warmed a bottle in the kitchen. Jason Joshua, or JJ, stirred and opened his eyes, searching for a familiar face. He blinked several times at the man smiling back at him and burst into tears. Jason stood and extended the baby to Shanna like a quarterback, attempting to hand off a football to the running back.

"You can feed JJ. Sit down, and I'll bring the bottle over," Shanna reassured him.

A minute later, tranquility returned as JJ enjoyed his late-morning snack of pumped breast milk. They named him Jason Joshua to keep the legacy of Jason's deceased little brother in the family but agreed to call him JJ to reduce confusion with two Jasons in the house.

Shanna sat beside her husband, leaned against him, and laid her head on his shoulder. "I'm so glad you are home and here with me now. A week ago, I was concerned I'd be doing all this alone."

Jason fed JJ, and his son fell fast asleep. The new father cradled JJ and leaned over until his head was on Shanna's chest. They sat silently for a full minute while Jason listened to her heartbeat.

"I missed that sound. It's just as I remembered."

Shanna pulled Jason's face toward her lips, and they kissed.

It took a week, but the roller coaster ride of events slowed, allowing Jason and Shanna to resume their return to normal life. A day after the Kellerman confession, the judge ruled to hold Jason under house arrest until he reviewed the recent evidence. The District Attorney, DEA, US Marshals, Arizona Department of Public Safety, and several local law enforcement agencies provided their preliminary reports three days later. Forty-eight hours after the judge received the reports, he dismissed the previous charge of Possession of a Controlled Substance with Intent to Deliver and all pending charges for assault, theft and vandalism Jason committed while trying to prove his innocence.

The DEA immediately volunteered to pay restitution to the owners of the stolen dump truck and Can-Am side by side, sensing bad press from two corrupt special agents. The US Drug Enforcement Agency also opened up an internal investigation to root out any other internal corruption and agreed to cooperate with the District Attorney to prosecute Donaldson and Kellerman. Last, the DEA gave Jason back pay from the time they terminated him at his conviction. It wasn't a lot, but it was something Special Agent Holland pushed for, and Jason appreciated.

Holland delivered the good news himself on the back deck of Jason's house. "I'm sorry for everything that happened over the last six months. I wish I could do more, but I hope this will help."

Jason took the envelope. "The money is nice, but I appreciate you went to bat for me with the Kellerman confession and all the follow-up reports. A lesser man would have thrown me under the bus because it could make the agency look bad."

Holland nodded. "I considered covering my ass for a few seconds. Two corrupt special agents inside the DEA are not a good look. It's a stain on the agency and will take some time to remove, but it has far more good people than bad, so the DEA will be alright. You were the one royally screwed over in all this, and I couldn't stand by and let it continue to happen to a good man and special agent."

The two men shook. Shanna joined them on the back deck with JJ in her arms. Holland complimented the new parents on their handsome son and turned back to Jason.

"I have more good news," Holland said. "Considering the judge dropping all charges against you, I convinced the boys back in Virginia to let you rejoin the team without losing rank or seniority. Special Agent Mulder, you can come back whenever you are ready. What do you think of that great news?"

Jason turned to Shanna and completed their non-verbal conversation in a glance.

"I appreciate the offer, but my days with the DEA are over."

"Are you sure? Do you need a little time to think about it?"

"No, I'm sure."

Holland nodded. "I suspected you may say that, so I arranged for a nice exit package to cover you and your new family for a few months while you look for something else."

"It was a pleasure working with you, and I appreciate everything you've done for me," Jason said. They shook hands again, and the special agent departed.

"That went well," Shanna stated.

"Yeah, it's been a shitty year except for JJ, but it's feeling like we're getting back on track. What time is everyone coming over?"

"They'll be here in a couple of hours. I wanted to be sure JJ got his nap in, so I told everyone to be here around six."

Jason nodded.

"Are you okay with everyone coming over? I know it was over-whelming with everyone here the night before your trial. Everyone is eager to meet JJ, and it's easier for me to do it all at once."

"Yeah, I'm good. I'm looking forward to showing off my new boy."

Two hours later, the off-grid home in Whispering Pines was buzzing with friends and family. After everyone enjoyed dinner, Jason and Shanna stood in the family room, surrounded by their guests.

"Excuse me, everyone. Excuse me," Jason shouted over the small crowd. Once it was quiet, he took JJ from his mom with his open arm and spoke.

"I want to thank everyone here for supporting Shanna, me, and JJ this year. It's been a tough year for us, but it's returning to normal now, and we couldn't have made it without you."

Jason raised his beer, and everyone lifted their beverages. "To family and friends."

"Are you going back to the DEA?" Noah asked.

Jason took a deep breath and shook his head. "No, I'm not going back. I loved the camaraderie with the guys, but the drug war is a bigger battle than I can fight. Narcos will do anything to pump more Americans full of their drugs. I admire the men and women fighting to keep our streets safe, but I know who I am. I'm better at protecting people than chasing down drug dealers."

"What will you do now?" Noah inquired.

All the eyes in the room shifted to Jason. He leaned over and kissed Shanna and then JJ's forehead.

"I'm not sure yet. I fought US Marshals, crooked DEA agents, exhaustion, starvation, and dehydration to get home to be a father and a husband, so I think I'll do that for a while."

***

Chapter 62

Scottsdale, Arizona

The adobe walls of the four-story apartment building danced with waves of silver reflected from the enormous community pool as Jason strutted through the courtyard with a moving box. A tall, gorgeous blonde wearing short shorts and a snug tank top gave him an appraising look while her dog sniffed around the grassy courtyard.

"Welcome to the complex," the woman said flirtatiously.

Jason took ten more steps and waited for Clay to catch up to him on the sidewalk. "I think you're going to like your new place, Clay."

Clay did a three-hundred and sixty-degree turn inside the luxury apartment complex in north Scottsdale and nodded. "I love it already."

They carried the boxes to Clay's fourth-floor apartment and placed them on the kitchen table. Brown and white moving boxes covered every available inch of counter space.

Jason crossed through the room that would transform into Clay's family room and walked onto the balcony. Clay followed him, and they leaned against the railing, soaking up the views of the rugged copper mountains standing guard over the city like granite sentinels.

"This place is great, but isn't it going to be a long drive to the 943rd for you during drill weekends?" Jason asked.

"Yeah, the drive will take three hours each way once a month, but I spend so much more time up here and in Washington, DC, since I started working for the Senator. It makes more sense to live in the Valley. Plus, I only have seven months left in the Air Force Reserve."

Jason's head snapped toward his friend. "I didn't know that. You're not going to reenlist?"

"No, the test of Special Recognizance in an Air Force Reserve Rescue Unit is over next June, so I'd have to move again if I want to stay in the reserve. I love my gig with the Senator's security team, so I will focus on that now."

"Good for you, man," Jason said. "I'm glad you found a job you're passionate about and enjoy. Is Senator Conrad like he appears on TV in real life?"

Clay nodded. "Yeah. He's a no-nonsense, straight shooter, but he's not an asshole. I like him."

"That's refreshing to hear," Jason said. They both turned back to gaze up at the mountains, where a pair of hawks soared in the warm afternoon air currents until Clay broke the silence.

"Senator Conrad is kicking off his reelection campaign next month, and we could use a few more good people on the security team we're beefing up for the campaign. It's a temporary gig through the election next year, but it's good for twelve months and could lead to a full-time job on his security team. It's a much safer gig for someone with a new family," Clay said. He elbowed Jason as if reminding him he was a new parent.

"Sounds interesting, but I'm not really into politics."

Clay laughed. "We're not making policy or voting on bills. Our job is to protect Senator Conrad and his staff, and that's it."

"That doesn't sound horrible, but don't you need special ops guys and snipers on the security team?"

"We already have enough of those. We need someone with EMT experience that can shoot and defend if the shit hits the fan and then patch us up if we take any casualties. Know anyone that can do that?"

Jason pressed his index finger against his lips. "Hmmm. I think I may know someone."

"Don't hurt yourself thinking too hard," Clay replied.

"Don't you travel a lot back and forth to DC? I don't want to leave Shanna for long periods of time a month after we have a baby."

"There will be some travel, but most of the campaign security will be around Arizona. I'll go to DC with the Senator when he returns to the Capital, but you'll stay here, scout future venues, and then hook up with us when we return. You can go home and sleep in your own bed on most nights."

Jason considered the opportunity. The Air Force and federal law enforcement were no longer opportunities for him, and the chance to work with Clay was appealing.

"Plus, the pay is almost double what you got at the DEA."

Jason backed away from the railing and turned toward Clay.

"Double? Seriously?"

Clay took the plastic straw out of his mouth. "I never joke about money." He returned the straw to its designated spot between his lips and turned his gaze back to the mountains.

Jason grabbed Clay's arm and rotated him a half-revolution to face him.

"How soon could I start?"

***

Thank you for reading Reverse Pursuit. I appreciate every reader.

While you're waiting for the next book in the Jason Mulder Thriller series, visit **RobertGoluba.com/BONUS** for two bonus stories. In OATH OF JUSTICE, see Jason protect his loved ones before he joins the Air Force and meet Josh and Gaby before they were taken from this earth too soon. In RAPTOR DOWN join Jason and a team of PJs as they go behind enemy lines to rescue a downed F-22 pilot and experience Jason's first kill.

If you'd like to read more thrillers by authors like Robert Goluba, visit **ACEThrillers.com**. ACEThrillers.com is a collection of action, crime, espionage, and related thriller authors sharing their current books, new releases, exclusive offers, promotions, and more. Find your next thriller at AceThrillers.com.

If you're ready to jump into Book 3 in the Jason Mulder Thriller Series, check out STRIKE BACK.

Strike Back: A Crime Action Thriller

A man uncovers a plot to assassinate the US Senator he's sworn to protect.

Jason Mulder wasn't expecting the extreme danger encountered in his new job. He joined the security detail for Arizona Senator Conrad's reelection campaign to spend more time with his young family. He's stunned when the Senator's new bill generates a long list of groups who want him dead.

Through skill and some luck, the Senator's security team of ex-special forces operators keep him safe...at first. But two brothers losing their family ranch won't stop until they eliminate the Senator in an explosive statement to America.

Can Jason find the people behind a string of deadly bombings before they move to a massive target that takes thousands of lives with the Senator?

Strike Back is the action-packed third book in the Jason Mulder crime action thriller series. If you like gritty investigations, epic battles with ruthless opponents, and ticking bombs that can change the face of America, then you'll love Robert Goluba's dramatic story of protecting the innocent from terror.

Strike Back is Book 3 in the Jason Mulder Thriller Series

CHAPTER 63

Robert Goluba is an author of crime action thrillers and suspense novels. He was born and raised in Central Illinois, where he attended college, served in the Army National Guard, and met his wife. At age thirty, after a self-diagnosed allergy to snow, he moved to sunny Arizona where he now lives with his wonderful wife, two kids, and canine companion. He published his first book in 2016.

He's currently working on his next book in the Jason Mulder Crime Action Thriller Series.

Visit **RobertGoluba.com** to learn more.

The Jason Mulder Thriller Series

Book 1, Cartel Hunter
Book 2, Reverse Pursuit
Book 3, Strike Back
Visit RobertGoluba.com to stay current with future books.